D0046402

CHARLOTTE
Cuts It Out

K. A. BARSON

Viking

VIKING

An imprint of Penguin Random House LLC

375 Hudson Street

New York, New York 10014

First published in the United States of America by Viking,
an imprint of Penguin Random House LLC, 2016

LIBRARY OF CONGRESS CATALOGING-IN-PUBLICATION DATA
Names: Barson, K. A.
Title: Charlotte cuts it out / K.A. Barson.
Description: New York : Viking, an imprint of Penguin Random House LLC, 2016.
Summary: When cosmetology student Charlotte Pringle, who has always wanted to run a beauty salon, realizes that she cannot do everything herself, she learns to be less controlling and more relaxed.
Identifiers: LCCN 2015022509 | ISBN 9780451468932 (hardback)
Subjects: | CYAC: Beauty culture—Fiction. | Friendship—Fiction. | Self-perception—Fiction.
BISAC: JUVENILE FICTION / Girls & Women. | JUVENILE FICTION / Family / Multigenerational.
JUVENILE FICTION / Social Issues / Self-Esteem & Self-Reliance.
Classification: LCC PZ7.B28048 Ch 2016 | DDC [Fic]—dc23
LC record available at http://lccn.loc.gov/2015022509

Printed in ITC Berkeley Oldstyle Pro

Designed by Nancy Brennan

1   3   5   7   9   10   8   6   4   2

For Sylvia

Charlotte and Lydia's Grand Plan

1. Win Winter Style Showcase. —> Earn stellar reps, bragging rights, and accolades.

2. Graduate high school with honors, college credits, and cosmetology licenses.

3. Get an apartment together and jobs in a top salon to pay for college.

4. Get associates degrees in business at Jackson College.

5. Build clientele. —> Earn enough money to open a salon together.

6. Be the bosses and live happily ever after.

★★ Bonus: Marry best friends. (At the very least, they will become best friends.)

Charlotte Pringle   *Lydia Harris*

one

39 days to the Winter Style Showcase

As I apply another layer of lip gloss and smooth my hair at the tiny mirror inside my locker, a deep voice whispers in my ear. "I don't mean to alarm you, but there's a severed hand sticking out of your backpack."

My hand jerks; my lips are a mess. Furious, I spin around so fast my skirt slaps my knees. "What the—"

It's him! For the past few weeks, this adorable, blue-eyed guy has greeted me every morning with a flirty smile, nod, or the occasional "Hey." Nothing more. In fact, I don't even know his name. So when I think of him (which is often) or speak of him (only to Lydia), I call him QT—shorthand for "cutie."

He takes a step back. "Uh, sorry."

"No, it's fine." I flash a smile and nonchalantly wipe the smeared lip gloss with my finger. "You just startled me."

He smiles back sheepishly, a blush creeping up his neck to his face, which makes his eyes look even bluer. "Can I walk you to class?"

"Sure." I slam my locker. "But it's right down the hall." I start to go, but I can't move.

My skirt is trapped in my locker door.

I try to pull it loose. I hear and feel a tiny rip. What if it tears away? What if I end up with half my skirt inside my locker, flashing my underwear in front of QT? That would be a nightmare, only worse, because I'm awake. I stop tugging and will myself to calmly open the door, holding my skirt slack so it doesn't tear more.

I quickly dial the combination, but in my panic-driven haste, I go too far on the second number. *Argh!* "Uh, just a sec." QT watches, clearly holding back a laugh. Now it's my turn to blush.

As I'm redialing, more slowly this time, he taps my backpack and asks, "So what's with the severed hand?"

The lock clicks open and I'm free. I turn and look up at him. He's got to be about six foot one, and he has the cutest little dent on the tip of his nose. "It's not exactly severed. It's from a mannequin. We're learning manicures this week."

"Ah, the fine art of cosmetology." He leans against the lockers. "I should've known."

Should've known? What does *that* mean? I raise my eyebrows and glare.

"Because your hair and makeup are always done, and you dress up pretty much every day. Around here, cos girls stand out." That's true. The medical programs at the Arts and Trades Center require solid-colored scrubs. The girls in child development are always in jeans, usually smeared with baby puke or smashed bananas. Fashion design girls wear their own creations, and some of them are pretty out there.

Almost everyone throws their hair in ponytails like they just don't care, except for the dance girls, who have tight, slicked-back buns. Worst of all is culinary arts—they have to wear hairnets!

The cos girls at ATC dress up every day. Our nails are perfect, our hair is in the latest styles, and, of course, our makeup is impeccable. If you're going to make other people beautiful, you need to start with yourself.

I'm pretty sure I hear him mumble something about cos girls—or was it me?—being hot, but it's drowned out by the bell. I don't ask him to repeat himself because that would be awkward, as if I'm fishing for compliments. I close my locker and we walk toward the cos lab. Since the halls have thinned out, the *tap, tap, tap* of my high heels is louder than usual.

"How do you walk in those things?"

"Skill," I say with a smirk.

"I bet you have—"

"Give it a rest, Reed." Some guy walks by and slaps him on the shoulder, grabs his arm, and pulls. "Come on. You can't afford any more tardies."

"Yeah," he says, catching himself from stumbling. He turns back and smiles. "See you around, cos girl."

I wave and strut into class. QT has a name, and it's Reed. I can't wait to tell Lydia.

— ✿ —

Except Lydia isn't there. I check my phone. No missed calls or texts. Something must be wrong. Lydia's never late, and if she wasn't coming, I'd know. What if she had a car accident? What if she's really sick? What if something's wrong with her dad again? I start to text, but Ms. Garrett interrupts. "Put it away, Charlotte."

"But, Ms. Garrett, Lydia is MIA. I have to—"

"Now."

I slip the phone into my purse and frown.

"Remember," she says to everyone, "you only have until the end of the week to get your paperwork and payment in for the Chicago hair show. Even though it's months away, we need to register early to get special group pricing and to lock in our break-out session choices. I've only received about a dozen so far, and I'd hate for you to miss out."

"Yeah, guys." I raise my voice. "I read that Tabatha from *Salon Takeover* will be there, and that guy from the Six-in-One shampoo infomercials, too!" Ms. Garrett shoots me a look, and Shelby Cox whispers something to one of the Emilys.

Shelby's mom is a cosmetologist, co-owner of a top salon in town, and high school friends with Ms. G—they were co-cheer captains, no less—so from Day One, Shelby's had the teacher's pet advantage over the rest of us, no matter that I'm just as good as she is at nails and updos. If Lydia were here, I wouldn't feel so uncomfortable. *Ignore them,* I tell myself. *Lydia will be here soon.*

Ms. G drones on about things she announced yesterday. I don't know why she coddles everyone. Isn't it our responsibility to pay attention the first time? I watch out the window for Lydia's yellow Volkswagen. Nothing. Where is she?

"Finally, the moment you've all been waiting for . . ." Byron James simulates a drum roll on the desk in front of him. "As you know, we're gearing up for the winter style showcase, and the theme for this year is . . ." More drum rolls. Ms. G waits for everyone to stop. "'Once Upon a Time in a Magical Fairy Tale.'"

We erupt in applause and cheers. A magical fairy tale theme is perfect! There are so many possibilities. My brain starts whirring—braided updos, tiaras, fancy nails, glittery fake eyelashes. For four Halloweens straight, Lydia and I have done each other's hair and makeup as Disney princesses. We're ready. We've got this.

Ms. G interrupts my pre-planning. "Remember that one-page bio you submitted the first week of school? Well, the catalogs are ready, and you'll get your copies tomorrow."

I can hardly wait. Lydia and I should be listed together in the cosmetology section, since we're a team. We wrote our bios together, highlighting our stellar skills: updos, including braiding, twisting, and curling; nail art; false eyelashes; manis and pedis; and dramatic makeup, specializing in eyes. Then we topped it off with leadership, enthusiasm, and attention to detail. We're sure to garner tons of interest from the other programs!

Ms. G walks around her desk and sits on top of it. Even though she's at least thirty-five, her pores are flawless and she's in really good shape. She starts talking about the seasonal events. The fall wellness fair is where the child development, culinary arts, and health programs put on a health fair for the community. The winter style showcase features cos and fashion design, and the spring recital is the music, dance, and theater extravaganza.

Since this means a lot of extra work on top of our classes, we "hire" each other and programs like building trades and graphic design for sets, signs, and brochures. Ms. G goes on about synergistic relationships between the programs and how we'll earn ATC bucks—the currency at Arts and Trades, which is really just credits—to trade goods and services with each other. We'll use the catalogs to shop for what we need. I doodle as I listen—high updos with strategically placed cascading curls, another design with braids and flowers—and take notes in the margins.

We'll need real money, too, for materials and supplies, so most programs will also have fund-raisers, where we offer our services to the community for nominal fees. In cos, we juniors will do manis and pedis, and the seniors will do hair services.

"You'll need to keep track of expenses and turn in reports. By the showcase at the end of the semester—which will be here faster than you think—your projects will be graded in English/communication, math/economics, civics/sociology, and computers, as well as for the cos program."

Toby, the slacker in the back row, raises his hand. Ms. G anticipates his question, because he always asks the same thing. "Yes, Toby," she says, "everyone *has* to do it." He starts to ask something else, but she cuts him off. "And if you don't, you'll open up a spot for someone on the waiting list." She gives him a smile, and he sits back and folds his arms across his chest.

Why anyone would try so hard to avoid doing what we're here to do is beyond me. How did he pass the faculty and senior student interviews and basic skills tests to get in here anyway? I know of at least two girls—one from Jackson High and one from Hanover-Horton—who were wait-listed. I'm sure both of them are more motivated than Toby. Where is Lydia? Without her, my *can-you-believe-this-guy* look is totally pointless.

Ms. G exhales loudly, getting back on track after being so rudely interrupted. "Plus, the showcase will broadcast on JTV"—our local Jackson TV station—"and the winners will get a prize package of industry tools and a one-thousand-dollar college scholarship, and be interviewed on the Channel 6 news, JTV, and MLive. So you'll appear on cable TV, network TV, and pretty much every newspaper in mid-Michigan. This project is a big deal."

TV interviews! What would I wear? Bright colors, of course. I look down at the tear in my flouncy chevron skirt. Prints are distracting on camera. I'll have to buy something new.

Shelby raises her hand and asks about the TV interviews. Even though I'd like to know more, too, Ms. G moves on. "There'll be plenty of time to discuss the details later. Starting today, every class will be about an element of the style showcase. You'll talk about ATC bucks, spreadsheets, and subcontracting in math and economics, for instance. For now, we need to get started on manicures. Everyone, get out your mannequin hands and nail kits and turn to page 657 in your text. You'll want to take notes."

We're almost up to Ms. G's demo when Lydia slips into her seat. I look at her in shock. No makeup, hair in a greasy ponytail. And she's wearing jeans and a T-shirt.

Are you okay? I mouth.

She nods, but doesn't make eye contact. I don't believe her. If she were okay, she wouldn't come to school looking like that. She would look like Lydia—her blonde ringlets meticulously curled and accented with a bow or a flower or something that matched her outfit perfectly. And she'd be wearing her trademark shimmery copper eye shadow, plus mascara and lip gloss. She's almost unrecognizable—like a "Before" picture. But at least she's here. I'm so focused on Lyd that I only half hear the rest of Ms. G's mani instruction.

Thankfully, I'm super skilled at multi-tasking, so I'm poised and ready when she says, "Partner up and show me what you've got. I'll be around to watch and grade shortly."

"Ms. G! Ms. G!" I wave my hand frantically. "May I use the little girls' room really quickly? Pretty please?"

"Quickly. The period's more than half over." She hands me the bathroom hall pass, which is a gigantic flip-flop with a gaudy yellow sunflower stuck on it. Somehow it's supposed to be a deterrent to loitering in the hall. Right now, I am determined to save my best friend from a fashion disaster, and it's going to take more than a cheap shoe with a flower on it to stop me.

Once I'm out in the hallway, I slip off my heels and run

barefoot past the restrooms, then through the heavy double doors to the parking lot, and straight to my car. The frigid November wind flutters up my skirt, and I put my shoes back on. Then I dig through my stash of extra clothes and accessories in the backseat until I come up with a workable outfit—a short color-block dress, black leggings, and black ballet flats. (Good thing Lydia and I wear the same size.) Perfect!

When I get back to class, she has our nail station all set up in the cos lab—the salon that connects to our classroom. Two walls of the cos lab are lined with back-to-back stations—mirrors, salon chairs, and workspaces that flip up to access the sinks. Another wall is lined with a high tiled bench with several jetted tubs underneath for pedis. Small nail tables in three rows of four fill the middle of the room.

I hand Lydia the clothes and the gigantic flip-flop. "It's okay," I assure her. "I'll cover for you."

To my surprise, she looks down at the pile as if I just gave her yesterday's garbage. "I'm fine. Let's just get this assignment over with."

Fine? Seriously? If someone posts a pic of her today, she'll regret it forever. I leave the clothes on a chair; she can change after we're done. Then I pull my makeup case and styling wand out of my purse. (Thank God Lydia chose a table near a post, so I have a place to plug it in.)

"Is there anything you don't have in there?" she teases.

"Nope."

"Got any snacks? I'm starving."

I fish out a protein bar and toss it to her.

She grabs the purse and rummages through it, pulling out a scarf, a spool of wire ribbon that I bought for wrapping presents, fake eyelashes and glue, two packs of barrettes, a headband, a wide-toothed comb, a few bangle bracelets, a bottle of mouthwash, roll-on glitter, some AA batteries, and a squirt gun. "Why do you need all this?"

"You never know." I shove everything back before she exposes some feminine hygiene product.

Ms. Garrett stops by our station. "Having trouble?" she asks.

"No," I say. "We just have a slight fashion emergency we need to tend to really quickly. We'll do the manis ASAP."

"Get moving, girls. You both need to finish before the bell."

"No worries, Ms. G," I call to her at the next station. "You know we've got this."

As I wrap Lydia's golden locks around the not-quite-hot-enough curling wand, she asks, "So what did I miss this morning?" That's more like it. Conscientious Lydia is back.

"Tons and tons." As I move the wand around her head like a deft fairy godmother, I tell her about the theme and my preliminary design sketches for the style showcase, and that we'll get our catalogs tomorrow. By the time I'm finished, the ringlets are all done.

Next, I put on my smock—this boxy black jacket with the ATC logo on it—and move on to her nails. I carefully review every step for her, but she watches the clock more than she watches me. Weird. She usually takes as many notes as I do in class, and manis are more complicated than they seem. I finish in record time and show Ms. G. She's impressed with my freehand zebra stripes, which are pretty snazzy, if I do say so myself.

When it's Lydia's turn, she skimps on the soaking time. Then she pulls out my favorite nail polish—Iridescent Iris—which means she's going straight from soaking to polishing. What about my cuticles? "Uh, Lyd?" I say, trying to be discreet. "Just because you overslept and slacked on your morning beauty routine—"

"It's not like it matters. You're going to redo it anyway. You always do." True, but we've got to have this down cold if we're going to ace cos and be prepared for state boards.

She shakes the polish and starts on my right thumbnail. "Oh, and I didn't oversleep."

She misses a spot. I resist the urge to take over and do it myself. "Huh?"

"I didn't oversleep. I've been up since five."

She uses too many brush strokes, so the polish is patchy. Wait, what did I miss? She'd better fill in the rest—both in the story and on my mani.

She continues painting my nails. "Mom had a huge cupcake order for some hospital event. You know, those high-fiber, naturally sweetened ones." We both wrinkle our noses. Truth be told, though, part of my nose wrinkle is due to the shoddy manicure. "We spent all night baking them, but needed to whip, frost, and decorate them this morning. It took forever!"

"Why did *you* need to do it?" I blow on my right hand while she finishes the left, trying not to let my disappointment show. "Where was Nutmeg?" Meg hates when we call her Nutmeg, but the name totally fits the senior baking assistant at Patti Cakes, Lydia's mom's bakery.

"She's working at Meijer now."

"What?" I'm shocked. "Nutmeg quit?"

Ms. Garrett shows up with her grade book. She gives Lyd's nails an approving glance, and raises her eyebrows at mine. I fib and tell her that they were perfect before I reached into my bag for my makeup case and smudged them. I may have overdone it, but she just nods.

"Lydia." Ms. G taps her nails on the grade book. She has perfect, squoval-shaped French-tip acrylics. "I still don't have your paperwork for the hair show."

"I know." Lydia rummages through the makeup case without looking up.

"Just a reminder that it's due by Friday."

"Yeah, okay." She takes out powder foundation, eyeliner, and mascara.

When Ms. G moves to the next station, I whisper-shout, "Oh my lanta, Lyd! You need to get that paperwork in. I can't go to the hair show without you. You're my PIC."

Lydia and I were in eighth grade when we came up with our Grand Plan to go to cosmetology school and get jobs to build our clientele while we earned business degrees. Then we'd open our own salon. My brother Oliver always called his best friend, Danny, his PIC—Partner in

Crime—so we started calling ourselves Partners in Cos.

"I know, I know." Lydia brushes foundation over her cheeks, forehead, chin, and nose. "But it's a lot of money, and I don't know if it's worth it."

"Not worth it?" I screech. People look our way, so I lower my voice. "It's the flipping Chicago hair show, and it's only a hundred seventy-five dollars—a bargain!"

"Maybe to you," she says, swiping mascara on her lashes.

The bell rings, so we hurry and clean up our station. "God, I hate that Ms. G never gives us enough time to clean up. Nobody does a good job. I had to dig through a dozen gunky Iridescent Iris bottles to find one that had the top screwed on tight."

"Lighten up," Lydia scoffs. "It's just nail polish. There's a lot more serious stuff in the world to freak out about."

"Yeah, like that outfit." We exit the lab, and I force Lydia into the bathroom to change.

When she emerges, finally looking put-together, I remember what happened before class. "Oh. My. Lanta! I forgot to tell you!" I say about an inch from her newly made-up face. "I found out QT's name!"

She arches an eyebrow. "A real name, or something you invented?" I am not amused. Since Lydia's never actually seen QT, she doesn't believe he exists. She claims that we're together too much for me to have flirtatious moments with someone she's never seen.

I scoff. "Real, of course!" I show her my skirt and tell her how it got trapped in my locker. She points out that torn skirts do not prove personhood. I can't deny that, but I tell her his name anyway. "Reed," I say. "One of the guys in his class called him that as he dragged him away."

"Whatever." She does this offhand gesture thing as we head to lunch. Add that to her weird attitude about the hair show, and if I didn't love her so much, I'd kill her.

two

The first thing I see when I get to work after school is my brother Oliver pleading with his wife, Nina, behind the deli/bakery counter. "Come on, honey, please . . ."

"I can't work another minute, Ollie." As usual, she pats her protruding belly. "It's just too stressful, and you know that's not good for the baby."

"What if we get you some more help?"

She stares at him as if he should know what she's thinking. I could tell him, as could everyone else at Pringle's Market: *I can't believe you're trying to make me do something I don't want to do.* She does this so often that "pulling a Nina" is store code for having a lame excuse. (But we don't say this in front of Oliver, of course.)

I try to slip past them to the break room to stash my things—and to avoid getting sucked into today's drama.

"Charlotte!" Oliver cries. "Thank God you're here."

Crapola!

I stop, pivot, and glower. My purse slips off my shoulder and I try to shrug it back up, but it slides down to my forearm and digs in. It weighs about a thousand pounds.

"Nina's quitting," he announces, clearly ignoring my *I'm-not-in-the-mood-to-deal-with-this* look. "Again."

I look at him. "You're getting divorced?"

Nina pulls off her green apron and huffs. "Of course not!"

"Then it's too late. As long as you're a Pringle, there's no quitting. Simple as that."

Nina's been working here since she was in high school. She knew what she was getting into when she accepted my boneheaded brother's proposal—in the middle of the produce section, no less. The only thing cheesier would have been if he'd asked her in dairy.

I fully expect her to bring up Mom, and I'm ready for it. Mom is a freelance statistician, but she maintains our website, negotiates with vendors, and works a register if we're slammed and she's here. Nobody can accuse Kimberly Pringle of shirking. But for whatever reason, Nina doesn't push it.

As I walk away, I hear Oliver say, "See? I told you Charlotte accepts you." I roll my eyes. *Spin it any way you need to, Ollie.*

I push open the break room door to find my father and grandfather ready to flee. As soon as he sees me, Dad visibly relaxes. "It's only Charlotte."

"Are they still at it?" asks Pops.

Ralph, the meat and produce manager, comes out of hiding.

"You're all cowards." I drop my backpack onto the floor. "Each. And. Every. One. Of. You." I hang up my coat and purse, and clock in. "And who's out there running the store while three grown men—the owners and manager of this store, I might add—are hiding from an itty-bitty pregnant lady?"

"That 'itty-bitty pregnant lady' is worse than a rabid wolverine," says Ralph. He's practically a Pringle himself— he started as a bagger back when Dad was in grade school and Great-Gramps ran the store. Then he went to Vietnam. While he was there, Great-Gramps passed away and Pops took over. He gave Ralph his old job as soon as he came back, and he's been here ever since.

"Tammy and Barb are out there," Dad says, not looking at me.

"And Tyler," adds Pops.

Of course they know how ridiculous they're being. Two cashiers, no matter how capable, and a timid bagger cannot run this store alone. And Mike, the night-and-weekend manager, doesn't get here until four.

Before any of us can get back onto the floor, Oliver slams in. "She went home," he announces.

"Is she coming back?" asks Pops. Is he concerned, or just looking for advanced warning?

"Doubt it." Oliver slumps into a chair like a worn-out teddy bear. "At least not today. She's really tired." He pauses. "It takes a lot of energy to grow a person."

A laugh escapes before I have a chance to stop it, not that I would have anyway. "That's Nina talking, not you, right?"

Now he's the one to glare. "That doesn't make it any less true."

"So who has today in the pool?" asks Ralph.

Around the store, we bet on pretty much everything: from the date the snow pile finally melts in the parking lot to how many days between Ralph's quarterly—or sometimes biannual—haircuts to how many times the UPS man sighs while dropping off packages, and anything else we can think of. It costs a buck to get into each pool. Winning isn't about the money, though, which is rarely over twenty dollars. It's about the bragging rights: Ralph correctly guessed my birth date more than sixteen years ago, and I'm still hearing about it.

Since I'm closest, I dig through the drawer under the microwave and pull out the file marked *Nina*. Then I flip through a sheaf of papers—*Date Baby Born, Hours of Labor, Baby Size.* "Ah, here it is!" *Days Missed for Being Pregnant* is a grid showing the dates from when Nina announced her pregnancy to two weeks past her due date, January 2nd. I look at today's square: it says *RWL*. "Uh, that would be you, Ralph."

"Thought so!" He pumps his fist in the air. "How much do I get?"

"I can't believe you people!" Oliver stands, and the chair topples backward. "Betting on how many days my wife will miss work . . ."

Pops rights the chair, and I count the squares between the last day Nina left work to today. "Twelve bucks." I count out a five and seven ones from the envelope and paper-clip it back to the form.

Ralph fans his winnings and cheers. Then he sees Oliver standing there. "Sorry, man."

"No," says Oliver, still pissed. "I can't believe you bet on my wife and didn't let me in on the action!" He grabs the paper from me. "How many squares are left?"

"Not many," says Pops. "Ralph keeps using his winnings to buy more."

Ralph flashes a sheepish grin. "Sorry. Can't pass up a sure thing."

Oliver chooses two dates, slips his money in the envelope, and puts it back with the rest.

"Okay, so where's Katie?" I return the folder to the drawer. "Can't she take over for Nina?"

"She didn't show up today," Oliver says.

"Oh," says Dad, as if he suddenly remembered. "She called in a little while ago. Her cat has diarrhea again."

Ralph makes a face like he just had to clean it up.

"Oh my lanta!" I yell. "Does *anyone* work around here anymore?"

Oliver leans in and says to Ralph, even though we can all hear, "Katie could use some of that Mylanta for her cat." All four of them bust a gut. Even as I shake my head and pretend it's not, I have to admit that Oliver's comment *is* pretty funny. I'd never encourage them with an actual chuckle, though.

Before I can leave, Dad, between giggles, tells me that Mom has a meeting in Kalamazoo, so I need to go home by four to feed and let out the dog, move the laundry from the washer to the dryer, and start dinner. "Is that all?" I ask with as much sarcasm as I can muster.

"You could stop global warming," says Oliver.

"Ha, ha. Very funny. Where's that mouth when you need to stand up to your wife?"

Oliver gives me the same stupid smirk he did when we were little. I can't believe he's married, much less a father-to-be.

"Oh, and could you cure cancer, too?" says Ralph.

"I'll get right on it." *Ignore them, and they'll stop.* Mom's advice. Sometimes it even works.

"And query Congress about the exorbitant price of rutabagas?" Pops deadpans.

Since I don't even know how to answer that, it's easy to ignore. I pull open the heavy door and try to stalk out, but it's not as dramatic as I hoped, because they all follow me.

There's a line at the deli/bakery, and some of the customers look pretty impatient. Dad gives me his puppy-dog eyes—a pudgy, wrinkly, bald bulldog puppy. "Since Nina and Katie aren't here—"

I force every bit of air from my lungs. "I need to take down the Halloween displays."

"Pops and Ralph will do it."

"They won't put the plastic jack-o'-lanterns away right. They need to be wrapped so that—"

"I'll tell them." He nudges me toward the day-old baked goods.

None of us likes dealing with irritated customers, but someone has to do it. Dad knows me, knows I'll step up, knows I always step up. He lightly tugs my hair, winks, and disappears down aisle one.

An upbeat Michael Franti song plays in the store. Pops says music soothes people and makes them buy more. Let's hope he's right.

"So sorry about your wait." I pull my hair back and wash my hands. Then I plaster on a smile as I tie my apron. "What can I get you?"

"A pint of German potato salad," snaps Mrs. Bandy, "and a half pound of smoked turkey." I scoop, slice, bag, weigh, and apply the UPC price sticker, and finally hand everything over the counter. She doesn't thank me. Mrs. Bandy must be immune to Michael Franti's infectious melody.

I hustle, and within fifteen minutes the line is almost gone. A woman wearing way too much makeup and the fakest-looking extensions I've ever seen tells me that she ordered a cake and is here to pick it up.

"Okay," I say, looking around for it. "When did you order it?"

"Yesterday," she says. "I talked to Nina."

"Let me give her a call." I grab the phone and motion for her to wait. The phone rings three times. *Please pick up. Please pick up.*

"Hello?"

"Nina, it's Charlotte." I turn away from the customer. "Is there a cake around here somewhere ready to be picked up?"

"Oh, yeah!" she says. *Whew!* "But I didn't get a chance to decorate it. The icing's made and in bowls in the cooler. You just have to frost it and decorate it."

She can't be serious! "You know I don't know how to do that!" I'm trying to keep my voice down. "You need to come back and finish it. Like, now. She's here."

"Sorry. I can't."

Before I can press her for an explanation, I hear a voice in the background that sounds as if it's coming in over an intercom. "Alicia, Nina is in the salon. Alicia, Nina is—"

"Gotta go." She ends the call. Not only did she hang up on me, but she's at a salon! She knows I'm perfectly capable of giving her a simple cut or a mani-pedi. If my own family doesn't trust me, how will I ever build a clientele? And why *is* she at a salon anyway, if she's so tired?

I'm seething, but I have to pull it together. *Your personal issues are not the customer's problem. Never look angry or incompetent in front of the customer.* I've heard Pops and Dad say these things a million times; they're part of my DNA. Yet here I am, wanting to throttle my sister-in-law and throw her under the bus and fire her and punch her in the face. All in front of the customer. I exhale slowly.

"It'll just be a minute," I tell extension-woman, who scowls and then gets on her own phone. I'm sure she's posting on social media about this.

I find the unfrosted cake in the cooler next to the icing. I set it on the counter in the back and search for the order slip. At least *that's* where it should be.

"I'm sorry, but it's not quite finished yet," I tell the woman.

"It was supposed to be done at three," she barks. Her face

is so overly made up that it looks as if it's on fire.

What I *want* to say is "Talk to Nina about that. Here's her number."

What I *do* say is "I know. And I'm sorry. But could you give me another half hour?"

She stomps off, complaining that the extra half hour feels like forever with all she still has to do.

I stare at the naked chocolate cake, the bowls of white, pink, green, and yellow icing, and the empty decorating bags and tips. Okay, so I have to frost the thing. Then I have to make flowers all around the edge and pipe *Happy Birthday, Paisley!* on top. I've never done it—that's Nina's department— but it can't be that hard. I've seen Lydia's mom, Patti, do it a million times.

In this very place, in fact.

When I was little, Grandma used to run the deli/bakery. But when she got sick and chemo took its toll on her, she hired Patti. Those first few months—the summer after Lydia and I had finished third grade—whenever Patti couldn't get a sitter, she'd bring Lydia to work with her. Those were the best days, because it gave me a break from stacking cans on the lower shelves or helping Ralph pull expired products from the dairy case. Instead, Lyd and I would braid each other's hair and play hide-and-seek in the meat cooler. We were the only kids we knew who played house in a grocery store. We've been best friends ever since.

Lydia! Of course! I call her cell. "Where are you?" I ask

before she can even finish saying hello. I hear music blaring.

"On my way home." She turns down the radio. "Why? What's wrong?"

"I have a pastry emergency."

"Be right there." She hangs up without another word. Except unlike Nina's, Lydia's hanging up is comforting.

I pace the entire ten minutes it takes for her to get here, on the verge of tears the whole time. Extension-lady walks past the counter three times, glaring. I would hide in the back, but I have customers. I slice a pound of honey ham for Dr. Pinson, scoop three containers of cranberry salad for Mr. Rehberg, and make a turkey and Swiss sandwich on white bread for our cashier Barb, who tells me about the time she dropped a cake on the floor while putting it in the cart, as if her story is supposed to comfort me. Finally, Lydia bursts through the automatic doors like a paramedic rushing into the ER. "I'm here! What's the problem?"

Within minutes, her hair's pulled back, she's gloved, and she has the cake frosted and the pastry bags loaded. I watch every step carefully. She whips out the flowers and the fancy script as if she's writing with a marker.

"Wow!" I knew she had skills from working with her mom all these years, but this is beyond good. "It looks amazing! You want a job?"

"Grassy ass." Lydia's sarcastic *gracias*. She laughs. "But I have my hands full with school and the bakery." She slips the cake into the box and sets it on the counter, just as extension-lady returns to pick it up. The woman doesn't say a word. She just loads it into her cart with her other groceries and wheels away.

"Have a nice day!" I call. No response. I turn back to Lydia. "Come on, work here. It'll be like old times."

"No way!" she says, much too quickly. "No offense, but there's no way in hell I'd work for you."

"Just because you start off saying 'no offense' doesn't mean that what follows is any less offensive." I shake my head. "Whoa! That sounded way too much like my mother. Anyway, you'd be working for Dad, not me."

"Yeah, right." She stacks the icing bowls in the sink. "I know better. No way, no how, no thanks."

I raise an eyebrow, trying not to be offended. "So I take it the answer is no?"

She laughs, and it breaks the tension.

"Well, if you ever change your mind . . ."

"Trust me, I won't." She peels off her plastic gloves and tosses them in the garbage. "I've got a lot of homework to do. I'd better get going." She grabs her purse and coat.

"Hey, Lyd." She turns back, and I say, "Thanks. You saved me."

Her face softens. "No problem. I've always got your back."

"Same here."

"I know." And she's gone.

three

When I get home, our Newfoundland, Buffy, is lying in a puddle. It isn't pee, though. She "swims" in her water dish, paddling waves onto the floor with her gigantic front paws whenever she's bored. Since Mom's been gone all day, she must have had nothing to do.

"C'mon, Buffy." I hold the door open to let her out. Only her eyes move. She looks at me and then back down. I jingle the bells that hang from the doorknob—her signal that she needs to go out. Still nothing. I bend down and yank on her collar, but since she weighs a good fifteen or twenty pounds more than I do, all of my pulling is pointless.

She looks at me as if to say, "Is that all you've got?"

I let out an annoyed sigh and give up, even though I know she needs to go out.

As usual, there's a list on the counter. Before I turn to it, I fill Buffy's bowl with kibble. Some of it bounces out and scatters across the floor. "C'mon, Buffy," I coax her. "Yummy lamb and rice nuggets stuffed with cornmeal filler and topped with preservatives. Mmmm!" Her head drops back down to the floor.

When she was a puppy, it took everything I had to keep her from knocking me over when I fed her. Now it takes everything I have just to get her to eat. I swear that she's just trying to get to me. Nobody else agrees. Mom always says that I've spoiled her by giving her attention when she doesn't eat, that the vet says she's healthy—a bit overweight, but healthy—and that maybe she should skip a meal or two. Pops says it's because she's getting old and slowing down, like he is, and eating is just a hassle. Dad agrees that she is just like Pops, but that they're not old, just obstinate. Oliver says that's what makes Buffy a Pringle. I say that that's exactly what I said—she's just being difficult—and then the whole conversation starts over again, with each of us explaining that's *not* what we meant.

Maybe she'll eat if I put some yogurt in her food. I wave the spoon at her so she can get a whiff. Then I stir it, scraping the yogurt and kibble around until each piece is evenly coated.

She doesn't seem the slightest bit interested. I move the bowl right in front of her, so she can eat without getting up. Still nothing.

"Whatever, Buff. I don't even care." Even though she and I both know that I do.

I pick up Mom's checklist. There's also a manila envelope marked *Some things to consider.* Knowing Mom, I'm guessing it has something to do with college. She's been relentless lately, pushing for me to go to a four-year university instead of a local college. I'm not even sure I need any college, since Lydia and I already have business experience and mentors. Adding an associate's degree to the Grand Plan was a compromise—give Mom an inch and she pushes for a mile. I set the envelope aside until after I start dinner.

First on the list is to put the chicken in the oven. Got it. Done. Easy.

Next is to assemble a casserole. Mom's already chopped the veggies and put them in the fridge. I read over the printed recipe she included. The steps are confusing and require me to sauté. What does that even mean? I'm not an Iron Chef! This is not assembly; this is *cooking*. Since all the ingredients end up in the same dish eventually, I decide to just mix them up and let the oven work it out—except for the mushrooms and onions, of course, because they're gross. I throw those in the garbage, where they belong. Then I cover the casserole dish with foil, put it in the oven, grab my list and the manila envelope, and head down to the basement.

Next on the list is laundry. I empty the dryer and fold the towels, sewn edge against sewn edge, in half and in half again and then in thirds. Then I stack them in the basket. Neat. Perfect. It's relaxing, like rolling a perm—even and methodical. Lydia doesn't understand why I like it so much. At her house they fold laundry any which way, edges crooked and uneven, slapped together haphazardly. What's the point of folding if the result isn't aesthetically pleasing?

I pull clothes out of the washer, hang up my favorite shirt carefully, and wince at my mother's jeans. She needs something more updated. These jeans are a serious style crime.

After I clean out the lint trap and start the dryer, I go back to the checklist and the manila envelope. I finally peek inside. Sure, enough—college pamphlets.

When Lydia and I announced in eighth grade that we were going to do the cos program, Mom was less than thrilled. She pretty much said that by the time eleventh grade came around, we'd change our minds. We didn't.

She had a huge attitude at the welcome meeting, which was held last year during the final week of tenth grade. We'd already taken our skills tests and had our interviews with both the staff and the graduating seniors. We, the chosen twenty-four soon-to-be juniors, had received our acceptance letters and were "invited"—along with our parents—to the mandatory informational meeting.

That's when it hit Mom that this was real, that we weren't just playing around. All week she tried to get me to change my mind. First, she talked about all the classes Oliver loved in high school and how sad it'd be for me to miss out on them. Then she mentioned how hard it would be to start at a new school halfway through.

Finally, as we were on our way to the meeting, she said, "There was a report on NPR about how people with college degrees earn a million dollars more in their careers than their less educated counterparts."

"Did they give sources for the data? You of all people

know how often studies are skewed just to prove a hypothesis." I threw Mom's statistical background at her. She didn't say another word.

That is, until we were at the meeting and Ms. Garrett said, "Completing our program, students earn up to thirty-four college credits, so those who wish to continue their education already have a head start."

Then Mom perked up and nudged me. "Did you hear that? College credits!"

Ms. G continued by outlining what it takes to become state licensed and explaining that we would be eligible to take the tests immediately following graduation. "Many of our graduates use cosmetology as a temporary or even back-up career. They get flexible salon jobs to help pay for college and go on to do something else if they choose."

College credits for *something else*. That's what she's held on to—and pushed—ever since.

I finally agreed to use the credits toward an associate's degree in business. But I have no intention of going further. What's the point?

I don't even look at the college pamphlets. Instead, the envelope goes into the recycling next to the dryer.

Back upstairs with my basketful of towels, I find Buffy lying in the same place, but her bowl is empty and licked clean, and every stray morsel from the floor is gone. She *was* hungry. I was right—she just messes with me to get her twisted canine jollies! I balance the basket on my hip and open the back door, jingling the bell, so she can go out and do her business, but she still won't budge. I growl at her.

After the towels are put away, I inspect the tear in my skirt. It's not too bad. A few stitches and it'll be as good as new—after I redo my nails. I grab the polish remover, cotton balls, and my home mani kit, flop onto my bed, and turn on Bravo to catch an episode of *Tabatha's Salon Takeover* before I start on my homework. I remove Lydia's botched polish and, while I'm at it, I do my feet, too. I've already seen this episode—actually, I've seen them all—and taken mental notes on how *not* to run things.

Lydia and I are on the same page about pretty much everything having to do with our salon. It's going to be upbeat, professional, and welcoming. Thanks to Tabatha and Ms. G, we also realize how important continuing education is. We'll budget for hair shows every year to keep up with the latest styles and techniques.

Mom's idea of education is different from mine. I get why she's so insistent. She went to college right out of high school, so to her, college is the only door to success. She wants me to have the opportunity to do anything. I just wish she could see that *this* is what I want!

Just as my hands and feet are perfectly polished in Iridescent Iris with black and light-pink polka dots, I hear the bell on the back door jingle—and not a little, like it does when someone comes home. A lot, like Buffy, Her Majesty, has summoned me—pronto!

I jump up, careful not to smudge my nails, and hobble gingerly on my heels down the stairs. I smell the roasting chicken and realize that I'm really hungry. By the time I get to the kitchen, I expect to see Buffy circling the table, like she does when she needs to go out, but no, she's sprawled on the floor again. That can only mean one thing. Yup. She peed on the floor, right by the door—her way of letting me know that I didn't hurry fast enough. She glares at me imperiously.

"Buffy!" I yell. "Bad dog!" I try to project authority as I stomp across the kitchen, but I'm still waddling on my heels with fingers splayed. I'm about as badass as a penguin. She must realize that I mean it, though, because she lumbers to her feet and follows me. Ha! At least I'm an *emperor* penguin!

I grab the roll of paper towels off the holder and turn around—except instead of taking my next awkward step, I slip in Buffy's emptied water bowl puddle and land right on my butt with one foot underneath me. The other foot slides under the leg of the table and scrapes the hell out of my toes, smearing purple nail polish all over the table and floor, and probably my skirt and underwear, too.

I scream, partly in pain, but mostly in frustration, and try to get up. Instead, I slip again. My nail catches the rip in my skirt, tearing the zig from the zag along my thigh. So much for repairing it! Now I'm wearing a chevron dust rag, and my whole back is soaking up dog drool water. Buffy bends down and kisses my cheek, leaving behind a rope of slobber.

Right then, the back door bells jingle again and Oliver and Nina come into the kitchen. Buffy barrels between them, practically knocking Nina off her feet, to get outside.

"Ugh!" Oliver says, noticing the pee puddle, then follows Buffy out to lock the gate so she doesn't get into the street. Nina rushes over—as fast as a hugely pregnant woman can rush, that is—and yells, "Oh my God, Charlotte! Are you okay?"

This would be hilarious if it had happened to someone else. Lying on the floor soaking wet and slimy, I turn my head and see Nina's freshly French-tipped toes in black disposable salon flip-flops. Just seeing them sends me over the edge. Nina didn't leave work because of pregnancy exhaustion. She wanted a pedicure—from a salon, not from me. And here she is, all polished and pretty, standing by the smeared, slobbery mess that I'm lying—no, more like wallowing—in.

I scoot over and wipe my Buffy-slimed cheek across her perfect little pedi.

Nina screams. "Ew! What was that?"

Laughing, I tell her, grab the paper towels from the floor, and clean up the rest of the mess.

Just then, Oliver shows up. "I latched the—" He notices something is going on. "What the—?"

"She slobbered on me!"

"What?"

"Charlotte wiped slobber on my foot," Nina says again, slowly.

Trying to process everything, Oliver keeps looking from Nina to me and asking her questions. Then she and Oliver argue about the cleanliness of a dog's mouth.

I toss out the paper towels and head back upstairs to do homework. On the way, I hear Oliver ask his phone if dog slobber is harmful to pregnant women. Even though I'm a total mess, the look on Nina's face was priceless. I can't wait to tell Lydia all about it.

four

By the time I get downstairs about an hour later, everyone is at the dinner table. The store must've been slow enough for Mike to handle alone, because Dad, Pops, and Ralph are here, too. Mom takes a bite of the broccoli rice casserole and almost instantly spits it into her napkin. "Charlotte." One word and a single look. That's all it takes.

I stab a piece of chicken with my fork and transfer it to my plate. Nina picks at her roll and the salad that Mom must've made when she got home, and Oliver shovels food into his face obliviously.

Dad asks Ralph to pass the salt. Mom intercepts it and gives him the *Moose-you-know-you-shouldn't-eat-salt* look. Then Ralph flashes him the *Sorry-but-I-tried* look. Dad takes the salt and sprinkles it on his food anyway. He smiles at Mom and soothes her by complimenting her dinner and calling her Angel 3.14, his pet name for her, which means "Angel Pi(e)." Ugh. This is what you have to deal with when your parents met in Statistics 101.

Mom returns her attention to me. "You didn't follow the

recipe I left for you." Translation: *You should do what I tell you—follow my instructions, look at those catalogs, forget hairdressing, and go to a prestigious university. Then you'll become something I can brag about.* Mom considers a hairdresser someone you hire, not something you become. No matter how often I tell her that *stylists* are *entrepreneurs* who dictate their own schedules and fees, she doesn't listen.

"I followed it for a while, but then I chose to forge my own path instead." I take a roll and drop it onto my plate. It bounces off and onto the floor, which is not exactly the punctuation I was going for. Buffy nabs it.

"Sometimes tried-and-true methods are more palatable." Mom primly pops a baby romaine leaf in her mouth.

I spoon some of the casserole onto my plate. "And sometimes they're pointless and boring." Then I take a bite. It's really gross, but I swallow quickly and grin.

We can all hear what Nina whispers to Oliver. "Are they still talking about this rice stuff?"

Oliver replies, "Not exactly."

He did what Mom wanted. He dual enrolled his last two years of high school, so when he graduated, he was able to finish college in only two years. Total waste of money, if you ask me. He'd be doing the same job at the store, with or without a degree.

He married Nina while they were both in college— Oliver was in his last semester, Nina in her first. Even though Nina quit school when she got pregnant, Mom still brags that "she'll be back at it as soon as the baby is weaned." Who

knows if that's true—especially since Nina hadn't even de-
clared a major yet—but Mom spins the brags her own way.
Too bad she hasn't figured out how to make my cos career
sound acceptable to her fancy friends from college yet.

"Did you look through everything I left for you?" Mom
pushes away her empty plate—empty except for the casserole, of course.

"Everything except the manila envelope." I grab another
roll and take a bite. With my mouth full, I add, "Buffy peed
on that."

Pops coughs. Is he choking, or laughing? He takes a
drink of water, then says, "Speaking of the rain in Spain." He
sets his glass down once he has our attention and has made
his point—time to change the subject. "Did anyone catch *My
Fair Lady* on AMC last night?"

Ralph takes another piece of chicken and passes the platter to Dad.

Mom isn't done, though. "Then you didn't see the itinerary for the college visits I set up for you?"

"It's a movie, Pops." Dad grabs a drumstick and sets the
platter down. "It's the same performance every time."

"Nope," I say to Mom. There's no need to visit colleges
I'm not going to attend.

"Shows what you know." Pops holds firm. "Movies change
every time you watch them, depending on your mood and
point of reference."

Mom pulls out her phone. "I'll e-mail it to you then, so
you can put it in your calendar."

Or not.

"I liked *Breakfast at Tiffany's* better," says Nina.

Mom hits Send. "Audrey Hepburn was at her best in *Sabrina,*" she says. Then she stands and starts stacking our dinner plates.

"Ah, *Sabrina!*" Pops beams. "Now *that* was a film!"

"Wasn't Rex Harrison in that, too?" asks Dad.

Pops shakes his head. "You're thinking of Harrison Ford. He was in the remake." He might mix up the details of the day-to-day sometimes, but when it comes to anything before 1995, I'd bet the store on all he knows.

My phone pings—Mom's e-mail. Out of curiosity, I click on it. One date jumps out. March 21—the weekend of the Chicago hair show! Which I have already registered and paid for.

"Mom . . ."

She doesn't hear me because she's clearing the table and everyone is talking at once—about their favorite movies and who starred in them, and if there have ever been any remakes. I take a bite of chicken and wait for a lull, but instead Oliver blurts, "Charlotte slobbered on Nina today." I swallow hard.

Everything stops. The chatter. The clearing. The last-minute chewing.

"Thanks, Oliver!" What an asshat! This is not the attention I was hoping for.

"Come again?" Pops asks. I'm guessing he thinks he heard wrong.

Oliver repeats himself. Then everyone looks at me.

"Get over it," I say. "It was just a little dog drool. Once that baby is born, you'll both be covered in all sorts of grossness."

"An infant can hardly be compared to a dog," says Nina.

"I don't know," I say. "Have you seen Oliver's baby pics? Woof!"

"All right," Dad says. "What's done is done. Let's clean up and move on. *Some* of us need to get back to the store." God bless Dad. He never takes sides.

"When are we going to hire someone to help in the deli/bakery?" Oliver asks.

Shut up, Oliver. If I don't tell Mom about the scheduling conflict now, who knows when I'll get another chance.

"I'm working on it," says Dad. "I should have someone within the week. Until then, it'd be nice if we all pulled together, huh?" He looks around the table at each of us, but gives me an especially meaningful look. Why me and not Nina? She's been practically running the place since Patti left. It's her responsibility. I know she's pregnant, but she's got two months to go. Lots of women work right up to their due date.

"Mom!" I yell louder than I intend, getting everyone's attention. She looks at me, eyebrows raised. "I have a conflict with one of the visits you set up. March twenty-first is the Chicago hair show. I already committed and paid—one hundred and seventy-five dollars. You signed the permission slip, remember?"

"No, I don't, but that doesn't matter." Mom brushes me off like crumbs on the table. "Scouting colleges is integral to your future. I'd say it's more important than some hair show, wouldn't you? I'm sure we can get your money back once we explain the situation. I'll talk to your teacher."

"No, Mom!" I'm nearly in tears. "I've already reserved my spot. It's too late to back out. I'm going to be a stylist. The biggest hair show of the year is much more integral to my future, especially after I win the showcase and get interviewed for the TV and newspaper."

Ralph changes the subject. "TV and newspaper?" He seems impressed.

"Yes." I jump on Ralph's curiosity and use it to plead my case. "The winner of the winter style showcase will be on the news—practically a local celebrity—the next day. Once I win, there's no way I can blow off the hair show. It would be like a slap in the face to my instructors, who work so hard for us to succeed in our chosen entrepreneurial field."

It's clear that Ralph is trying not to laugh at how hard I'm working my angle.

My mother, however, is unimpressed. "It's a long shot. Your school's pretty competitive. Lots of talent. I'm sure plenty of people want to win that showcase."

Thanks for the vote of confidence, Mom. "But *I'll* win," I say.

Dad winks at me. "Confidence is key, kiddo."

"And what am I supposed to tell your grandmother?" Mom asks, picking up the silverware. "I have it all set up for you to stay with her that weekend."

"Tell her the truth," I say. "There's a conflict. Isn't that what you were going to tell Ms. Garrett?"

Mom and I glare at each other, neither of us willing to budge.

Ralph leans into Pops. "I smell an opportunity."

Oliver sniffs dramatically. "Oh, yeah! A bet! Now we're talking."

Nobody cares about a disagreement—until there's a wager on it. Then everyone's interested and wants in on the action.

"What are the terms?" Ralph asks. Dad grabs a sheet of paper and a pen from the buffet and hands them to Ralph.

"Simple. If Charlotte wins the showcase, she can go to the hair show," Oliver says. "If she doesn't, off to Grandmother's she goes. Lucky you," he says to me.

"Let's up the ante a bit." Dad taps the table. "If Charlotte places—first, second, or third—she can go . . ."

Mom tries to object, but Dad reminds her how competitive and talented my school is, so she backs down. "And if she comes in first, she can choose her own career path, including college." He's looking right at Mom. She's fuming. I love it. Way to go, Dad!

"So if she doesn't place in the top three, she does what I want her to do?" Mom clarifies.

Dad looks at me, and I nod. I'm not worried, because I'm going to win. I can barely contain myself. Not only will I win and be on the news, but I'll also have Mom off my back. Bonus!

"So it's settled, then," says Ralph. Then he recaps the terms, writes them down on a legal pad, and drafts a pool so everyone can place their bets. Wagers need to choose my exact place. The higher I place, the higher the buy-in for the square, which will weed out the dollar warriors. This is gearing up for high stakes—not only is it the highest buy-in in Pringle history, but my entire future is on the line.

Either I look nervous or Dad realizes how serious this has become, because before Mom and I sign the terms agreement, he asks, "Are you sure you want to do this?" He's probably also worried about being caught in the middle if one of us reneges.

Mom takes the pen and signs her name. Then she hands the pen to me with a sly smile, gathers a pile of dishes, and heads to the kitchen. She's sure she's going to win, which makes me even more determined.

"Charlotte, you don't have to." Dad puts his hand over the paper. "I'll talk to your mom. I'm sure we can work out a compromise, where you can go to the hair show and visit your grandmother another time."

Is Dad just trying to keep peace or does he doubt me, too? Even if we could work something out, Mom will still be on my case about college and every other life decision. It needs to stop now. And winning the showcase is the way to do it.

I move Dad's hand and sign my name. It's a done deal.

five

38 days to the Winter Style Showcase

The stack of catalogs on Ms. G's desk distracts me the whole time she talks about our fund-raiser. This Thursday and Friday morning, we'll be in our salon doing manis and pedis to raise money for the showcase. We'll have mini fund-raisers every other Friday morning after Christmas vacation to raise money for general cos supplies.

"In your computers class today, you'll be creating flyers," continues Ms. Garrett. "Personalize them, print them, and hand them out. You'll earn ATC bucks for every client service you perform. You get credit for every person who requests you, plus you'll all take turns with walk-ins."

The top ATC buck earners will receive a selection of makeup and hair care samples. I don't care if they're samples of things I use or not—I want them!

Shelby must, too, because she asks a bunch of questions. *Forget it, Shelby. They're mine.* Winning the fund-raiser is the first step to winning everything. And it's not like Shelby needs it. Although she could use a little heat protectant spray; her ends are fried.

Toby makes some lewd comment about being paid for his services, and Ms. G sends him down to Mr. Finn, our principal/dean/disciplinarian/guidance counselor. We have a lot to cover today, she warns. We all sit up a bit straighter.

"And now, let's talk about the winter style showcase. Mark your calendars—it's in six weeks." I've had it marked since the first day of school.

She *finally* passes out the catalogs, and everyone starts flipping through them. Our cos teams will join with the fashion design teams to present a live portfolio—three or four models displaying our talents—as well as create a bunch of written reports and give a PowerPoint presentation. Lydia and I, of course, are a stylist duo. "PICs, baby!" I cheer, high-fiving Lyd when I see us on page 114.

We slide our desks together and study the catalog so we can fill out our partner preference forms. The fashion design class is doing the same. After school today, the teachers from both programs will meet to match us up, partly based on our choices, partly based on whom they think will work well together.

"What do you think of them?" I point to a fashion design team who call themselves the Runway Divas. All of the design teams have names; none of us in cos do. I wish we'd thought to name ourselves. It's the first way to make a statement. I'll have to suggest it to Ms. G for next year.

"Yeah, sure." Lydia, who is back to looking like herself, fiddles with the ties on her jewel-green tunic. She doesn't seem very enthusiastic.

"Okay?" I give her a chance to express her disapproval. She doesn't, so I put them on our list. "We have to pick two more." I check out the photos and read through the descriptions. "Definitely not the Denim Duo." I wrinkle my nose.

"Country theme," Lydia and I say at the same time.

"No country, no way, no how!" she adds. *There's* the strong reaction I was looking for.

"Anyone jump out at you?" I ask.

"How about Neon Taffeta?"

"Eh, I don't know," I say. "They seem kitschy."

"I know!" She beams. "Kind of creative, like they'd stand out."

"I want to stand out because we're the best, not the loudest and tackiest."

She gives me a look. "How do you know they're tacky?"

"I can just tell. Okay, next . . ."

"Five minutes!" Ms. G announces.

"Oh my lanta!" I hate being rushed, and scramble to find the perfect choices, but none of the words sink in. "Lydia, help! We need attention to detail, stellar skills, and extra flair."

"You choose." She's flipping through her catalog, not even in the fashion section anymore. "I don't really care."

"*Don't care?*" Lydia knows that apathy is a hundred times worse than vulgarity. "Are you mad because of what I said about Neon Taffeta? If you want them, I'll put them down."

"No, it's fine. We'll find someone else." She goes back to the fashion section. "How about them?" She points to a random listing.

I raise my eyebrows. "Leather and Lace?"

"So they're kind of badass," she says. "What's wrong with that?"

"Nothing. If you're into skulls and Harleys and Ed Hardy, which we aren't."

"Then do what you want." She closes her catalog. "I. Don't. Care."

Ugh! What is *with* her? I try to find the team with the most strengths, but they all start jumbling together. So many of the listings say the same things—*team players, flexibility, proficient in this stitch or that stitch*. None of it screams *winning team*. I decide to judge them by their names. Classic Elegance and Enchanted Velvet seem to best fit my style—and Lydia's, of course—and the showcase theme. Lyd just nods when I tell her. She doesn't even look at their profiles.

I hand our form to Ms. G just as she calls, "Time's up!"

We spend the rest of the morning taking a test on pedicures. I whip through the short answer procedure questions, even though the building trades guys are making a ton of noise down the hall—pounding, sawing, drilling. Why isn't their room down near automotive mech?

The true/false part is trickier than I thought, so I take my time. Yes, sodium hydroxide's pH is highly alkaline. Or is it highly acidic? It's highly something.

Lydia sighs heavily several times, which tells me that either she didn't study or the noise is getting to her, too. Everyone else seems to be equally distracted—except for

Shelby, of course. I raise my hand and ask Ms. G if I can close the doors. As I get up, I see that Lydia's hardly written anything.

I hurry back to my seat and a few minutes later, while I'm pondering the percentage of bleach in a basic disinfecting solution for tools and foot spas, Lydia hands in her test. I still have another page to go. She's quick, but this is quick even for her. I turn back to my paper and refocus. I need to ace this.

I'm one of the last to hand in my paper. When I get back, Lydia is thumbing through the catalog again. "Find a better team?" I whisper. "She might let us change our form."

She shakes her head. Ms. G shushes me. I'm looking up some of the questions in the text to check my answers when the bell rings.

"Just as I thought." Lydia taps my catalog. "There's nobody in here named Reed."

"What?" I open it up and realize I don't even know where to start. There's no index, and I don't know which program he's in. "You must have missed him. There are a lot of people in here."

"I checked them all." She grabs her backpack and slips her purse onto her shoulder. "See for yourself."

"I will." I put the catalog in my purse. "Is culinary arts doing lunch today or are we sneaking out for BOGO Tuesday tacos at Loco's?"

"Culinary arts day is Thursday this week—Mediterranean flatbread pizza and Greek salad. Today is the same mystery casserole the regular cafeteria had the first week of school. So, tacos, duh," she says. "*Ándale.*" Her Spanish accent is so appalling it's funny, but when it comes to choosing food, Lydia is an aficionada.

I was kind of hoping that we'd run into Reed so I could prove that he's real, but I'm not willing to choke down "chicken surprise" when I can get a delicious, authentic taco— half-price—instead. Hopefully, we'll run into him later.

Rachel, a sweet girl from custodial services, waits by my locker, smiling. She rarely says anything, but she always smiles. On the first week of school, in front of everyone in the hall, some little bunhead told her she had a staring problem and to "take a picture, it'll last longer."

Without thinking or breaking my stride, I snapped, "Maybe if you didn't use shitty boxed color, your roots would last longer." Even though her roots *were* hideous, I wouldn't have brought them to her attention if she hadn't been such a rip-roaring bitch.

Ever since then, Rachel stops by my locker at least once a week to show me something. Last week it was a cute hairstyle in *Glitter* magazine. Today it's her French braid. "My cousin did it," she tells me.

"It's a great look for you," I say. "Practical, yet pretty."

She smiles and runs off toward the cafeteria hugging her brown bag lunch. She doesn't say good-bye or anything, but she never does.

"That braid was super crooked," Lydia says halfway to the parking lot.

"I know, but she was so proud of it. It's not her fault that one of us didn't do it. Not everyone is as awesome at braiding as we are."

"True." Lydia stops suddenly. "Hey! Hear that?"

I pause, pretending to hear the sombrero-wearing cat mascot of Loco's Tacos calling. "Oh, hells yeah." Then I yell, "We're coming, Loco!"

— ✳ —

In mathematics and economics—which Lyd and I call "icks"—that afternoon, Mr. Sims, aka Mr. Comb-over, gets us all jazzed talking about ATC bucks. It turns out that we don't just earn them at the fund-raisers—we earn them whenever we do manis and pedis in the ATC salon (along with real money for the cos program to buy supplies), and also if another program subcontracts services from us for their own showcase. The wellness fair is coming up, which is the showcase for child development, culinary arts, and all the medical programs.

I wonder which program earns the most ATC bucks each year? My Pringle gambling gene makes me want to set up a pool.

I'm already scheming ways to be the school's highest earner and win the pool, even if it only exists in my head. First, we need to get a jump on "marketing," as Mr. Comb-over calls it. I text Lydia, even though she's sitting right next to me. **Let's go to the mall tonight to hand out flyers.** A moment later, my phone flashes: **kk.**

Just like Ms. Garrett, Mr. Comb-over pushes subcontracting for our showcases. We'll hire the construction program to build the set, musicians and artists to add personalization to our individual parts, and digital arts to help with our signs, brochures, and PowerPoint presentations. The programs will also hire culinary arts to provide refreshments after the showcase.

They must have had a teachers' meeting about the word "synergy." "All the programs support each other, just as all businesses and consumers support the economy—it's the perfect micro example of the macro synergy in the country's industries," he lectures. By the time he finally gets to the good stuff—spreadsheets, cost analysis, and how we'll get interest on ATC bucks—I'm tempted to write an analysis of the synergistic relationship between his comb-over and hairspray.

There is more synergy talk in civics/sociology with Mrs. Roberts, as well as an overview of everything we're being graded on related to the showcase. Not only does it include the actual makeup and hair and overall concept, creativity, and professional presentation, we're also being graded on our speech and the level and extent of subcontracting, teamwork, and leadership we present. We have to write a million reports, too, which, along with the visuals of our presentation, will make up a gigantic winter style showcase portfolio. It'll count for one-third of our overall semester grade in each class.

And then there's something else, not related to the

showcase: community service. According to Mrs. Roberts, even though it's required, we don't earn ATC bucks for it, only bonus points.

"Bonus points?" I ask, raising my hand.

"You need twenty hours of community service to graduate." Mrs. Roberts's wrinkled beige sweater looks as if she pulled it out of last week's laundry basket. "This is a good time to do it, because the number of hours you put in could be the deciding factor in the event of a tie, and it's a big part of your civics grade, too."

I can't imagine what kind of community service relates to cos. Raising my hand again, I think out loud. "So what do we do? Give random makeovers to people at the mall, or something?" Several kids laugh. "No, seriously. That would beautify the community, right?"

"I'm sure you'll come up with something a little more"— Mrs. Roberts thinks about her next word for a really long time—"impactful." More laughter. But at least I'm asking about it, unlike anyone else.

Finally it's time to head to computer class and make the flyers for the "marketing" we're going to do at the mall. I know how to do this—I've done flyers for Pringle's a million times. This one has to have real style, though, so Lyd and I use clip art, word art, and colorful fonts.

"Girls." Mr. Tim—and yes, we know that name sounds like a mega-star hairstylist, but he's our wannabe-hipster computers teacher—looks at our screen. "You've got a lot going on there. Sometimes simpler gets more attention."

"I hear you." I enlarge the cartoon balloon that says MANI/
PEDI ONLY $10!!!!

"We should make the font for the date and time bigger
and bolder," suggests Lydia. "And maybe make the balloon
yellow?"

"Well, I'm glad you *heard* me, at least." Mr. Tim walks on
to the next computer station.

I change the font and balloon. Personally, I think the
peach looked better, but I'm a team player, so I give in.

We use the color printer—and every piece of lavender
copy paper in the cabinet. "The mall. Seven. Be there," I say
to Lyd with a grin.

— ✳ —

I wait at a table by the Twisted Pretzel for fifteen minutes before
I text her. After another five minutes with no reply, I call and
get voice mail. I pull the ATC catalog out of my purse and
look at the names and faces on every page. No Reed, but there's
the guy who pulled him away from me—Trent Rockwell,
Digital Design. With that mop of hair and his droopy brown—
or hazel?—eyes, he reminds me of a basset hound.

I look closer at each digital dude, but Lydia's right: Reed's
not there. She shows up as I'm trying to figure out why.

"Hey! Sorry I'm late." Lydia collapses into a chair. She's
out of breath, her hair is a disaster, and she has green frosting
on her sleeve. "I have so much to tell you. I've been running
nonstop since school let out. The bakery is freaking busy."

I hand her a napkin and point to her sleeve. Food-smeared

clothes and messy hair aren't exactly our best advertisement. "Your mom hasn't found a replacement for Nutmeg yet?"

She grins. "Just call me Nutmeg 2.0."

"You can't do it all." I pull the flyers out of my purse, along with my wallet, a compact mirror, and a hair clip. "Has she placed any ads?"

"It's okay. I don't mind."

I hand her the mirror and clip and get up. "I need a pop. Want anything?"

"No thanks. I'm good." She peeks in the tiny mirror and tames her stray locks with her fingers and the clip.

When the girl at the Twisted Pretzel—her name tag says Ann—hands me my Diet Mountain Dew, I hand her a flyer. "We're doing a fund-raiser for the ATC cos program. If you know anyone who'd want a mani or pedi, come in on Thursday or Friday morning and ask for Charlotte or Lydia." I point to the bottom of the page. "Only ten bucks!"

"Okay, thanks!" She smiles and takes it. Who knows if she means it, though.

"Don't forget to ask for us." I swipe my card and smile. "We get credit."

Back at the table, Lydia is talking to a couple of guys. When I walk up, they say good-bye and head toward the main entrance.

"Who was that?" I ask, taking a sip of my pop. "The guy in the Carhartt coat is cute."

"I know, right? Just some guys from ATC. They're in the computer programs. One of them is talking to Emily."

"Which one?"

"Which guy, or which Emily?"

"Both."

She spills what she knows—Emily R. met the goatee guy at a party a few weeks ago—even though I really don't care. What I really want to know is how Lydia knows all of this when I don't. Yes, she's friendlier with people than I am, but she usually keeps me in the gossip loop.

We traipse through the mall, handing out flyers to everyone we see and to the clerks in every store that will take them. Some won't, especially if they sell their own nail care products.

When we're done, I'm famished. I suggest Applebee's, since it's right there, and they have the best mozzarella sticks.

"I don't know," Lyd says. "I'm not really hungry."

"Have you already had dinner?" I know perfectly well she hasn't, especially if she's been busy.

"It's just that . . ." She's acting all weird, not even looking at me.

"What?" I say a bit too loudly. I lower my voice. "You have something else going on?"

"No."

"Then what?" We're standing in the middle of the mall right outside Snapz! People are starting to stare.

She whispers, "I don't have any money right now. I spent it at lunch."

She spent it all? She got water with her tacos, and her total was less than two bucks.

"Is that it?" I grab her arm and start toward Applebee's. "I'll cover you."

Right after the server brings us our drinks and disappears, Lydia says, "I'm pretty sure I failed my pedi test."

"I doubt it." We pull the papers off our straws. "It was super easy."

"Maybe for you." She takes a sip of her water. "I'm just not sure I'm cut out for this."

"Of course you are!" I look at the menu, although I don't know why. We always order the same thing—chicken tenders from the 2 for $20 menu. "You've just been too busy at the bakery. I'll help you before the next test. No worries." I look around for our server. "Where'd she go? I'm starving."

She must have been right behind me, because suddenly she appears. "Sorry about that. What can I get ya?"

Lydia says, "A cup of the chicken tortilla soup."

"We're not getting our usual?" I ask.

Lydia blushes, but I don't know why. Ordering food isn't embarrassing. "Come on. You don't want the *soup!*" Then I say to the server, "No offense."

"None taken, hon." Her messy ponytail wags as she shakes her head. "I wouldn't eat it, either."

"See?" I don't wait for Lydia to answer. I order our tenders and our mozzarella sticks with two ranch dressings, no marinara. When the server leaves I ask Lydia, "What's the matter?"

"I told you I don't have any money," she says, more into her water than to me.

"And I told you that I'd cover it. You can pay another time. No biggie."

"That's just it. I'm not sure when . . ."

I wave her off. "Whenever. We're PICs, remember?" Lydia nods after a second, and I change the subject. "I looked through the whole catalog, and you're right. Reed isn't in it at all. I've figured it out. He's an undercover cop trying to bring down the weed dealers in automotive mech."

Lydia laughs. "Oh, okay, Sherlock."

"Yeah, and speaking of the catalog." I pull it out of my bag. "I've marked everyone we're going to need to subcontract for our presentation."

"Shouldn't we wait for our designers?"

"We can't wait for a second. We *need* to win this." Then I tell her all about the bet. "So this is so much more than a school project to me. My whole future depends on it."

"God, Charlotte!" says Lydia. "It's one thing to bet on melting snow and a bagger's hiccups. Are you sure you want to risk everything on a contest?"

"It's too late. I already signed. I can't go back now. We just have to make sure we win."

Lydia shakes her head. I don't know why she's so worried. Even if by some strange twist of fate we don't win, we're sure to place.

The server brings our mozzarella sticks. I thank her and rip open a container of ranch. "So I was thinking of a fantasy Candy Land theme, since you're so good with sugar flowers. Wouldn't those look fantastic in a piecey updo?"

"Yeah, probably." She dips a mozzarella stick.

"And then the dresses can be shimmery with crystals all over them to look like candy, too," I continue. "Using glitter and shine spray, we could make the models look as if they're made of sugar."

"As long as nobody throws water on them," Lydia says while chewing. "We wouldn't want them melting, melting, melting." She cackles like the wicked witch from *The Wizard of Oz*.

"Very funny." I peel off some breading and pop it in my mouth.

She pauses to wipe her hands. "This all sounds really great, but won't the fashion girls want to design their own dresses?"

"Oh, they can," I say. "But our ideas are going to blow them away. They can use them as a starting point."

"Uh-huh." Lydia sounds apprehensive. "Um, but I wonder—you know, you just have this way of taking over sometimes . . ."

"I do not!" I polish off the last mozzarella stick, stack the plates, and gather all the debris from the straw and napkin wrappers. "But someone's got to be in charge of this thing. We only have thirty-eight days, and I don't want to go into the first meeting without a plan."

Our food comes, and while we eat I tell Lydia about my plans for subcontracting. I have ideas that include quite a few of the programs. "To be *synergistic*." We both roll our eyes.

"But we're going to have to cover some of the costs with actual cash, right?" she asks. "We can't subcontract everything. Remember last year? Some of those presentations were pretty extravagant."

In eighth grade Lydia and I attended the ATC visitation and fell in love with the cos program. We've attended every winter style showcase since then—observing, critiquing, planning. Last year, when we heard we'd actually been accepted, we made our parents go, too. I can't believe it's finally our turn to shine.

"Maybe a little, but it'll be ninety-nine percent ATC bucks." I count out the financial plan by holding up my fingers. "First, there's the fund-raiser, which we're going to own. Next, the fashion designers will add their own supplies and ATC bucks to the mix. Finally, don't forget about all the makeup and hair care tools we already own."

"I don't know. It still sounds expensive."

"It shouldn't be too bad." A little ketchup drips between my fingers.

She takes a sip of water. "I, uh, need to talk to you about that. It's kind of about this dinner, too."

"Okay." I wipe the ketchup off my hand with my napkin.

"You know how my dad was sick?" She picks at her thumbnail, leaving little peelings from yesterday's mani on the table. It's a nervous habit, and she's tried to stop, but it's not great if you're going to be a professional stylist. At least she doesn't bite them anymore.

"Uh-huh." My hand is still sticky, so I look through my

purse for a wet-nap. Lydia's dad suffers from serious depression. He was hospitalized for nearly three weeks last summer, and it was several more months before he was working again full-time. Wait! What is she saying? I stop what I'm doing and look at her. "Oh, no! He's not sick again, is he? Oh, Lyd."

"No! No, it's nothing like that." She fidgets with the salt and pepper shakers. "He's doing much better. Great, actually. It's just that . . ."

Then her phone rings. Lyd takes the call, and I take the salt and pepper shakers and put them back with the dessert menu. After listening for a few moments, she says, "I'll be right home," then hangs up. "That was Mom. More bakery stuff."

"So, quick, tell me about your dad," I say. Is he still hassling her mom about working so many hours? Are they getting divorced? Is he really as *great* as she says?

When he was sick, it was so hard on them. Some days he didn't get out of bed, and then he'd be up all night. The meds made him look and act like a zombie. They couldn't get the combo and dosage right until he was hospitalized.

"It's no big deal, really." She leans in and whispers. "It's just that things are a little tight right now until the hospital bills are paid off."

What is she talking about? I told her I'd cover dinner. The project? It's not like it's going to be that expensive.

"You have insurance, right?" I whisper back. "That should cover most of it. Besides, what do your parents' bills have to do with you? You have a job. Your mom's paying you, right? It's not like they'd have to pay for the showcase or anything."

"Yeah, yeah. You're right." She stands and grabs her coat. "I have to get home. You sure you got this?"

"I said I would. PIC, remember?" I pick up the check. "Sure everything's okay?" She nods, but doesn't entirely meet my eyes. "Then get out of here." I pluck my debit card from my wallet. "Say hi to your parents. I'll see you tomorrow."

"Thanks." She smiles and leaves.

After I get home, I spend the rest of the evening creating a detailed plan for our presentations, complete with a time-line and checklists. To win the showcase, we need to get a jump on things. And Lydia is so distracted by bakery crap, she's going to need all the direction and support I can give.

Charlotte's Vision for the Winter Showcase

★ Our team wears coordinating outfits.

★ Props: giant candy "forest" added to fairy-tale background, sugary accents.

★ Wow-factor prop: Snow machine.

★ Music: whimsical flute music for the PowerPoint and speech/model presentation.

★ PowerPoint first: behind-the-scenes pictures of our work throughout the semester.

★ Speech/Model Presentation next: Required—ONE model each. However, to fully showcase our skills, we—our fashion designers, Lydia, and I—will go above and beyond and style TWO each. On stage, we discuss the techniques we used as the models walk and turn.

★ Thunderous applause!

★ We win first place!

★ I win the bet!

★ We are so legendary that we become the standard by which first place is judged in upcoming years.

six

37 days to the Winter Style Showcase

Wednesday morning Ms. Garrett tells us that we've been matched with our fashion design teams, and the lists are posted in the multipurpose room. We'll have our first meeting there. I'm so excited that I don't even check my hair and makeup first. Everyone races down the hall.

I find Lydia's and my name and look across the list to . . . Runway Divas!

"Woo-hoo!" I yell. Then I jump up and down and high-five Lydia. "We got our first choice!"

Within minutes, we've tracked them down—Gabriella, who is not "Gabby," she tells us right away, and Shea. "Which rhymes with 'hey,'" she says with a singsong voice and a wave.

Gabriella is dark-skinned, with big brown eyes and the longest, curliest eyelashes I've ever seen. They're real, too; I know my falsies, and these are legit. Her hair is cropped short, which really accentuates her eyes. The girl is straight-up gorgeous.

Shea, on the other hand, has long, straight reddish hair,

and her skin's so white she's practically translucent. The contrast between the two Runway Divas is almost comical. It's not like Shea's ugly—she's got kind of an ice princess thing going on—but even with all the makeup she's wearing, she pales in comparison to Gabriella, both literally and figuratively.

I begin by introducing Lydia and myself.

"So," Gabriella says before I get a chance to even open my binder, "Shea and I have the costumes all planned out. We're thinking short dresses with jagged hemlines."

"And wings and Chuck Taylors." Shea squeals. "Like punk pixies!" She waves her hands in the air. I wish she would fly away and get off my nerves.

"Pixies?" I snap. "What are we supposed to do with their hair?"

"Pixie cuts," Shea snaps back. "Duh!"

"We can't cut hair yet. We're only juniors," explains Lydia, the voice of reason. Didn't anyone go over the rules with them? "We're doing hairstyles, accessories, and semipermanent color only."

"Let me show you what we have in mind," I say, pulling out my notes. After the two of them and Lydia have a copy of the plan—which I made at home last night—I begin. "We were thinking a sweets theme, using candy flowers and shimmer to make the models look sugary." I show them the picture on the third page, a cream-colored dress that looks as if it's made of frosting that I found online. "Wouldn't it be cool to do the skirt like this, with some of the flowers made from ribbon and others out of actual sugar?"

Lydia looks at the picture. "Ooh! The top looks like it was frosted with a serrated spatula. Love it!"

Shea wrinkles her tiny, pointy nose, as if my idea stinks.

"Why couldn't we combine all of our ideas?" Gabriella inspects the picture. "We have three or four models to present. One could look like a shimmery, sugary pixie—with an updo—and another could wear a frosting dress. These ribbon flowers are easy."

"I can do sugar flowers in my sleep," Lydia says.

The next thing I know, she and Gabriella are brainstorming how *they* can pull off *my* idea! Shea and I are left glaring at each other while they babble about frosting and ribbon and "pops of color." I thought this was going to be two teams working together, and anyway, if it's my idea, I should be in charge. I'm fuming. And Shea? Talk about a Runway Diva. I don't even want to talk to her. She must feel the same way about me, because she pulls out her phone and starts texting.

"So what are you guys going to do?" Gabriella asks. *You guys?* What?

Shea doesn't even look up from her phone. "I've already designed my dresses. I'm sure Charlotte can figure out some hair to go with them."

Gabriella and Lydia exchange glances. What, are they *friends* now who can read each other's minds?

"You know, Shea," suggests Gabriella, "you already planned on using sheer fabric. There's no reason the two ideas can't be merged and coordinated beautifully."

"Whatever."

Knowing that a big part of our grade is teamwork, I decide to make the best of this disaster. "Hey!" I say. "How about we subcontract little kids from child development and ballet dancers to be our models? One could wear your pixie dress"—I look at Shea—"and they'd all dance and twirl across the stage en pointe, like they're flying." Gabriella nods as if she agrees. My "propensity for adaptation" will certainly be highlighted in my report.

"Perfect! Like Sugar Plum fairies!" Lydia exclaims. "Not to mention *synergistic*." I grin. About time she rejoined Team Charlotte.

Shea thinks about this for a second, slips her phone into her pocket, and almost smiles. "It might just work."

We decide to stockpile as many ATC bucks as we can before our next meeting, to get an idea how much we'll have to spend on subcontracting. PIC has met the Runway Divas and prevailed.

~ ✖ ~

Friday is the second day of the cos fund-raiser. Lydia's and my marketing efforts paid off—Thursday was nonstop, client after client, and there was even a line at one point. Several teachers and administrators, including Mr. Finn, came in for services. The salon was buzzing. The first hour or so, I kept track of how many clients each team had—we were neck and neck with Shelby and Taylor, and Joelle Sims and

Tasha Green, and the Emilys were right on our tails—but then I got focused on my work and lost count. I expect today to be just as busy.

I haven't seen Reed for days, but I do see the guy who pulled him away the other day. The basset hound guy. He's taller than I remember—like seven feet—and thin. His hair is dark and curly, and he still needs a cut. What was his name? Oh, yeah, Trent. "Hey," I say, joining him as he walks down the hall.

"Hey, yourself," he says.

Then I realize that I'm not sure how to ask about Reed without looking like a creepy stalker. "So, have any of you digital dudes been subcontracted for the winter style show-case yet?"

"Digital dudes?" He laughs. "Yeah, some of us have, even though we're not all dudes. Why?" He stops and looks at me as if he's trying to figure out whether I'm hitting on him. He gives me a crooked smile, and a lock of dark, curly hair flops into his eyes. They're hazel. He's not bad looking, but he's no Reed. Maybe I can introduce him to Lydia.

"Just taking a survey," I say, looking away. "And . . . I noticed you're not all listed in the catalog."

Something in his face changes, and he stops smiling. He knows why I asked. "Oh, you mean Reed?" I don't say any-thing, but my look must give me away because he adds, "He started the program late—a week or two after the bios were turned in, I think."

"Oh, okay," I say. "That makes sense."

The crowd flows around us. "So you want to know if he's already taken?" he says, with a bit of an edge.

Is he talking about the showcase or romantically? I want to know the answers to both, of course, but I don't appreciate his attitude. "You don't know me or what I want," I sass. Then, a second later, "But now that you mention it, is he?"

"You're going to have to ask *him*. And, by the way, you have a couple of tarantulas on your eyelids." And he strides away, not even looking back once. Forget him. He's too arrogant for Lydia.

When I get to the cos salon, things are in full swing. Ms. Garrett is on the other side of the reception area unlocking the door to the parking lot. Shelby and Taylor are folding towels at Shelby's hair station, and Joelle and Tasha are tossing out dried up nail polishes. Byron grabs his nail kit and cuticle oil from the supply closet. Even Toby is working, setting up his manicure station. Lydia is already there, too, wearing her smock and sitting in a pedi chair along the far wall with her feet on each side of the foot spa in front of her. "Hey, can we talk?" she asks.

"Sure. I'm sorry. Things have been crazy this week." I sit down on a rolling stool and let my purse slide down my arm to the floor. I spin to look in the mirrored wall, batting my lashes. "Do these look like tarantulas?"

She half laughs. "Uh, no! Why?"

I don't think so, either. "No reason." Trent's an idiot.

Lydia peels nail polish off her thumb again. "I haven't known how to—"

"Charlotte. Lydia," Ms. G pages from the reception desk. She's only a few feet away, but she says paging is more professional. Personally, I think it's obnoxious, but nobody asked me. "Your first appointment has arrived."

"Talk later?" Lydia must really want to tell me something.

"Sure. Of course." I turn on the hot water for my foot bath, and go introduce myself to my client. I've already met her, though—it's Ann, from the Twisted Pretzel. Her friend Raynee introduces herself to Lydia.

"Hey!" I say. "Thanks for requesting us."

"No problem." Ann's already hung up her coat, and follows me back. "I usually do my own pedicures, but since neither of us has class until later this afternoon, Raynee thought it'd be fun to have a spa day."

"Great idea!" I show Ann to my station.

"We might even splurge for manicures," Raynee says, lowering her feet into Lydia's foot bath, "if you have time."

"We'll make time," I say. *Cha-ching!*

"Cute shirt," Lydia says to Ann. "Snapz!, right?"

"Actually, it's part Snapz! and part Raynee Gilbert." Ann holds her arms out like she's presenting a fabulous prize on a game show. "Raynee alters most of our clothes."

"You? Wow! That's amazing!" As usual, Lydia is instantly comfortable and making conversation with Raynee as if they're old friends. They talk about sewing and how it's a lost art and clothing sizes and how they don't fit anyone, really.

It's not as easy for me, but I try. "What school do you guys go to?"

"Officially, Northwest," says Ann, "but we're taking dual enrollment courses three days a week at Jackson College."

I set up my scrub, lotion, and tools on the tiled area around the foot spa. "That's cool. My brother did that, too."

Lydia pulls out her pedi note card and sets it next to her. Raynee notices, but doesn't say anything. I'm super embarrassed. "We're students, so we're still learning," I say quickly. "We want to make sure we don't skip anything." I leave out the fact that we should know how to do a simple pedi blindfolded by now, and that *I* do.

"No problem." Raynee scrolls through her phone.

Lydia and I set up the rest of the tools and lotions on a towel while Raynee and Ann relax, soaking their feet in the warm, sudsy, lavender-scented water. Music plays in the background, like in a regular salon. Around us, several others—even some guys—are getting the salon treatment.

When I start buffing the rough spots on Ann's feet, she pulls away and giggles. "Sorry," she says. "I'm really ticklish. That's why I've always done my own pedis."

"No problem." I smile and apply more pressure. "Is this better?"

"Actually, it is!" She seems really impressed. "Thank you. I was worried I wouldn't be able to do this." Then she turns to Raynee and says, "I'm going to have to send Mom, Jackie, and Chris in here. She's really good. And my feet really needed it."

I smile as I move around each toenail with a curette. "That's my purpose in life. Ridding the world of calluses and unsightly toe jam one foot at a time." Ann and Raynee laugh, and Lydia just shakes her head.

Even though I joke, I really do feel as if I'm doing something important. People feel better about themselves when they're well-groomed, and when they feel better they're nicer, and when people are nicer, everyone around them is happier. So the way I see it, I'm promoting world peace. Well, maybe I wouldn't go *that* far. But who couldn't use a little self-esteem and mood boost?

I remind them about our upcoming fund-raisers—every other Friday, starting right after Christmas break—and tell them I'd really appreciate any referrals. They say they'll definitely let their friends and family know, and I get to work with a nail rasp. Lydia fumbles with her cards, then looks at her tools and shrugs. As nonchalantly as possible, I hand her the rasp and slowly demonstrate one-direction filing. She follows my lead.

"Guess who's coming for Thanksgiving?" Ann asks Raynee.

"Jon?" Raynee wiggles her eyebrows.

I pretend I'm not listening, but I am. Not only does cosmetology make the client feel good, it allows me to eavesdrop freely and without disdain. Today is the best day ever.

"No! You know he has his own family dinner." Ann air-swats her. "Tony!"

"Really?"

"Really." Ann beams. "Gram invited him, and he accepted."

"That's so cool."

I guess I'm not very good at pretending to not listen, because Ann explains that Tony's her older brother, and he's spent a couple of years away from their family.

I'm glad that someone at least is looking forward to Thanksgiving. While I love having the day off, Grandmother Vanderpool will be coming. She's so formal, which always makes us more tense than grateful. Even Mom is tense, and Grandmother Vanderpool's her mother.

They continue to talk about Ann's family as I lotion and massage and paint her toes. She chose Iridescent Iris, too. I knew I liked this girl.

When they're both done—and Lydia has, thankfully, done a decent job—Raynee decides that yes, they'll splurge on the manis, too. She loves the Harvest Pumpkin color I suggested.

While they talk about double-dating with their boyfriends, I look over at Lydia, who's concentrating on Raynee's right hand, and imagine spa days in our own salon with us gabbing about our boyfriends—or maybe even husbands, down the line when we're fully established.

We've never let guys come between us. It's kind of our rule—we don't date anyone unless the other approves, and we don't bail on plans with each other for a date or a boyfriend. And if we're both in a relationship at the same time, it's important that our guys like each other, too. The few times it's happened, we've all hung out and it's been awesome.

This gets me thinking about Reed, and how I want Lydia to meet him before he asks me out—*if* he asks me out, which I hope he does, soon.

After we finish the girls' nails, they ask for more flyers to pass out to people they know. We hand them a whole stack and thank them for supporting us. They thank us and tip us each five bucks, even after they pay the ten to the salon. I can't believe we're getting paid for doing something we love so much!

The rest of the morning flies by so fast that I'm shocked when Ms. Garrett tells us to clean up our stations because the bell is about to ring.

Once class is over, we head out to the hall together.

Lydia sighs and rubs her temples. "That was rough. We barely had enough time to finish one client before the next one showed up."

"I know. Wasn't it great? I bet we set a record! Shall we sneak out for lunch to celebrate?"

"Can't," she says. "I have a meeting with Mr. Finn."

"Finn? Why?" I stop walking and some kid from auto tech runs into me.

"Hey, watch it!" he snaps. "Hey, Lydia, did you say you're meeting with Finn?"

I growl at him, as if he were my dog Buffy not wanting to go outside.

"Easy, killer." Lydia laughs. Then to the guy, she says, "Don't worry. Her growl's worse than her bite. Yeah, I am. Why?"

He gives me a sideways look as he says to her, "Can you

tell him his car is ready? We changed the oil and fixed the broken windshield wiper."

"Sure. No problem, Jake."

Jake walks off toward the cafeteria.

"You know that guy?" I ask. "And why are you meeting with Finn?"

"Sort of. We've talked a few times. He's nice. I can't explain about Finn now, but it has to do with the stuff I need to talk to you about." She takes a few steps down the hall, turns around, and walking backward, says, "Let's hang out this weekend."

Now I'm super curious. She's tried to talk to me a few times, and nobody meets with Mr. Finn on purpose. Maybe this has to do with being late on Monday? "For sure. Text me."

Except that doesn't happen. First of all, Lydia isn't in any of our afternoon classes. And when she texts, I'm working and can't get back to her. By the time I remember, it's late, so she doesn't reply. Sunday is pretty much the same. If something were really wrong, I'd know, right? When her dad was sick, we talked (or texted) practically nonstop. We'll catch up on Monday. After all, if whatever she needs to talk about were really important, she'd come to the store.

I am the queen of the deli/bakery, a dubious honor. Dad still can't find anyone reliable to supervise, and Katie—whose cat is better—isn't great on the counter by herself. By her own admission, she's more of an assistant.

Nina didn't really quit, of course. (She's fake-quit at least four times this year. And yes, there's a pool for that, too.)

She's there sometimes, but we really need someone full-time; two people at the counter is best. I can only work after school and on weekends. If need be, Dad or Pops will fill in for me, but it's not their thing. Needless to say, instead of hanging out with Lydia and getting the low-down on her meeting, I spend my weekend elbow-deep in deli meats, cold salads, doughnut batter, frosting, and sprinkles—not to mention Katie's repetitive stories and pictures of her cat's "hilarious" antics, which all look the same except for the various outfits (yes, she dresses up her cat), and Nina's whining about being kicked in the ribs.

My life's a constant party.

seven

32 days to the Winter Style Showcase

On Monday, I get to school early, hoping to grab some time with Lydia. After tossing in my coat, grabbing my books, and doing a quick lip gloss check, I slam my locker, turn around, and come face to face with Reed. Clearly, early arrival has unexpected benefits. "Hey."

"Hey." He leans into the lockers. "I hear you want me."

I laugh out loud. I can't help it. What a cliché! Even if it is sort of true, I'm not about to fall for that line. "Get over yourself." I *tap, tap, tap* away in my turquoise sling-backs, hoping he follows.

He does. *Yes!*

"I meant as a graphic designer for your showcase." He acts offended. "What did you think I meant?"

I give him a *don't-play-with-me* look, and he smiles. He is so freaking adorable!

"Okay, seriously." He starts fast-talking. "I need the sub-contracting. We don't have our own showcase. Our grades are based on what we do for everyone else's show."

"Well, we do need a graphic designer." I'm in professional mode now. "How are your skills?"

"The best."

"You're in."

"Don't you need to check with the rest of your team?"

"Officially, yes, but I'm not worried."

"Cool," he says. "I'll put your name on my schedule. How do you spell it?"

Good one. I haven't told him my name. I decide to play his little game. "The standard way." He smirks. He knows I've caught him, but I decide to let him off the hook. "Charlotte. Charlotte Pringle."

"I'll do it right now, Charlotte Pringle," he assures me.

"Perfect." I get the last word because we're at the cos classroom door. I leave him standing in the hall. *Score.* I don't care what the rest of the team thinks—as far as I'm concerned, Reed's our graphic designer.

Lydia's not in class yet. I take out my phone to text her and see she beat me to it, an hour ago.

I NEED to talk to you. Call me ASAP.

Oh, no! We never hung out—or even talked—this weekend like we'd planned. Maybe something really is wrong. I press her pic in my favorites and wait for her to answer. Voice mail! *Ugh!* I hang up and call again. Again, voice mail. I text: **Where are you? What's wrong? I'm at school.**

The first bell rings. No Lydia. I turn around every few seconds, but only non-Lydia people are coming into class. I walk to the door and scan the hall. She's not there. I go to the window. I don't see her Volkswagen, but since I can only see half of the parking lot, that's not definitive. I return to my seat.

I overhear one of the Emilys say to Taylor, "Did you hear about the fashion design girl who got booted for turning in a dress from Younkers as her own design?"

"I heard that Younkers' CEO called from New York and threatened to sue the school," says the other Emily.

"That's not true," says know-it-all Shelby. "Nobody got booted. She's just *moving* to *Yonkers, New York,* with her parents. It's no big deal."

The first Emily is skeptical. "How do you know?"

"Because she was our designer," says Shelby. Taylor nods.

The other Emily asks something else and Shelby answers, but I can't hear because the second bell rings and she's whispering. Shelby and Taylor lost their designer? What does that mean? There weren't enough fashion designers to match up with all of us, so one team only has one—Shelby and Taylor's. I'm just about to turn around and ask some questions of my own, but right then Ms. Garrett rushes into class, muttering something about being late because of a meeting.

"I have the results of the fund-raiser!" she exclaims as soon as we're settled. She even waves spirit fingers—once a cheerleader, always a cheerleader. My heartbeat flutters like Ms. G's twinkling acrylics, and I'm not sure if it's from anticipation about the results, or because I'm worried about Lydia.

Where is she? Why does she *NEED* to talk to me? If she was just running late because of bakery stuff or something, she probably wouldn't even text, let alone use all caps. Something is going on.

"Your first ATC bucks deposits have been made into your team accounts. You'll use them to pay your subcontractors. Negotiate with your team about how you'll distribute your funds."

Taylor raises her hand to ask about accessing the accounts. She wasn't listening last week, when we went over all of this? Great. Now Ms. G needs to explain it again, and it takes forever.

Finally, *finally,* she's done going over the online forms and "banking." "Now for our winners . . ." Desk drum rolls. I'm nervous, even though I know we're going to win. *Just say our names, already.* Ms. G pulls out a piece of paper like she's reading the Oscar nominees. "In third place . . ." The drum rolls stop. "The Emilys!" Both Emilys stand and bow and we all cheer. Ms. G hands them little prize bags.

"In second place, Shelby and Taylor!" They both walk to the front, but instead of taking a bow, Shelby just stands there in her cute peacock-print pumps looking pissed. She grabs her prize without even looking at it. She didn't win, and she obviously wanted it as badly as I do.

This must mean that we've won! *Where is Lydia?*

"And our winners for the big fund-raiser event are . . . Charlotte and Lydia!" We each get two bags—one full of hair care samples and another full of makeup and nail polish. Ms. G gives all four bags to me as everyone claps and cheers.

Shelby gives a half-assed clap. I curtsy twice, once for me and once for Lydia.

As happy as I am to win—and I have to admit that our marketing at the mall was brilliant—I can't fully embrace it until I know Lydia is okay and she celebrates with me. This is the first step toward our shared future. I console myself by imagining the two of us winning the showcase—together.

Next, Ms. G hands back our pedi tests. As she gives Shelby hers, she winks at her. Teacher's pet! How obvious! At least I got an A. As much as I'd like to know Lyd's grade, since she was so worried, I'm even more concerned about where she is.

The whole time Ms. G is lecturing about chemical hair treatments and what they do to the integrity of the hair shaft, I glance between my phone and Lydia's seat, willing her to appear. The clock above Ms. G's desk is excruciatingly slow.

At the sound of the classroom phone, I jump in my seat. It rarely rings and it's so freaking loud. "Excuse me," Ms. G steps away from her PowerPoint to answer it.

Everyone is quiet, trying to figure out what's going on.

"Yes . . . It's fine . . . So it's finalized, then? . . . I'm sorry to hear that. . . . Yes, I understand. . . . As we discussed? . . . Yes . . . Right . . . I'll tell her." I can't figure out anything from that and based on my classmates' confused faces, they can't, either.

Ms. G hangs up the phone and says, "Charlotte, Mr. Finn would like to see you."

The whole class erupts with, "Oooooh!"

Me? Mr. Finn wants to see *me*? Never in my life have I been called to the principal's—or vice-principal's, or anyone's—office. Ever.

I stand up and smooth my skirt, looking at Ms. G expectantly. "Should I take all of my stuff with me?" I ask. She nods, so I pick up my purse and backpack. Everyone's eyes follow me as I walk out. I can almost feel them.

As I close the classroom door behind me, I hear Ms. G return to her lecture. My first thought is, How am I going to get the notes I'll miss since Lydia's not there? My next thought: Does this meeting with Mr. Finn have anything to do with *why* she's not there?

In ninth grade, Jordy McCann was called to the office in the middle of pre-algebra because his mom was in a bad car accident on I-94. I didn't know him that well, and I'd never met his mom, but still I felt so bad for him.

What if something happened to Lydia?

Tap, tap, tap. My heels are so loud and echo in the empty hallway.

Or did something happen to her parents? Wasn't she trying to tell me something about her dad the other day? She said he was doing great, didn't she?

Tap, tap, tap.

Was she hiding something? Or is this completely new?

Tap, tap, tap, tap, tap.

Then I think of Jordy McCann again. Maybe it has nothing to do with Lydia. What if something's happened to *my* parents? Or to Pops?

I pick up my speed. *Tap—tap—tap—tap.*

Why does the office need to be a million miles away? I can't walk fast enough.

By the time I get there, I'm out of breath and practically in tears. I rush in so fast that the heavy wooden door slams behind me. A bit more of a dramatic entrance than I'd meant, but I can't help it.

"Mr. Finn called for me," I manage to blurt out to the secretary, who looks as if she's never seen a freaked-out girl before. "I'm Charlotte Pringle."

"Charlotte. Yes." She holds open the gate that separates the waiting area from the inner workings of the Arts and Trades Center's main office and points to a door that's slightly ajar. "He's waiting for you in there."

The office staff's and administrative students' eyes follow me. I know they hear my heels tapping, but I wonder if they also hear my heart pounding through my eardrums, and if they know what's going on, and do they feel bad for me, like I did for Jordy McCann?

I knock lightly and open the door. Mr. Finn, who's sitting behind a gigantic, imposing desk, indicates an empty chair and says, "Charlotte, come in. Have a seat."

As I walk across the geometric-patterned rug, I brace myself for whatever horrible news he has for me. Then I see Lydia. Lydia! She's in one piece, every golden spiral curl in place. I resist the urge to hug her and tell her that we won the fund-raiser. I sit and give her a huge smile of relief.

She presses her lips together and looks away. Uh-oh. Something *is* wrong! My heart speeds up, and I feel sick to my stomach.

"Charlotte, I'm not sure how much you already know." Mr. Finn laces his fingers together like he's praying or something. *Nothing. I know nothing.* "We've had a few, uh, changes within some of the programs." He moves his prayer hands back and forth in a chopping motion as he talks.

"Okay."

"One of our fashion design students has left the program," he says. So at least part of what I heard this morning is true. "Which means we've had to do some juggling to accommodate everyone in cosmetology."

Still not picking up what you're putting down, Mr. Finn. Why doesn't he get to the point?

"Since your team obviously needs to be adjusted, too, we—the fashion design instructor, Ms. Garrett, and I—have decided to move Gabriella to Shelby and Taylor's team. I've talked to each of them this morning, and they're good—"

"Wait! What?" I look back and forth between Mr. Finn and Lydia. "Why does *our* team need to be adjusted?"

"Because Lydia has switched to the culinary arts program," Mr. Finn says slowly, as if I should already know this, which I don't. I most certainly do not. My face must give me away, because he turns to Lydia and says, "I thought you told her."

Lydia? Culinary arts? *Switched?* What? *When?* The geometric shapes on the rug seem to vibrate. I stare at them, trying to steady them. And myself.

"I was going to tell you," Lydia chokes out, barely audible. "I mean, I tried. Kind of." Her voice is more normal now. "I don't know." From the corner of my eye, it looks as if she's searching her lap for a cheat sheet that's not there.

I should say something—ask questions, try to figure this out—but I don't know where to start. All the way down the hall, I imagined all sorts of bad things that could have happened. I tried to prepare myself for anything. But not this. Lydia, my BFF—my PIC—has blindsided me.

I stare at Mr. Finn's praying ax hands. "For Lydia to make a smooth transition to culinary arts . . ." he begins.

Lydia. Transition. Culinary arts. His words echo along with my throbbing pulse while his hands chop away at my world.

"She'll need to focus on the wellness fair, which is their showcase, of course, and it's coming up in less than two weeks."

Wellness fair. Showcase. Two weeks.

"We've decided that the two of you can continue as a team, even though you're officially in different programs."

Continue. Team. Different. Programs.

"You'll assist her at the fair, and she'll assist you in your showcase. Of course, once the empty spot in cos is filled from the waiting list, that student will also be on your team. Unfortunately, because the fashion design program is so new and doesn't offer a state certificate, there is no waiting list. So your team, as well as Shelby and Taylor's, will need to function with only one fashion designer."

Blah. Blah. Blah. Blah.

"We realize this is unusual, but the program directors both speak highly of your ability to lead and to adapt. Look at the bright side—while it may feel as if you've lost a team member today, by the time of your showcase, you'll still have four people dedicating their time and talents to your team." Mr. Finn forces a grin that makes me wince.

Blah. Blah. Blah. Yeah. Yeah. Yeah. Bright side?

I've got to get out of here before I get sick.

"Do either of you have any questions?" he asks. I can't speak. Lydia is dead silent. Mr. Finn clears his throat. "Well, then. Please talk to your program directors should any questions or problems arise. My door is always open as well." Then he chuckles, and stands up. "Well, usually, anyway. Sometimes, it's just cracked."

Chuckle. Cracked. Chuckle. Cracked.

Cracked.

That's when I realize that's exactly how I feel. Cracked.

I stand, too. I think Lydia does as well, but I'm not looking at her.

Mr. Finn walks around the desk and escorts us to the door. My ankles wobble as I concentrate on moving across the cushy geometric shapes.

I'm not sure what Mr. Finn says next, but I'm pretty sure it's some sort of *see-you-later* pleasantry, because the next thing I know I've hoisted my backpack and purse onto my shoulder and my heels are *tap, tap, tapping* down the hall as fast as possible.

Without even pausing at my locker for my coat, I burst through the heavy double doors that lead to the parking lot. The last time I was out here alone during school, I was helping Lydia avoid a fashion disaster. Back when Lydia dressing like everyone else at ATC was unthinkable. Back when I thought Lydia and I were PICs with a Grand Plan. Back when things made sense.

The damp, cold November wind slaps my face. It feels good after being in that suffocating office. As I hurry to my car, icy, smoky puffs billow from my mouth like cartoon thought bubbles. If I were in a comic strip, they would be filled with expletive symbols.

I sit in the driver's seat. My pounding head falls forward and rests on the steering wheel. Then a rap on my window makes me jump. It's Lydia.

"Can we talk?" she mouths.

I roll down my window about halfway, but don't unlock the door. "What?"

"I know you're mad—"

"Mad? I wouldn't call it mad." Although maybe I would— in the Mad Hatter sense of the word. What happened in Finn's office resembled a tea party in Wonderland. Then I laugh a strange little half-laugh. Maybe I am mad. In the anger sense of the word.

"I've wanted to tell you for a long time, but I didn't know where to start. And then you agreed to that bet. I was scared of how you'd react." She rubs her hands up and down her bare arms. Even though it's less than forty degrees and feels like it could rain—or snow—any second, I don't invite her inside the car and I don't offer her any of the sweaters, hoodies, or jackets from my backseat, either. If I'm cold—and I am—then she should be colder.

A long time? Lydia's known about this for *a long time?* How long is "a long time"?

I take a deep breath and glare at her. "How about 'Charlotte, I'm switching programs. Charlotte, I'm throwing away our Grand Plan—our dreams for our future. Charlotte, I'm ditching you.'" With the last "Charlotte," my voice cracks.

Cracks. I need to get out of here. I start my car.

"Where are you going?" Lydia steps back as I shift into gear.

"I don't know." What I do know: I'm keeping her prize bags.

I pull away and leave her standing in the parking lot as the first few raindrops dot my windshield.

eight

Although all I really want to do is take some Advil, climb into bed, and pull the covers over my head, I decide that I'm not Nina. I'm going to go to the store and work. At least at Pringle's Market, I know what to expect.

Except as soon as I walk through the sliding doors, I don't see Katie or Nina or Dad or Pops in the deli/bakery. Instead, behind the counter is a raggedy stranger with the crappiest black dye job I've ever seen. It's obviously boxed color—and wrong for her skin tone, too. She's on her cell phone. I knew Dad was interviewing this morning, but I didn't realize he'd hire someone so quickly.

I start to say hello and tell her that I'm just going to drop my stuff in the break room and I'll be back to help her, but I don't get the chance. As soon as I say, "Hey . . ." she holds up her index finger in a terse *wait-a-minute* gesture.

I resist the overwhelming urge to go back there, rip the phone out of her hand, bury it in coleslaw, and have Dad fire her immediately. Considering the day I've had, I'm in no mood for this. She clearly thinks I'm a customer, so I don't tell her otherwise. Testing: how long will she be on the phone while a "customer" waits?

My phone pings. I wrestle it out of my purse. It's a text from Mom: **Where are you? Just got robocall from school.** I'll deal with that later.

A couple of regular customers in the produce section keep glancing over, clearly perplexed as to why I'm on this side of the counter. I simply smile and continue to wait. Mr. Cho smiles back and hands his toddler a grapefruit, but Mrs. Lambert pretends as if she isn't looking.

"He still won't stop?" Raggedy-hair girl leans against the stool by the chicken rotisserie. "Please!" She laughs. "I know. It's not funny. I don't know what to say. At least he's cute. Right?"

I clear my throat to remind her that I'm still here, and she turns her back. She flipping *turns her back* on me!

What's going on today? First, my best friend blindsides me, and while my head is still spinning, everything is haywire at the store, too. Is there any place where things are as they should be?

That's it. I'm done.

Juggling my purse and backpack, I go behind the counter, pick up the store phone, and press the intercom button. *Now* the girl decides to pay attention to me. "Hey, what are you doing? You can't—"

"Moose Pringle to the deli, please. Moose to the deli," I page. Then I slam the phone onto the receiver and glare at her.

Before either of us can say anything, Nina rushes out of
the break room. As soon as she sees me, she stops dead. Her
eyes dart back and forth between me and the girl. The girl
notices Nina and *her* eyes dart between Nina and me, trying
to read what's going on. If this were a western, Nina would
be pulling innocent children—like the littlest Cho—out of
harm's way. She knows I'm about to blast this girl, even if she
doesn't know why. Damn! Why didn't I wear my red cowboy
boots today?

"First of all," I say, forcing myself to be calm. "I realize
you don't know who I am, but that is not the point."

"Who *are* you?" Her lip curls on one side.

I ignore her attitude. "Around here we do not ignore customers. Ever! And you shouldn't be taking personal calls,
but if by some chance you are, if someone comes up to the
counter, you hang up. *Immediately!*"

Mom and Dad weave through the people around the
deli/bakery/produce area pretending to be engrossed in romaine and citrus and day-old strudel.

"Charlotte?" Mom translation: *What are you doing here?
Why are you holding your gigantic purse behind the deli counter? And, most of all, why are you making a scene in front of
customers?*

I follow Mom's head-jerk summons to the break room.
Nina rushes to Raggedy Rude Girl. Before I get out of earshot, I hear the girl say, "You said she wouldn't be here until
three." So Nina *did* tell her about me. Then why did she ne-
glect to tell her how to behave around customers, especially

if she was going to leave her alone behind the counter?

Not giving Mom a chance to start in, I say, "That girl needs to go. She's a total liability. She was on the phone and ignored me for almost two minutes!"

"Give her a chance," says Mom.

"I did," I protest. "And she blew it."

"It's her first day, puddin' pop." Dad tries to be soothing, but it's condescending and pissing me off.

"Why aren't you at school?" Mom asks accusingly.

"So you're not going to fire her?" I ask Dad.

"You've said yourself that we really need someone back there. Take her under your wing. Train her. The Pringle way."

I growl.

"That's my girl." Dad pats my head as he opens the door to leave. "Her name's Hannah, by the way." His work here is done.

Ralph slithers past Dad without saying a word. He pulls a sheet of paper and a pen out of the drawer and sits down at the table.

"So?" Mom presses. "Why aren't you in school?"

"I have a headache." It's the truth, even if it's not the *whole* truth. There's no way I'm going to tell my mother, who doesn't want me to be in the cos program in the first place, that my PIC just threw me under the bus.

"Take some Advil." Mom translation: *That's not an excuse.*

"I did," I lie. "It didn't help. Nothing can help. I have the biggest headache in the history of all headaches."

"Maybe you should go home and go to bed, then." Translation: *Pull yourself together.*

I scowl. I *am* together. As far as she knows, anyway. "I have to set up the Opening Day display," I say.

"Did it already," says Ralph, still writing.

"Did you find the mossy oak wrapping in the—?"

"Yup."

"The hunting-themed beer cases?"

"Stacked by aisle twelve."

"Did you arrange the—?"

"Beef jerky, disposable hand warmers, and bright orange knit caps, all asymmetrical and aesthetically pleasing." He doesn't look up. "Of course."

I start to protest, but Mom interrupts me. "Go home, feed and let out Buffy, and check the Crock-Pot. If it's bubbling, turn it to low. If it's not, leave it alone. Put a drop of lavender and a drop of peppermint oil behind your ears and lie down. I don't know what's going on with you, but you're wound way too tightly. Even more so than usual." She kisses my head and returns to work.

What's going on with me? Oh, nothing much. It's just that my whole future rests on a Grand Plan that my best friend flushed down the toilet on a whim. That's all.

Ralph slides his paper over to me. "Want in?"

It's a new pool. *Hannah's Last Day.* "RWL" already takes up five squares. He pulls a five-dollar bill out of his wallet and puts it in a "Hannah's Last Day" envelope. This is Ralph's way of saying that his money's on me. I smile, pull out a five, and match him.

— ✳ —

Buffy must sense my mood because she doesn't mess with me today. She eats, goes out, and returns promptly, probably because it's all-out raining now. Once I take some ibuprofen, remove my makeup, and change into my yoga pants and hoodie, I curl up to watch TV in my bedroom, flipping the channels between HSN and QVC. Buffy climbs up beside me. Even though she's not supposed to be here, when she rests her humongous head on my thigh, I pet her. Sometimes I think she's the only one who truly gets me.

I never actually watch the shopping shows. They're just background noise and visuals while I do other things. Watching for more than five minutes is mind-numbing. I try to find something else, but there's nothing on that's even barely decent.

I've never missed school unless I was really sick, so I'm not sure what to do. I try putting the essential oils behind my ears like Mom suggested.

My head is still pounding and the rain is really coming down. I hear it pelting my window—perfect napping weather, or so I hear.

I slide under the covers and close my eyes. Buffy jumps off the bed and flops onto my shaggy magenta rug, which makes me think of that crazy geometric rug and Mr. Finn, and then Lydia. I roll over and cover my head with my pillow, willing my brain to come up with something else.

Hannah is a sweet girl's name, not a bitchy slacker girl's name. I can't believe Dad hired her.

Not that, either!

I turn on some music. Maybe that'll clear my mind. A song by Cake comes on. Cake reminds me of the cake fiasco last week, and how Lydia saved my ass.

"Lydia! Ugh!" No matter how hard I try to distract myself and clear my head, I keep going back to Lydia. And, now, I also want cake.

Buffy lifts her head and looks at me like, *Do you mind? I'm trying to sleep here.*

I flip off my phone dock and yank the covers back. It's no use. There is nothing relaxing about doing nothing! I grab my phone and earbuds and stomp down the stairs, through the living room, and into the kitchen. Once I start rummaging through the cupboards, Buffy barrels down the stairs and sits by the treat jar. There's no cake anywhere, not even a Little Debbie snack cake. I growl and give the dog a peanut butter nugget. There's no point in both of us suffering. Then I throw on my running shoes and tromp down to the basement.

Mom has clothes drying on hangers all over the workout equipment. I move some of them, draping them over the washer before I step onto the treadmill and push the power button. I start off at a walk as I sync the music.

Even with it streaming directly into my head, I can't stop thinking. I ramp up the speed.

What am I going to do without Lydia in cos? The Grand Plan was designed around getting our cosmetology licenses together. *Together.* We were supposed to win the showcase and go to the Chicago hair show *together.* She would be by my side as I won the bet and stepped into our future. We were supposed to do all of it together.

And she made the decision to leave cos without me. What kind of friend does that? Even if my life weren't tied to what she does, who makes that kind of major decision without running it by her best friend? She never gets bangs or layers or even highlights without talking to me first. How could she alter the course of both of our futures without a single word?

The more I think about it, the angrier I get and the faster I run.

How could I have been so stupid? I thought I had my whole life planned and under control—but how under control could it be if so much depends on other people? On one other person. PICs, my ass. No more Partners in Cos. I'm flying solo now. And I can do whatever I want.

What *do* I want?

First, I want to slow down and stop sweating so much before I keel over. I turn down the speed and catch my breath.

Do I still want to continue cosmetology without Lydia? I'm not sure I can do it alone. The days she's not there are hard enough—putting up with Toby the slacker and Shelby and her groupies. How can I sit through class after class without her? How can I win the showcase alone? If I have to follow Mom's plan . . . I shudder just thinking about it. I haven't even thought of any other career choices since Lydia and I created the Grand Plan.

As I slow to a walk, I see the manila envelope I threw away last week still sticking out of the garbage bin by the dryer.

It wouldn't hurt to take a peek.

Sitting cross-legged on the cool concrete floor, I look through Mom's college pamphlet collection. Wow, she put a lot of effort into this. There are brochures for nearby universities—some public, some private—and a few from schools in other parts of the country. Everyone in the pictures looks so posed and happy.

I pretend I'm the girl in the Ferris brochure wearing a white lab coat and looking into a microscope. "Yes, I'm looking at bacteria in cow spit, and I find it fascinating!" I check out her hair. What, don't science majors have time for root touch-ups? Geez! "You're in a brochure representing your future alma mater, honey," I say to her. "Do it for them, if not for yourself."

"Who are you talking to?" Mom startles me. I didn't hear her come home, let alone down the stairs.

"Oh my lanta! Don't sneak up on people!" I put my hand across my chest. "You about gave me a heart attack."

"Sorry." She pops out my earbuds and lets them drop into my lap. "Feeling better?"

I'm not sure if it's the Advil or the essential oils or the

run or just the break, but my head isn't pounding anymore. "Yeah."

"Glad to see you're finally looking at those." She scoops up the clothes I'd draped over the washer. "They're not too messed up from Buffy's pee?"

"Huh?" Then I remember my snide remark at dinner last week and half laugh. "No."

"Lydia called the store looking for you," she says. "She said you weren't picking up your phone. Is something going on that I should know about?"

Maybe it's because we're among laundry soap and college brochures, and the moment weirdly reminds me of a mother/daughter heart-to-heart from a TV commercial—Hallmark or Folgers or possibly Tampax—but I open up about my meeting with Mr. Finn and Lydia's switching programs.

"Culinary arts, huh?" she says. I nod. "That's a much better fit for her. She's got a knack for working with food, and there's always a need for that somewhere. I'm glad to see that *she's* looking at the future realistically."

I'm not sure what I was expecting—a hug, an understanding shoulder squeeze, or comforting words that somehow hint that she's on my side—but Mom's reaction won't make it into a commercial anytime soon.

So the situation still stands. With or without Lydia, I have to prove to Mom that cosmetology *is* a realistic career. So what if the Grand Plan fell apart? My resolve strengthens.

Step one: create a new and improved Grand Plan—the Grander Plan.

Dad can't get away from the store, and Mom has some wine-tasting thing tonight, so I take my dinner, a bowl of chili from the simmering Crock-Pot, to my room. I grab a spiral notebook from my backpack and start making a to-do list.

Charlotte's ~~and Lydia's~~ Grander Plan

1. Win Winter Style Showcase. —> Earn stellar reps, bragging rights, and accolades.

  ★★ Bonus: Win the bet and ~~tell Mom where she can shove those brochures~~ prove that I'm capable of choosing my own path.

2. Graduate high school with honors, college credits, and cosmetology license~~s~~.

3. Get an apartment ~~together with Lydia~~ and a job~~s~~ in a top salon to pay for college.

4. Get an associate's degree~~s~~ in business at Jackson College.

5. Build clientele —> Get enough money to open a salon ~~together~~.

6. Be the boss~~es~~ and live happily ever after.

  ★★ Bonus: ~~Marry best friends. (At the very least, they will become best friends.)~~ Have a hot, non-annoying boyfriend~~s~~.

—✳—

After a long shower and thorough moisturizing, I see I have several missed calls from Lydia and a text. **Please call me. Please.**

Might as well deal with it. I tap her picture in my contacts.

"Hey," I say when she picks up. I doodle flowers and scrolly vines on a new page in my notebook.

"Hey." She takes a deep breath and talks fast. "Listen, I'm *so* sorry that I didn't tell you before Finn did."

"You said you wanted to talk this weekend, but you didn't try very hard." I draw a version of Shea's pixie dress.

"You were working, and it was really busy at the bakery— there was never a good time—" She pauses. "Those are just excuses."

"Yeah," I say, letting the word hang in the air.

"I know. I'm sorry. I was wrong. So, so, so wrong not to tell you. I was just afraid how you'd react."

"So waiting until it's a done deal and having Finn break it to me was supposed to ease the blow?"

"I didn't think about that. I'm a chickenshit coward and a rotten friend."

"At least we agree on that."

She laughs. I don't.

After a long, awkward silence, she asks, "Do you have to work tomorrow?"

"Yeah, but Dad finally hired someone for the deli-slash-bakery—whom I hate, BTW—so I plan to avoid that whole area of the store." I write REED in big block letters.

"You've never liked *anyone* your father's hired. That Kayden girl, who you claimed was the Antichrist. Geoffrey, that old guy with the fake British accent. And Daryl, who ended everything he said with *You know what I mean?*"

"Hey, Kayden was evil. Geoffrey was from Kalamazoo. And you agreed that Daryl was annoying. You know what I mean?"

She laughs. "I guess. So what did this new girl do?"

Even though I'm still pissed at her, Lydia is the only person I can really talk to. I tell her the whole story while I color in each letter of Reed's name with a different design.

"That bitch!" she says when I get to the part when I page Dad. And it's just the right thing to say to make me feel better—about that part of my life, anyway.

My phone beeps—low battery. After I plug it into the charger, Lydia says, "So how about I meet you at the store around four-thirty, pick up a few groceries, and make dinner at my house? As a peace offering."

I agree, as long as there's cake.

nine

31 days to the Winter Style Showcase

Cos without Lydia feels weird. It's like half of me is missing. There's no one to roll my eyes at when Toby says something idiotic; no one to sympathize with me about Shelby. Worst of all, I'm on my own for all the partner exercises. Ms. G assures me that Lydia's spot should be filled by the end of the week. She means well, but my PIC can't be replaced by some random person who didn't make the cut originally.

I sit in my usual seat in the front row and swear I feel everyone watching me, hear them whispering about me. I'm not cut out to be a loner. I'm a leader, and leaders need people. Lydia is my people.

It's BOGO taco day. I text Lydia: **Loco's calling.**

She doesn't reply until the bell is about to ring. **Can't. Finishing a soufflé. Working through lunch. Sorry.**

By now, I feel committed to Loco, since I've been thinking about his crunchy tacos all morning. I'll grab a couple for Lydia, too, and take them over to the ATC kitchens. It's better than eating alone.

I pull into Loco's, on my way to the drive-thru. A few digital dudes are getting out of a vintage black Camaro. Then I see the driver—Reed! No way am I driving through. I whirl into the space next to them, do a quick hair-and-gloss check in the mirror, get out of the car, and make my way to the restaurant.

Reed holds the door open for me. What a gentleman! "Thank you." I smile.

"No problem." He winks.

We all wait in line together—Reed, me, Trent, and another guy they call Birch. If Trent's a tall, skinny basset hound, Birch is more like a bulldog—burly, with wide shoulders and chest and a tiny waist and butt.

"Is that your car?" I ask Reed.

"Yup." He inches closer to me as the line moves forward. "It was my brother's, but he sold it to me when he went into the Marines. You like it?"

"I do." I look directly at him. "It's hot." We hold eye contact for yet another flirtatious moment. Why couldn't Lydia be here to witness this?

Trent orders six tacos and a large Pepsi. Whoa! That's a lot of food. Up close, I realize that he smells like peppermint and clean laundry. He takes his drink cup, moves off to the side, and waits for his order.

I order two tacos for me and two for Lydia and a small Diet Mountain Dew for us to share—to go. When I pull out my wallet, Trent says, "That's a Dooney and Bourke."

Wow! I've never known a guy to recognize designers,

especially not handbag designers, before. "Yeah, it is. I got it for Christmas."

"My mom has a couple of them." He moves to the fountain pop dispenser and fills his cup with Mountain Dew. I'd love to take a pair of scissors to his hair. The shaggy hound look does not suit him.

"Hey!" I drop a hint to Reed. "Have you seen that new James Bond movie yet?"

He says he hasn't. Then he orders two tacos and a side of chips and cheese.

I'm just about to ask him if he'd like to when Trent interrupts. "I've seen it. Daniel Craig is probably the best Bond ever."

"Seriously? You think so?" I say. "Better than Roger Moore, Pierce Brosnan, and Sean Connery?"

"Heck, yeah. He's not pretty like those other guys. He's more believable."

He's crazy. Pretty? Nothing about James Bond is *pretty*. "You have no idea what you're talking about."

"I could kick all their asses," proclaims Birch.

And within seconds, the conversation degenerates into all the tough-guy actors, old and young, whose asses Birch feels equipped to kick—Chuck Norris, the Rock, Clint Eastwood. I shake my head, fill my drink cup, and take a sip. Anybody can talk big in the Loco's Taco line.

By now Trent's food is up. He smirks at me and takes his tray to a table by the window. Ugh, that smirk. Rather than get caught in another argument with him, I turn to Reed, and turn on the charm.

"So, Reed," I say, "what's going on this weekend?" *Take the hint, dude.* Movie + weekend + girl = date.

He smiles mischievously—so freaking adorable! "My brother's coming home on leave." His food is ready, and so is mine. "We're probably going to MSU to party at his old frat house."

"That sounds like fun."

"It usually is." He grabs his tray, and I take my paper bag. "What about you? What are you doing?" he asks.

Waiting for you to ask me out. (No, that sounds too desperate.) *Same as you, going to a party.* (But that makes me look unavailable.) I need something more mysterious, as if I could have plans, but nothing definitive, in case he does ask me out. "Not sure yet." I stand with one hand on the exit door.

"Bring over some hot sauce, will you?" Trent calls. Can't he see we're having a conversation? He can get his own hot sauce—or ask Birch to do it.

"Okay," Reed calls back. Then, before he gets it, he gives me another wink. "See you around, Charlotte."

"Later, Reed." I bounce out the door.

He doesn't ask me out, but I can tell he's close. Guys don't want to make a move when their friends are right there and interrupting. My ex-boyfriend Matt and I flirted for the entire summer before he finally asked me on a date. He was shy, though. It shouldn't take nearly as long with Reed.

By the time I get back to the ATC kitchens, lunch is almost over. Lydia removes her soufflé from the oven, and I ask her to free her curls from that hideous hairnet. She rolls her eyes, but she does it. I tell her about Reed while we scarf down our cold tacos. I expect her to tease me as usual about his not even being real, but instead she tells me about her crappy morning—burning her first soufflé and having to start over. Good friends listen, so I do, but it all feels so rushed.

We check our teeth for stray lettuce as the bell rings and then head to "icks" class.

Later, when I get to work, I do everything I can to avoid Hannah. First, I redo the Opening Day display—as usual. I know he thinks he's helping, but Ralph's idea of aesthetically pleasing and mine are clearly not the same. He just stacks and groups everything together. I prefer merchandise to be spread out so that when customers take items, it doesn't look as picked over. No matter how many times I show him how to do it—or Dad, or Pops—they never listen.

I spend the rest of the afternoon stocking the dairy case and removing anything past its expiration date. Few things are more exciting than old sour cream and yogurt, except maybe creating a pool predicting how many items need to be thrown out—or as Dad puts it, "written off."

Some Pringle's Market bets are long-range, and involve buying squares on a calendar, such as the birth date of Oliver and Nina's baby. Some allow people time to buy in, but close on a certain day, like who will win *America's Got Talent,* the Stanley Cup, or Best Picture at the Oscars. (Or Mom's and my showcase bet.) One of my favorites, though, is a "quick pick." That's a one-dollar same-day bet. We have pre-printed lists with all the employees' names, and room for write-ins for quicker picking. Someone walks around the store, takes the bets, and collects the cash. The only stipulation is that you have to pay that day. Since gambling isn't exactly legal in Michigan, Dad won't let us do this in front of customers, but we have our workarounds.

Expired food is a pretty common quick pick. To keep it on the down low, we use code. Tammy is scanning a huge order and has a long line of customers. "Can I get a QP on dairy for today?" I ask her.

A piece of hair falls from her usual clip. She tucks it behind her ear and checks her smock pocket quickly—probably to make sure she's got a buck—and replies, "Fourteen?"

I check the list to see if anyone's chosen that yet. Nope. "Perfect. Thanks." I'll put a check next to her name once I get her dollar. She's good for it. The other two cashiers buy in, too.

Tyler mumbles "eleven" while methodically bagging at the end of the checkout.

I smile at Mr. Skrocki, who's holding his debit card and waiting, and write down Tyler's guess. "Got it."

I find Mom, Dad, and Oliver in the office. Mom's on the phone, but holds up a hand. "Five," I say. "Got it." She gives me a thumbs-up, never skipping a beat.

Dad, who's engrossed in balancing the books, guesses zero. He says it's "the power of positive thinking." Oliver calls it "wishful thinking," and guesses twenty-two. I leave as Dad and Oliver debate whether or not attitude contributes to reality.

Pops sits on a stool in customer service and waits on an old guy he calls Bud. Once Bud pockets his lottery ticket and pack of smokes and walks away, I ask, "QP on dairy?"

"I didn't pee on anyone . . . today," says Pops, straight-faced. "And who's Darry?"

"Pops!" I laugh and pray nobody heard him. Is he joking, or did he hear me wrong? With Pops, you never know, so I repeat, enunciating carefully, "Quick. Pick. On. The. Dairy. Case?"

He guesses two and then asks, "Did you forget Nina and the new girl?"

"No," I say. I didn't forget, exactly. It's more like deliberate avoidance.

Pops knows exactly what I'm doing. As I walk toward produce, he calls, "Stop, drop, and roll, Charlotte."

When I was in kindergarten, we had a Fire Safety Day at school. We had to color a picture of what we were supposed to do if—God forbid—we were ever on fire. There were giant bubble letters to color that said *Stop, Drop, and Roll.*

Then the teacher, Ms. Rhodes, read a picture book supplied by the local fire department. It showed all these dangerous scenarios of a fictional kid named Ted doing stupid things and catching himself on fire. Then she'd ask, "What should Ted do?"

All the kids shouted, "Stop, drop, and roll!"

Not me. I raised my hand and questioned Ted's motives and family situation. Why was he lighting a barbecue grill?

Where were his parents? Why were they using candles—didn't they have lights? If he had fire safety at school, shouldn't he know better?

Ms. Rhodes told me that these were all *excellent* questions, and then asked, "What should Ted do if he makes a mistake and finds himself in a scary situation?"

"Call 9-1-1," I answered.

"Before that." She was relentless.

"Jump in the lake."

She explained how running just fans the flames and creates a bigger problem, and that there's an important step before water and calling 9-1-1. She asked the rest of the class what that was and they screamed in unison, "Stop, drop, and roll!"

Then she asked me again what Ted should do.

By now, I was pissed. I said, "Ted should go to a different school, because his teacher didn't teach him to watch out for fire."

That night, at the dinner table, Mom announced that Ms. Rhodes had called her. "Charlotte, you *knew* the right answer," she said.

Pops stuck up for me. "She's a smart girl and a free thinker," he said. "She'll figure things out for herself."

Ever since then, when he thinks I'm being too stubborn for my own good, he reminds me to stop, drop, and roll.

I wave him off and head for the produce department.

Ralph hands me a dollar bill and says "seven" before I open my mouth. He's never missed a pool that I can remember. Once, when I was about fourteen, I asked about the seemingly never-ending supply of singles in his front pocket. He explained that they were "for bets, for tips, and for the titty bar." Nina was standing right there, and she had just started at the store, so I figured he was going for shock value. I played along and called him a skeevy old bastard. Ralph guffawed and said he might be offended if 1) It wasn't true, and 2) It wasn't coming from a "spoon-licker"—his term for a spoiled brat who has everything handed to her, but takes it for granted. I called him a few more choice words after that.

Nina relayed the whole story to Oliver, who told Mom, and I got in trouble, which is one reason I am not a fan of Nina's—another reason I walk by her and Hannah again as if they aren't even there.

I spend the next hour and a half behind the dairy case reading tiny stamped dates and putting them in chronological order. Little detailed jobs like this always put me in a better mood; they're my specialty around the store. Oliver, of course, says it's a control thing.

Lydia arrives just as I'm finishing up and figuring out the winner. I give her a chance to get in the pool before I go around and collect, but she passes. While I do that, she grabs the things on her shopping list. She's checking out when I pay Tyler, the winner of ten smackers.

Tammy's hair is in her face again. "Here," I say, handing her a pack of little barrettes I had in my purse from when Dad put half of my hair care section in the health and beauty aisle on clearance. He claimed the items weren't selling well enough to take up so much space, but I'd argued that he didn't give the display enough of a chance. He didn't listen, so I bought up most of the stock I'd painstakingly ordered and arranged.

"Wow! Thanks!" She smiles and immediately swipes her stray hair back, clipping in a barrette. "My bangs have been driving me crazy all day."

"No problem." I shoulder my purse. "Growing them out takes patience. But they're looking good."

Tammy winks at me, thanks me again, and hands Lydia her receipt.

In the parking lot, before we head to our cars, I ask Lydia if she saw Hannah. She says, "Yup. I went right up to her and said, 'Bitch, you mess with my friend and you mess with me!'"

"You did not!" I jingle my keys.

"I know." Then she laughs at her own joke. I laugh, too.

— ✳ —

Walking into Lydia's kitchen feels like putting on yoga pants and slippers after a long day of skirts and heels. Lydia unloads the groceries and chops a bunch of veggies, then starts whipping up something with cucumbers and avocados. I turn on QVC, mute it, and get the music going. We sing along to some old Christina Aguilera song while I clear off the papers, mail, and miscellaneous debris from the kitchen table, piling it into a neat stack on the sideboard. No matter how uncomfortable things have been lately, the pull of decade-long habits is too strong.

"So I have this idea," Lydia says. She hands me a bowl of what looks like guacamole. I dip my finger in it, but before I can lick it, she pushes my finger into my face, smearing the goo on my cheek. I instantly stick my hand into the bowl to fling a huge wad at her, but before I can, she yells, "Don't! It's a face mask!"

I freeze mid-fling. "Wait! What?"

"It's a face mask," she repeats. "Since I need to do a booth at the wellness fair next Friday *and* since I'm coming from cos *and* since you're my partner, I thought my project could be skin food."

"Skin food." I look at the mixture in my hand. It smells yummy—fresh and light.

"Yeah." She gives me a smile. "What else would a foodie and a cosmetologist present at a health fair?"

"Kool-Aid hair dye?" Then we both crack up.

In middle school, we both wanted colored streaks in our hair. We were talking about it at the store, and Tammy told us that her daughter used unsweetened Kool-Aid and vinegar to color hers. "It's easy," she said dryly, "if you want to look and smell like an Easter egg."

Neither of us could think of anything we wanted more than Easter-egg hair, so we grabbed a handful of raspberry and grape Kool-Aid packets right before Lydia's mom picked us up. We were smart enough to realize that the stuff would stain, so we changed into swimsuits and decided to put it on in the shower.

By the time Patti realized what we were doing, their bathroom looked like a crime scene at Willy Wonka's. Deep pink and purple splashes and streaks were everywhere, including our arms, legs, necks, and torsos.

We had no skills, so instead of highlights or streaks, we had chunks and sections of variegated pinks and purples. Since we both have light hair, those bright colors grabbed hold and hung on tight. It was horrible, and we loved it.

"Then we discovered hair chalk . . ." Lydia reminisces.

"Easter-egg hair 2.0," I say. "I loved that stuff. Still do. But then we learned to foil . . ."

". . . and we used Mom's food coloring and pastry brushes."

"That was the biggest mess ever."

"It wasn't *that* bad." She covers the guacamole-facial bowl with plastic wrap.

"Not like when I got that curling thing from TV—"

"—and got my hair so tangled in the bristles that we had to cut it loose."

"At least bangs were in style," I say.

"We tried so many crazy things. What were we thinking?"

"PICs," I say, laughing, then instantly regret it. We're not PICs anymore. There's this weird awkward moment. Is she thinking the same thing I am? What are we now?

Lydia breaks the tension. "So we can't really do full facials. People aren't going to want to mess up their makeup." She returns to her pile of chopped veggies and deftly adds them to some oil in a pan.

"True." I pull out a stool at the kitchen island and sit.

"So I was thinking that we'd have a batch mixed up to show the consistency and how great it smells." She stirs the veggies. The garlicky aroma makes my stomach grumble. "People can try it on their hands, like at the cosmetics counter. And we can give out recipe pamphlets."

"Perfect for subcontracting to a graphic designer," I suggest with a sly grin. If we hire Reed, I could work with him for both Lydia's and my projects, for lots of quality bonding time.

"Exactly. But . . ." She stops stirring and removes the pan from the heat. "Don't be mad. . . ."

"What?" I brace myself for *another* bomb.

"I already hired a graphic designer." Then she starts talking really fast, spewing explanation. "I started so late, and the wellness fair is only two weeks away. I had to move quickly." She gets out another pan and pours cream into it. "We had a big meeting with some of the other programs to finish up the subcontracting details, and since I'm working on my own right now—everyone else is in teams—I feel so weird, you know?"

Yes, I do know—thanks to you.

Is she trying to say that she made a mistake? That she really belongs in cos, with me? I don't ask, though. I just listen to the rest of her story. She's my best friend, PIC or not.

Lydia puts water on for the pasta and stirs the sauce. "Well, at the meeting, Mrs. Barbara, my CA teacher, introduced me to a graphic designer. Since he was available, I jumped on him."

"You jumped on him? Go, Lyd!"

"Not like that. God, Charlotte. You know what I mean."

"You haven't had a boyfriend since Cody. Maybe you need to get back out there." Cody and Lydia dated from ninth grade into tenth and then off and on for a few months. He messed with her head a lot. He was super moody, so when we'd all go out, she never knew if he was going to be charming and fun or sullen and critical. Actually, taking sides when Cody and Lydia fought was one of the reasons why Matt and I broke up.

"I'm out there." She whisks the sauce with fervor. "I talk to guys all the time. I just haven't found the right one."

"What about this graphic design guy? What's his name? Does he know Reed? Is he cute?" I grab a piece of zucchini from the pan on the counter and pop it in my mouth.

"I don't know. I guess so, but let it go. I just met him, and the one convo we had was about the booklet he's creating for us. I'm supposed to bring him the finished recipes on a flash drive by the end of the week. So you're okay that I hired him?"

I finish chewing before I speak. "Looks like I have to be. It's already done." Yes, I'm disappointed that I won't be bonding with Reed over cucumber and avocado clip art, but there's always the winter style showcase. *Take that, Pops. I can stop, drop, and roll sometimes.*

Besides, in my mind I've already raced ahead to Lydia and her mystery man and Reed and me as potential friend-couples. I don't mention any of that to her, though. She's clearly not ready to go there—yet. And until Reed asks me out, we're not, either.

The next thing I know Lydia and I are sitting in her dining room wearing guacamole facials and eating "penne à la Lydia," featuring, in Lydia's words, "a garlic cream sauce and a sautéed vegetable medley."

"You sauté? Look at you being all Iron Chef," I tease, but I'm genuinely impressed, given my recent rice casserole debacle.

Lydia laughs. "Of course."

I really want to ask her why she changed programs, but I'm not sure I want to know. What if it was because of me? She doesn't want to work at the store with me; maybe she doesn't want to work in a salon with me, either. I don't want to think about it—just like Lydia doesn't want to think about boyfriends.

Instead, I rave over her food and we plan out the rest of our booth. Lydia says that since child development is also involved in the fair, there will be tons of kids there, so everyone has been encouraged to include something for them, too. We decide to do face painting and include an edible paint recipe in our brochure. Lydia already has the recipes figured out, which are amazing. She even included one for Kool-Aid hair dye!

"And then there's the party the night after the fair." Lydia sprinkles more parmesan on her pasta. "Everyone from CA, CD, and the health programs, plus all the subcontractors will be there."

"That sounds like so much fun!" I key the event into my phone calendar, devour another forkful of pasta, and imagine us whooping it up together with our digital design dudes.

"I know, right?" She puts her fork down, and we return to plans for the presentation.

We discuss how the booth should be decorated—in greens, with silk flowers. Lydia will borrow them from the bakery's window décor stash, since they won't be in use this time of year. We'll create posters with pictures and explanations of all sorts of skin-enriching foods. Lydia says we've already done more than a lot of the culinary arts teams. Maybe, I think, we'll have a shot at winning *both* of our showcases.

After we put the leftovers away for her parents, we dive into the richest, creamiest crème brûlée I've ever had—and I've eaten a lot of Patti Cakes desserts. "Wow!" I say, my mouth full. "This is awesome. Your mom really outdid herself."

"This isn't from the bakery," she says proudly. "I made it last night."

"No way!"

"Way!" She beams. "I know it's not cake, but—"

"Who cares? This is delicious! You really *are* an Iron Chef!"

As I devour my dessert, I remember what Mom said about Lydia having a knack for working with food. And I have to admit that she does. But did she have to leave cos to do it?

We spend another hour or two watching QVC, criticizing the hosts' hair and reminiscing about our own hair disasters—like Lydia's sixth-grade perm and my first attempt using a razor to texturize. We also gossip about people from school—who's dating whom and who's breaking up with whom—and talk about food. I tell her about my rice casserole, and she cringes. She tells me about these new cookies they started making at Patti Cakes, and how everyone seems to like them. I love how we can go from TV to hair to school to cookies so effortlessly. But there's something else there now—a ginormous elephant in the room with us.

In the way best friends have, Lyd seems to read my mind. She turns so she's facing me on the couch. "You're here, and things seem okay between us. Are you still mad about, you know . . . ?" She chews on her lip. She sometimes does that when she's nervous, especially when her nail polish is all peeled off, which it is.

"A little," I say, sounding snippier than I intended. Maybe because I'm madder and more worried—about why she left and where that leaves me—than I'm admitting. "I just don't get it."

"I know," she says to the afghan on the back of the couch. "It's just that—well, I started baking to help Mom, I started cooking to help around here, and I started cos because of us. But lately I've been thinking about what *I* want. You know, what do I want to do every day—as a career—once school is over . . ."

I don't want to hear this. I don't want to believe that when Lydia imagines her options for the future, the better choice excludes me. Not once have I ever thought about working without her. I can't even fathom it.

I watch TV and try to tune her out as she goes on about

how rolling perms and filing feet and cutting hair don't excite her like rolling dough and filling pastries and chopping food. For her, cos skills are great for personal maintenance and style, but not something she wants to do all day, every day. All I hear are Mom's words in Lydia's voice: *A fun hobby, but not a real career. Blah, blah, blah.* It's bad enough that my mother feels this way, but Lydia, too? I can't take it.

When she starts talking about her dad and how glad he is that she's working with her mom, and how her family and the school have been so supportive, I become completely engrossed in the woman on TV modeling denim blazers that are perfect for travel. They're covered with pockets on the outside *and* the inside. One woman slips her makeup case, wallet, and smartphone in them to show how convenient it is.

"Who would buy that?" I think out loud.

"Are you listening to me?" Lydia asks.

"Of course," I say, still glued to the TV. "You're happier cooking, your dad is better, and your parents are proud of you."

"Uh-huh, and . . . ?" As if there's more.

"And I'm glad everyone's happy." I don't look at her. I can't.

Without a word, Lydia picks up our dessert dishes and goes into the kitchen. She has no right to be mad at me— I'm not the one who left, she is. I'm not the one who has unconditional family support. She is. I'm not the one who lied and pretended to be all in on a *frivolous* career plan. But before I say anything I'll regret, I decide to change the subject. After all, as hurt and betrayed as I feel, Lydia and

I have to do the showcases together. And she's still my best friend . . . isn't she?

The QVC models are now modeling flowy, stretchy pants. Since the volume is muted, I can't hear what the hostess is saying, but by her overexaggerated expressions, she's clearly amazed at how stretchy and flowy the fabric is. So stretchy. So flowy. So amazing! Everyone should want them—now!

"You know what we need to do," I call out, desperate to change the mood.

"What?" Lydia calls back.

"We need to go shopping for matching outfits for Friday." I turn around on the couch, toward the kitchen. "They can be in the same colors as the booth, which will pull every-thing together. Plus, it'll be fun. Snapz! has some really cute stuff right now."

She stands in the doorway. "I thought we'd just wear black dress pants and our black cos smocks. That would look professional, and we'd still match."

"Except it wouldn't be fun. I think we need some fun, don't you?"

"It just seems pointless to buy a new outfit for one after-noon." She drops into her dad's recliner. And then I remem-ber what happened at Applebee's.

"First of all." I shake a mock-scolding finger. "There is no such thing as a pointless new outfit. Especially one you can wear again. Which we will. Second of all, I'll cover you. What's the problem?"

"Thanks, but there's no problem," Lydia says. "I just don't think it's necessary."

"Okay, whatever!" Now I'm mad again. And not just because of the clothes. She acts like my suggestion is ridiculous. Like *I'm* ridiculous. I want to scream, but I go with snide instead. "I'm sure that attitude will save your dad a fortune when you get married. Why buy a dress that you'll only wear once?"

She sighs. "It's not exactly the same thing."

"You're right." I jump up and walk into the kitchen, grab my coat and purse from the table. "It's not the same thing. Your wedding is hypothetical and in the unknown future. This is real and important *now*."

"You're not going to bully me into getting new clothes just because you want them." Lydia's voice is ice-cold. I am *not* bullying her. I'm trying to salvage our friendship and make the showcase—*her* showcase—the best it can be.

"Whatever. Go naked, then!" That's all I can think to say before storming out.

I calm down on the drive home. So what if she doesn't want a new outfit? I realize that I reacted to more than just what we're going to wear at the showcase. I text her an olive branch: **Thanks for dinner. It was delicious.** ☺

She texts back: **You're welcome.** No smiley. Sarcasm?

I reply: **See you tomorrow.** ☺

No reply. Whatever. At least I tried.

ten

25 days to the Winter Style Showcase

Since Lydia's dinner made more tension than amends, the rest of the week was super boring. She claimed she wasn't ignoring me and that she was just busy with the wellness fair, but if that were true, she'd have asked for my help. And she didn't.

On Friday, while the rest of the class practiced their up-dos on one another, I had to use a leftover mannequin head that someone had already rolled into a perm. Combing out a Sasquatch would have been easier. But I did it. The complex braiding, sweeping, pinning, and curling really impressed Ms. G.

After she marked my grade in her book, she casually said, "Your new partner—Mackenzie Moore—will be starting on Monday. Isn't that great?"

I topped my do off with a heavy mist of hair spray. "Really? Yeah, great."

My new partner. As if a PIC can simply be plucked from a list and instantly replace my best friend since elementary

school. Still, if I'm going to continue in cos without Lydia—
and I am—and if Lydia isn't coming back—and it doesn't
look like she is—having a partner in class has to be better
than this Sasquatch mannequin. Maybe Mackenzie Moore
won't be so bad. Maybe she'll be great, like Ms. G says. Maybe
I should make an effort.

I spent the whole weekend planning my first impression—
that is, when I wasn't working. I foiled a few highlights
around my face and redid my nails. Then I went shopping
for a new outfit. I considered inviting Lydia, but I didn't want
to be accused of bullying her into getting new clothes again,
so I went alone. But just like being in cos, primping and
shopping just isn't the same without her.

But today is bursting with possibility. I'll meet my new
partner, so my full showcase team can finally get rolling. We're
a little behind, but we should be up to speed soon. Lydia's
final meeting before the wellness fair—which is Friday—is
at the same time as our showcase meeting. Even though
we're technically still supposed to help each other, we can't
be both places at once, so we text and decide to stick with
our own events and recap for each other afterward.

Mackenzie Moore shows up just before the team meetings. At first I think she's a teacher, because she's dressed
in khakis and a blue turtleneck sweater. Her hair looks
clean and brushed, but it has absolutely no style—it just
hangs there—one length, mousy brown, a few inches past
her shoulders. She's also wearing zero makeup. None. Is

this girl really interested in a cos career?

Ms. G introduces Mackenzie to the class and asks her to tell us a little about herself.

"Well," she starts, and then giggles nervously. "My name is Mackenzie Miranda Moore, and I'm in eleventh grade. Just like all of you. Except Mrs. Garrett, of course."

This is my new partner? I think I'll stick with the Sasquatch head.

"Ms.," Ms. G corrects.

"What?"

"Ms. I'm not Mrs. I'm Ms. Garrett."

"Miss?"

"Ms." By the look on Ms. G's face, she's feeling the same way I am. She moves on. "So what made you choose cos?"

"Nails," she says simply. Ms. G prompts her for more. "I like to do nails, and I'm really good at it. I'm also good at styling. And cutting, too. I cut all my Barbies' hair when I was a kid."

If she's so good at nails, why aren't *her* nails done? And when she says that she's good at cutting and styling, does she mean just on her dolls? *Everyone* here cut Barbie hair as kids—probably even Byron and Toby! Mackenzie's hair has clearly never been styled or cut, other than a trim. What exactly does she know how to do?

Ms. G has her take a seat—Lydia's—while she goes over a few announcements. "The style department"—which is cos and fashion design—"will cover the fairy-tale backdrop.

However, if your team is using music, I need your forms with the song title and artist no later than next Monday, so we can purchase the permissions. If you're using props beyond what we provide, you'll need to pay the stage helpers, who will be from custodial arts."

"How much will that be?" I ask as I raise my hand. "And do we still need to turn in music choices if we're subcontracting a live musician?"

"Nominal," answers Ms. G. "Five ATC bucks each. We want to encourage you to go all-out. And yes, but note that on the form. We need to double-check copyrights and permissions for the sheet music."

"Where's the form?" Toby asks.

"All forms are on MyATC. Click the showcase tab and then forms," says Ms. G.

"What about a snow machine?" I ask. "Will that cost extra?"

"Yes," she says, "and I'm sure that will be substantially more. It belongs to the performing arts department. I'll check with them and get back to you."

I thank her and smile. She wants all-out? We're going all-out and then some.

Ms. G dismisses us for our team meetings. "Go to the cafeteria, because the wellness fair folks are in the multipurpose room." Everyone leaves, but Ms. G calls me over to meet Mackenzie.

"You're in good hands," Ms. G tells her after she introduces me. "Charlotte will show you the ropes and help you get caught up." She flashes me a *please-be-nice* smile that looks remarkably like my mother's.

The only thing I say to Mackenzie is hi before she launches into a play-by-play of Finn calling to tell her she got into cos. I walk as fast as I can to the cafeteria. She practically has to run to keep up, because she's several inches shorter than me and her mouth is using up all her energy.

When we get there, Shea is seated at a table by the far doors. We make our way around the perimeter and I introduce them.

Shea and I recap our theme and preliminary plan for Mackenzie. This is our team, sans Lydia.

"Because of the setbacks, we need to get moving on subcontracting, pronto." I fan through the ATC catalog. "We need ballerinas, kids, a flute player, artists, builders, and a graphic designer." I make a list as I talk, borrowing from my Grander Plan.

"I used to make candy with my grandma every Christmas when I was little," Mackenzie announces. While I'm wondering what that has to do with anything, she launches into a long random story.

When she pauses to ponder whether she was eight or nine that particular year, I interject. "We don't have a lot of time, and we need to cover a lot." In other words, *wrap it up.*

Mackenzie looks at me as if *I'm* the one being rude. "I'm just trying to help," she snaps. "Jeez! Anyway, I can make the candy flowers, I think. Or at least my grandma can. I don't know. Do we have to do everything ourselves?"

"Yes, we do," I say. "And we have the flowers covered. Lydia is doing them."

"Who's Lydia?" She looks around the table.

I keep my explanation brief, but it sparks a litany of questions: Why isn't she here? Why is she on our team if she's not in cos or fashion? Why did she leave cos? I answer the first couple, but by the last question, I'm annoyed. First, we're wasting time. Second, I don't know the answer. Third, even if I did, I'm not going to divulge Lyd's personal deets to someone I just met. "Start thinking of ideas for your models, okay? We'll probably each do two styles. We should coordinate, but not copy, don't you think?"

"I can do pretty much any hairstyle," Mackenzie says, sweeping her hair behind her ears. "Braids . . . twists . . . pin curls . . . waves . . . ringlets . . ."

"Good," I say. "That'll give us plenty of options."

Shea moves on. "Back to subcontractors. I know most of the ballerinas, so I can handle that part." She has a notebook and is taking notes. This is good. She's on top of things.

"Buns . . . bouffant . . ." says Mackenzie.

"Also," Shea says through Mackenzie's rambling, "Ms. White said the graphic designers will be here as soon as they're finished with the wellness fair groups."

"Cornrows . . . dreadlocks . . ." Mackenzie continues to no one in particular.

Reed's coming here? How did I not know that?

"That's good." I run my hands across my head, smoothing any stray frizzies. "I have a graphic designer I'd like to use."

"Mohawk, odango . . ."

I turn to Mackenzie with my list and the catalog. "Would you like to help—wait, odang-*what*?"

"Odango," Mackenzie corrects me. "You know, the way Sailor Moon has her hair. It's big in anime. I might do that as one of my styles."

"Good to know. And we can talk about *that* later." I open the catalog and slide it across the table. "Can you help us with *this,* please?"

Mackenzie flips through the pages and names everyone she knows, but none of it seems relevant to our project. Shea and I look at each other—we're on our own here.

A woman with a clipboard—a secretary from the main office, I think—comes around and asks for our list of subcontractors. She has runners on deck to fetch them from their programs to join our meeting. We don't have a list; we didn't know we needed one. The woman reiterates what Shea said—graphic design, along with building trades and multimedia art, will be here soon. But for less common subcontractors, we need to specify.

I look around. Other teams have their lists ready. "When was this assigned?" I ask.

"Last Monday. You've had a week." She looks at me as if I'm a slacker! I'm mortified. Monday? That was the day I met with Finn and Lydia. The day I left. I totally forgot to check what I missed! Shea met with Finn, too, and she had a dentist appointment that day, too, so she didn't know, either.

Then clipboard woman says, "All subcontractors need to be finalized by the end of program today."

Today? *Crapola!* I thought we had more time. Full-blown panic sets in. We ask for a few more minutes. She agrees, but seems perturbed as she moves to the next table.

I take the catalog from Mackenzie, and Shea and I pore over it, scrambling to make a list. We were able to make informed choices on ballerinas—thank God Shea knows them. The flutists and child development people were pretty much random. We chose two of each, hoping to do a quick interview before making our final choices. To expedite the process, I deliver the list to the woman and smile in an attempt to redeem myself.

While waiting for the subcontractors, we discuss hair and dress ideas, which launches Mackenzie back into her random list of styles. Shea pulls out her portfolio, but before I can see her sketches, my phone flashes a text from Lyd.

I need you. Come to the multipurpose room ASAP. Please.

Oh, no! Something must be wrong. I try calling her, but she doesn't answer. As much as I hate to bail on our team, I can't ditch Lydia, even after everything that's happened.

I relay the situation to Shea. She encourages me to go and assures me she can handle the subcontracting. I hesitate. Will she make the best choices without me? I quickly discuss interview questions, ideal answers, and basic criteria for the people we need. She doesn't take notes, but says she's got it. I insist that she get Reed as a graphic designer. She says she'll do her best. I give her my cell number and ask her to keep me updated.

Clipboard woman is suspicious, but lets me go with a handwritten hall pass. I know she's even more convinced of my slacker attitude now, but I don't have time to prove otherwise. I throw open the door. The hall is swarming with building trades, graphic design, and multimedia arts students, armed with folders, notebooks, laptops, and large messenger bags, all headed into the cafeteria.

"Charlotte? Where are you going?" Reed holds the door open as people stream past us.

"My friend needs me," I say. "I should be back soon. Find a redhead named Shea back by the far doors. Tell her I sent you. She'll get you signed up on our team."

"Sounds good to me." He winks and smiles.

When I get to the multipurpose room, Lydia isn't there. I search the room, ask a few people—the ones wearing hairnets—and eventually find her in the building trades lab by a small pile of wood with two other people. She looks as if she's about to cry.

"I'm sorry," says a girl wearing brown Carhartt pants and a green long-sleeved tee.

"We need to go." A guy in a ponytail nudges her. "The other meeting will be over soon."

The girl says, "Let us know what you decide. We can still do it, but we need to know today. We're wrapping up this showcase and starting on the next one by the end of the week."

Lydia nods, and they leave.

"What's wrong?" I ask.

She bursts into tears. "I'm having a panic attack, and I need you to talk me down."

"Okay." I speak slowly and calmly. "Slow down, breathe, and tell me what's going on."

She takes a few deep breaths. "I want an arbor as the entrance to our booth. Remember the flower garland from the bakery I planned to use?" I nod. "Well, I thought I'd drape it on the arbor and also use it for the posters."

"Great idea—"

"Except I got in too late. The wellness fair is in four days, and they're not ordering new supplies until next week—for the winter showcase. All that's left are these scraps."

There are a few longer boards, but mostly, the pile looks as if it's ready for a bonfire. I can't imagine anyone— including a fairy godmother or a genie—turning that mess into an acceptable doorway. I don't say that, though. Instead, I ask what the building trades people said.

She tells me that they can do something, that it won't be as good as if they'd had weeks to build it, but that it could work—especially if she covers most of it with flowers.

"There you go." I try to sound upbeat.

She picks up a short piece of wood and drops it. "It's going to be a Franken-arbor."

Then I receive a text from Shea: **Your graphics design guy is in. Not so sure, though. He's kind of a tool.**

Yes! Reed is on board! But wait. "Kind of a tool"? What does she mean? I hope she hired the right guy.

I reply, **Why? What happened?**

Lydia sits on the dirty cement floor as tears stream down her cheeks. "This is all just too much. What was I thinking? I'm in way over my head."

Finally, she's come to her senses! Moving to CA may have been impulsive and stupid, but it's only been a week. Maybe we can go to Finn and put everything back the way it was, make it all right again.

I try to sit next to her, but my skirt isn't long enough to fully cover my butt and legs against the cold floor. I try to adjust it, but it's not working. I end up in a weird pose, sitting on my heels, which hurts my knees. I lean to put my arm around Lydia to comfort her and end up falling into her shoulder.

"What are you doing?" She gives me a half-annoyed, half-amused look.

"I'm trying to help you, but my skirt and this floor just aren't a good combo." I stand and brush sawdust specks from the back of my clothes. Then I grab a stool from a nearby workbench and boost myself onto it. "So, do you want me to go with you to talk to Finn?"

Another text from Shea: **Nothing, really. Just full of himself for someone who spells like a third grader. Not my type. Are you two talking?** Followed immediately by another: **Anyway, subcontracting is done.**

Reed can't spell? That could be problematic. Unless Shea is exaggerating a few typos. I'm not too worried. Extra proofreading sessions mean more time with him.

"Finn? Why would I talk to *him*?" She stands, dabs her eyes with the edge of her shirtsleeve, and sifts through the wood pile.

I text Shea, asking who she chose and ignoring her question about Reed and me. She texts back the names and why they're the best, to which I reply: `Thank you!!! I owe you big-time!`

Lydia is visibly annoyed that I'm texting instead of talking to her.

"The sooner you talk to him," I say, "the sooner we can get you out of those ridiculous hairnets and back to cos where you belong."

She stops cold and stares at me. "I *am* where I belong. I'm overwhelmed with the project, not with the program. Just because I didn't tell you everything doesn't mean that I didn't put a lot of thought into changing. God, Charlotte. *This* is why I can't talk to you."

My phone lights up with a final text from Shea: `No problem. See you at the next meeting.`

I read it but don't reply. Lydia sighs and walks away.

I let her go. I can't believe she thinks she can't talk to me! Who did she reach out to when she was freaking out? Me! Who left my meeting the second I got her S.O.S.? Me! Who talked her through her meltdown? Me! Who's getting no credit for being a good friend? Me!

Charlotte's Vision for the Winter Showcase

★ Our team—Shea, Lydia, Mackenzie, and me—wears coordinating outfits.

★ Props: giant candy "forest" added to fairy-tale background, sugar flowers created by Lydia, built by building trades, decorated by multimedia art, and placed by stage helpers.

★ Wow-factor prop: Snow machine.

★ Models: Four ballerinas and (two to three?) children (as flying and frolicking fairies).

★ Music: whimsical flute music for the PowerPoint and speech/model presentation.

★ PowerPoint first: behind-the-scenes pictures of our work throughout the semester, designed by Reed.

★ Speech/Model Presentation next: Required—ONE model each. Shea designs all four dresses; Mackenzie and I style TWO each, plus our mini fairies. On stage, we discuss the techniques we used as models dance and turn.

★ Thunderous applause!

★ We win first place!

★ I win the bet!

★ Reed and I double date with Lydia and her guy.

★ We are so legendary that we become the standard by which first place is judged in upcoming years.

eleven

21 days to the Winter Style Showcase

The next few days are weird. I've hardly heard from Lydia. I texted a few times to check in and offer help, but each time she said she had everything under control. I asked if she even wanted me at the fair, and all she said was **Of course. Don't be so melodramatic.**

Mackenzie is getting on my very last nerve. Not only does she say random things, but the girl wears khakis every day. She must have a closetful of them. Nobody should have *boring* as a signature style. And her skills are even worse than her wardrobe! First she criticizes Ms. G's braiding technique, as if she knows more than the teacher. When we practiced on each other, I did it Ms. G's way and it looked great. She did it her way on me, and it fell apart by lunch!

Then Ms. G tells us to partner up to practice foiling. Except I can't practice on Mackenzie, because her parents refused to sign the permission slip that allows other students to cut or chemically process their kid's hair. She has virgin hair—never been treated in any way, except trimmed. After the braiding mess, I said that if I had to work on a mannequin, so did she.

Ms. G couldn't argue with that. When I saw Mackenzie's shoddy highlights, I thanked my lucky stars.

There's nothing happening with Reed. No new conversations, or flirting by the lockers; just a quick "hey" as he rushes to class. Gauging from how busy the halls are, more than half of the ATC is involved with the wellness fair.

Finally, on Friday, Fair Day arrives. We're excused from afternoon classes in order to set up. Everything needs to be perfect before the doors open to the public at five.

The multipurpose room is a madhouse. I wade in, cos smock over my arm. Before I plunge in to help Lyd, I take a look around. Booths—colorfully decorated L-shaped table configurations, with banners hanging on the wall behind them—line the perimeter of the room. Many have wooden stands on which we can hang informational posters, signs, and more decorations. I see why Lydia felt pressure to compete. Building trades and graphic design did a great job.

One side of the room is devoted to the medical programs. There are a blood pressure exam station, booths about different disease screenings and awareness, scales and information about BMI and a healthy diet, and, of course, the sign-up for the blood drive. The vampires—what we call the phlebotomy students—are in their element, working side by side with the Red Cross.

Giant tumbling mats are set up side-by-side, covering the middle of the room. There are plastic climbing structures, a slide, and a games area marked with signs: bean bag relay, musical chairs, and hopscotch. They even have folding chairs along the edges for parents to watch from. It's so bright and colorful. The best part is the bounce house in the corner.

The other side is for culinary arts. Some of the stations look almost like kitchens—there are hot plates, Crock-Pots, toaster ovens, microwaves, and a popcorn machine. The apple booth has cider, caramel apples, and mini applesauce cups and smells so sweet and cinnamon-y.

Our booth is decorated with green tablecloths and flowers. The arbor is already in our "doorway." It looks much better than I thought it would, even before we add the floral garland. Lydia freaked over nothing, and she says *I'm* melodramatic. On the wall behind us, the banner reads NATURE'S FACIALS—FOR DELICIOUSLY SMOOTH SKIN.

"When did you come up with that?" I ask.

Lydia looks up from organizing the bowls and grins proudly. "Last week. Sounds tempting, huh?"

Instead of answering, I put on my smock.

"What?" she snaps. "My project uses food for skin care. Mrs. Barbara liked it a lot."

"Her and Hannibal Lecter." I try not to crack up, and fail.

"Jeez and crackers!" She spreads a black drop cloth across the floor to catch any face paint spills. "Is *anything* ever good enough for you?"

"Yes, lots of things," I say, taking the other side of the drop cloth and tugging it so it'll be even with the booth beside ours. "Our 'Franken-arbor' looks fantastic. Your crème brûlée. Iridescent Iris nail polish. Pretty much anything from QVC's Dooney & Bourke show. See? I'm not picky." Lydia tugs back, tucking her end under the booth's side wall. "Cute digital dudes named Reed."

I feel Lydia start to pull again, so I lean backward and bend my knees. All of a sudden, the cloth goes slack and I lose my balance, landing on my butt. *Bam!* A wooden brace from the booth next to ours digs into my butt cheek and my eyes smart with pain.

"Sorry," says Lydia flatly. "I thought you had it. Are you okay?"

"I'm fine." I squinch my eyes to hold back the tears. Everything hurts when I stand up. At least I'm not wearing a skirt today.

Then I notice everyone watching. Trying to hide my embarrassment, I throw my arms up like a gymnast at dismount and yell, "Ta-da!" I get a few smiles, and a moment later the chaos starts up again.

"So how many folding chairs do you think we'll need?" Lydia asks, moving on so quickly that I'm wondering if she let go on purpose.

"Two or three," I say, resisting the urge to rub my sore backside. It hurts like hell.

She grabs two chairs from the cart manned by a couple of custodial services guys a few booths down from ours and sets them up. The whole time she's scanning the room.

"What are you looking for?" I pull out the color bowls I borrowed from cos and arrange them on the inside of the booth.

"Carter was supposed to be here by now," she says. "He has the recipe guides."

"Carter?"

"He's the digital design guy I hired." The way she smiles leads me to believe there's more going on than recipe booklets. She opens a canvas bag and pulls out a long string of floral garland.

"Lydia . . ." I mock-scold, already imagining the four of us hanging out.

"What?" She tries to pretend she doesn't know what I'm asking, but she sucks at it. I stare at her, waiting for her to come clean. "There's not much to say . . . yet. We've only been talking for a week." She drapes the garland along the top of the arbor and hides her face behind the cascading orange and yellow blooms.

"But you've been talking?" I grab the strand and shake it playfully. She smiles. "Cool! Go for it, Lyd!" I say, but really, I can't believe she hasn't told me before now. That's not like her—well, not like the old her. That's not like *us*. I've shared every detail about Reed, even when he was simply QT. Why hasn't she gotten excited about our double-dating prospects, too? What's happened to us?

I wait for more details about Carter, but she moves on to the face creams and paints.

Just as we're finished decorating the booth, putting up the posters, and stirring the paints and creams, Trent shows up. He's got a camera dangling from his neck, and he hands Lydia a box—her brochures.

"Where's Carter?" she asks, clearly disappointed.

"He's finishing up another job in the lab," he says, "but he'll be here eventually." He nods to me, and I give him a brusque nod back. "Hello" would have been nice.

Then he explains to Lydia that he's taking pictures of the fair, and asks if she needs any for her PowerPoint, which won't be presented until the week of the winter showcase. Ours play *during* our show. I pretend not to listen to their small talk. He's telling her how much he likes photography, how it's kind of his hobby, and how he's getting extra credit for it because ATC will use his work on their website.

"He's nice," Lydia says when he finally leaves. "Not too hard on the eyes, either."

"What about Carter?"

She shakes her head. "What about him? I'm just stating the obvious."

"Uh-huh." *For someone who seems pretty into himself,* I think.

My last boyfriend, Logan, acted like he was into me, but when it came right down to it, he cared more about his friends and football and his stupid classic car. Our relationship only lasted a month. And Matt was *too* into me. Whenever we weren't together or hanging out with Lydia and Cody, he called and texted constantly and stalked my Facebook and Instagram. Maybe Reed will be different, a happy medium.

Lydia starts to wonder where Carter is again, but thankfully the doors open and within minutes, the place is swarming. Our customer service experience helps, as our friendly smiles and hospitality kick in.

The girl in the booth next to us, where they're making antioxidant smoothies, looks as if she's close to tears. Some little kid spilled his smoothie all over the floor, so she's trying to clean it up while her partner is asking where she put the bananas. People are walking right through the mess and tracking it all over.

We get decent traffic, and people are taking the recipe guide—freebies always draw traffic. A woman with two small boys walks past. Her hair is perfect. That's no small thing; I usually think everyone's hair could use a little something. Her color is clearly professional—multi-tone highlights with all-over level eight or nine, without any evidence of damage. Nice!

The older boy pulls on her and asks to get his face painted. She asks what's in the paint. I tell her, "Corn starch, coconut oil, and natural food coloring." She agrees and asks the younger boy—Alex—if he wants to get his face painted just like Cameron. He hides behind her leg.

While I paint a spaceship on Cameron's cheek, the woman asks, "Are those fake eyelashes?"

I smile and nod. "They add a little pizzazz to pretty much any style." I dab a little orange into the star on the spaceship to give it dimension.

"They look so natural," she says.

Natural? There are tons of sparkles on them. Last I checked, people don't naturally have sparkly eyelashes, but I don't argue. She's probably talking about my stellar application skills, not to be confused with my application of stellar objects on foreheads. Ha! I chuckle under my breath.

"What's so funny?" asks the boy.

"Nothing," I say, finishing up. "You're just so dang cute." He smiles. Then I ask his mom, "Where do you get your hair done?"

"At my salon," she says. "Catch-a-Ray, near Vandercook. We all trade hair services."

"You own a salon?" She nods and introduces herself as Kristina. Then I tell her that I'm in the cos program, and she tells me that she went to ATC ten years ago and asks me to give Ms. G a hug for her. We talk for a while about my future plans and how she built her clientele and bought her salon. She's living my dream. Before they leave, she hands me her card and tells me to come by after I graduate.

I thank her and put the card in my purse where I won't lose it. Just talking to Kristina brings my Grander Plan into clearer focus.

I spend the next few hours painting kids' faces while Lydia slathers green goo on people's hands and talks about how nourishing it is for the skin. These women (and men, too) are eating it up. Figuratively, of course. Nobody actually tastes it, even though Lydia assures them that it's safe to eat.

Rachel, the girl from custodial services, lingers at our booth for a while, too. Eventually, I realize that she wants her face painted, but she doesn't actually ask outright—she just watches me work on the kids. Then, when I clue in, I ask if she'd like something, and, after some discussion, end up painting a tiny pink heart just under her right temple. I accent it with a stick-on sparkle.

After she leaves, I watch her move from booth to booth, smiling and touching the heart every so often. It's nice to see her happy. Simple changes to your appearance really can give you a boost. Mom might think it's superficial, but she's not here, witnessing it.

Other people from the store are here, though. Barb and her husband bring their nieces, and Tyler, the bagger, is here with his grandma. He's carrying a bunch of brochures—I see one on colon health and another about breast self-exams. Several regular customers file past, too.

There's about an hour left when a mother and daughter come up. The girl is about thirteen, and she's wearing a knit cap pulled down so low it almost covers her eyes. The mom looks completely exhausted, as if she hasn't slept in years. When Lydia massages the mask into her hands and talks about the benefits of avocado oil, you'd think she'd found the Fountain of Youth. The daughter sighs, glares, and says, "Come on, Mom! You promised we'd leave by six and get dinner at Napanelli's."

"Just a minute, sweetie. I want to find out about this."

The girl pouts. She has the biggest, roundest blue eyes I've ever seen. Something is different about them, though, but I can't figure out what. To buy some more time for the mom, I try to make conversation with her.

"I know you're too old for face paint," I say, "but I could

do your makeup, if you want." She shrugs. I turn on my sa-lon charm. "Come on. Why not?"

Her mom overhears. "Go on, sweetie. It'll be fun."

The girl almost throws herself into the chair. Her arms are crossed, her lips pressed tight. I sanitize my hands, open my purse, and pull out my makeup bag and the samples I—*we*—won from the fund-raiser. Then I lay out brushes, moisturizer, powder foundation, blush, eye shadow, eye liner, and mascara across the table.

"I can't wear mascara," the girl says matter-of-factly. "I don't have any lashes." That's it! I knew there was something different about her eyes. She doesn't have lashes, or brows.

"That's okay. I wasn't going to use that anyway. It's mine, and using someone else's mascara is as gross as using some-one else's toothbrush." She scrunches up her face in disgust. "Exactly!" I say.

I open the tube of moisturizer. "Wait a second," she says. Then she pulls off her cap.

She's bald. Her head is beautifully shaped, and there are tiny, baby-fine wisps of blonde hair just beginning to sprout. "I have cancer." The way she says it, it's like she's trying to shock me. She watches my face intently, coldly. I've seen that look before. I've *given* that look. She's testing me. Is she try-ing to see if I'll feel sorry for her, if I'll look away?

Challenge accepted. "You also have gorgeous eyes and amazing cheekbones," I say with authority, keeping my eyes locked on hers, which widen ever so slightly. Clearly, that's not the response she expected, and she drops her guard a bit. I suppress a smile, and squeeze some moisturizer into her hand. "Rub that all over your face evenly; it makes your skin softer, and it's a good base for the foundation." As she does, she watches me. I open the foundation and pick up a brush. "This is organic. It's made with powdered minerals and tints. Your skin color is close enough to mine that it'll work."

When she's ready, I brush on the foundation, which blends perfectly. Then I follow with a few strokes of bronzer and blush.

"How do you get the sparkles on your eyelashes?" she asks.

"They came like that." She gives me a Buffy-confused head tilt, and I laugh. "They're fake," I say, which gives me an idea.

"You know," I say as I crack open a sample of lip gloss, "I don't have any unused mascara, but I do have a new pack of false eyelashes, if you want. They're not sparkly, though."

By then, her mom is watching us.

"Can I, Mom?" she pleads. "Please."

The woman hesitates, and I'm sure she's going to say no, so I quickly add, "They peel right off."

She gives in. The girl's lips tighten again, but this time she's holding back a smile.

Turning her chair so her back is to the room, I rub sanitizer all over my hands again and squeeze a tiny dot of glue between my thumb and index finger. I tell her to close her eyes, and then I use a Q-tip to spread a thin, even layer across the edge of her lids. I press the lashes into place.

While they're drying, I brush on some rose-gold eye shadow, then open up the brown eyeliner and draw in some faint brows. "Just a few finishing touches." I dig into my purse to find a spool of wide ribbon, some glitter, and a stray bangle bracelet. Everyone should have a little sparkle. I cut off a long piece of ribbon and tie it around her head like a headband, finishing with a bow on the side.

She fidgets in her chair and sits on her hands. "What's your name?"

"Charlotte." I roll a little glitter across her lids, and slip the bangle onto her wrist. "What's yours?"

"Sarah." She looks from her wrist to me.

"It looks better on you," I say. "You can have it."

After I turn her chair around, I hand her a mirror. "Ta-da! The beautiful Sarah, fully accessorized." Her whole face lights up in a grin so wide that it shows a missing top tooth about halfway back.

"Oh!" Her mom covers her mouth, and starts to tear up.

"I don't even look sick," says Sarah, still beaming.

"It's not that," her mom chokes. "It's just been so long since I've seen you smile."

Lydia stands back and looks as if she's going to cry, too. I notice that a few people are watching. Before Sarah leaves, she hugs me. A little makeup magic has completely transformed the sullen girl of thirty minutes ago.

Once they've moved to another booth, a tiny older woman in a pink pantsuit comes over. Her hair is too dark for her age and skin tone, but it's perfectly coiffed in a classic roll-set style.

"I saw what you did. It was quite remarkable. How would you like to do it again?"

I hope she's talking about Sarah, and not falling on my butt earlier. "What do you mean?"

"Every year around Christmastime, Allegiance Health hosts an event to raise awareness"—she leans in and whispers "And money," then resumes a normal volume—"for the pediatric oncology department. It's held on the hospital campus so everyone, including inpatients, can attend." I nod, still not sure what she wants, and a little distracted by how much she uses her pink-manicured hands when she talks. "Sometimes young patients who lose their hair are so self-conscious that they refuse to go. Maybe if you brought in some of your—"

"Accessories?" I offer.

"Yes, accessories!" Her hands flutter with each syllable. "Maybe that would help persuade them. After all, it's their event. I'd hate for anyone to miss out."

I think of a roomful of girls like Sarah, and what I could do for them. "Sure, I'd love to," I say. Then I glance over at Lyd, who's busy cleaning up the bowls and straightening the brochures. "Can my friend Lydia help, too?"

"Of course," says the woman. "That would be wonderful. One more thing, just so you know." More over-the-top gesturing. "To work with our young people, we'll have to run a background check on you both, and you'll have to sign a confidentiality agreement. We do this with everyone. HIPAA laws." She says this as if I know what HIPAA is.

I make a mental note to look it up later. "I'm sure that will be fine."

As I put the ribbon and glitter back in my bag—and keep scanning the room—she goes on and on about past events and how people with money give more to charity before the first of the year "so they can write it off, you know." At the word "charity," a light bulb goes on in my head. This can be my service project! It's cos-related and helpful to the community. Plus, it's something I would like to do. Win-win-win.

Then I see him.

Reed is here! He's over by the eye-test booth talking to Trent. I realize again how tall Trent is. But even though Reed's almost a foot shorter, that's tall enough for me. Trent points to our booth and Reed begins walking toward me, weaving through the thinning crowd. Ms. Pink Pants keeps talking, and I reply automatically, hurrying her along as I watch Reed come closer.

"I'll get everything cleared through the administration and staff . . ." she's saying.

"Right, right."

"You'll probably need several hours with the patients . . ."

"Right, right."

"And you're welcome to attend the dance afterward . . ."

"Right, right."

"Well, I won't keep you," she says finally. "I'm sure you

have better things to do than talk to me all evening."

"Right, right."

She stops suddenly, hands freezing mid-gesture.

Oh, no! I laugh nervously. "I mean . . ."

"It's fine, dear." She touches my arm as if to dismiss the awkwardness. Then she pulls out a little notepad and pen, both matching her pink suit. "May I get your contact info, please?"

As I write my name, e-mail, and cell number down, my heart races. Reed is just a few booths away. I hand back the notepad, and she hands me her business card. She looks at my info and says, "Charlotte Pringle. Any relation to Bill?"

Oh, great. She knows my family. Pops or Dad? Probably Pops, since few people even know Dad's real name. "Uh . . ." I'm so focused on Reed that I suddenly realize it looks as if I'm totally clueless. "Yeah," I say, collecting myself. "My dad and my grandpa are both Bills."

"I'm guessing it's your grandfather I know," she says. Figures. Her and the entire town. *Pringle's Market: Serving Jackson since 1945.* She launches into how she knows him— the VFW or the IGA or something—and Reed is almost here. Will she *ever* stop talking? Maybe she's related to Mackenzie.

Luckily, another older woman saves me. "Excuse me. Anita?"

I take advantage of the interruption and escape. Ms. Anita Pink Pants calls after me, "I'll be in touch, Charlotte."

"Thanks so much!" I flash a quick smile and wave just as Reed gets to our booth.

"I'm so sorry I'm late," he says, checking his phone before slipping it into his pocket.

"It's all right," both Lydia and I say at the same time.

We look at each other.

"Charlotte, this is Carter. Carter, this is Charlotte."

Carter? Wait. This guy isn't Carter—Lydia's Carter. This guy is Reed. My Reed.

There must be some mistake. Or a mix-up. Like in a movie or hidden camera show. Maybe Carter and Reed are twins. Please tell me they're twins. I can deal with that. In fact, it's perfect. Lydia and I are interested in twin brothers. Yay! Right?

"We've already met." He laughs. "We talk all the time."

No, we haven't. I know your twin brother, Reed. Not you. I haven't met you.

"Charlotte, what's the matter with you?" Lydia seems annoyed. I can't imagine what I look like. I hope I don't look like I feel, which is confused. And weird. And confused. And stupid.

Trent comes over to the booth as I say, "Carter? I thought your name was Reed. He called you Reed that day in the hall." I point at Trent.

Lydia says, "Reed? Did you say Reed?" Now that I see her face, I know what mine just looked like. What it must still look like. She turns to me. "QT?"

I nod slowly. It's hot in here, stuffy. I can hardly breathe.

"Cutie?" Reed, or Carter, or whatever the hell his name is, seems amused. "My name is Carter Reed. My guy friends call me Reed, and most everyone else calls me Carter." Then he looks at me. "So that's why you've been calling me Reed? I just figured you were being like one of the guys."

One of the guys? Is he serious? I have never, ever, ever tried to be *one of the guys!*

If I'm one of the guys, then what's Lydia? His girlfriend? The guy who I was hoping to make my boyfriend, so we could go out with Lydia and *her* new boyfriend, turns out to *be* her new boyfriend! How could I be so stupid?

Lydia and Reed—*Carter*—and Trent are watching me, but then quickly look away. They're embarrassed for me. They're pitying me. I think of how Sarah tested me to see if I'd look away. *I'm embarrassed,* I tell myself. *I don't have cancer.* In comparison, this is nothing. This. Is. Nothing.

But when I see Reed—oh, God, will I ever be able to call him Carter?—it doesn't feel like nothing. I turn to the bowls of crusted-over face paint on the table. Lydia already cleaned up her stuff while I was talking to Ms. Pink Pants. All that's left is my mess. All over the place. Staring at me.

I stack the bowls and brushes on top of one another, take them to the garbage can, and dump them in. Even though the bowls are for mixing hair color, and they aren't disposable—and they don't belong to me—I don't care. I'll buy new ones.

When I start shoving makeup back in my case, Trent comes over. "Can I help?"

"No, it's fine." I tighten the cap on the foundation before putting it away. "I've got it."

Lydia tugs on the drop cloth I'm standing on. "Oh, sorry," she says. I step off, and she and *Carter* fold it up. Together.

"You sure?" Trent asks again.

"Uh-huh," I say. Then I pull off my smock. "Hey, Lyd, if you have everything under control, I'm gonna take off, okay?" All that's left is cleanup and awards. Right now, I don't care if we win. Right now, it doesn't look like there is a *we* anymore.

"Sure, okay," she says, as she takes down the silk flowers and hands them to Carter.

I look at Reed—Carter—as nonchalantly as I can. What did I miss? He's been flirting with me for weeks. Hasn't he? We've had this *thing*—this playful banter practically every morning. He was interested in me. So what's this? Why is he with Lydia like *they* have a thing?

I want to ask him. But that would be so trashy, like reality TV. And I am not the desperate chaser girl. If he doesn't want me—and only me—then he can burn in the fiery pits of hell, with a bad perm. And a mullet.

I need some air. I'm out of here.

Trent follows me, his camera bouncing on his chest. "You sure you're okay?"

Sure. Okay. Sure. Okay. Why are those the only words anyone can say? The only words that do not fit me or the situation right now.

"Why wouldn't I be?" I stop in the middle of the hall and glare up at him. I wish he'd stop talking to me and look away, but he doesn't. Instead, he seems to be looking at me even more closely, searching my face—for what, I don't know. His eyes are kind of green, almost the exact color of his polo shirt. Now the staring is getting awkward. I'm waiting for an answer to my question, and it's like he's waiting for *me* to answer it. Or to break down. Or something.

I give up and walk away, my two-inch heels echoing with each step. Halfway down the hall, I turn back, and he's still there. I keep going. Before pushing through the double doors, I check again, and he's gone.

twelve

20 Days to the Winter Style Showcase

That night, no matter what I'm doing—fielding Mom's questions at dinner, searching Pinterest for showcase ideas, or working on spreadsheets—I can't stop thinking about what happened at the fair.

Fortunately, the week leading up to Thanksgiving is always super busy at the store, so all day Saturday I focus every brain cell on turkey and stuffing mix, canned pumpkin and mashed potato flakes, and displays and customers.

I'm doing pretty well, too, until my phone reminds me of the party tonight for the wellness fair programs. Lyd invited me the night she cooked dinner for us. I'd forgotten all about it. Is she still planning on going? And if she is, do I want to go, even though Carter Reed will probably be there?

"All available cashiers to the front," Barb pages. "All available cashiers to the front." I spend the next three hours running a register and vacillating about whether or not I should go. Should I reach out to Lydia? I hate how things are. What's going on with her and Carter Reed? Are they a thing? She wouldn't let a guy come between us, would she? No matter how she's been acting lately, I'm sure she wouldn't do that. By the time the crowd thins, I've pretty much convinced myself to call her after work, make amends, and go to that party.

My stomach grumbles, and I have a slight headache—I was too busy to each lunch—so I decide to grab something from the deli before I head home.

Box-dye Hannah and Katie have their own huge lines of customers, and are too busy to say anything as I slip past them and go into the back.

So are Nina and Oliver. "Don't be mad," Oliver says, as Nina boxes up a pumpkin spice cake. "I didn't even know we were having a baby when I bought the tickets!"

"So what am I supposed to do?" Nina whips green-and-white bakery string around the box and ties it off. "I don't want to miss it, and I can't go alone. You have to bring a partner to every class. *Every* class. Not just the ones that are convenient for *them*."

Usually I don't want Oliver and Nina to see me, but this time I wait, hoping they notice and shut up. They don't. So I wash my hands, grab a giant croissant from the bread bin, and head to the fridge for turkey, cheese, mayo, and lettuce.

"I'll be at the first one," he says. "And the last two." His face is red and he looks like hell. His green Pringle's apron is smeared with some red jelly-looking stuff—probably cranberry salad.

"The first one is just an introductory class—what to expect the final weeks of pregnancy, complications, communicating with your doctor, and how to know when to go to the hospital. The *next* class is the most important—when they cover labor! That's when I'll need you."

"I'll be there for *actual* labor." He cups both of her shoulders in his hands. "Isn't that more important? Come on, Neen, these tickets were really expensive, and the guys had to buy them a year in advance, and—it's just one class!"

"Is this how it's going to be, Oliver?" She pulls away from him and starts crying. "Are you always going to put Red Wings games and other shit ahead of your daughter?"

I do *not* need to hear this. I slap my sandwich together and put everything away as fast as I can.

"Can't someone else do it this once? Please!"

Before I wrap the sandwich in a paper towel, I take a quick, gigantic bite. I'm starving.

"Who am I going to get? You know I can't ask Allie. Asking her to go to a childbirth class after everything she's been through is just mean." Nina's practically hysterical now. "And my mom is too far away. So who else is there? Huh?"

"What about my mom?" And now Oliver finally notices me. "Or Charlotte?"

I stop chewing.

"Charlotte?" Nina says this as if we are being introduced for the first time.

"Why are you looking at me?" I say with my mouth full.

Oliver grins like a cartoon dog with a bone. "Yeah. Charlotte."

I finish chewing and swallow, hard. "I'm, uh, busy that day."

"We haven't said which day yet," he points out.

"Well, I'm pretty busy every day." I run my tongue over my teeth, feeling a gummy croissant and mayo film all over them.

"See, Oliver?" snaps Nina. "She doesn't want to." Then she flips from hysterical and whiny to pissed-off. "It's fine! *Go* to your damn Red Wings game. I don't need either of you." She grabs the pastry box so hard that the corners crumple. Then she stomps out to the counter like some pregnant Godzilla.

"Nice, Charlotte," Oliver says dryly. "Would it kill you to think of someone besides yourself for one minute?"

"Said the guy who's leaving his pregnant wife to go to a hockey game," I counter. "Not my commitment. Not my responsibility."

I finish my sandwich in the break room, away from both of them.

Before I'm even done, Mom storms in. "Oh my lanta! Where's the fire?"

"'Oh my lanta' is right." She gives me a look. "I know Nina's not your favorite person, but would it kill you to help her out? It's only a few hours of your time."

I can't believe this. Oliver is an *expectant father,* and he ran to Mom as if he were ten. "If it's so easy, why don't *you* do it?"

Mom's baby blues cloud over and her jaw tightens. "It looks like I'll have to," she says coldly. "Because that's what *families* do—help each other out." If she's trying to guilt me into it, it's not working. She turns to leave, then stops. "Oh, and you're grounded for the rest of the weekend."

"Grounded? Because I can't cover for Oliver? You can't be serious! I have plans with Lydia." Maybe. But I don't tell her that.

"Not anymore, you don't." She shakes her head. "And it's not because of the class, it's because of your snippy attitude. I'm your *mother*. You don't have to like me, but—"

"Good." The word slips out before my mind can stop it. Why did she come in here and hassle me to begin with? I do *not* have an attitude. None of this was my fault.

Her eyes are like lasers. "Want another week?"

I don't say anything, but I don't back down, either.

She pushes open the door, then turns around for a parting shot. "I'd do it, too, but that would be more like a punishment for the rest of us." And, with that, she's out.

Funny, Mom. You're so clever. Not!

She might have grounded me, but she didn't say that Lydia couldn't come over. Maybe we can mend fences with a makeover/movie sleepover. I really need to vent about Mom. As soon as I pull into our driveway, I call her.

"Hello?" I hear Lydia's laughing voice, loud music in the background.

"Lyd?" I open the door and Buffy rushes out past me. I brace myself to keep from toppling.

"Hey, Charlotte. What's up?" She sounds distracted, like I caught her at a bad time. Who's with her?

"Where are you?"

"Steak 'N Shake," she says. Then to someone else, "Just a sec. I'm on the phone."

"You sound busy." I drop my bag, slip off my shoes and coat, and flop onto the couch.

"What? Sorry, it's loud in here." There's a long pause and then it gets super quiet. "Okay. This is better. What did you say?"

"Mom's being stupid. She freaked out because I won't go to some childbirth class with Nina." Buffy batters at the door. I get up to let her in.

"Really? That sucks," she says, as if she's thinking about something else.

"I know!" I open the back door. "So do you want to—?"

It's loud again on her end; people are laughing. "Sorry, Charlotte, I've got to go."

Go? Go where? To that party? Without me?

Cold air rushes in with Buffy.

"Okay, well . . ."

She hung up.

". . . bye," I say to no one.

The old Lydia would never have gone to a party without me. The old Lydia would have said, *I'll be right there*—like we've both done lots of times. The old Lydia cared about how I felt.

"Guess it's just you and me tonight." I toss my phone onto the end table. Buffy hops up on the couch and settles in. "Romantic comedy or action thriller?" I ask her. Movie night with Buffy is more fun than some lame party, anyway.

About nine o'clock, Mom and Dad bring home a pizza. I'm still pissed off—and full of turkey croissant—so I'm not really hungry. One little crispy pepperoni is too irresistible, though, so I pick it off. When I go back for another, Mom yells at me. "Don't just pick at it. Take a piece." I leave instead.

Grounded or not, there is no way I am going to bed before ten on a Saturday night. I turn on QVC and open my Grander Plan notebook and the ATC catalog. Time to find someone who isn't Carter Reed. But before I begin, I scroll through Facebook.

My aunt Kathy and uncle Scott—Dad's sister and her husband—have posted several check-ins and pics. They live in Traverse City, but they travel a lot. They're in Florida through the holidays.

There are pics of the wellness fair, statuses about weekend plans—by the sounds of it, everyone is having fun, except for me and my cousin Jonah, who lives in Texas and is sick with a cold—memes about the holidays, and pics of Katie's cat in a Pilgrim costume.

Wait! What's this? *Lydia Harris is now friends with Carter Reed.* As of twelve minutes ago. I check all of her social sites, and sure enough, she's now following him on every one. So much for not dating him. So much for never letting a guy come between us! In the time it takes for my blood pressure to rise, my browser refreshes, and the pictures start. Lydia doesn't post them, but she's tagged in them.

There's one with her laughing with a lot of people I don't know.

Another one of feet—Lydia's orange shoe next to some guy's boot.

Next, a selfie. Lydia is making duck lips, and the guy she's with looks like a goon. *It can't be,* I think, zooming in. But yes it can. It's Reed. *Dammit—when will I learn?* Carter. It's *Carter.*

Lydia's with Carter, right now. At the party. They're laughing together and bonding.

Apparently, she's made her choice, and it isn't me.

thirteen

18 days to the Winter Style Showcase

I'm so busy at the store on Sunday that I barely have time to think about Lydia and Carter and their goofy pics and all their bonding and inside jokes that probably make me look like a fool—well, maybe I think about it a little. Okay, maybe a lot.

By the time I get to cos the next morning, I'm a bit pissy. First thing, I ask Ms. G if I can change graphic designers. "The one we have just isn't going to work," I say. She asks why and I tell her I'd rather not go into it. She says that unless there's a really good reason, the assignments are already set. I say I do have a good reason, but it's personal. She tells me that working with people with whom you have personal differences is called professionalism.

Before I can object further, she hands me a piece of paper—a quote from performing arts for the snow machine—tells me to discuss it with my team, and to contact Mr. Rollins, the PA director, for a subcontracting agreement by the end of the day. The quote includes a mandatory PA stage helper to operate it. It's pricey, but worth it. Then she tells me to sit down so she can start class.

Ms. G announces that since the wellness fair is over, all our focus should now be on the style showcase. She wants to hear our project ideas—probably so she can steer the worst ones away from disaster, and make sure that we're all actually working on something—so we go around the room. Even though I always sit in the front, she weaves up and down the rows, so it takes a while to get to me. Mackenzie isn't here yet, so again, I'm on my own.

Joelle and Tasha are planning an ambitious mythology theme—with Medusa's snakes done in braids, Hera's hair fanned out in peacock feathers, and Nisus's hair dyed purple. Their skills are fierce, especially with braids and color. I'll have to keep my eye on them.

Byron and Toby are doing something with robots—gray body paint, metallic silver suits, futuristic hair—which has a lot of potential, but no doubt Toby will squander it by doing everything at the last minute. The Emilys have a country theme, which I expected—complete with side braids and cowboy boots, no doubt.

Someone else is doing badass bikers, with funky hair and black leather. There's a Celtic fantasy with long velvet capes and magic rings; that could either be pretty, or cosplay gone horribly wrong. There's a 1960s flower power idea that seems way too simple—what skills does straight hair with daisy headbands show off? A woodland fantasy theme that sounds like a *Snow White* rip-off.

Then it's Shelby and Taylor's turn. "Well," says Shelby, "we got a new fashion designer because our first one moved away. Our new designer, Gabriella, had this really great idea—our dress is going to look like frosting, we're going to accessorize with fondant, and top it off with a massive bouffant, so she looks like a cupcake."

Wait a second—that's *my* idea! Gabriella stole my idea and gave it to Shelby and Taylor! I stand up to protest, but Ms. G makes me sit down until they're finished. I can feel the steam coming out of my ears.

Taylor continues, "Everything will be pink—retro fifties, with a pink Cadillac prop, lollipops, and that old song 'Sugar Pie Honey Bunch.'" All pink? They took my idea and turned it into Pepto-Bismol. I guess that's apropos, since it's nauseating.

I raise my hand. Ms. G nods. *Finally.* "First of all, my— *our*—theme is Sugar Plum Fairy, and that was *my* idea for a frosting-like dress and candy accessories. Gabriella was my and Lydia's designer and—"

"There *have* been some unusual circumstances," Ms. G interrupts, "but I think your ideas are different enough that they can exist in the same show and not seem redundant." *Different enough?* That's not exactly fresh and original. "You're not doing bouffant, right?"

I'm reluctant to give too much info; Shelby and Taylor might steal those ideas, too. "We're doing several styles, and yes, at least one will be an updo—not bouffant *exactly,* but—"

"I'm sure it'll be fine," says Ms. G. "Anything else?"

"Yes," I say. "That song is from the sixties, not the fifties, and it's called 'I Can't Help Myself.'" Pops plays a lot of classic Motown at the store.

Taylor asks if she should change the song. I tell her she might want to consider it—and her theme as well. Shelby rolls her eyes and says nobody will know and that I'm just being anal. I mutter that I'd rather be anal than an asshole, and *bam,* I get sent to Mr. Finn's office. Who knew Ms. Garrett has robo-hearing?

I relate the whole story in detail to Mr. Finn. Not only does he listen with his fingertips pressed together, but he also bites his lower lip so that it squeaks when he breathes, like a deflating balloon. It's really distracting.

When I'm done, he simply tells me to refrain from *any* name-calling, even under my breath. I tell him I will and ask him if I can switch graphic designers.

"Is there a problem with the one you have?"

"Yes."

He waits expectantly. I don't elaborate. "Does it involve bullying, harassment, or anything else that would require my intervention?"

I mull that over for a second. As much as I'd love to get my way, I can't lie. "No."

"Have you discussed this with Ms. Garrett?"

"Sort of." He waits for more explanation. "She said no."

He stands. "Then that's my answer as well. Thanks for

stopping by," he says as if I came over for tea and crumpets, instead of being booted from class for calling Shelby an ass-hole. I shoot him a half smile and head to my locker. Team meetings will be starting soon, and I want to mentally prepare, especially since I'm stuck with Carter Reed.

— ✳ —

Determined to make the best of it, I settle myself at a table in the multipurpose room with my binder, the detailed time-line, and checklists, and wait for the rest of my team, includ-ing the subcontractors, to show up.

I'll put the showcase first and not let anything with Lydia or Shelby bother me—just like a good leader should. If every-thing goes as outlined, I'll win, be able to go to the Chicago hair show, get Mom off my back, and prove to everyone that I know what I'm doing. Cos isn't just a superficial hobby; it's a viable career choice, and I excel at it. Just thinking about it makes me feel as if I drank a whole pot of coffee.

Shea shows up first with both arms full of some kind of stiff, glittery fabric and what looks like a half-sewn dress. No matter what I think of her, I'm impressed. This girl is ready to get down to business. She drops the pile onto the table, sits down, and takes a deep breath. "Okay, so here are our designs. Four dresses, each different, but each com-plementary."

Just then, Mackenzie barrels in like a pint-sized, khaki-wearing tornado. "What's up, guys?" But before anyone can answer, she tells us about her morning, starting with sleeping through her alarm, continuing with every mundane thing her sister said at breakfast, and ending with some story about *almost* hitting a deer on her way here.

"Okay." Shea opens her notepad and shows me a drawing. Again, I'm impressed despite myself. It's really good. She smooths out the pile of glittery fabric. "We're using this. It's metallic, so it'll look like sugar, like you wanted."

Another design, which complements the first one, is shorter, asymmetrical, and has cap sleeves instead of straps. It's really pretty. Mackenzie claims it as hers, and starts talking about doing either an elaborate French braid or that Sailor Moon style she mentioned last week.

Ignoring her, Shea flips the page. Another terrific drawing. "And this is my pride and joy. It's a ball gown with hand-sewn sequins and beads. The skirt is supposed to look like a multi-tiered cake. I know you don't sew, but let me tell you, these stitches are a bitch. It's about half finished now, but it's too heavy to drag around."

Finally, she shakes out the dress she brought. It's a raggedy-looking tulle and taffeta thing. "This one has that jagged hemline I told you about. It's really complicated, and will actually take longer than the others, so I—I mean *we*—should get extra points for it. The skirt looks like petals, too. Isn't it adorable?"

The designs are mostly good, and Shea seems really excited, but I can already see the problems. I take a closer look at the last dress, drape the tulle across my fingers, and choose my words carefully. "So are these petals finished?"

"Yes," she says. "They're supposed to be rough."

"How is rough complicated?" I wonder aloud. "Isn't it just cutting?"

Shea rakes her hands through her hair and sighs. "Seriously?"

"There's no need to be snippy," I say. "I'm just being honest. This project means a lot to me."

"It means a lot to me, too," she snaps.

"You know ballet dancers are wearing the dresses, right?"

"Of course. So?" She closes her notebook and folds the dress in half, then drapes it over a chair.

"Well, one of the metallic dresses is too fitted to move in, and with all of the beading and sequins, the floor-length gown's going to be heavy and cumbersome." I don't add that the metallic fabric looks better suited to Byron and Toby's robot theme than my sugar plum fairy. Still, I have to ask, "Where are the ribbon flowers? Didn't we talk about ribbon flowers?"

"Uh, Gabriella took that idea, remember?"

Shelby and Gabriella may have the best design idea—mine—but that doesn't mean we can't come up with a better version. I try to explain this to Shea, but she's too pissed off.

And then, as if this meeting weren't going downhill fast enough, Lydia and Carter come in, laughing like their lives are just one big party. Once the majority of the team arrives, we begin introductions. I pass out instructions outlining where to be when and what to do to prepare.

First are the ballet dancers, who are wearing black

leotards and yoga pants. Two of the girls, Kayla and Kaylee, have tight, slicked-back buns; the third has short hair and a black fabric headband.

"Aren't there supposed to be four?" I ask Shea, then turn to the girl in the headband. "Uh, where's your hair? You had long hair in your catalog photo."

"Yes," says Shea. "Where's Lindsay?"

Headband girl answers Shea first. "She backed out. She's Clara in *The Nutcracker*, and rehearsals are brutal." Then to me, "I cut it. So?"

Isn't it obvious? "So, this is a hair show. I can't braid it, curl it, or put it up."

"I wish someone would've told me!" Shea fumes. "What are we supposed to do now?"

"It's fine by me if I only have one model," Mackenzie says. *Way to settle for the minimum requirement, partner! Especially when the rest of the class is going above and beyond.*

"What about a wig?" suggests one of the other ballerinas. (Is it Kayla or Kaylee? I'm not sure which is which. And they've both got those slicked-back buns.) "Or extensions?"

"It's against the rules to use wigs because they come prestyled." I click my pen open and closed, open and closed. "And she doesn't have enough hair to hold extensions."

Shea, in an attempt to keep the model, says, "A pixie cut *does* go with our theme."

I ignore her. I doubt she'd be so accommodating if she had to work with a model who couldn't wear clothes!

Clearly, I'm going to have to replace headband girl.

When I tell her, she says, "Good luck with that so close to *Nutcracker,*" gets up, and leaves.

In a matter of minutes, we're down to two models. I ask Kayla and Kaylee about replacements, but they just shake their heads, purse their lips, and shrug. I look at Lydia, Shea, and Mackenzie, hoping for some assistance, some reassurance, something. After all, they're my co-leaders, aren't they? Shea is in a texting frenzy, no doubt telling off Lindsay for bailing, but promises she'll figure something out. Lydia is having a side convo with Carter Reed, and Mackenzie is braiding a piece of her own hair. How can a team with this many leaders be so lame? This is not how I pictured my winning team. They act like there's nothing at stake.

Suddenly, a disheveled girl in a ponytail and jeans runs in and takes a seat. She introduces herself as Melody from child development. "I'm sorry I'm late. We had a crisis with some biting toddlers."

"Come on, you guys, we have a lot to do." I clap my hands to get their attention. "We haven't even met our whole team yet, and we've already lost a member—two, if you count Lindsay. Let's get focused, okay?" I finish the introductions as I hand out the rest of the instructions.

"What's this?" asks Carter. "I know what I need to do."

"You do?"

"Yes." He opens his laptop. "In fact, I brought a sample PowerPoint to show you."

We all huddle around the tiny screen and watch as pictures scroll and pixelate and change in all these funky ways to an annoying Taylor Swift song. The photos are fine, but his font is inconsistent, and I count at least four spelling and capitalization errors.

"This is your best work?" I say.

He looks as if he doesn't understand the question.

"Here we go," Lydia mutters. What is that supposed to mean? Is she too into this guy to see that his work is sub-par? Shea snickers.

Again, I choose my words carefully. "It's just that I see a bunch of spelling errors and problems with the fonts."

Carter gives me a look as if he's thinking, *My work is fine. This girl's just pissed off that I'm into her friend.* "It's a *sample* of my work."

I tap my pen on the table. "Fair enough. But I'll need to go over the prelim PowerPoint with you, make sure everything's okay." Now he and Lydia give me a look like I'm just trying for another chance with him.

Seriously? I'm way past that. We're talking about my future here. "Moving on," I say.

"What do you need us to do?" asks the building trades guy in a grungy Craftsman hat. He's sitting between a guy holding a flute case and a girl splattered in yellow paint. As I explain how I want the set built and decorated, I ask Mackenzie to coordinate the music with the flutist. The form is due today. The rest of my team goes back to their discussions as if my "interruption" never happened.

"It says here that you need a few little girls in sparkly ballet costumes and fairy wings to frolic across the stage."

Melody points to her instructions. Finally, someone is paying attention! "Where are they getting these costumes?"

"Shea?" I refer the question.

She looks up from her phone and I repeat what Melody
said. "I could throw together tutus using elastic headbands
and leftover fabric from my petal dress," Shea says. The
words "throw together," "leftover fabric," and "petal dress"
do not add up to a winning combo.

"Do any of the kids have Halloween or ballet recital costumes they could reuse?" I ask Melody, grasping at straws.

Shea sighs, annoyed, and returns to her phone. Melody
makes a note on her instructions. "I'll see what I can do.
No promises, though." Then she says, "So you're doing their
hair?" I nod. "When?" I tell her that morning. "Um, you'll
need to communicate all of this to their parents. And get
permission."

None of that had occurred to me. I convince Melody
to be a liaison with the parents and to make the appointments. She says that will cost more, and I agree to pay—it'll
be worth it to make sure everything is right. Then she asks,
"Do you just need kids, or do you need some of us to help
corral them?"

Corral them? What are they, cows? Yet one more thing
I hadn't considered. Kids are always melting down at the
store. We'll need professionals to handle that. "Having some
of you there to help would be great."

"Anything else?" she asks. I like this girl.

"Could you bring them to the meeting next week? I'd like to meet them before the showcase."

"More like criticize them," Shea says under her breath. But before I can respond, the bell rings and every chair in the room scrapes back as people stand and gather their things.

My team practically runs from the table. I call after them, "Hey, wait! We still need to talk about the snow machine. I have a quote."

"Do what you want," Shea says over her shoulder. "You're going to anyway."

Lydia and Carter crack up. *Ha! Fine! I* will *do what I want, thank you very much.* So much for teamwork.

"Please be prepared for the *next* meeting!" I yell to a closing door.

Other than her "Here we go" comment, Lydia doesn't say a word. She doesn't stay after to explain why she and Carter are so lovey-dovey, or why she ditched me on Saturday. She doesn't stick up for me or help me at all. She just acts like the rest of them and exits in a hurry. With Carter.

I watch as they leave the room, and realize that even in the months before she switched programs—all through summer and early fall—Lydia's been acting like a different person. Like someone who has secrets. And those secrets have affected me. What else is she hiding?

Mondays are pizza days, so the lunch line is really long. Taylor and one of the Emilys are behind me. "Is Lydia seeing that Carter Reed guy?" asks Emily. At first I think she's talking to Taylor, but she's not. She's talking to me.

"I don't know," I say. Which sounds weird and defensive, but I really don't know. The last thing Lydia actually said was that they're weren't anything, yet. But her actions, online and at school, have been the complete opposite. Even other people have noticed.

"We're not trying to spread gossip or anything," says Taylor—which means they are—"but you should know that he's been seeing my friend Brianna from J-High since freshman year. He cheats on her all the time. I don't know why she puts up with it. If Lydia's hanging out with him, she's only going to get hurt. He always goes back to Bri. Always."

"Maybe this time it's off for real," I suggest. He does seem interested in Lydia. But until the wellness fair, I thought he was into me. Were there other girls who thought the same thing?

"I almost fell for him myself," Emily puts in, "until Taylor introduced me to Brianna, and I heard everything straight from her. He's a real jackass." Whoa! Well, there's my answer.

"Have you guys told this to Lydia?"

"No." We're getting close to the front of the line. Taylor fishes her wallet out of her backpack. "We figured she'd rather hear it from her best friend. Less embarrassing, you know?"

"Yeah." But if I did tell her, I don't know if she'd believe me, or if she'd think I just want him for myself. Hell, I don't even know if we're still friends, let alone best friends. What kind of person drops her best friend for a guy, no matter how cute he is? Maybe she deserves what she gets.

After we get our pizza, they ask if I want to sit with them. Shelby and the other Emily are already at their table. "No," I tell them. "Shelby hates me."

Taylor snorts. "No, she doesn't. She thinks *you* hate *her.*"

Why would she think that? I've never done anything to her.

"Come on." Emily takes my arm.

I stand my ground. "She called me anal."

"You *were* being anal." How rude! I was not! I scowl, but Emily doesn't seem affected. She tugs again.

I don't have much choice. I don't know—or care—where Lydia is. She's probably with Carter. So I either need to sit with them or sit alone. Since I'd rather saw off my arm with dull thinning shears than sit alone, I join them. It's awkward. The Emilys ask about everyone's meetings. Just as Taylor starts to answer, Shelby interrupts, throws a few pepperonis on her tray, and gives her a look—a *don't-talk-in-front-of-the-enemy* look. Did she think I wouldn't notice? I chew my pizza and avoid eye contact with her. After I'm done with my lunch, I make excuses and leave as fast as I can, with only a quick smile and wave to Emily and Taylor.

"Icks" class is no time to break it to Lydia that her possible boyfriend is a cheating jackass—and I confess that I'm not even sure I want to—so I don't say anything. Besides, she makes it clear that she doesn't want to talk to me, because she sits two rows behind where we always sit.

Mr. Comb-over assigns "Expense Projection Reports" based on our presentations. I suggest we call them "budgets," since that's all they are. He says that's fine. Someone in the back says something, and a bunch of people laugh. One of them is Shelby. This is the girl who thinks I hate her? Fine. I flash her a dirty look.

The first step is to create a balance sheet from our most current ATC bucks statement. When I check the escrow account that Lydia and I share—shared?—there's a major discrepancy. The balance is less than half what it was last week. Mr. Comb-over shows me how to check the transaction history. And there it is: a huge transfer to Carter Reed. Another to someone in building trades, and yet another to multimedia art. Each one is dated the day before the wellness fair.

I whip around to where Lydia is working on her final report. *"You stole my ATC bucks?"* It comes out much louder than I intended.

Joelle says, "Oooh!" and several people around her snicker.

Pink-faced, Lydia pulls over her chair and whispers, "I didn't *steal* them. I needed them for the wellness fair—the expenses were higher than I expected. I'll pay them back to the account before the showcase."

Everyone is pretending not to listen, but they suck at it. They're hanging on our every word. So I don't even try to keep quiet. "How? Since the fair is over, there won't be any more culinary arts fund-raisers, and you're not in cos anymore, so you can't work in the salon. We're over two hundred dollars in the hole, and I can't subcontract without it. You could have told me this before the team meeting, you know."

"I don't have all the details figured out yet," she admits, "but I won't leave you high and dry. You know that."

I glare at her. "Do I? Because the way I see it, you've left me high and dry a lot lately."

Toby says something about being high. Byron laughs, and Shelby tells them to shut up.

Lydia takes a deep breath, and by the look on her face I can tell that whatever she's about to say is going to be nasty. I'm geared up to retaliate with what I heard about Carter, but Mr. Comb-over walks up and tells us to get back to work.

As Lydia takes her chair back to her computer station, I say, "Don't forget to include embezzlement in your final report."

That prompts a few more whispers and snickers, but I don't care. Lydia shoots me a look, but doesn't say anything. After all, it's true. Her project was fine because she dipped into our shared account, and she didn't tell me because she knew I'd be screwed. She had to know that she couldn't put back her share of the balance. Is she trying to get back at me or something?

Now I have to figure how to write a budget with almost no money. I'm not sure it's even possible. There has to be a way around this, but I'm not sure what it is. I close the program and log out of my account. I'll do the report later.

Then I reach into my notebook, pull out the quote for the snow machine, and rip it in half.

Considering how busy we are this week—even during the times that are usually dead—and how awful school was, I should have just skipped and gone to the store. I head over as soon as the last bell rings.

The store is packed, of course. There's a line at the deli, even with both Katie and Hannah hustling to keep up. After I take my stuff to the break room and clock in, Dad flags me down and asks me to pitch in. He's clearly frazzled, so I don't argue.

I tie on an apron and get right to work. Mrs. Donnelly asks for two pounds of shaved ham, a pound of Swiss, two medium-sized containers of three-bean salad, a container of German potato salad, some tabbouleh, and two dozen onion rolls. "Nolan's home from college, I take it?" I say, laughing as I scoop beans into a plastic tub.

"How can you tell?" She gives me a big smile. "Between him and his brothers, the vultures are picking my kitchen bare."

Once the salads are done, I box up the rolls and slice the meat and cheese. "Happy Thanksgiving," I say, handing it all over.

Before I turn to the next customer, I notice what Katie's doing. She gets out the roast beef, slices it, and bags it. Then she scoops a salad. Then she goes back to the cooler to slice cheese. She's completely scattered, running all over the place. Has she always been this spacey?

"Katie?" I say. She stops and looks at me. "Ask for the full order. Then do the meats and cheeses at the same time, before moving into the salad case. If you consolidate the steps, you'll look less like a turkey running around with your head chopped off."

"Okay," she says, but she does the same back-and-forth crap with the next customer. Now I know how Ms. Garrett feels when she has to repeat everything a thousand times.

"Stop! Watch me." I help the next few customers so she can see what I mean. Then I say, "Got that?" She nods. "Good." I smile as I say it—positive reinforcement.

A few minutes later, Hannah uses the same spoon for both the chicken salad and the macaroni salad. I intercept the container of macaroni salad before she gives it to the customer, telling the woman we're going to use a fresher batch. Thank God, she doesn't balk.

I take Hannah into the back, along with the bowl of macaroni salad from the case, and toss the container in the garbage. "Now dump out the rest of the macaroni, wash the bowl, and refill it," I tell her. "It's contaminated. And redo this order without crossing spoons." I start to tell her how to sanitize the bowl, but it'll take less time to just do it myself. "Never mind. I've got it."

"It's not like it matters," she says in a monotone. "They're both made with the same mayo."

Her tone and attitude make me want to slap her. "It's not about the mayo. It's about walnuts. There are walnuts in the chicken salad. How do you know that whoever eats that macaroni isn't allergic?"

She looks suitably mortified. "Whoa! I didn't think about

that." Then she winces. "I'm sorry. I was up all night, and my brain is a little mushy."

It's not my problem that she was partying all night. "We owe it to our customers to give them what they order without any added bacteria or allergens. We want repeat business, and they won't be back if they're in anaphylactic shock!" Didn't anyone train her? "Next time, pay closer attention."

When I get back to the counter, Katie is missing. "Where'd she go?" I ask no one in particular. The waiting customer shrugs. I apologize and help him.

Hannah reappears with the macaroni, and we settle into a rhythm. I keep an eye on her. After a while, I page Katie, but Tammy shows up instead. She whispers, "She's in the bathroom crying."

I sigh. "Why?"

"I thought you'd know. When Barb tried talking to her, the only words she could make out between sobs were *Charlotte, turkey,* and *head chopped off.*"

"Oh my lanta! I was just trying to help her be more efficient."

"Did you threaten her?" she says.

Before I can say anything, Hannah comes over with a refilled container of cranberry sauce. "Yes, she did," she answers with a snide grin. "And if the cops need a witness, I'm available."

Tammy laughs and pats Hannah's arm. "I knew you'd fit in here."

Fit in? Is she serious? This girl doesn't even know the basics—about deli, or hair.

"So what *did* happen?" Tammy asks.

Hannah's rendition makes me out to be an overbearing bitch. I try to explain and interject some truth into the story, but she keeps cutting me off. Tammy appears to be buying it. I can't believe it. She's known me a long time.

Hannah asks if Katie is all right, and Tammy says she is, but that she went home. Home? Seriously? I'd hate to see how she'd react if I really had yelled at her.

By the time Tammy turns to go back to the registers, it hits me. I call after her, "Wait! There's a pool, isn't there?"

Tammy hurries away as if she didn't hear me, but I know damn well she did. Soon I see her slip some cash to Ralph over by the sweet potatoes. "I can see you!" I yell, attracting stares from everyone shopping in produce and the deli/bakery.

I don't have time to hassle them because we get busy again, but I glare at Ralph whenever we make eye contact. He's not afraid. Why should he be? I'm really not as mad as I'm pretending; I just wish I could've gotten in on the action. I wonder what the bet was. How many minutes it takes Tammy to get the story of what happened? How many times Katie posts on social media when she should be working? I can't wait to find out.

fourteen

15 days to the Winter Style Showcase

I wake up Thanksgiving morning to the smell of roasting turkey, cinnamon, and simmering cranberries. Mom's been up and cooking since the butt-crack of dawn. Part of me feels kind of guilty that I'm not down there helping her, but she didn't ask. I stretch luxuriously in bed. No school, no work—Thanksgiving is one of the few days I can sleep in and take my time with my hair and makeup.

By the time I come downstairs, Dad, Pops, Oliver, and Nina are drinking coffee and watching the parade on TV. Nina's wearing a sweater that's clearly stretched beyond its limit—I can't imagine what her skin looks like. And she still has a whole month to go!

I'm about to join them when Mom appears from the kitchen, stepping over Buffy, who is sprawled out across the doorway. "Charlotte, I need your help." Cooking! Just what I was afraid of. She takes off her apron, tosses it onto the kitchen table, and stands in front of Dad, blocking his view of the TV. "Moose," she says, and he's forced to look at her. "When the timer rings, pull the pie out of the top oven, please. Mother will be here soon, so I need to get ready."

"Gotcha," says my dad. But as soon as she steps away, he's glued to the TV again.

I wait for my orders. Mom motions for me to follow her—upstairs, away from the kitchen. No cooking—excellent!

A print blouse and dark brown pants are hanging on the outside of Mom's bedroom closet. Every time Grandmother visits, I serve as Mom's fashion consultant. "Which would look better—this, or this?" She takes out a chocolate-brown-and-cream sweater dress. Then she pulls out a striped corduroy jumper . . . thing. "Or this?"

"Put that away and don't *ever* get it out again. Unless it's going to Goodwill." I pick up the sweater dress. "This. You need leggings with it, though. What colors do you have?"

"Black, and black."

I shake my head. You can't mix black and brown without something to tie them together. When I return with my brown leggings, she's in the dress, but she's tying this hideous scarf around her neck. It has cornucopias on it! I stop her mid-tie and take it away. "If you wear that, I'm getting emancipated."

She laughs. "Fair point. But you know she'll say something if I don't."

"So what?" I counter. "Even she knows it's ugly. Remember when she gave it to you? She said she won it at a charity auction, and that if you didn't like it, maybe *one of those girls at the store* would appreciate it."

Mom winces; we all do when Grandmother talks about

the people at Pringle's. It's as if they're the staff of Downton Abbey, and we're the Crawleys.

Store legend—that is to say, Tammy, who's been at Pringle's since Dad was in high school—has it that Mom used to be almost as bad. She had no idea how things worked, but since she'd just gotten married to the boss's son, she tried to take charge. Needless to say, it was a disaster. One day, during a rush, Tammy couldn't take it anymore. She quit and walked out, leaving Mom with a line of customers and no backup cashiers. After she learned how to run the registers—and yes, the customers were *super* pissed—she quickly developed a new appreciation for the Pringle's staff.

She apologized to Tammy and begged her to come back. Now the two of them are dear friends.

"Charlotte, promise me you'll make an effort to get along with Oliver and Nina today. I really don't want another lecture from your grandmother."

"I'll see what I can do," I say lightly, as I rummage through her jewelry.

She starts pulling up the leggings. "Man, these are tight. What size are they?"

"They're medium."

"Medium?" She stops. "I can't wear medium."

"They're stretchy. Keep pulling." I slip a long chain with an owl pendant around her neck, and step back. "Perfect. And pick up some brown leggings next time you're at Keehn's. I'll never understand how you can buy a dress without getting all the accessories at the same time."

Mom tugs and wiggles and hops up and down. "There's something else I need to tell you."

Uh-oh. I brace myself.

"Nina invited someone to dinner," she continues.

That's it? That's normal; we always have a few extra people. Ralph has been at every Thanksgiving dinner as long as I can remember. No Pringle's friend or employee is allowed to dine alone the fourth Thursday in November. Ever.

But wait a minute. "Who?" I ask.

Mom finally gets the leggings all the way up, and adjusts the dress. She's stalling.

"Mom, who did she invite?"

She looks in the closet for a pair of boots.

"Your brown ankle boots," I tell her. "Who is it?"

"Hannah," she says into the closet.

Before I can react, the doorbell rings. Mom shoves her feet into the boots and runs downstairs like the house is on fire. Then I hear the smoke alarm.

It *is* on fire!

I take the stairs two at a time.

It's chaos. As Buffy circles the table and barks, Mom pulls a charred, smoking pumpkin pie from the oven, but I think she's emitting more smoke than the pie is. "Moose! You were supposed to *take the pie out*." She glares at him, keeping her voice down; Nina and Oliver and our guests are right there in the entryway. If we can hear Grandmother quizzing Nina about her due date, the baby's gender, and name possibilities, then they can probably hear us, too.

I let Buffy out and hold the door open to let some of the smoke clear.

"Stop, drop, and roll." Pops twists the cap off a bottle of beer and takes a swig.

"I never heard the timer go off." Dad fans the smoke detector with a pot holder. "I swear."

"*I* swear—" Mom starts.

"Kimberly!" Grandmother says from the kitchen doorway. Her level nine ash blonde hair is in her signature angled bob with a stacked back. She's also impeccably dressed—stylish brown pants, a cream cashmere sweater, and just the right amount of bling around her neck. You'd never know she was almost seventy.

In a split second, Mom composes herself, puts the pie down, turns, and gives her a hug and kiss. "What's that smell?" asks Grandmother.

Before Mom can reply, Dad cuts in. "It isn't a Pringle Thanksgiving without at least one disaster." He grins and opens the window over the sink.

"Happy Thanksgiving, Mother!" Mom says with effort. "Where's Mr. Vanderpool?" Mr. Vanderpool has been married to Grandmother for over thirty years. We don't call him "Grandfather." Mom doesn't call him "Father." We all call him "Mr. Vanderpool." Grandmother's rules.

I let Buffy back in and close the door. She makes a beeline for Grandmother and starts sniffing and nosing her hand for affection.

"Oh, he's in the foyer speaking to that man who handles the produce at your market." *That man?* She *knows* his name is Ralph; she's only had Thanksgiving dinner with him for the past ten years. "Kimberly, dear, you look marvelous! How do you do it all?" All the while, she's pulling her hand away from the dog and cringing.

Mom smiles and puts her arm around my shoulders, then grabs Dad's forearm. I see her nails digging in, but he doesn't flinch. "I have a lot of help, Mother."

"Can I offer you a cocktail, Grandmother?" I say dutifully and guide her to the living room, so Mom can regain control of the kitchen.

"What time is it?" she asks.

"Almost noon."

"Perfect! How about a gin and tonic?"

Dad scoots past me. "I'm on it."

Pops, Ralph, and Mr. Vanderpool are on the couch with beers, chatting it up, when the doorbell rings again. Buffy barks, but stays in the kitchen. Nina answers it and hugs Hannah, who is carrying an infant seat with a blanket over it. A baby? Hannah's a mom?

She pulls the blanket away and there he is—a sweet, sleeping little bald guy in an orange onesie with a turkey on it. He's really cute all scrunched up in there. Hannah, on the other hand, is a hot mess. No makeup, baggy jeans and a faded long-sleeved tee, box-dyed hair in a ponytail. Her roots are coming in.

"Oh! What's his name! How old is he? Can I hold him?" Nina moves in to take him like Hannah has brought her a present.

"No!" Hannah snaps. Nina steps back in shock. About time she realized that the girl's a bitch. "Um, I mean," Hannah backpedals, "the longer Caden stays asleep, the better. Trust me."

Nina recovers and asks Hannah what she'd like to drink. When she waddles into the kitchen to get a Sprite, Hannah and I look at each other.

"I told Nina you wouldn't want me here, but she insisted," she says.

"Of course she did. It's Thanksgiving." I go into the kitchen and let Mom order me around. I set the table and get out serving bowls and spoons while she finishes the gravy. Oliver fills the bowls and places them in the warming drawer.

Mom will not let the burnt pie go. She talks about the smoke smell and wonders aloud if we'll have enough dessert for everyone and complains how nobody ever listens to her. Dad says he'll go get another pie. "Having access to a closed grocery store is the best perk of owning it," he says, and escapes out the back door.

Less than an hour later, all of us, including the baby, who is still asleep in his car seat, are sitting around the table. Mr. Vanderpool says the world's longest blessing. He not only thanks God for our food and the friends and family with whom we share it, but then launches into a litany of all our country has to be thankful for, which is a weird mash-up of the Bill of Rights and random Facebook memes.

Then Caden starts fussing. Hannah tenses, her head still bowed, clearly unsure if it's appropriate to disrupt the blessing by getting up. When Mr. Vanderpool finally says "Amen," there is almost an audible sigh of relief. (I'd lay bets on Ralph.)

Hannah plucks the baby from his seat. He looks around the table at all the strange faces, opens his mouth, and proceeds to wail at the top of his lungs. Not just crying— stiff-bodied, red-faced, eyes-tight screaming. We all wait for him to calm down before filling our plates, but that doesn't happen. She paces and jostles and jiggles and pats and coos, but the baby just gets louder and louder. Buffy anxiously follows her. Pops takes her out as the rest of the table quietly serve themselves and pass the dishes, bowls, and platters around.

"I'm sorry." Hannah looks as if she's going to cry, too. "He gets like this a lot. The doctor says it's colic, but nothing I try seems to work. We should go."

Mom stands. "Don't be ridiculous." She holds out her arms for Caden. Hannah balks, but Mom insists. "Charlotte was colicky. I'll take him in the other room and rock him. You should get some time off. Sit, please. Relax. Enjoy." Hannah obeys, and Mom disappears, but we can still hear Caden's muffled screams. Hannah keeps glancing toward the closed door.

"Boy, was Charlotte a screamer!" Pops recalls as he sits down at the table, takes the green beans from Dad, and spoons some onto his plate. "That's what destroyed my hearing."

"That, and too many rock concerts in the sixties," says Ralph, with his mouth full of stuffing. Grandmother looks aghast. She might be appalled by his bad manners, but I'm appalled that they're bashing my infant self in front of me.

"Charlotte was colicky?" Nina pats her belly. "Is that hereditary?"

"It wasn't colic." Dad rests his elbows on the table. "Even back then, she was vocal when something wasn't done her way."

Hannah chokes on her pop and coughs. Oliver cracks up.

Thanks, Dad!

"So when did she stop?" Nina asks.

"She hasn't," Ralph answers. Everyone, even Grandmother, laughs. Since when did this become Bash Charlotte Day? "No, seriously. I won the pool and everything."

I put down my fork. "What pool?" My voice is ice.

Ralph is clearly enjoying this. "It started the first time your mother brought you into the store. You were fussy. She called it colic and said it would eventually stop. We named the pool 'When Charlotte Cuts It Out,' and it was supposed to be a date—you know, like we do—but I decided to kid around, and wrote 'never.' Years went by and the pool got buried and eventually lost. It resurfaced a few years ago. Since all the dates were long past—except mine—I won."

I stare at him. Is this for real? There was a bet about when I'd finally *stop being difficult*? That started when I was a *baby*? And the winner guessed *never*?

Oliver tries to hold in laughter, but he sucks at it. Nina

mouths, "Stop!" Hannah and Ralph both look away from me.

"The turkey is delicious," says Grandmother, changing the subject.

"Yes, it is," Dad agrees. "Kimberly's a great cook."

Then the table gets quiet, except for the clinking of silverware on china. There are a few more comments about the food. Pops and Mr. Vanderpool talk about the president and how different the world is from "their day," while Grandmother asks Nina—again—when her due date is.

Little Caden is still screaming. I feel for him. I want to scream, too.

"Kimberly's food is getting cold," Grandmother announces. Translation: Kimberly is the lady of the house and the person who cooked the food. She shouldn't be rocking *the help's* baby.

Hannah starts to stand. "You're right."

"I'll go," says Nina. "Take a break. You never get one."

"Thanks so much. I mean it." Hannah takes a sip of pop as Nina goes to relieve Mom. "I've had a hard time keeping sitters because he cries so much."

Oliver swallows hard. "Really?"

"Yeah." She toys with the green beans on her plate. "Actually, that's what I was doing when I first met Charlotte." She looks down, not at me. "I'd only been working three hours when my sitter called and said she couldn't take it. I know his crying can be nerve-wracking, but I have to work. I'm on my own."

Her sitter quit? On her first day of work? She's on her

own? I assumed she was talking about a guy that day, not a baby. And ignoring a customer for no good reason.

"You poor dear," says Grandmother. "I don't mean to pry, but what about the baby's father? Or your parents?"

Hannah looks up now. "I'm from Ohio. Mom's in Akron. Dad's in Kent." She takes another sip. "When Cody—Caden's dad—found out I was pregnant, he moved here because he heard there was work, and he could support us. After Caden was born, I moved here, too, thinking we'd be a family. Stupid. He wasn't looking for work. He was running from me. He still is, I guess. Except I'm not following anymore. I can't face my parents. Dad said if I left I couldn't come back.

"Don't get me wrong," she adds quickly. "Caden's the best thing that's ever happened to me. It's just that it's so"—her voice cracks—"hard."

She leaves the table in tears just as Mom returns.

"Charlotte," she barks, "what did you do?"

My head snaps up. "I didn't do anything!" Except totally alienate a girl who has nobody.

Dad, Pops, and Ralph nod in corroboration, so Mom drops it. "Wow, that boy has some lungs. Cute as a button, though."

She sits down and starts to eat. Everyone else is done—everyone but Dad and Ralph, that is. They'd keep going until someone takes the food away or it's gone, whichever comes first. Nina comes in, telling us that Hannah is trying to feed the baby. He's still wailing. Poor Caden. Poor Hannah. Poor us.

Then Grandmother says, to my surprise, "Oh, Charlotte!

I've been busy making plans for your visit. I've even made arrangements for you to stay in the Notre Dame dorms on Friday night with my neighbor's daughter. She's a mathematics major." I clench the edge of the tablecloth in my fist. *What?*

"How lovely, Mother." Mom carefully dabs at her mouth with her napkin, as if she's the Queen of Manners. And Stealth Scheduling.

"I'm so sorry," I say, knowing I'll pay for it later but not caring. "I have a conflict. My class at school is going to the Chicago hair show that weekend, and I've already paid in full. Didn't Mom tell you?"

"She most certainly did not." Laser glares dart around the table. From Grandmother to Mom, from Mom to me—I feel the holes boring into my skull. I avoid eye contact. I think of the sign outside the ATC metal fabricating shop: ARC WELDERS IN USE. PROTECTIVE EYEWEAR REQUIRED. We need a sign, too: PRINGLE FAMILY THANKSGIVING IN PROGRESS. TRENDY SUNGLASSES REQUIRED.

"That's because the schedule hasn't been decided yet," Mom says, through clenched teeth.

Hannah returns, and I realize that the crying has stopped. Caden's finally dozed off. She starts to help Nina clear the table, undoubtedly picking up on the tension. I'm sure Nina will fill her in once they're in the kitchen. Mr. Vanderpool's head nods sleepily. Pops nudges him and he snaps to, but within a minute he nods off again.

"Maybe not officially," I finally have to admit. "But

it's pretty much a done deal. I know I'm going to win the showcase at school—that's our end-of-semester presentation, Grandmother. Everyone will expect me in Chicago. It would be improper to rebuff the invitation, especially after I've committed." If I speak formally and focus on etiquette, maybe I'll win her over.

"I see." Grandmother is clearly appreciative of my good manners—take that, Mom!—and impressed by my commitment, but she's obviously annoyed.

Mom smiles meaningfully. "There's a saying about counting chickens, Charlotte."

"There are also hundreds of sayings about hard work and a positive attitude *paying off.*"

Ralph gives me a thumbs-up. "That's what I'm betting on, kiddo."

"Could someone please explain what's going on?" Grandmother demands. "If Charlotte won't be coming in March, I'd like to know now before I waste my time preparing."

Oliver fills her in on all the details of the wager. Dad just shakes his head, and Mom looks as if she wants to crawl under the table.

Grandmother makes a pained face. "I'm not sure I fancy being the booby prize."

"Booby prize," Ralph snickers. Pops elbows him.

I take a deep breath. "It's not like that, Grandmother. Mom and I have different opinions about priorities, but no matter what, I'll make time to visit you. Even if it's not that weekend."

"I understand, dear." She pats my hand. "Your mother and I had similar discussions when she was your age. I'll wait to do anything else until I hear a more concrete itinerary from *you*." I promise to keep her informed. Grandmother is now my ally. Chalk one up for Team Charlotte.

"Where's Lydia?" Pops asks when Nina and Hannah start passing out pieces of pie topped with whipped cream. Lydia always came by with something scrumptious from Patti Cakes on Thanksgiving. It was tradition. She ate with her family, had dessert here, and stayed the night—for the girls' movie, Black Friday strategy session, and shopping the following morning.

"She's not coming this year." I pass him a piece of pie, hoping he doesn't ask why.

"Pie? Coffee?" Nina asks. Pops takes my plate and a cup from Nina. He's distracted from Lydia, thank God. Mr. Vanderpool says he shouldn't, but he does, devouring every crumb and downing two cups of coffee.

Mom and Grandmother gossip about people I don't know. Hannah and Nina swap pregnancy stories. Oliver and Mr. Vanderpool discuss the economy, while Dad and Ralph talk about work. Pops oscillates between the economy and work convos, but somehow he's able to apply the cost of rutabagas to both.

I pick at my pie and think about what Ralph said. He's betting on me. Counting on me. Those who bet on me as a baby—that I'd eventually outgrow being difficult—lost. My stomach sinks. There's a lot riding on my winning the showcase—not only money, but dignity and respect. As PICs, Lydia and I were unbeatable. Now, though, everything's different, harder. I hope I don't let everyone down.

Within minutes, the guys are around the TV in varying degrees of sleepiness. Football scores blink across the screen. Caden wakes up screaming again, so Hannah straps him in his seat. Before she leaves, she tells me she likes my hair. "It always looks so nice."

"Thanks." I smile.

She twirls her ponytail. "I'm lucky if I get a chance to wash mine. I haven't had the time or the energy to style it since Caden was born."

"That would be tough," I say above the baby's crying. "If you want, I could touch up your roots sometime, throw in a few highlights, and show you some good wash-and-go styles."

"Really?" Hannah looks genuinely excited as she hoists Caden's seat onto her arm. "I'd love that."

I open the door for her. "I've been pretty shitty to you. It's the least I could do."

She looks as if she might hug me, but thinks better of it. "Thanks, Charlotte."

If someone had told me two weeks ago that I'd be glad Hannah came for Thanksgiving, I would never have believed it. But I am. She's so much different from what I imagined.

After the kitchen's cleaned up, Grandmother, Nina, Mom, Buffy, and I slip into Mom's home office to watch a movie.

We have an extensive collection of classics—everything from *Gone with the Wind* to *The Breakfast Club,* including an array of Alfred Hitchcock and nearly every James Bond flick. Nina says she's never seen *Beaches,* so Mom insists we remedy that.

A movie about best friends and loss? Without Lydia? No thank you! But I'm not going to go into it with Mom, Grandmother, or Nina, so I get a head start on our weekend shopping strategy by perusing Black Friday ads on Mom's computer instead.

Once the movie is over and every one of us is a blubbering mess—yes, even me, despite my efforts to tune it out—we make our lists. Friday is mall and chain store shopping, which we keep hidden from Dad. If he thinks we're spending money at big-box stores, he'll come unglued. We make up for it on Saturday, when we buy local—Toy House, Anna's, and Picture This. We take a break on Sunday, regroup, and finish up online with Cyber Monday. By Tuesday, our shopping is pretty much done.

"Three a.m., as usual, then?" Nina folds up her list.

Grandmother gasps. "You're still *bargain* shopping—in the middle of the night?" She takes the throw blanket off of her lap and drapes it over the arm of the chair.

"Yes," Mom answers both of them.

"It's an adventure." Nina, who had been curled up on the end of the couch, stands and shakes out her foot as if it's asleep.

"It's tradition," I say, mindlessly scratching Buffy's ear, as she rests her head in my lap. Mom started going with Aunt Kathy and her friends back when Oliver was a baby. When Kathy moved Up North, Mom started taking Lydia and me. Nina joined in the year she and Oliver got married. Some years Patti joins us, and other times Tammy from the store, too.

"Are Lydia and Patti coming?" Nina asks.

"Not this year." I offer no further explanation.

"Tammy's sister is in town, so she won't be coming, either." Nina stretches her arms up and returns them to her belly.

"Looks like it'll just be us Pringle girls." Mom puts the DVD back on the shelf. "You're always welcome to join us, Mother."

"No, thank you," says Grandmother. "Nobody is out at that hour, except for hobos and hooligans. It's not worth getting trampled for discount gadgets."

Nina and I look at each other and stifle laughs. Trampling hobos and hooligans? What news station has Grandmother been watching?

"Oh, Mother! Times have changed. The hobos and hooligans get their trampling done on Thanksgiving now." Mom says this with such a straight face that Nina and I can't hold it in anymore.

"You make fun." Grandmother stands, smooths her pants, and adjusts her sweater. "But when you're on the underside of one of those shopping buggies, don't come crying to me." She walks out and announces to Mr. Vanderpool that it's time to go home and feed the cat.

"Oh my lanta!" I fold the blanket Grandmother had on her lap. "I don't know where to start with that."

"Charlotte," Nina says in mock seriousness. "If you're ever trapped underneath a shopping buggy, you can always come running to *me* for help."

I laugh and thank her, and Mom shushes us both before she leaves to pack up leftovers for Grandmother and Mr. Vanderpool.

Usually, on Thanksgiving, Lydia spends the night. We watch more movies—a classic marathon of James Bond, Alfred Hitchcock, or Molly Ringwald. She makes us fancy turkey sandwiches with cranberry sauce at midnight, we sleep for about an hour, and then do each other's hair before shopping.

This year I throw a piece of turkey on a buttered roll and go to bed early with QVC on in the background.

fifteen

14 days to the Winter Style Showcase

"I told you to dress inconspicuously," Mom hisses as we sneak out the back door at the butt-crack of dawn, trying not to disturb Dad and Buffy. Buffy is the most important. If she wakes up, I'll have to feed her, let her out, and wait for her to want back in. We don't have time for that if we're going to get the best doorbuster deals.

"I did." I climb into Mom's Accord. "What's wrong with what I'm wearing?"

She starts the car. "You do this every year! First of all, there's nothing inconspicuous about those hot-pink UGGs. And your hair and makeup is quite, uh, flashy. We're trying *not* to draw attention, remember?"

"I'm going shopping. There will be tons of people there. I can't go out looking like"—I buckle my seat belt and look her up and down—"well, you. I know it's seriously early, but you didn't even try." Her ponytail is poking through the back of her faded blue Lake Michigan cap. If she's wearing makeup, it's so faint it's pointless. And her jeans and baggy sweatshirt are better suited for yardwork, not shopping.

"The point is to be inconspicuous," she repeats, and pulls out of the driveway. "I don't want to deal with your father if someone sees us."

Our first stop is Meijer. They sell practically everything, including groceries. Dad hates them. He considers anything even remotely big-box as evil, "running the little guys out of business." Mom always tells him that they're a local-*ish* chain, but then he switches gears and calls them our competition. We don't go there often, but when we do, we keep it on the D.L.

"Well, you look like a shoplifter. Or a hobo." I try to keep a straight face, but I can't.

"My point! *This* is how you blend in!" Mom strikes a pose as she pulls up to Nina and Oliver's apartment building. Nina is already standing in front, wearing a dark coat, a hat, and sunglasses—although, to be honest, she's so huge you could spot her from space.

After she hoists herself into the backseat, I say, "Sunglasses?"

"*Too* inconspicuous?" She takes them off and puts them in her pocket.

"Oh my lanta!" I turn and the seat belt digs into my neck. "Mom's dressed like a hobo, and you look like a shady hooligan! Grandmother was right!"

Mom and Nina laugh.

"Except *we're* the ones people have to watch out for." Mom pulls into the parking lot.

"Forget trampling." Nina pats her belly. "I'll just roll right through the crowds."

Then we all crack up.

Our strategy at Meijer: In and out as fast as possible. Nina is after a seriously-on-sale diaper pail thing that's supposed to make dirty diapers smell like lavender—"Good luck with that," I tell her—and a Red Wings sweatshirt for Oliver for Christmas. Mom has her sights on a new vacuum, even though she's pretty sure that with that price, there won't be any left, and a Crock-Pot for Nina—although she tells Nina it's for Tammy to keep it a surprise. I'm on the lookout for a new purse; the straps on mine are starting to fray from the weight of all the stuff I carry around. After we snag our respective deals, we'll meet at the checkout.

I beeline to Accessories, where I find an adorable hobo bag for $8.99, down from $49.99. I giggle and decide to buy two—Mom definitely needs a hobo bag for Christmas. They're not designer, but I don't care—they're cute and have more than enough room. Besides, at less than nine dollars, it would be wrong not to buy them. I get tan and black for me and brown houndstooth for Mom. While I'm in the department, I grab a pair of brown leggings, too. Four minutes in and I've already got one person checked off my list.

I wander over to the baby department. Nina is rummaging through some novelty onesies while holding the diaper pail box on her hip as if it's a baby. A yellow onesie with *My Auntie Rocks* scrawled across an electric guitar screams out for me to buy it. I show Nina. "Only two bucks!"

"Perfect!" She grabs two more with sayings like *Daddy's*

Princess and *Too Cute,* then says, "We'd better get going." We weave through the browsing shoppers with carts and the display racks to the beat of "Jingle Bell Rock," which is playing overhead.

Just before the aisle that leads to the checkouts, I stop dead. About two feet in front of me is a display of half-priced pumpkin pies, and the person stocking it is none other than Nutmeg, Patti Cakes's former assistant manager. As Nina barrels toward the cashiers, I try to back away, so Nutmeg doesn't see me. And not just because I'm a Pringle at Meijer. I'm also kind of mad at her for bailing on my best friend—former or not—and her mom.

"Charlotte?"

Busted!

"Nu—Oh, Meg! Hi!"

"Hey, I haven't seen you in ages!" She hugs me. "How are you?"

"Great!" I give her a fake hug back. "And you?"

"Okay, I guess," she says, as she stocks. "I'm sure you heard I got laid off from Patti Cakes. It's not so bad here—I just wish I could get more hours. Part-time doesn't pay the bills. I might have to find a second job."

Clearly, Nutmeg takes my "And you?" a bit too literally. But—wait. Did she say she got *laid off*? Why would Patti let her go? Nutmeg was great at her job, and judging by all the hours Lydia's been putting in, Patti Cakes clearly has the business. It doesn't make any sense, but since Nutmeg thinks I already know, it would be awkward to ask. I listen to her go on about her bills and hours, hoping she says something that clears it up.

Why didn't Lydia tell me?

Mom and Nina call to me from the checkout. They're up next. I excuse myself, give Nutmeg another fake hug, and slip into line, ignoring the glares and rude comments from the tiny gray-haired lady behind us.

Black Friday shoppers can be nasty.

While Nina and Mom *ooh* and *ahh* over froofy baby dresses in Keehn's, I head to Claire's for accessories—for the showcase, the hospital event, and, of course, for me— and then to Snapz! to check out the doorbusters. Lydia's always so much better at finding deals than I am. On Black Friday last year, she got a pair of earrings, a tank top, a peppermint-scented candle for her mom, a tractor calendar for her dad, two pairs of patterned leggings, and some really cute shoes, all for less than thirty bucks. I spent a hundred dollars, and all I got were the same shoes as Lydia's—in a different color—a scarf, and some perfume. It's really weird doorbusting without her.

And just as I'm thinking about Lydia, I do a doubletake. I could swear I see her in Snapz!, looking at an oversized greenish sweater. Except it can't be her. She'd never wear that color—we've talked a million times about how no one with our skin tones looks good in chartreuse— and I've never seen the person she's with before, either.

I walk in. The Lydia doppelgänger sees me and freezes. It *is* Lydia!

"Lyd?" I say. Translation: *What are you doing here? I thought you weren't shopping this year.*

"Uh, hi," she says. Translation: *I was hoping I wouldn't run into you. This is awkward.*

"Hi," I say. Translation: *So this is how it is? You're throwing away our plans* and *our traditions?*

And me, too.

I stand there, waiting. I'm not sure for what. An explanation, maybe? Don't I deserve one? A punchline? Is this a joke? If so, I don't get it.

"Well, we've gotta go." She quickly folds the sweater, throws it back on a display, and pulls her friend toward the door. She didn't even introduce us.

Just before they're out of earshot, the girl says, "I thought you were going to get that sweater."

I don't hear what Lydia says, which is probably best.

I wander through the mall, trying to ignore the lump in my throat.

Why won't Lydia even talk to me? What did I do?

I guess she's not avoiding shopping entirely. Just shopping with me.

By the time I meet back up with Mom and Nina, I'm more pissed than hurt. And she thinks she can pull off chartreuse? Fine. She deserves to look boxy, washed-out, and hideous.

Mom, Nina, and I tackle Target and still finish by seven. Then—in another tradition—we head to Roxy's Café for breakfast. I show them all the ribbon and sparkly jewel stick-ons I found for the hospital fund-raiser. Mom nods and says, "That's nice," but I can tell she's engrossed in her receipts. "You know, that vacuum was even less expensive than I thought." *Way to show an interest in my career, Mom.*

The server takes our orders—my grilled cinnamon roll, chocolate milk, and coffee; Mom's coffee, sourdough toast, and hippie hash (veggies and potatoes grilled and topped with an over-easy egg—a Roxy original); and Nina's Denver omelet and milk. After she leaves, Mom says, "I'm glad we Pringle girls get a day like this now and then." Translation: *See how pleasant it is to be nice, Charlotte?*

"That's for sure," Nina says. "Hard to believe that by the time next Black Friday rolls around, there'll be another Pringle girl—she'll be almost a year old by then."

Another Pringle girl. My niece—she'll call me Aunt Charlotte. Mom will be Grandma, and Dad will be Grandpa. Oliver will be someone's dad.

Shopping for lavender-scented diaper pails and goofy onesies is one thing, but adding another person—someone we don't know—to our family in just a few weeks doesn't feel quite real. I had years to adjust to Nina before she married Oliver. Not that I had a choice, but at least I knew what to expect.

What if this kid cries all the time like Caden? What if she winds up looking like Oliver in a dress? There's a fifty-fifty chance. I imagine his big schnoz on a little baby; no amount of accessories could camouflage *that*. Or what if she's a little brat? She'll be a Pringle. What kind of monster would I be if I didn't love this baby?

"Charlotte, are you okay?" Mom asks. "You look a little green around the gills."

"Yeah, uh, I'm fine." The server brings us our drinks. I sip at the bitter coffee until there's enough room to add some chocolate milk. "I'm just tired. And hungry."

But what I really am is off-kilter. Soon I'll be related to a little girl I don't even know. And Lydia—someone I thought I knew better than anyone except myself—has become someone I don't know at all.

Is it too much to want to know what to expect?

I take another sip of my chocolate coffee. That, at least, is perfect.

sixteen

11 days to the Winter Style Showcase

When I get to school Monday morning, I'm determined to clear the air with Lydia. Are we friends or not? How can she go from being my PIC to blowing me off at the mall in just three weeks? What am I missing here?

The Allegiance fund-raiser is this weekend, and Lyd and I need to fill out the paperwork for the background check ASAP. Maybe that's the best—and least confrontational—way to start the conversation. But she doesn't stop at her locker before the bell rings, and I have to get to our team meeting. At least I'll see her there.

I commandeer a table in the multipurpose room and spread out my things. Again, Shea is the first to arrive. She walks in carrying a binder and a sketchbook, but no actual dresses.

"We might have a problem," I say as soon as she's seated. She gives me a look. "What now?"

"Remember at the first meeting when we agreed to stockpile our ATC bucks?" She nods. "Well, how much do you have?"

"Not that much," she admits. "Our tailoring fund-raiser

didn't go that well. I guess nobody wants to pay five dollars to get a zipper replaced on their pants when they can just pick up a new pair on the clearance rack at Keehn's for twenty. I thought we'd get more hemming, but we didn't." She fiddles with her hair. "I don't know. Maybe we didn't advertise enough, or something."

I grab a pen from my purse and click it open. "What's the bottom line?"

She opens her binder to her budget and shows me. Her balance is measly, even less than mine. We're doomed. This is what I get for counting on other people to pull their weight. I feel sick.

Within minutes, the room fills with people, and the rest of the team joins us at the table. I notice that Carter and Lydia come in together, and sit practically on top of each other. Melody, the child development girl, has three little girls with her, just as I'd asked at the last meeting. She has all of them scrunch together in one chair. They appear to be well-behaved, so at least one thing seems to go our way.

I tell the team about our financial situation—or lack thereof. Mackenzie asks a ton of questions, most of which are annoying and a waste of time.

Finally, the guy from construction trades says, "I already started the props you ordered. Are you saying you're not going to be able to pay me?"

"Uh, I, uh . . ." I stammer. "How much have you done so far?"

"I have most of the materials, and I've cut the wooden lollipops. The PVC should be here later today or tomorrow, and then all of it needs to be assembled, primed, and painted. That'll be more labor costs."

He shows me his report and points to an entry about halfway down the page. "This is where I am today." Then he points to the bottom of the page. "Here's where we'll be by the showcase—exactly where I said in my quote."

"We don't have that much." Shea looks at the number, too, and shakes her head.

"What *do* you have?" He is not pleased, and I can't blame him. I agreed to the contract when I still had all of our ATC bucks from the cos fundraiser—or thought I did, anyway.

I open my binder and show him today's total. "We have a little more than that," I add, indicating Shea, "but not much. I'm sorry. Plus, I need to pay all of these people"—I sweep my hand around the group—"and our music permissions and stage helpers."

"I can't believe this!" He slaps the table. The other teams turn from their discussions to stare. "You just cost me a buttload of ATC bucks. Finn is going to hear about this. I'm outta here."

"Me too," say the flutist and the artist at the same time, and follow him out. When the little girls see all this, they get up, too, and run toward the door, with Melody giving chase. This must be what she meant by "corralling."

"They're dropping like flies." Shea shakes her head. "What are we going to do?"

"I don't know," I admit.

"What about the rest of us?" asks Kayla (I think). It's suddenly really hot and stuffy. If I'd worn leggings, the way Mom wanted me to—because it's late November, and freezing—I'd probably pass out.

Everyone's eyes are on me. Well, not *everyone's* eyes. Carter's and Lydia's are on their phones. They're texting. Probably each other. Probably about me. I want to take their cells and chuck them across the room, but I have too many other people to deal with first.

"Without models, we have no showcase," Shea points out. "As it is, we only have two." So she didn't find any replacements, like she'd promised. I let it slide; we can't afford more models now, anyway.

I write down my balance, add Shea's, and subtract what I owe the building trades guy, the cost of stage helpers, our music license, and two ballerinas. What's left can either cover the kids or Carter, but not both, and the PowerPoint is required. Damn it. Carter's already gotten so much of our ATC bucks stash—not to mention my best friend—that I resent having to give him anything more.

And what are we going to do about music? Our form was for flute sheet music. We can't afford to pay the musician now, so that's out. "Does anybody have any ideas of what we can do for music?"

"I do!" Mackenzie starts scrolling through her phone.

Melody returns with the little girls in tow. None of them has melted down yet, thank God. "I can't do this by myself," she announces. "And if we add another person to help, it's going to cost more." We don't have more, and she knows it. "How about this?" she continues. "If it's just me and only one of them, you'll still have the effect you want, and it'll reduce your cost by two-thirds."

"Deal!" I really like this child development chick, even if she does dress like my mom on Black Friday. She and Hannah have that in common. What is it about kids that is so damaging to personal style? If that happens to Nina, I'll stage an intervention.

"So this is our team." I gesture as if I'm unveiling a brand new sports car on a game show. Even though our team— Shea, Mackenzie, Lydia, Carter, Kayla, Kaylee, Melody, one kid, and me—more accurately resembles Ralph's rusted-out 1995 Ford Taurus. "We may be small, but we're mighty," I say, possibly trying to convince myself more than them.

"Here it is!" Mackenzie says so loudly that she startles one of the little girls. "It's by a band from Ireland that my brother is into." She plays it so we can all hear. It's lively and it fits our theme. The Kays—Kayla and Kaylee—both agree that it's the right tempo for what they'd like to do.

"Perfect! Can you get a revised form to Ms. G today?" I ask her, hoping it's not too late to change.

Mackenzie nods, as she tells the Kays the story of when she first heard the song coming from her brother's room and how she ran in and demanded that he download it for her.

The kids are getting antsy, so Melody excuses herself. Apparently, it's snack time.

"Shea? Do you have new sketches?"

"I do." She opens her book. "I haven't started sewing yet, because that didn't turn out so hot last time." There's an edge to her voice.

We all huddle together to see them—except for Lydia and Carter, of course. Shea shortened the floor-length gown to knee-length and made the metallic skirt shorter and more angled. The dancers agree that they'll be able to move easily now. "And I'll serge the petals' edges so they're not so rough," she says.

I have no idea what she means, but it sounds good. "These are much better," I tell her. "Although I have a few suggestions." She gives me a look. "Can you use a more iridescent fabric, instead of the metallic? I don't want anyone to get us confused with the robot theme."

"I already have the silver fabric, but I can put a layer of iridescent taffeta over it."

"That should work."

"You think so?" She clasps her hands under her chin and bats her eyes. "You really think so?"

I ignore the sarcasm. "Yes, I really do. I think they'll look great. Nice job."

As they say, a little praise goes a long way. Her expression softens, and I swear she smiles.

After some brainstorming, we all decide that one of the dancers will do a quick-change backstage—"We do it all the time during our shows," one of them says—so Shea can still present three dresses.

Mackenzie says she's only doing one style. "My style is so spectacular, it'll be more than enough to wow the judges." I hope she's right, but so far, other than some pretty cool nail designs, none of her skills have impressed me.

I still need to figure out how to do four hairstyles on two heads. *Think about that later,* I tell myself. *Just keep going.*

Shea takes the ballerinas to the fashion design lab for measurements. As they leave, I can hear her say, "We have less than two weeks, so we'll have to work as fast as we can."

And then there were four.

I take a breath and force a smile. "Carter, what do you have to show us?"

"What do you mean?" He looks confused, and I notice he doesn't have his laptop with him.

"She means—" Mackenzie starts.

"The only thing I've seen is that sample PowerPoint from the last meeting," I finish. "What do you have in mind for this project?"

He sighs. "Probably something pretty similar, but with different pictures." He doesn't say "duh," but it's certainly implied.

Mackenzie opens her mouth as if she's about to say something, but I beat her to it.

"If we're going to pay you more than we already have," I glare at him, "we're going to need something a little less generic."

"You haven't paid me anything yet." He scowls. That little

dent on his nose is butt-ugly. How did I ever think of him as QT?

"Lydia paid you a ton for that box of brochures," I point out as nicely as I can. "Some of that money was mine." Mackenzie nods as if she knows what I'm talking about.

"Charlotte!" Lydia snaps. As in: *Don't tell him that. It makes me look bad.*

"We already agreed," he says. "I thought this was a done deal."

"I think we need to renegotiate." I keep my voice cool, yet authoritative. "We agreed"—I put verbal quotes around it—"before I saw your work. I thought I was paying for something more professional."

He straightens up. "More professional? That was for a friend of mine, and she got an A. So it couldn't be that bad."

"I get As all the time," Mackenzie adds. "It's not that big a deal." Random, but at least she's trying to be on Team Charlotte.

Lydia looks mortified. I don't care.

"I disagree," I counter, and point out all the errors I can remember. Then I add casually, "Was that for Brianna or some other girl?"

Mackenzie asks Lydia, "Who's Brianna? Is she on our team, too?" Lydia shakes her head.

Carter's eyes widen and his jaw tightens. "You are such a bitch!"

I gasp as if I'm offended. "I am? I had no idea. Thanks for enlightening me."

He stands up. "Find another digital designer. I'm done."

I pretend I'm unfazed. "Like I'd pay you for something I can do better myself." He stomps out and slams the door. The teacher in the back goes after him.

"That didn't go well," Mackenzie says, stating the obvious.

"What was *that* all about?" Lydia looks pissed. "Who's Brianna?"

"Carter's girlfriend," I answer. "I would have told you, but it's hard when you don't talk to me." So much for being nonconfrontational.

"Oh, like you'd know if Carter has a girlfriend!" She leans in and glowers. "You didn't even know his name a week ago. You think *I'm* bad? You can't have him, so nobody else can, either?" She shoulders her purse.

"Oh, okay, Lydia." I throw up my hands. "At least *I'm* honest with *you*. I talked to Nutmeg on Friday, and she said—"

"You talked to Meg? Where?"

"At Meijer."

"*You* went to *Meijer*?" She knows Dad's opinion of Meijer. "Why can't you just leave me alone? Why do you have to pry into everything?"

"What are you talking about? I didn't pry. I just ran into her. I didn't ask anything, except how she was. She's the one who said—"

"Ooh, a cat fight!" Toby bounces in his seat like a kindergartner.

"Shut up, Toby!" Lydia and I say at the same time. If we

weren't so pissed at each other, we'd probably laugh and high-five. But there is nothing funny or high-five-worthy going on. That's when I notice that the whole room is paying attention.

I lower my voice. "Lydia, what's going on with you? Everything's so messed up."

"Everything's *been* messed up," she retorts. "You've just been too clueless to see it."

What is she talking about? I am not clueless! Up until a couple of weeks ago, everything was fine. Unless she was lying and hiding things from me even then.

"I've tried talking to you, but you don't listen. You know, not everyone lives in 'The World According to Charlotte.'" She even uses air quotes.

The World According to Charlotte?

The supervising teacher returns and asks the two of us exactly what's going on. I'd answer, but I'm not even sure myself. I scan the room; a lot of people are still watching us, as if Lydia and I are today's entertainment.

Even Mackenzie is speechless.

I push past the instructor, muttering that I need to take a break—not waiting for an answer or a hall pass—and make a beeline for the girls' room, to the farthest stall. I cover the seat with toilet paper first, then sit down to pee. It takes less than a minute, but considerably longer to get my head together. I flush and dab the corners of my eyes with toilet paper so the tears don't streak my makeup.

My phone pings a reminder: Ms. Pink Pants. I figured I'd have Lydia's info for the background check by now. I rub hand sanitizer on my hands and shoot her an e-mail to say that Lydia won't be joining me. I don't give a reason.

The bell rings, but I can't move. It's lunchtime, and there's no way I'm showing my face in the cafeteria. No way.

The door to the bathroom opens. I lift my feet so that nobody will know I'm in here. One girl uses the toilet while the rest stand by the mirror.

"Can you believe all that? Talk about clearing a room. Charlotte's team couldn't get away from her fast enough." The voice sounds familiar. I try to peer through the crack in the stall, but I can't see.

"I know, right?" Another familiar voice.

"You guys'll win for sure now," says a girl whose voice I don't recognize at all.

"I don't know." I'd know *that* voice anywhere. Shelby! "Charlotte might be intense—"

"Anal."

Hey!

Shelby laughs. "Yeah, exactly." *Rude!* "But she's got mad skills. My updos don't come close, and she can freehand nail designs better than stencils."

Wait a second, *Shelby* thinks *I* have skills? If only Mom could hear this—that talent she talks about recognizes *my* skills.

The door opens again. They're leaving. "I still think you're going to win."

"I hope so," says Shelby as the door closes.

Maybe Lydia is right. I am clueless—at least about some people.

When we were kids, Lydia and I used to play a game called Opposite Land. "Good" really meant "bad," and vice-versa. We'd talk about how much we loved the dentist, and hated the water park, or how candy was horrible and dog food tasted good. With Lydia being all bitchy and Shelby complimenting me, I feel like I'm in Opposite Land for real.

Shelby thinks I have mad skills. For some reason, this makes me feel better about everything that happened today.

Just before the bell rings, an announcement comes over the PA: "Charlotte Pringle, please report to the office. Charlotte Pringle, Mr. Finn would like to see you." Great. Either the building trades guy or Carter has been trashing me. Or else that teacher turned me in for being out of class without a pass. I rearrange my clothing, wash my hands, and run out of the bathroom without even drying them.

As I march down the hall, I notice everyone looking at me, yet again. Some people are grinning. Some are out-and-out laughing. *Ignore them,* I tell myself. One girl in a plain ugly bun claps her hand across her mouth. *Grow up! She's just jealous.* I lift my head high. Even without a team, I have a chance of winning the showcase. I have style. I have swagger. I have skills.

Rachel comes up to me. "I need to tell you something."

"In a little while, okay?" I keep walking. "I need to see

Mr. Finn." This is the third time I've been called to his office in the past month. This time I'm not scared. This time I have things to tell him, too.

Tap, tap, tap. More snickering. I can't believe how fast rumors travel in this school. Has everyone already heard about the scene this morning?

I pass Trent at his locker. He slams it and runs up beside me, yanking off his hoodie, just before I get to the office. I feel his arms around my waist. *What the hell?* I swat him away. He leans in, as if he's going to whisper in my ear. Or, oh my lanta, is he trying to kiss me? "What are you doing? Quit it!" I pull away and run into the office.

"Mr. Finn wants to see me?" I say, a little out of breath.

Mrs. Ellenwood tells me to go in. But as I pass her desk—before I can get to Mr. Finn's office—she whispers loudly, "Oh, Charlotte, honey, you have toilet paper hanging out of your skirt."

Another secretary looks up and adds, "And there's some more stuck to your shoe."

I look down at the little white paper tail trailing from my heel.

Their words travel in slow motion—
from their mouths—THIS—
through the air—CAN—
into my ear—NOT—
and through every nerve and synapse—BE—
to my brain—HAPPENING.

Pow! It all registers.

Oh, God! I reach back, yank out the wadded-up and trailing toilet paper, and smooth my skirt, as if smoothing it down can erase the fact that I just paraded down the hall in front of the whole entire school with toilet-paper streamers flapping behind me.

seventeen

10 days to the Winter Style Showcase

The meeting with Mr. Finn isn't what it could have been. I'm pretty sure the construction trades dude did talk to him, but he doesn't say so. He simply says he's "checking in" on how things are going—you know, "since my team is *unusual.*"

"Oh, Mr. Finn, you have no idea!" I give him a censored recap of everything, mainly detailing how few ATC bucks my team has and how we should, in the interest of fairness, be given a stipend, since two of our team members weren't able to do any fund-raising.

He listens intently and seems to be thinking over what I said. *Come on, Finn. Come on!* Finally, he says, "*In the interest of fairness,* I'm afraid I can't simply *give* one team additional ATC bucks. Imagine, if you will, that your team wins. How can we defend against any accusations that you had an unfair advantage?"

Is he serious? He's denying me more money because of how it might look? He doesn't care about me or my team. He's just covering his own ass, as usual. I gear up to tell him so, but then it hits me. Finn thinks my team will win.

And he's right. When I win, I want to make sure every-one knows that I overcame my disadvantages and earned it. I thank him for his faith in my abilities and walk out of his office with my head held high.

But then, as soon as I hit the hallway, I get a few stares and snickers and want to run and hide. I can't, though. I have a test in "icks" class, and I need to revamp my vision for the showcase—one that amazes everyone, especially the doubters, scoffers, and haters. I decide to fly under the radar for the next couple of days, until someone else does some-thing even more stupid. Then everyone will forget about my scandalous TP parade and move on.

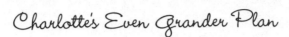

Charlotte's Even Grander Plan

1. Win Winter Style Showcase —> Earn stellar reps, bragging rights, and accolades.

★★ Bonus: Win the bet and prove everyone wrong!

2. Graduate high school with honors, college credits, and cosmetology license.

3. Get an apartment and a job in a top salon to pay for college.

4. Get associate's degree in business at Jackson College.

5. Build clientele —> Get enough money to open a salon.

6. A. Be the boss and live happily ever after.
   B. Have a hot, non-annoying boyfriend.

Charlotte's Revised Vision for the Winter Showcase

★ Our team—Shea, ~~Lydia~~, Mackenzie, and me—wears ~~coordinating outfits~~ whatever we want. Mackenzie will probably wear khakis. That is the least of my problems.

★ Props: giant candy "forest" added to fairy-tale background, sugar flowers ~~created by Lyd, built by building trades, decorated by multi-media art~~ ALL DONE BY ME and placed by stage helpers.

★ ~~Wow-factor prop: Snow machine~~ ☹ NO ATC BUCKS! ☹

★ Models: TWO ballerinas and ONE child~~ren~~ (a flying and frolicking fairy). I plan to do TWO hairstyles on my model, though.

★ Music: ~~lively, whimsical flute music~~ Recorded Irish music for both the PowerPoint and speech/model presentation.

★ PowerPoint first: behind-the-scenes pictures of our work throughout the semester, designed by ~~Reed~~ ME.

★ Speech/Model Presentation next: Required—ONE model each. Shea designs ~~all four~~ THREE dresses; Mackenzie ~~and I style TWO each~~ styles ONE model, I style ONE model, plus TWO hairstyles and our mini fairy. Onstage, we discuss the techniques we used as models dance and turn.

★ Thunderous applause!

★ We win first place!

★ I win the bet!

★ ~~Reed and I double date with Lydia and her guy.~~ NEVER NEVER NEVER!

★ We are so legendary that we become the standard by which first place is judged in upcoming years.

eighteen

9 days to the Winter Style Showcase

Wednesday morning, Ms. Garrett calls Shelby and me up to her desk. "I got a phone call yesterday from Anita Worthington at Allegiance." Ms. Pink Pants? How does she know Ms. G? Turns out, actually, that she doesn't. "She wanted to tell the head of the cos program about the fundraiser for the pediatric oncology department and how she found you, Charlotte. Pretty impressive. Way to represent ATC cos!" She holds up her hand, and I high-five her with a smile.

This is great—but I have no idea why Shelby's here, too. Ms. G goes on: "Apparently the idea has gotten such a positive response that Mrs. Worthington wants to make sure she has more than one stylist there." She looks at me. "I guess Lydia backed out?" I nod. I don't tell her that I didn't give Lydia a choice. "She asked me to recommend another conscientious, trustworthy student." Now she looks at Shelby. "And I thought of you. Are you interested?"

She starts telling Shelby the details, but all I can think is *Why? Why would Ms. Garrett do this to me?* She knows Shelby is my biggest competition in the showcase. It's bad enough that she has Gabriella—and my ideas. Now she can see my "mad skills" up close, and be able to copy them.

Before I can object, Shelby says, "Of course! I'd love to!" The next thing I know, she's at Ms. G's computer, filling in the paperwork. A few clicks later, it's a done deal. I'll be spending next Saturday night with Shelby Cox.

"Thanks, Ms. Garrett," she says before returning to her seat. "And, thanks, Charlotte. I'm really looking forward to this."

I nod with a tight smile. *Yeah, I bet you are.* She already has my best dress idea. Why does she need to grab my service project, too?

⸺ ✳ ⸺

When I get to work that afternoon, Hannah has a huge smile on her face. I don't think I've ever seen her smile, at least not like this. "What's up?" I ask.

Nina says, "Charlotte, I'm so glad you're here. I'm pooped. I need a nap before class tonight." She hugs Hannah. "I'm so excited for you. See you later."

"Sleep tight. Thanks for everything."

"No problem." As I stand there, baffled, Nina grabs her coat and purse from the back. "I'm glad it all worked out," she says as she leaves.

"Me too."

Once Nina's gone, I ask Hannah, "What worked out?"

"Everything." There's the smile again. "Nina convinced

me to call my mom." A customer comes up, and Hannah stops mid-explanation to wait on her. She does everything right. Maybe she's going to work out after all.

"Sounds like it went okay," I say when she's done.

"It's better than okay." She's practically bouncing. "I gave your dad my two-week notice today. I'm moving back to Ohio by Christmas!"

"Moving? Really?" Just when I'd adjusted to her—and maybe even started to like her a little—she's leaving. What are we supposed to do now? Nina's about to have the baby, so she'll be off work for months. That leaves just me and Katie, which translates to just me. What a disaster!

"What's the matter?" She pulls out an almost-empty container of cranberry salad. "I figured you, of all people, would be thrilled."

"Nothing. Yeah, well, no. I mean . . ." What do I mean? A few weeks ago, if Hannah had quit, not only would I have been happy, but probably a few dollars richer, since I bought up a bunch of squares in the pool. But getting to know her and her story—she's just a tired, overextended mom, not a slacker party girl—has changed things. I was just getting to know her, and now I won't have the chance. "I'm glad you're working things out with your family, but—well, I've just gotten you trained so that you're not a total liability."

Hannah laughs. "If I didn't know better, I'd think you're going to miss me."

"Maybe I am, okay?" I snap.

"Wonders never cease," she says as she refills the

cranberry salad. "Can you do my hair before I go?"

We're scheduling a time to do it—the Monday afternoon before Christmas—when Mom texts me to come to the office ASAP. We're not too busy, so I do.

"What's up?" I ask before I realize that she's on the phone.

She motions for me to stay put, says good-bye to whoever it is, hangs up, and says, "We have a slight situation. Don't say a word until I'm finished telling you about it."

Already this is not looking good.

"Oliver's on his way to Detroit. The Red Wings are playing tonight."

Right. Nina said she had birthing class. It's *that* night. The class he needs to miss, so Mom is standing in.

"Nina needs someone to go to class with her." I raise my eyebrows. "That was work on the phone. All hell is breaking loose. I thought the study was done, but the reports are contradictory, so we need to meet tonight to figure it out. Otherwise, there will be major lawsuits—" She stops mid-explanation. "Anyway, long story short: I can't go."

"I already said I couldn't do it. And I already served my time, remember?" I plant my hands on my hips.

"First, yes, you did. Second, you 'served time' for talking back. I *do* remember." Mom stands now. She means business. "Hannah said she'd do it."

"Great. So what's the 'situation'?"

"In order to go, she needs a babysitter." Mom cocks an eyebrow. "Which would you prefer—the class, or Caden?"

"None of the above."

She glares at me as if that's not an option. I glare back.

"Charlotte, please." Her tone is less *I'm begging you* and more *I've had enough*. When I still don't budge, she pulls out the big guns. "I'm going Christmas shopping next weekend. While my love is deep and unconditional, my generosity is not."

"Blackmail? How unbecoming!" I hold my hand to my chest dramatically.

"I prefer the term *leverage*," she says in a tone reminiscent of Marlon Brando in *The Godfather*.

"Well played."

"Thank you," she says. "So you'll go?"

"Do I have a choice?" I ask, still trying to think of a loophole.

"You always have a choice," she shoots back in a way that implies I don't—again, like Brando.

"I'm going back to work," I say, turning to leave. I will not admit defeat. She knows I'll do it. That's enough.

"Thank you, sweetie. I love you."

I'm not sure if I hate her or want to be her. I let the door slam behind me.

— ✳ —

When I get in the car two hours later, Nina immediately says, "I'm sorry. I know you don't want to do this."

"It's okay." I try to sound sincere, but I suck at it.

The ride to the hospital is pretty awkward, but it's nothing compared to the looks I get when I walk into the classroom with Nina. She introduces me and explains that Oliver has Red Wings tickets. Some of the dads and a couple of the moms say they'd rather be at the Joe with him. The laughter makes things a little less weird, but only slightly.

"Let's get started, shall we?" The instructor's voice is too even and gentle. While I'm sure she's trying to sound comfortable and reassuring, it just comes off as creepy to me. Her pajama-like gauze outfit and long, wispy gray hair aren't doing her any favors, either. I want to tell her that it would look thicker if she cut it, but I decide that's probably not her goal.

Everyone sits on the floor like kindergartners. Most of the women lean into their husbands. Nina and I are between a young woman and her mother—the only other "non-couple"—and a bearded guy whose belly is bigger than his wife's. We listen to the instructor drone on for over an hour about the stages of labor.

I knew it was an exhausting process—I've seen enough TV shows and movies—but she makes it sound terrifying. The early stage alone can take twenty-four hours. And that's only the beginning. The description of active labor and then its final part, transition, sounds like torture, not the "miracle" Ms. Smooth-talker refers to it as. Contractions coming closer and closer together, harder and harder, until eventually there is no break in between. And this excruciating pain could go on for hours!

There is no way I'm going through that—ever.

And while I do enjoy an extensive vocabulary, I could

have lived my entire life without learning the definitions of the words "effacement," "dilation," and "episiotomy." By the time we get to the birth itself—and watch a movie depicting so much detail that I might need counseling to recover—all of the partners are in shock and the mothers-to-be are visibly panicking.

After the movie, the instructor clues in and switches gears. "We're going to practice the breathing exercises I introduced last week," she says, "so, Moms, I'm going to ask you to find a comfortable position. You can recline against the foam wedges"—which are in a pile in the corner of the room—"or sit leaning forward, whichever puts less pressure on your pelvic bone."

The other "birthing partners" and I collect a few wedges each and bring them back. Ugh. When was the last time these things were washed? Nina props them behind her to make a forty-five-degree angle and leans back.

"Partners, I'd like you to sit next to these beautiful women. I want you to breathe along with them. Take a deep cleansing breath. In, in, in through your nose. Fill those lungs." Her arms extend out and then up in some sort of yoga ballet. I hear and feel all the air being sucked from the room. Is this what a cult is like? Nina breathes in and looks at me with desperate eyes; I quickly inhale and hold my breath.

"Now, release slowly through your mouth, letting go of the stresses of the day." The dad next to me exhales a cloud of chili-and-cigarette-smelling breath, jacking up my stress level. Is it nine o'clock yet?

After a few more "cleansing breaths"—frankly, toothbrushes and mouthwash would have been a better choice—the instructor tells us we're going to simulate how these techniques actually help with pain control. The moms are supposed to close their eyes or choose a focal point and concentrate on slow, deep breathing while we, the partners, squeeze their knees, lightly at first and then harder and harder until we're squeezing as hard as we can.

Finally, something fun! I get to make Nina as uncomfortable as I feel.

Nina closes her eyes and slowly inhales and exhales. At the signal, I grab hold of her knee. This might be the first time I've ever touched her voluntarily. I begin gently. When she doesn't flinch, I increase the pressure, and soon I'm squeezing so hard that my knuckles are turning white. Nina doesn't react at all.

Whoa! She can't feel this? I apply even more pressure. Pain shoots up my arms. Then they start to go numb. She keeps breathing evenly and comfortably.

When Ms. Smooth-talker tells us to let go and for the moms to breathe normally, Nina says, "That was stupid. I hardly felt a thing." Seriously? Nina's a lot tougher than I've ever given her credit for.

Then the instructor tells us to lean in and squeeze our partner's knees like we did while they were concentrating on breathing—except now she tells the moms *not* to focus on breathing. As soon as I increase the pressure, Nina jumps and yelps. "Hey! Ow! Ow! Ow! Stop it! You didn't do it that hard before."

"Yes, I did!" I tell her, letting go. "Harder, even."

"Really?"

I nod. Similar conversations are going on around us. Apparently, this breathing crap really works. Who knew?

The instructor reminds the moms to practice their breathing whenever they can. "It'll be more effective if you're used to doing it. In the heat of contractions, you don't want to panic. Once you lose control, it's tough to regain it."

One woman says she's getting an epidural as soon as they'll let her, and Ms. Smooth-talker looks at her as if she just kicked a puppy, which instantly transforms her from Ms. Smooth-talker to Ms. Judgy-hippie. But she recovers and says, "Everyone must find her own path."

While the moms talk in groups about diaper services, breast pumps, and stretch marks, and the instructor and a couple of the dads collect the foam wedges and pile them in the corner, I talk about the squeezing exercise with a few more dads. We all agree that it was pretty impressive.

Afterward, Nina sits in the car but doesn't start it right away. I'm just about to say something when I see tears dripping down her cheek and her shoulders trembling. Then she's full-out, gulping-for-air sobbing. "I can't do this, Charlotte."

"It's okay," I say. "I can drive."

"Not drive," she cries. "Have a baby! I can't. I can't do this."

This is not a typical Nina meltdown. This time I see her point. There is no easy way to give birth. Even I was freaked out during the class.

I try to keep things light. "I don't think you have much of a choice," I say, indicating her belly. "You've kind of come too far to go back now."

"I know." Then she starts sobbing even harder.

"Hey, now." I touch her arm, which has a death grip on the steering wheel. "You don't have to think about it today. You're not in labor, right?" She shakes her head. "Then just take it as it comes, one breath at a time. I know you don't believe me, but I was squeezing the hell out of your knee, and you took it like a champ. So you *can* breathe through a lot of it."

"You think so?" she says as she catches her breath.

"I know so." I put my seat belt on. "And there's always an epidural."

She pulls a tissue out of the console, wipes her eyes, and starts the car.

"And Oliver will be with you."

"Ollie's an idiot," she says matter-of-factly.

"No argument here."

Suddenly she's sobbing again. No, wait—those aren't sobs, they're giggles. She's laughing. "Oh, God. I can just see it," she manages. "He'll pass out." I can see it, too, and then we're both cracking up.

I hand her another tissue. She blows her nose, takes a deep "cleansing" breath, and collects herself. "I'd kill for some Rocky Road ice cream."

"No need for violence," I say. "We don't close for another two hours."

She backs the car out of the lot, and soon we're in the break room digging into a pint of Rocky Road, mimicking Ms. Smooth-talker/Ms. Judgy-hippie. All in all, the evening hasn't been as bad as I imagined.

But I will never, ever admit that to Mom, or Oliver.

nineteen

6 days to the Winter Style Showcase

Shelby picks me up around 4:30 on Saturday afternoon for the hospital event, wearing her signature peacock-print pumps. I usually prefer to be the driver, but she caught me off-guard yesterday.

We were practicing rolling perms, and even though I technically have a partner, I was stuck working on a leftover mannequin some senior had already used to cut asymmetrical layers because Mackenzie wasn't in class. The weatherman predicted a major blizzard—the Snowpocalypse!—so Mackenzie's mom made her stay home. They'd been predicting the storm all week. Pringle's Market sold out of bottled water, batteries, and Pop-Tarts, which is often a sure sign that bad weather is on its way. We haven't seen more than a few flurries, though.

ATC is so different than it was three months ago. I started the year with a PIC, determined to show everyone what I could do. Now, not only do I have an unreliable partner, but everyone seems to be avoiding me. I pissed off my entire showcase team, so I can understand that. And God knows how many people witnessed my post-bathroom walk of shame. But does everyone else have to avoid me, too? Somehow, I have become social kryptonite.

I no longer linger in the halls. I eat lunch in my car. I spend a lot of time on the library computers trying to figure out a way to make the presentation work with reduced resources. So it's a surprise when Shelby stops me on the way out of cos on Friday and asks if I'd like her to pick me up. The word "sure" just pops out of my mouth, and the next thing I know I'm giving her my address and cell number.

Shelby's car is an older Ford Escort, but the inside is adorable. She has a tiny chandelier hanging from the rearview mirror, and the ceiling, visor, and part of the dashboard are one gigantic picture collage—silly selfies, childhood pics, and random school wallet photos of her friends at all different ages. I avoid the awkwardness of hanging out with Shelby Cox on a Saturday by looking at all of the pictures.

"Wow!" I stop at a selfie of Shelby and a woman with an adorable angled razor cut and bright pink and green peekaboo highlights in the front.

"That's my mom," she says, turning the radio station to a song by Cage the Elephant.

"Her hair is cute," I say, noticing the beveled salon mirror in the background. I wish my mom would let me do something more adventurous to her classic bob, other than cover grays with her natural color. "How did you get all those pics to stay up?"

Shelby stops at a light a few blocks from the hospital. "A combo of thumbtacks and tape. It hides the fact that my car is a piece of crap."

"It works," I say and immediately regret it. I mean that her car looks nice, but it sounds more as if I'm agreeing that it's a piece of crap. "I mean—"

"I know what you mean." Shelby laughs, letting me off the hook.

We're quiet the rest of the way. If I were alone or with Lydia, I'd belt out the lyrics of the song on the radio. Instead, I sing along in my head as Shelby taps her fingers on the steering wheel.

After we sign in, a security guard shows us to our "salon." It's a small room, clearly used for meetings; there's a long, empty table and a tall stack of chairs in one corner. No mirrors. No sinks. No problem; I've worked with less. After we unload our bags, Shelby says, "I'll be right back. I've got to get something out of the trunk."

Okay, I think, and start emptying my purple duffel bag. I lay out zippered makeup bags full of samples—some left over from winning the fund-raiser, some collected from Birchbox, and others bonus freebies from Industry Source orders. There are disposable mascara wands, Q-tips, rolls of ribbon, roll-on glitter, and false eyelashes and glue. I've also brought paper towels, my curling wand, combs, and several sprays with varying degrees of hold and shine.

Shelby returns with a giant box. It's full of hats and

boas and scarves, and even a few really fun wigs.

"Where did you get all this stuff?" I drape a bright blue boa around my neck.

"From under my bed."

"No, seriously."

"I *am* serious." She sets the hats out on the table. "My sisters and I used to play dress-up and put on all these crazy shows at the salon. Do you have any idea how boring it is to spend your whole childhood waiting for hair to process?"

"More than you think." I laugh. "I grew up in a grocery store."

Something sparks in her eyes. "That's right! Then, yeah, you get it."

Yeah, I do. In elementary school, kids used to think that because we owned a grocery store I could just grab anything I wanted any time and eat it—as if it was my own gigantic, personal pantry. Of course, it isn't like that. Even back then, I had to "buy" what I wanted from my employee food allowance, which isn't very much. It really pissed me off when other kids still didn't get it, so after a while I stopped trying to explain it.

I realize that I've been thinking about Shelby's life the same way—as if it's one giant makeover party, just because *her* family business is a salon.

Who knew I have so much in common with Shelby Cox?

Mrs. Worthington—who I can't call Ms. Pink Pants today, because she's wearing a black pencil skirt and a sequined Christmas sweater—shows up.

"Thank you so much for coming!" she cries. Before I can say, "It's our pleasure," she barrels on, addressing not me, not Shelby, but Trent Rockwell, who's come into the room behind her. What's *he* doing here?

Judging by the camera around his neck, taking pictures. Seems he got a haircut, too. His hair isn't in his eyes anymore, so now I can actually see them. They *are* hazel, and his lashes go on for days.

He waves. "Hey, Charlotte. Hey, Shelby."

"I see you know each other," remarks Mrs. Worthington.

"Hey, Trent!" Shelby's trying to pull a chair from the top of the pile, but they're stacked too high. Trent goes over and easily takes it down. The two of them start unstacking the rest of the chairs and setting them around the table.

I set up a hair and makeup station by unzipping my bags and grouping like items together while I half listen to Mrs. Worthington explain every detail of the event—most of it a repeat of her e-mails. As Trent adjusts the settings on his camera, I notice the interesting pattern on his cable-knit sweater—it changes from black to gray to white. Then my eyes travel up past the red T-shirt peeking out around his neck and land on his face. He's watching me watch him. How embarrassing!

I look away, but then back over at him. What's he thinking? Is he thinking about me? I don't need to wonder for long. He mouths, "What?" As in, *What are you doing? What are you looking at? What do you want?*

I quickly return to my station, rearranging products and

pretending to be listening carefully to Mrs. Worthington.

Her monologue is cut short by nearly a dozen patients and two nurse escorts. Suddenly the room feels very small. For some reason—maybe because I met her first—I imagined they'd all be like Sarah, but of course they're not. Some are young kids, while others are closer to my age. Some have hair. Three of them are boys.

Sarah lights up as soon as she sees me. She comes over with a few of her friends, girls about her own age. She's much paler than she was at the fund-raiser, and I wonder if she's not feeling well. Since we're here to help them focus on being kids rather than patients and I'm sure they get badgered enough, I don't ask her.

"Well, I'll leave you to your transformation while I check with the caterers," says Mrs. Worthington. But no one is listening. The kids are all too busy picking through Shelby's accessories display. One guy replaces his knit hat with a Viking helmet, then exchanges it for a top hat.

"Look at this!" A girl puts a sparkly tiara on her head, but she doesn't have any hair for the combs to attach to, so it slides off. Instead of getting mad, though, she hands it to the girl next to her. "Here, Marley. You should have them put your hair up and wear this."

Marley, who appears to be about ten, takes the tiara. "Yeah, okay," she says, and brings it over to me. "Can you do it?" Even though her hair is in a medium-length bob, it's still more than most of the other kids have.

"Updos are my specialty," I say, smiling and leading her

to the closest chair. Then I pull another chair over to act as my station, and dig through my bag for a comb, bobby pins, and hair spray. Shelby helps dole out the hats, boas, and other stuff. Kids try things on and pass them around, and she and the nurses attempt to keep some semblance of order. It doesn't help, though. Everyone is excited, so it gets really loud as the kids all talk at once, laughing while figuring out what they want.

I comb through Marley's bangs. "You have really pretty hair."

"Thanks," she says. "I hope it grows back curly."

"Can it do that?" I ask, surprised.

"Some people say it can. I start chemo tomorrow, so it's probably going to fall out soon. That's why my mom wants to take a ton of pictures tonight."

As if Trent has superhero hearing, he comes over and starts snapping pics. Marley makes funny faces and we all laugh. Then he holds the camera over his head, clicks, and turns around for a behind-the-back shot. Marley giggles all the way up from her toes.

Suddenly, a commotion grabs everyone's attention.

Sarah's doubled over, near the door, throwing up. It's clear that she was trying to get to the bathroom, but couldn't make it in time. When she straightens up and sees every-one watching, she bursts into tears and runs out. One of the nurses hurries after her. The other leaves to find a custodian.

The mood in the room immediately changes—from laughing and yelling to complete silence. Shelby and Trent and I exchange quick glances. This isn't like school, where an embarrassing thing happening to someone else is funny. There's a disgusting, stinky reminder of cancer on the floor, and no way to avoid it.

So I don't. I say loud enough for everyone to hear, "Cancer sucks ass."

One of the younger kids giggles nervously, probably because I said "ass."

An older boy—about fourteen or fifteen—nods. "Cancer sucks ass."

One by one they all proclaim it, louder and louder until their voices overpower the stench.

And each time, the rest of them cheer as if they're unleashing some ancient, forgotten power.

As if they're reclaiming control.

As if they're Mel Gibson's countrymen in *Braveheart*.

They're not alone.

They're not weak.

They're decked in glittery wigs and feathers and floppy hats.

And they're fierce.

When the nurse returns with the custodian and his rolling mop bucket, the whole room is one uproarious *cancer-sucks-ass* chorus. Once she realizes what they're saying, she tries to quiet the kids down, to scold them—but then the energy of their defiance gets to her, and for a second she looks as if she might cry. But she doesn't. She just lets them chant.

Even though Shelby is busy reorganizing her disheveled

box of accessories and Trent continues to take pictures as if nothing out of the ordinary is happening, they both look as if they're on the verge of either smiling or crying. I feel the same way.

By the time the mess is cleaned up, the group has settled down, but their spirits are up again, which energizes Shelby and me to go all out on their hair and makeup. She finishes up with the hats, wigs, and scarves; I do false eyelashes, curls, braids, and glitter. We both do makeup. The guys get into it, too. They wear hats—one a fedora, one a top hat, and the third a newsboy cap—and let us brush on the tiniest hint of bronzer. Finally, we give the nurse a rainbow wig and a feather boa and add a few sparkles to her eyelids and cheeks.

We all pose for several pics, and everyone looks fabulous, if I do say so myself. Shelby and I grin at each other.

The nurse who went after Sarah returns to tell us that she's refusing to go to the dance. "Would it help if I talked to her?" I ask.

She looks dubious. "You could try, but I don't know. She's had a pretty rough week."

"Yes, she has," agrees a girl sporting a mesh headband with peacock feathers. "But you should. I'll come with you."

"I'll come, too," says another girl.

"And me," says Marley.

"We'll all go," declares the fedora-wearing boy who started the "Cancer sucks ass" chant.

Shelby, Trent, and I look at one another, then at the

nurses. The patients are already out the door, on their way up to pediatric oncology. As we follow them, I feel a twinge of guilt. How could I have felt so sorry for myself this week? That was nothing compared to this.

As resolved as the kids are to talk to Sarah, she's not budging. "Get out!" she yells at the crowd in her hospital room. She pulls the covers over her head.

The kids all start talking at once, doing their best to convince her. Sarah emerges from under the covers, but she just glares and refuses to talk to anyone. I notice how her eyes keep darting to the older boy in the fedora, though.

I sit on the edge of her bed, lean in, and whisper, "I saved some lashes for you—some really sparkly ones."

"I don't want them."

"You sure?"

She shrugs.

"How about I get them and then you can decide?"

She shrugs again.

I start to get up, but Trent stops me. "I'll go," he says. "Where are they?"

After he leaves, Sarah calls one of the nurses over and whispers in her ear. The woman orders everyone out. "Let's go back downstairs," she says. "Mrs. Worthington will wonder where you went." Reluctantly, they obey, but not before each one says something encouraging to Sarah, or gives her a smile.

I stand up, and that's when she asks, "Will you stay?"

"Of course." I sit back down.

Shelby says, "I'll meet you downstairs."

The room is empty, except for Sarah and me. "Can you make me look like you did at the fair?" Her voice, just above a whisper, cracks.

"I have even more stuff now," I say as convincingly as I can. She's much paler than she was that day, and her eyes have dark circles around them. "We can go totally glam, if you want."

A smile threatens to break through her scowl. I've got her!

Trent walks in, carrying my bright purple duffel bag as if it's a sack of potatoes. He looks goofy—but in a sweet way, not a stupid way.

"Thanks." I've been meaning to say that to him ever since my walk of shame, but I haven't had the guts. Just looking at him is embarrassing, knowing what he saw—and how he tried to help. And how I thought he wanted to kiss me and swatted him away.

I quickly dig out my glue and a new pack of sparkle lashes and get to work. As I spread the glue on the edge of Sarah's right eyelid, I casually ask, "So what's his name?"

"Who?"

"You know." I wipe off the excess with a Q-tip. "The hottie in the fedora."

She doesn't answer, and I realize it's because Trent's still there, watching. "Oh, sorry!" he says. "I don't mean to stare. I've just always wondered how she puts those tarantula things on."

Sarah almost smiles. "Don't worry," I tell her, and give him the side-eye. "You can talk in front of Trent. He won't say a word. Right?"

"Right." He zips his lips. "Okay if I take a few pics? They would be great for this project Charlotte's doing." Sarah shrugs, then nods.

Then Trent looks at me. "If you want them, I mean."

I not only want them, I need them—especially if I'm going to have to do my PowerPoint presentation myself. So I lean in and pose, but I still can't look directly at him. He snaps the picture. Then he tells me to ignore the camera, that candid shots are best. Pretty bossy.

As I finish Sarah's eyelashes, she says, "Felix." She blinks a few times, then opens her eyes. Even though I'm not finished with her makeup, the blue of her eyes is hard to miss framed in the curly lashes. She's stunning! "His name is Felix," she says. "You really think he's hot?"

I tell her to close her eyes again and I finish with some shadow—a neutral coppery rose on the lid and a pale pink highlight on the brow bone. "Sure I do. He's got that Bruno Mars vibe going on. Don't you think?"

"Maybe." She blushes. "I don't know." I catch a glimpse of sweet and shy before her face clouds over. "After what just happened—"

"He'll worry that if you're not feeling better," Trent cuts in, "he'll miss a dance with the prettiest girl here tonight."

"You're just saying that," she retorts. "There's nothing pretty about puking in front of a guy. It's horrible."

"Yeah, well, imagine this: This girl at school was in the bathroom during a break last Monday." I lean in and whisper, "You know, doing what you do in the bathroom."

She makes an *Ew!* face. I continue in a dramatic narrator voice, "Suddenly, she was paged. To. The. Principal's. Office." Sarah is listening, wide-eyed.

"But there's something she didn't know. You know what that was?" I pause.

"What?" She shifts her weight toward me on the bed, which pushes me closer to her.

"She had . . ." I look her straight in the eye. "Toilet paper! Hanging from her skirt! And trailing from her shoe!"

"And it was wet, too," Trent chimes in.

It was wet? *Oh, God!* I hope he's exaggerating for effect.

Sarah's gaze shifts to him. "Did you see?"

He smiles. "I tried to tell her, too, but she pushed me away."

"Rude," says Sarah.

"Yes, it was," I admit, looking at Trent, who's still smiling. Then, turning back to Sarah, I say, "You know who else saw?"

She raises her eyebrows.

"The *whole* school." I gesture emphatically. "Everyone."

She has a look on her face that is somewhere between amused and mortified.

"You know who that girl was?"

"You?" she says with a slight grimace.

I nod.

"Did that really happen?"

Before I can reply, I notice that she's not looking at me, but past me, at Trent. I turn around. He's nodding, too, and doing his best not to bust out laughing. I can't blame him.

Then Sarah finally does laugh, and Trent can't hold it in anymore.

"It isn't funny." I cover my head with part of her blanket, but she pulls it away. My face is burning. "See? We all do embarrassing stuff and live to tell about it." Then guilt washes over me. How can I say that to someone whose life is as uncertain as hers?

She doesn't seem to have the same reaction. Instead, between giggles, she asks if she can have lots of sparkles.

As I'm finishing Sarah's eyes and makeup, Shelby comes in.

"You look great!" she tells Sarah. *Shelby thinks I have mad skills,* I remember. "I thought you'd want to accessorize a little." She holds out the almost-empty bag. Happily, there are still some good things left, and Sarah chooses a wide headband with a huge red flower on it.

All put together, she looks adorable. She preens in the mirror a little, but she still doesn't feel so hot, so her nurse gives her something for the nausea.

"The other kids are at the dinner now." Shelby sits on a rolling stool. "They hope you're okay, Sarah." She turns to Trent and me. "When Mrs. Worthington came to get them, they asked her if we could stay for the dance, too. She said she hoped so, but I told them all that I'd have to check with you guys."

"Oh, please come!" Sarah bounces a little, but stops, looking a little green. She adds a final "please, please, please!" before she lies back down.

How can we refuse?

The three of us agree to go, and even though we're hungry—at least I am—we decide to keep Sarah company instead of eating. She's not up for the banquet, and we weren't included in the head count.

Once I fish a couple of energy bars from my purse, Trent heads to a vending machine and contributes a pack of pretzels and some M&Ms. Shelby asks the nurse where we could get something to drink, and she brings us ice waters, a few apple juices, and several individual packages of graham crackers.

"That's all I could find," she apologizes. "It's the weekend."

We thank her and divvy up our hodgepodge feast onto paper towels. Sarah even eats half of a graham cracker and a few ice chips while we debate the merits of the latest Melissa McCarthy movie, which morphs into a game we dub *Funny or Stupid*. We take turns saying movies, and the other three have to guess if that person thinks the movie is funny or stupid. We add our own opinions, too, of course. Even though I love movies, I don't know Shelby, Trent, or Sarah very well, so I'm horrible at the game, which Sarah finds hilarious.

About an hour later, after I've refreshed Sarah's makeup, we follow the nurse as she wheels Sarah down to the banquet.

The conference room is on the fifth floor and seems to take up nearly a whole wing. Twinkle lights wrapped in tulle adorn the ceiling and pillars. The large round tables are covered with fancy tablecloths, and in the center of each table is an evergreen and candle centerpiece. It's hard to imagine this as a hospital meeting room tonight.

The DJ is in the corner playing old music that Pops would call peppy while the caterers clean up and tear down the food tables near what I assume is the dance floor. Nobody is dancing. Most of the older people sit at their tables; only a few are mingling. The kids are sitting at two tables in the corner, looking bored out of their minds.

Mrs. Worthington hurries over to us, beaming. "Charlotte, Shelby—thank you so much. The children look so . . . festive." Trent is already snapping away.

"Thanks for the opportunity." Shelby sets her purse on her chair. "It's been fun."

"I love helping people feel good about themselves," I add. "Everybody deserves that—especially these kids."

"I couldn't agree more," says Mrs. Worthington. "I'm delighted that you-all could join us. I hope you'll encourage the kids to get out on the dance floor."

I give her a big smile. "No offense, Mrs. Worthington," I say politely, "but I don't think they're going to dance to this kind of music." By the look on her face, I'm guessing she chose the music. "Would you mind if I requested a few songs?"

She recovers quickly. "By all means, dear. The event is for the children, after all."

I march over to the DJ stand and ask if they have anything from this century. "We have everything," one of the guys says. "What do you want?" I list about ten bands off the top of my head.

"You got it, babe," the other guy tells me. I am no one's "babe," but I shelve the argument in favor of the music, thank them, and walk away.

The next song is one of my suggestions. Even though it's current and perfect to dance to, the kids are suddenly shy.

"Oh, no!" I announce. "You are all getting out there. We didn't come all the way down here to spruce up some wallflowers. You are divas and hotties and dancing queens and jumping beans and—please don't make me keep going here!"

Shelby looks at Trent, who mocks, "Jumping beans?" Everyone laughs, and the ice is broken. Shelby, Trent, and I pull some of the kids to their feet, and the rest follow. All of us—including the nurses in their pink cat and blue moon scrubs—shake it on the dance floor.

The songs keep coming, and we have a blast. Once an old disco song comes on, a few of the donors join us as well. Shelby, Trent, and I dance and sing together with the patients like we're all old friends. Everyone—whether they're dancing or sipping from crystal goblets and tapping their toes under the table—seems to be enjoying themselves.

Sarah gets tired and has to sit down, but we bring over her wheelchair so she doesn't have to miss out. Marley starts to push it around, but Sarah's stomach can't take it, so she stops.

The next song is slow and the kids scatter like glitter in a wind gust. I take a second look, and realize that Trent is on the dance floor with Sarah, who's gotten out of her wheelchair. I don't know what he's saying, but she's smiling. They're swaying slowly, probably to keep her stomach steady.

Felix is watching. Ooh! I think he likes her, too. "You can cut in, you know," I say casually.

"No, that would be rude." He doesn't take his eyes off them.

"If you like her, go after her." I give him a little playful push. And, to my delight, instead of resisting, he goes.

Soon he's dancing with Sarah, and Trent is walking back to the tables. He's smiling. "It worked."

"What?" I ask.

He leans close so I can hear him above the music. "Sometimes seeing the girl you like smile at someone else . . ." He trails off.

"What?"

"Makes a guy know what he wants." He looks away. Is he still talking about Felix and Sarah?

The next set of fast songs gets Mrs. Worthington and even more of the rich hospital benefactors out on the floor. Some of the accessories get passed around, and a bald man in a suit sports the rainbow Afro and giant sunglasses while his wife shimmies with a boa to a Daft Punk song. A few songs later, an older guy does the twist to Lady Gaga. It's so cute.

I'm catching my breath when a slow song comes on. I start back to the table, but then feel a tap on my shoulder.

"I wasn't sure how to get your attention," says Trent. "The last time I touched you, you slapped me." I wince inside yet again, and—yet again—can't bring myself to look him in the eye. "Want to dance?"

Why do I feel fluttery all of a sudden? I've danced with guys before—tons of times. It's no big deal. *It's just Trent. Stop it!* "Okay," I say.

He takes my hand in one of his, and places his other at my waist. He's so tall that I could lean right into his chest. I could, but I don't.

"Now, is this so bad?" He smiles, and it's kind of sexy.

I shake my head. Then, finally, I make eye contact. "You know, I'm really sorry about the other day," I tell him. "I just didn't know what you were doing."

"I know." We take small steps, and sway to the music. "I should have said something instead of swooping in on you. It all just happened so fast."

"Thank you for trying." And I don't look away.

The lights. The music. His warm, strong hand in mine, on me. His hazel eyes flecked in gold and rimmed with dark lashes. I'm caught up in the moment. He leans in a little closer as the music winds down. He's going to kiss me. He's going to kiss me. *He's going to kiss me!* And I'm not only fine with it, I want him to. All fluttery again, I tilt my head back and close my eyes—ready.

The song ends. No kiss. Trent's still holding me, but he somehow seems to step back. "Charlotte? What are you doing?"

I open my eyes.

After a moment, a sly expression crosses his face. "You thought I was going to kiss you."

"No!" I say a little too forcefully. Warmth spreads up my neck. I'm blushing. How could I be so stupid? "I was just into the music."

He raises his eyebrows. "If you say so."

"Aargh!" I start to pull away. "You're so—"

He keeps hold of my right hand. "I'm so what?" The amused expression on his face makes me want to slap him.

Instead, I swat at his chest with my free hand. "Annoying." *Adorable.* "Cocky." *Considerate.* I search for something else—something especially pointed—but his expectant, playful smile isn't helping. "Tall." *Tall.*

"*Tall?*" He laughs. "Is that all you've got?"

I yank my hand out of his and stomp away, leaving him in the middle of the dance floor grinning like a goon.

twenty

After it's all over and we're driving home, Shelby suggests stopping at Mondo Burger. Only the drive-thru is open, so we have to eat in the car. We don't care; we're starving.

"That was a blast!" Shelby says. She pulls into a parking spot and turns off her lights, but keeps the car running.

I nod with my mouth full of cheeseburger, and watch snowflakes hit the warm windshield and melt into tiny droplets.

"The kids looked really tired at the end, though." She tears open a ketchup packet and squeezes it on her fries. "I hope it didn't wear them out too much."

Another nod from me. I'm especially worried about Sarah—but she looked so happy when Felix wheeled her into the elevator. She deserves something good to counter all the crap.

They all do.

After a sip of pop I say, "It was nice of Mrs. Worthington to publicly thank us at the end."

"I know, right?" Shelby wipes ketchup off her hand with

a napkin. "I'm glad you were able to thank them for the opportunity for all of us. When they all stood up and clapped, I got kind of choked up, and then I got embarrassed. But you kept it together. Like always."

"No problem." Wow! Shelby thinks *I* keep it together? Did she miss my outburst at the last team meetings and the walk of shame immediately afterward? "Telling people how I feel isn't really a problem for me. Not saying something is harder."

Shelby laughs nervously. She could probably say something really snarky, but she doesn't. Instead she says, "Like when Ms. Garrett waits until two minutes before the bell rings to have us clean up. I so want to tell her that if she gave us more time, the supply room wouldn't be such a mess."

"I know!" I pull the tomato off my burger, wrap it in a napkin, and reassemble. "I've said the same thing to Lydia no less than a million times." Except Lyd always laughed off my comments, saying she was glad for the extra time and telling me to lighten up.

"I mean, do you know how many bottles of nail polish got gunky because people didn't make sure the tops were on tight enough?" Shelby seems genuinely angry. As if she agrees with me, unlike Lydia, who would only say that sarcastically, pointing out how unimportant nail polish is.

"Over a dozen."

"Fourteen!" Shelby looks as if she's seeing me for the first time. "And we'd have more time to clean up if Ms. G didn't have to deal with Toby. How did he get into cos in the first place? All he does is mess around." It's like she's listing all of *my* biggest cos pet peeves.

"He's so obnoxious," I add.

"Right!"

While we eat, we talk about the projects we've done so far and how Shelby thinks we should have had more time for finishing touches. I totally agree. Then she tells me about her ideas to make Posh Salon and Spa, her mom's business, better. Her mom won't listen, though—not about changing things, and especially not about letting Shelby go to college. Unlike me, she really *wants* to.

"She says it's pointless to spend all that money when I'm just going to end up back at the salon, working for her." Shelby twists a straw wrapper between her fingers. "She loves it here. So does my little sister. But I just want . . . I don't know . . . more." Then she talks about going to college in a big city. "I'd still use my cos license, to help pay for college and to get experience. Then I'd *really* like to do hair for movies or TV. Good luck telling my mother that."

Pringle's is just as much a family business as Posh. The difference is that Mom, Dad, and Pops have never expected me to do what they do. They've never made me feel trapped there. I think of the college catalogs in the downstairs garbage, and feel like such a spoon-licker.

"The salon's not that bad, though. At least I get paid." Shelby sips her pop. "Not like Lydia."

Where did that come from? Ever since Lydia started helping out at Patti Cakes, she's always been on the payroll.

"Oh!" Shelby sees my face and backpedals. "I shouldn't have said anything. Shit. I just figured you knew, since you've been best friends forever. Please, please don't tell her I told you. Shit."

Wait, what? How does *Shelby* know anything about Lydia's life? She goes on, clearly trying to make up for her misstep. "My dad is her mom's accountant. I overheard my parents one night—he's not supposed to talk about clients—I shouldn't have been listening. Shit." Shelby winces. "Please don't say anything."

I gather the wrappers and shove them into the bag. "I won't," I assure her.

Shelby doesn't need to know that Lydia and I aren't really talking, anyway. But every time I turn around I'm learning about something *else* Lydia's been keeping from me. Why didn't she say anything? I've always been there for her.

Haven't I?

"Seriously." Shelby is desperate. "I know we're not really friends—that you pretty much hate me—but—"

"I don't hate you." Well, not all the time. Shelby looks skeptical. "Hey, *you're* the one who rolls your eyes and talks about me and laughs with Taylor and the Emilys. And you're the one who called me anal."

"I don't talk about you or laugh." No way am I going to bring up what I heard in the bathroom. First of all, I don't want her to know I was eavesdropping from a stall, and second, what she said wasn't mean or gossipy. "If I'm laughing, it's probably at either Comb-over or Toby." She meets my eyes. "I'm sorry I called you anal—but, honestly, sometimes you are. Like a know-it-all teacher's pet."

I glare at her. "Me? *You're* the know-it-all teacher's pet! Ms. Garrett loves you because she knows your mom."

"Pssht! More like she answers all of your questions, but brushes me off because she knows my mom. Why do you think my team was the only one shorted a designer right off the bat?"

I hadn't thought of that; she might have a point. Rather than surrendering, though, I throw another example her way. "She asked you to demo the perm rolling yesterday." I adjust the heat vent away from me. It's getting warm in here.

"Because my mom told her that I'm weak at rolling perms." Shelby turns the heat to low. "Did you notice how she picked apart my technique?"

"No," I say. "But I did see her wink at you when she handed back the pedi tests."

"You're right. She did wink at me," she shoots back. "But she gave you first prize for the fund-raiser a minute before that!"

Just when I'm about to jump out of the car and call my dad to pick me up, she starts laughing.

"What's so funny?"

"This is just like me and my cousin Tiffany. Our moms say we argue because we're so much alike—both bossy first-borns."

Shelby and I, so much alike? No way! As she's laughing, I consider. She thinks I'm a teacher's pet. I think she is.

She thinks I hate her and talk about her behind her back. I assumed the same about her. She's my biggest competition in the showcase. She told her friends I had "mad skills." In other words, we have the exact same problems with each other. In addition to cos aspirations and family businesses, we're both apparently annoying as hell.

Oh my lanta, she's right. There's no way I'm admitting it, though.

She starts the car and pulls out of the parking lot. "So what's the deal with you and Trent?"

Great! My second or third least favorite topic. "No deal. He's the most irritating person on the planet." Then I smile. "Besides you, of course."

"Aww," she coos. "You're in love."

I huff and scowl, and she laughs like a demented hyena.

Could all of this possibly be the makings of a friendship? Me and Shelby Cox?

If someone had predicted it a month ago, I'd have called that person a liar. But so many unexpected things have happened lately that I guess anything's possible. A lot is going to depend on the outcome of the showcase, though.

twenty-one

4 days to the Winter Style Showcase

Monday is the last meeting before the showcase. In a perfect world—the one outlined on page one of my notebook—the only thing we'd have left to do is a practice run-through. Instead, I'm not even sure if anyone on my team will show up today, since we've already lost the building trades guy, the artist, the flutist, two ballerinas, and Carter, the digital design disaster and all-around asshat.

And I have a ton left to do. I sit at a table in the multipurpose room and look over my list. I have to get photos from Trent and the rest of the team, write my speech, create the PowerPoint presentation, paint and assemble the rest of the props, finalize my plans for hair and makeup, gather everything needed to make that happen, keep up the records for all of my reports, and follow up to make sure everyone else is doing what they're supposed to do.

Melody from child development and the little three-year-old ballerina, Lily, show up first, which is weird because Shea is always early. Lily is wearing a tutu, a sweater, leg warmers, and pink light-up tennis shoes. The ballerinas,

Kayla and Kaylee, are next. They sit down and immediately tell Lily how cute her leg warmers are and ask her about her recital last year.

Shea still isn't here, and it's almost our turn to use the stage for the run-through. I go over to Shelby and Gabriella's table. "Hey, guys, sorry to interrupt, but can I talk to Gabriella for a sec?"

"Yeah, sure," says Shelby. "Everything okay?"

I purse my lips and shrug. I'm not sure. Gabriella stands and looks at me expectantly. She's wearing gold shimmer on her eyes. Nice choice with her coloring.

"Do you know where Shea is?" I ask.

"She's sick." She starts to sit back down.

"Oh, no!" I say. "Is it serious? Will she be back soon?"

"I don't know," she says, standing again. "She was here on Friday."

"Okay, thanks," I say. Gabriella returns to her meeting, and I go back to my table.

What are we going to do? We're supposed to finalize all of our plans today and run through everything. The only person with a dress is Lily, and she provided it herself. I hope Shea just has a little bug and will be back tomorrow, dresses in hand. I text her: **I hear you're not feeling well. Get better soon.** ☺

I tell the others that Shea isn't here and then text Lydia: **Where are you?**

The teacher supervisor tells us that we're next for run-through, so we head to the auditorium. Toby's team is just leaving. There are at least a dozen people, it seems. His models are wearing silver robes and full futuristic makeup, including blue metallic lipstick. They're laughing and high-fiving, and Toby is wearing a tinfoil hat on his head. He shields his models from us by standing between us, flailing his arms and putting his hat on one of the models' heads. "Don't look! Don't look!"

I shake my head and walk past him. I get it. The closer we get to the competition, the more secretive everyone is getting about their project's details. But *me* steal from *Toby?* Never! Although his team is bigger and *actually here,* and his models already have their styles in place. Oh my lanta! Even Toby has his shit more together than I do. Looks like I'm in Opposite Land, for sure.

I talk to the stage team, which are a few guys from custodial services and a couple guys from building trades, and tell them about the props I'll be bringing on Friday.

One of the building trades guys says, "Yeah, I know about those." Translation: *You're the girl who screwed over my classmate.*

"*That* was not my fault," I argue. He shrugs me off. Then I show him where I want the props positioned. They're supposed to put them in place while the stage is dark between presentations.

"Got it," says the building trades guy who made Lydia's arbor.

"Lights check," says a familiar voice from the speakers in the sound booth. Trent? "We've been using these . . ."

Soft, faint lights come up across the stage. ". . . for the other groups. With spotlights at the podium and on the models. Does that work for you, Charlotte?" Definitely Trent!

"Yes, that should be great," I call. "Can you do two lights on the models when little Lily here is on stage, too?" I tap Lily's shoulder.

She smiles and says, "Are you talking to God?"

I hear Trent cracking up as he says, "No problem." Great! As if he's not cocky enough already, now he's going to have a God complex. Everyone on stage laughs, too. Lily looks embarrassed.

I crouch down next to her, point to the sound booth in the back of the auditorium, and say as loudly as possible, "No, he's not God, just a goony high school guy. Say hi to Lily, Trent."

Bright lights inside the booth come on, so we can see Trent on the other side of the window waving and making a goofy face. His friend Birch is there, too.

"See what I mean?" I say.

Lily laughs. "Uh-huh. He doesn't look anything like God."

I agree, even though I have no idea what God looks like. Or how Lily does.

The lights in the sound booth go dim again. "Is your PowerPoint uploaded yet?"

"Not yet," I call. "Still working on it."

"Taking it down to the wire, I see," he says. "Music?"

"I have it here," Mackenzie calls, holding up her phone.

"So you don't need anything from me, then?"

"Nope, not a thing!" Then I remember that I *do* need something. Pictures! I flinch and smile sheepishly. "Well, maybe some pictures for my PowerPoint . . ."

"I'll send you the link to the thumbnails," he says. "Make me a list of the numbers of the ones you want. Then I'll e-mail you the files without watermarking."

"How much—"

"Just get me a list and we'll work it out later," he says. "Now for the run-through."

He's so bossy. But I don't say that because I'm grateful that he's willing to help.

Mackenzie plays the song from her phone. Melody tells Lily to follow the ballerinas and to do what they do. The Kays, one at a time, dance en pointe and leap across the stage. They're graceful and amazing. Lily does an adorable job imitating and following them.

"Can you repeat that, but stop about here," I ask, standing near the middle of the stage, "and turn slowly while we discuss your hair, makeup, and costume?"

"Like this?" Kayla nails it.

"Yes! Perfect," I say.

Kaylee suggests a move that circles around and exits from the same side she enters, so that it'll save time for the quick change. She shows us, and it's fantastic. It allows for more stage time for Lily, too, so I say go with it. Mackenzie agrees.

Finally, we simulate the quick changes and repeat the

process with the "new" styles. Everything goes beautifully, even though we're missing the snow machine, live flute music, the props, the models' actual dresses, makeup, hairstyles, and our final speeches.

After we're done, I notice I have a text from Shea: **Thanks! Hope to see you tomorrow.** Good! That shouldn't put us too far off track. I'm sure Shea has her part handled. (I hope so, anyway.)

Mackenzie and I thank everyone and set up salon appointments for Wednesday for the Kays and Lily. We need to make sure the hairstyles will work, and give them time to get used to them. I text Lydia again. Is she on Team Charlotte or not? Finally, I head to Building Trades to gather the partially done PVC and wooden candy props that I've already paid for.

If I have any hope of pulling this off, I don't have a moment to spare. I have a ton to do and less than four days to do it.

— ✳ —

The store is pretty slow after school, so I start writing my speech in the break room. Or I try to. Considering how things are going, it's par for the course when I run out of blank paper halfway through. I rummage through the drawers under the microwave but find nothing usable.

I stop by the service desk, but Pops doesn't have anything but a tiny notepad. The song "Sweet Caroline" by Neil Diamond comes on overhead—for the third time in the past hour. "What gives?" I ask Pops. "Are you playing that song on a loop?" It's one of his favorites. He used to sing it to Grandma—Caroline Pringle.

"Not me." He shakes his head. "Must be Oliver. He's been singing it the past few days. Probably stuck in his head from the Wings game the other night."

I laugh. "Singing it? The only words Oliver knows are the chorus echoes."

Then Pops starts singing along as I walk away, "Sweet Caroline . . ."

"Ba ba ba!" I sing back at him from an aisle away.

He smiles and sings the next line.

Next stop: the office. Which, happily, is empty, so I can riffle through Dad's desk. No blank paper, but I find a couple of files . . . including a bright green one with my name on it.

Bizarre, I think, and open it.

It is full of betting pools about me.

I wonder why they aren't in the break room with the rest of the pools. Then I realize: I am not supposed to be looking at these. They are secret.

The first is a QP: *How many times Charlotte says, "Oh my lanta!" in a shift.* This one is dated three weeks ago. The winner was—no surprise—Ralph, who guessed eleven. Ha! I didn't realize I said it that much, but I guess it is kind of funny.

Next: *When Charlotte redoes the displays.* There's a sheet for every display from Opening Day through New Year's. So *that's* why Dad and Ralph always get to them first! Do they do the displays wrong on purpose just to watch me change them? Are they laughing and high-fiving each other behind my back every time?

Then: *Number of times Charlotte makes an employee melt down.* It's from last year. I count one, two, three . . . twelve, thirteen . . . There are fourteen entries, each with the person's name and the date. Shit. There are a lot of repeats—and a couple of them don't even work here anymore. Am I the reason why?

It's like picking at nail polish. I have to sift through the pages to see if there's one for this year, and there is. The most recent entry is *Katie, November 23.*

I feel sick.

I knew Katie was in the bathroom crying. I knew there was a pool. Worst of all, I even thought it was funny—thinking everyone else was on my side.

The entry before that reads *Hannah, November 9.*

On Thanksgiving, Hannah had told us how her sister had bailed out of babysitting on her first day. Which is why I'd caught her on the phone, and called her out for ignoring customers. And made her cry.

I wonder if I want to see what the next pool is.

Just then, Ralph walks in. He starts to speak, but as soon as he sees what I'm looking at he backs out the door. "Hold it!" I say. "What do you know about these?"

He raises his right hand. "I plead the Fifth."

"Two questions," I say. "And I want the truth." He waits, eyebrows raised. "One, how long have these pools been going on? And two, am I really that bad?"

"Since you officially started working here—so about five years—and yes. Yes, you are."

Ralph has always been straightforward, but not like this. This is a punch in the gut.

"I'm not one for hugging or nice words to make people feel better." He reaches into the drawer in front of me and pulls out a roll of masking tape. "I start betting pools."

Then he leaves me alone with the evidence.

I don't need to ask what he means. I already know. When Mom didn't think I had what it took to win the showcase, Ralph got a wager going. Then when I was upset about thinking Hannah was a slacker who ignored customers, he started another one. Both times there was comfort in knowing his money was on me. He—and everyone who bet with him— had my back. But really, he was betting that my spoon-licker ways would earn him a few bucks.

A sure thing.

Then he'd include Katie and Hannah and everyone else on the *Charlotte-made-me-melt-down* sheets. Once they'd made the pool, he'd show them, turn it into a joke. A game. A way to let them in on the future action and show them that they weren't alone. I look down at the file in my hand. The damning evidence is right here. Names, dates, calendar squares with circled winners.

It's like a secret club. One that I thought I was a part of—and I am, but not in the way I'd assumed. One that shows how people *really* feel about me. One that exposes how I really am.

If I'm such a bitch, why hasn't anyone said anything to me and told me to cut it out?

I know the answer to that, too. Mom and Dad have, more than once. I just blow them off. Oliver has, and I've blown *him* off, too. And then there are Pops's "Stop, drop, and roll" comments.

Nobody else at the store can say anything—because they can't. Because I'm a Pringle.

I *am* a spoon-licker. Oh, God.

Just a few days ago I was crying in the bathroom, feeling like everyone was against me. Seeing the list of people I've done that to makes me want to hide and cry again.

Maybe I should add my name to Ralph's pool. *Charlotte, December 7.*

~ ✖ ~

And then there's the showcase, four days away.

I return to the break room and look at the reconfigured list in front of me, and all that I have to do. And that I've created a situation where I have to do it all by myself.

There's a reason why most of my team has left. I thought I was a speak-her-mind, get-things-done, strong woman. What I am instead is a keep-your-distance, whip-cracking-tyrant, Grade-A bitch.

It's too late to apologize and turn back the clock. The only thing I can do is put all of my energy into streamlining the presentation and making sure it, at least, works. *Maybe I can actually pull it off,* I tell myself. Maybe I can still win—or at least place—and get to go to the Chicago hair show and earn the right to direct my future.

If my life were a movie, this would be the musical montage where the heroine figures it out and works and fights her way to the top. I can hear the *Rocky* theme song in my head. I channel Baby from *Dirty Dancing,* practicing that lift until she nails it and shows everyone that "Nobody puts Baby in a corner." I imagine Julia Roberts in *Pretty Woman,* shopping, pulling herself together, and proving those snooty boutique bitches wrong—"Big mistake. Big. Huge!" I am Elle Woods in *Legally Blonde,* pulling out all the stops, winning the case, and freeing her framed sorority sister.

I have what it takes. I can do it. I will do it.

But first, I need a sandwich. I'm hungry.

⁓ ✳ ⁓

Monday night, I stay up until after 2:00 a.m. painting a primer coat on the unfinished wooden candy cut-outs that I'll paint tomorrow to look like lollipops. It's freezing in the garage, so I hurry. Luckily the PVC pipe for the candy canes is already white, so I don't have to paint that. While they dry, I add "learn how to make candy flowers" and "make them" to my to-do list, since I still haven't heard back from Lydia. Then I rewrite my speech for the third time. The first two times I read it aloud, it sounded robotic, forced, and ridiculous.

When that's done, I start blocking out the PowerPoint. Trent e-mailed the link to his pictures like he said he would. Because it's last-minute and because he refused to give me a firm quote, I'm sure he's going to gouge me, so I plan for only the pictures that will maximize my message and skill set. With so few pictures, the slides look as skimpy as my ATC bucks account, but they'll have to do. I make a list to give to him tomorrow.

Please, please, please, I pray to any god who might listen to spoon-lickers who deserve every rotten thing that happens to them. *Let someone come through for me.*

twenty-two

3 days to the Winter Style Showcase

Of course, I oversleep. I take a five-minute shower, and my hair is in a legit messy bun, not a strategically styled messy bun. I throw on an outfit I just wore last week, hoping nobody remembers. I don't even have time to put on eyelashes—just mascara. I guzzle a gigantic travel mug of coffee on my way to school.

Thank God I'm not in heels today. Right before first bell, I race down the hall and come to a skidding halt at Trent's locker. I thrust my list at him, catch my breath, and say, "How much will you charge me for these?"

He takes it and says, "Good morning to you, too. You're not wearing tarantulas on your eyes today. Looks nice."

I do not have time for his sarcasm.

He sighs, then takes a look. "What are you going to do with these?"

After I explain the revised PowerPoint, he shakes his head. "No offense"—which tells me he's about to say something offensive, and here it comes—"but stick to cos, because that's one crappy presentation."

I can't glare at him, as much as I want to. I need him, so I adopt a reasonable tone. "What am I supposed to do, then? You know that *other* digital dude called me a bitch and bailed."

"Find someone more reliable." He's so damn cocky!

Two can play that game. "Like who? You?"

"Maybe. For the right price."

The right price? He's expecting me to pay for filet mignon on a BOGO Loco's Tacos budget.

"What about just the pictures?" I ask.

"One ATC buck each." Wow! That's reasonable. Surprising.

"Deal. Can you get them to me by tomorrow?"

"You'll have them by noon." He stuffs the list in his pocket and practically saunters away.

The bell rings, and as I race to class, I think: *Why does he have to make everything so difficult?* All he had to do was tell me how much the pictures would cost. Instead, he tells me my idea is crap, and acts like he's God's gift to the digital world.

Lydia sits with Carter at lunch and then completely ignores me in computers and "icks," so I ignore her, too. Whatever. I can't think of anything I've done wrong. I did my best for her showcase, and she hasn't done a single thing I need her to do for mine. She's lied—*a lot*—ditched the Grand Plan, and thrown away our friendship—for a guy, and a dumbass guy at that. Spoon-licker or not, if I've been horrible to Lydia, I can't see where.

Shea is nowhere to be found, so I track down Gabriella, who tells me that she's still sick.

I text Shea: **Still not feeling OK? Anything I can do?**

Three days to the showcase, and no dresses! I report the problem to Mr. Finn, who says he'll check into it and get back to me. I fill him in on everything, including my frustration. He says he understands.

After work, I put a coat of white paint on my candy props and leave them to dry. Shea hasn't texted back, and there are no e-mails from Mr. Finn about Shea, but I have to assume he's on it—the showcase is important to her, too. She wouldn't just bail.

Then I thumb through my store of fashion magazines and scour the Internet for inspiration. I load my Pinterest board with fantasy makeup and hairstyle images. I need the perfect pair of looks—one that can be quick-changed into the other. I decide to do an ombre color—from natural to bright pink—with curls. For one dress, I'll pin up the curls. Then all Kaylee has to do is remove the pins, shake out her head, and give it a quick spray. Voilà! Two styles, one head. It'll be impossible to change makeup that fast, so I'll just have to make it doubly awesome. I decide on sparkly lashes with fancy eye shadow to look like rainbow wings, swirly eye-to-cheek appliques, and deep to bright ombre lips to coordinate with the hair. Fabulous!

Hair and makeup planned out—check.

I drive to Michael's to get the paint and brushes I need to finish the candy props. The circles will become lollipops when I add twisty rainbow spirals, and red stripes will make the PVC pipe sticks into candy canes. No biggie.

But there are too many options. Acrylic or oil paint? Tube or jar or plastic bottle? What kind of brushes? Finally, I ask a woman in a red vest. I go into great detail about the size and shape and the materials, and the white base coat.

After all that, what does she say? "I don't work here." And she walks away like *I* just inconvenienced *her*! *Hello! You could have stopped me!*

They should have a big sign on the sliding doors: RED VESTS WORN BY AUTHORIZED PERSONNEL ONLY BEYOND THIS POINT.

I have to repeat it all for a legit Michael's vest-wearing employee, and leave about seventy-five dollars poorer. Still, I've got what I need—and I know I can do this. After all, I have "mad skills" when it comes to freehand nail designs (thank you, Shelby Cox). This is just on a bigger scale.

But it turns out that three-foot wooden circles aren't exactly like one-inch nails. Everything is much more visible, and the brushes are harder to control, especially in the cold garage. My lines go from fat to thin to fat again, and there are blobs and missed spots. So much for uniformity.

The paint fumes are giving me a headache, too. I decide to take a break and grab some dinner.

"There's some leftover ham and au gratin potatoes in the fridge," Mom says, letting Buffy out and getting ready to go to bed.

"Thanks." I pull the Tupperware from the fridge and grab a plate.

"What are you doing out there anyway?" Mom fills the coffeepot with water and pours it into the reservoir.

"Painting props for Friday," I say. I scoop some food onto the plate, cover it with a paper towel, and put it in the microwave.

"What does that have to do with cos?" She puts coffee in the filter and sets the timer for morning. "Wouldn't another program handle those?"

"It's art, Mom. It's all related. Don't you know anything about synergy?" I have no idea what that means, but I say it with great conviction.

The truth is, she's right—not that I would give her the satisfaction of telling her so or admitting that I'm struggling. None of this has anything to do with cos, but it's my only hope of having a presentation at all.

As I'm devouring my potatoes, Mom lets Buffy in. "Well, you look like you could use some sleep, so don't stay up too late."

"Thanks! Like that's possible," I mumble, mouth full, but Mom doesn't hear me because she's halfway up the stairs. Buffy sits next to me with a sympathetic expression. I tell myself that at least *she's* on my side, but I have a sneaking suspicion that if I weren't eating, she would've been in bed before Mom.

The rainbow twists on the lollipops are a mess. The colors bleed together, and the harder I try to fix them, the worse it gets. I'm left with what looks like a bunch of preschool paintings that not even a mother—*my* mother—would display on the fridge.

I turn my attention to the candy canes. I can't keep the angle consistent as I wind around the first PVC tube, and I have no place for the thing to dry without smudging the paint on one side. (I don't realize this until I'm almost finished.) I end up chucking the tube across the garage, getting red paint on the floor and the lawn mower. (Good thing it's already red. Maybe Dad won't notice.) I brew Mom's coffee, drink two cups, and keep going. The other three look just as bad, but by the time I'm done, I don't care.

It's almost three a.m. I start to look over my speech again, but realize that the letters are all jumbly. I take a shower to wake up.

Then I fill a bag with the tools and makeup for tomorrow's practice. I need to tweak my speech. I need to work on the PowerPoint. And I still need to figure out how to make candy flowers, not to mention actually making them.

Wrapped in a towel, I lie on the bed with my laptop and scroll through recipes. I don't understand half the words. What's gum paste? A ball tool? I don't even cook—how on earth am I going to do this?

I find a site where I can buy sugar flowers. But they're thirty dollars each, and I need twenty. *Six hundred dollars?* Forget it. There are instructional videos, aren't there? I find one, click play, and lay my head down to watch.

Buffy's barking wakes me up—but it's the middle of the

night, and she only barks like that at the garbage guys. Then I hear the rumble and clang of the garbage truck.

What the hell? I paw for the clock. 7:44 a.m. My appointment with Kaylee is at eight!

I jump out of bed, throw some clothes on, grab the hairdo bag, and run, leaving Buffy slobbering and barking, and the garbage truck in the dust.

I catch a glimpse of myself in the rearview mirror of my car. My hair is sticking up all over and has a weird part in the middle. The right side is a ratty mess from falling asleep with a wet head. I am not fit to be seen out in public, let alone school. I try smoothing it down, but it boings back up.

At the first stoplight, I dig through my purse for a brush and a hair tie. I tame the mess as best I can in the forty-seven seconds I have before the light turns green. Of the other eight lights on the trip to school, only three more are red. I use one for eyeliner, one for mascara, and one for mouthwash. I spit out the window, and it trails down the side of the door. I can hear Oliver now: "You spit like a girl." I start to answer the Oliver-voice, but stop myself. Have I totally gone bonkers? Judging by the look on the man's face in the car next to me, the answer is yes.

I run into class five minutes late. Kaylee is talking to Ms. Garrett. "There she is," she says. Ms. G gives me a look. The rest of the class is already working, either on makeup or hair color.

Even though I'm frazzled, I do my best to pull it together and be professional. First, I get Kaylee a magazine to read

while I set up. Before I style her, I'm going to do the semipermanent pink ombre. It'll be bright for the show, and gradu-
ally fade out after about fifteen washes.

Except there are no color bowls left in the supply room.
Every single one is being used. When I ask Ms. G, she says,
"I don't know where they went. It's like they grew legs or
something."

Oh, no! I know where they went—into the garbage. I
"borrowed" them for the wellness fair, and tossed them after
the Carter Reed debacle. I had planned to replace them . . .
Now I'm screwed.

I rummage through cupboards for something else that
might work. There are tiny Dixie cups, but the paper would
disintegrate in two seconds. The only other thing is a gigantic Halloween serving bowl covered with witches, Franken-
monsters, and ghosts.

I mix up the color and return to my model. She looks uncomfortable when she sees the monster bowl. "What's that?"

I try to laugh as if I'm in control, and reassure her she
doesn't need to worry. It doesn't work. My laugh is more like
a cackle, my hair's a wild mess, and I'm cradling a freak-
ishly ghoulish bowl. Kaylee vaults out of the chair. "I can't do
color. Okay? No color!"

"But this is a showcase of my skills," I plead. "If I don't
do color, the style will be too simple." What am I going to do
now? Then I see Toby across the room applying silver hair
chalk to his model. The skill level isn't the same as foiling,

but it's better than nothing. And it's totally temporary. The only thing is, I'd have to do it again on Friday.

"I don't care. If I came home with pink hair, my dad would freak out." We lock eyes. It's a stand-off. "I'm not sitting down unless you agree to only style," she repeats. "No cutting. *No color.*"

"What about chalk?" I offer as a compromise.

"Chalk?"

I explain that it's a lot like pastels that artists use, only it's designed for hair. It washes out immediately, so her dad shouldn't care. She agrees and sits back down.

First, I section her hair, twist and color each piece. Then I dry it and create a magnificent updo with twists and strategically placed curls. I'm able to use a larger palette—pink, blue, purple, yellow, *and* green—than if I'd applied actual color, so I'm pleased.

When she sees it, she loves it and actually thanks me. Then I explain where the flowers will be, how to remove them and pull out the bobby pins, and what to do to get the next style. (If there *are* flowers—but I don't say it out loud because I'm trying to stay positive.) She follows my directions, and it looks amazing, if I do say so myself.

Finally, I do her makeup, showing her where the appliqués will be. Because the makeup is so dramatic (and I don't want everyone to see), she removes the lashes and washes her face immediately afterward. I arrange for her to come back first thing Friday for the final style and makeup.

"What about the dresses?" she asks before she leaves. "I only had one fitting. Shouldn't we make sure they fit and practice the quick change?"

"I agree." I gather my bobby pins and slip them into the container. "Until I hear from Shea, though, I don't know. She has them. Maybe tomorrow?"

Kaylee shrugs. "Let's hope." And then she heads to class.

I text Shea again: **Haven't heard from you. Hope you're okay. Models are asking about dresses.**

Mackenzie is just getting started on Kayla's hair. She's globbing the pink and blue highlights on too thick, especially by the scalp, and since her foils aren't wrapped well, the color is bleeding all over. What a mess!

Ms. G is talking to a couple of models at her desk, so she doesn't see what's happening.

I need to do something—fast! I call Mackenzie over to the pedi area to avoid freaking Kayla out, and choose my words carefully. "Do you need any help with your highlights?"

"No, I've got it," she says.

"I think I should help," I offer. "The colors are bleeding."

"Seriously?" Mackenzie is offended. "You are so critical. Fine!" She hands me the comb she's holding. "You do it."

Melody and Lily are standing in reception.

"I'll do Lily's hair, then," says Mackenzie, "if that's okay with you."

I nod. Then I hurry over and ask Kayla if she'd mind if we started over, and if I did it instead. She's not thrilled, but she agrees. I'm hoping that I've caught it early enough, before the color grabs hold too much. I wash her hair thoroughly with clarifying shampoo, then dry it. There's a purplish tinge, but it actually looks fine with our theme. While I'm foiling the back, Ms. G comes over and asks why I'm working on Mackenzie's model.

"I'm just helping out," I say.

"More like taking over," Mackenzie corrects me from the next station. She's braiding Lily's hair, but the little girl is squirming so much that it's very uneven.

Thanks for throwing me under the bus, Mackenzie! Maybe I should tell Ms. G why I needed to step in.

Ms. G looks at me, but Tasha calls to her before either of us can say anything.

"I'm just about done with the foils," I say to Mackenzie. "Then you can wash it out and do the style."

She rolls her eyes. "So kind of you to let me finish *my* client."

Kayla looks uncomfortable. So does Melody.

Lily is bouncing in her seat, oblivious to the tension.

God, I wish I were three.

While Kayla is processing, I overhear Taylor and Shelby say Lydia's name.

"I know!" says Shelby. "Somebody should talk to her . . . see if she's okay."

"What about Charlotte?" asks Taylor.

"What about Charlotte what?" When someone mentions my name, that's as good as an invitation.

They don't seem to mind. "Brianna had a convo with Lydia on Twitter last night." Taylor pulls it up on her phone so I can take a look. "It's pretty effed-up, if you ask me."

The Tweetversation went like this:

@BriannaBanana: @LydiaHarris14 Didn't you notice his FB relationship status? Or did you just not care? #HesTakenBitch

@LydiaHarris14: @BriannaBanana @CarterReed says he's never on FB and everything there is old news. #TakeItUpWithHim

@BriannaBanana: @LydiaHarris14 Old news? Check the date.

Then there's a screenshot of a text from Carter: I'm not talking to Lydia. I swear. She's just some girl from school. She's not even cute.

I need to find Lydia. No matter what's happened between us lately, she's still my best friend, and what Carter Asshat Reed did is not okay.

twenty-three

As soon as the bell rings, I practically run to the cafeteria, but Lydia's not there. I check the parking lot. Her car's in its usual space, but she's not in it. She's not at her locker, either.

The only other place I can think of is the culinary arts kitchen.

She's alone, wearing a white apron and the ugliest blue hair net I've ever seen. Tears are streaming down her face as she kneads and pinches some pink Play-Doh-looking stuff. The kitchen smells like sugar and bleach.

"I've heard blue hair nets are the must-have accessory this season," I say.

She looks up from her work and gives me a half-assed smile. "Have *you* checked a mirror today? You look raggedy."

Harsh! I'd call her out, but I'm not here for that. Besides, she's right.

"I also heard about what happened."

"Great." She punches the dough. "I'm sure the whole school knows."

"Probably. But at least maybe they'll stop talking about

my toilet paper streamers, so yeah, thanks for that."

"You're welcome," she says sarcastically. "It's the least I can do." Then she stops mid-dough-punch and full-out sobs. "Oh, Charlotte! How did everything get so messed up?"

I walk around the counter, put my arm around her, and poke at the dough with my free hand. "How should I know? I don't even know what you're making."

She half-laughs, half-sobs. "Not that! Us. You and me. And my life in general."

I shrug, grab a tissue out of my purse, and hand it to her. "I know about as much about your life lately as this tissue does."

I don't tell her that everything I *do* know I've heard from Nutmeg and Shelby. Stuff I'm not even supposed to know. Stuff that doesn't make sense.

"I've tried talking to you so many times," she says, "but you just wouldn't understand."

I lean against the stainless steel worktable that spans across the wall of ovens. "How do you know?"

"Because your family's never been broke." Translation: *Because you're a spoon-licker.*

I have no idea what to say.

After a moment, she goes on. "I told you we were having some money problems because of when Dad was sick." I nod. "But it's worse than I let on. Mom's losing the bakery, and since the house is tied to the business, we might lose that, too. That's why we had to lay off Nutmeg. I've done everything I can to help, but it's just not enough."

Losing the bakery? "I'm so sorry, Lyd." *What can I do? How can I fix this? I could ask Dad to lend them some money. Or something.* "Maybe my father could—"

"Stop it!" She shrugs off my arm and steps away. "This is why I can't talk to you! You just swoop in and take over!"

"Okay! Geez! I was just trying to help. I don't want you to lose . . ." I can't bring myself to finish the sentence—to say *lose your house.* I can't. *Lydia and her family, homeless? That only happens to other people, doesn't it? They'd find some- where to live—right?* "Anything," I finish lamely.

"I know." She rests her elbows on the counter. Her voice is quiet, almost toneless. "You can't help it. It's just not as simple as a loan or a job working for someone else again. Mom built Patti Cakes and made it successful, and now her dream—*our* dream—could be gone, just like that. All be- cause of one rough patch."

I was mad because Lyd abandoned our Grand Plan. Maybe it was never her *plan.* "The *bakery* is your dream?"

"Yeah," she says. "Mom's *and* mine. Ever since Patti Cakes started." *That was four years ago. Way before we even applied to ATC. How had I not seen this?* "I tried to tell you that I'm not cut out for cos—that I didn't want to run a salon—but you never listened. You didn't want to hear it, I guess."

Lydia was so excited when the bakery first opened. She ordered customized aprons for Patti, Nutmeg, and herself. I figured she was just happy for her mom. But now, I remember her talking for hours about the new con-

vection oven and that monstrous mixer thing.

I tuned her out then. And probably every other time she blabbered on about cooking.

"Why did you sign up for cos, then?" I pull up a stool and sit down. "And let me keep talking about the Grand Plan?"

"I thought it would be fun. And I still want to get an apartment together and take classes at JC." Lydia abandons her pink dough, pulls up another stool. "But it wasn't all fun. It was hard. Really hard."

I remember Lydia struggling with her skills test when we first signed up. She did it, but she worried that she'd bombed. And then, more recently, her pedi test. She never did get her mani and pedi steps mastered. It was all right there. But I was so focused on what I wanted, I never even saw her struggling, or heard her complaining for what it was—she was out of her element.

"I know I should have told you, but I didn't know how." She traces lines in the flour sprinkled on the table. "I knew you'd be blindsided, whether I told you or Mr. Finn did. I just took the chickenshit way and let him do it."

Watching Lydia draw in the flour reminds me of the geometric design in Mr. Finn's carpet and the day he told me that Lydia had changed programs. I *was* blindsided. But if I'd been paying attention, I wouldn't have been. "That's not chickenshit." Would I have ever listened otherwise? I'm not sure.

As if she's reading my mind, Lydia says, "Even if I'd had

the guts to tell you, I'm not sure it would've sunk in. I tried telling you about Dad and the problems with our finances, but you didn't get it. And then, when I tried again before the wellness fair, all you said was that we needed new outfits."

"God, Lyd." My stomach knots, and not because it's lunchtime. "I didn't know." I thought I hadn't done anything to her. That I was in the right. That *I* was the good friend.

"That's what you do." She returns to the dough, pinches off a bit, and rolls it into tiny little balls. "You assume people should act or be a certain way, unless you see a reason to cut them slack."

I sweep the flour into a pile with the side of my hand. What people? What way? "What do you mean?"

"Like Rachel from custodial arts. She's in special ed, so you're always nice to her. And that girl with cancer. You have patience with them, but with everyone else . . ."

"So now I'm wrong for being *nice*?"

"No!" She smashes a few of the dough pellets into tiny pancakes. "I mean that everyone has something—a reason to be kind to them. Some people's crap is just not as obvious, like some disability or disease. But it's still there."

Like Hannah's. And Shelby's. I only saw what I wanted to see. "So that's why you said that 'not everybody lives in the world according to Charlotte.'"

"Pretty much." She gets up, walks over to the sink, and washes her hands. "And, like I said, that's why I did cos in the first place. The world according to Charlotte can be fun.

It's dress-up and makeup and playing and saying whatever and doing whatever without worrying about money or caring what anybody thinks."

"Yeah." *Saying whatever and doing whatever and not caring.*

"Honestly, I liked hanging out with you and pretending I still lived there." She sits down beside me again. "For a while, anyway."

"And then Carter Reed came along . . ."

"Yeah, that was stupid." She covers her face with her hands. "And *I* was stupid. And I'm sorry. It's just that he was nice and cute, and he chose me—at least I thought so—when I really needed something good to happen. I'll never let a dumbass guy come between us again." Then, as if she suddenly remembers what she was doing before I came in, she perks up. "I have something to show you." She jumps up, runs to the back cooler, and brings out a large sheet cake box . . .

. . . and through the window I see a bunch of beautiful candy flowers.

I take the box, set it on the counter, and open it. They're gorgeous! "Wow! Did you do these?" She nods. "For me? Are they made of gum paste?"

"Of course!" Then she stops short. "Wait, you know about gum paste? Whoa! I'm . . . surprised." Then she grabs a wad of pink dough and says, "I have a few more to do. Maybe that'll help make up for Carter and ditching you and everything?"

"It's a start," I say, and grin. Lydia may be the one apologizing, but she's not the only one at fault. "You could also forgive me. I'm sorry I wasn't there when you needed me."

"Deal." She pokes my arm with her finger and leaves a pink doughy dot.

The longer I look at the flowers, the more impressed I am. They're the first thing that's gone right with my presentation in a long time. *Watch out, Shelby Cox! Lydia's back on Team Charlotte, and we're coming up on your peacock-print heels.*

— ✳ —

Now that Lydia and I have cleared the air, I feel much better. Except for the fact that Shea still isn't in school. She hasn't texted me back, and nobody seems to know anything except that she's sick. I can't finish my speech without her input, so that's on hold until then. But I'm beginning to worry. I hope she's better soon. Time is running out.

When I get home from work, I take a look at the props. They look horrible—full of inconsistent lines, drips, and globs. Maybe the stage lights will be dim enough that no one will notice. That's what I tell myself, anyway.

I sit at the kitchen table with my laptop to work on my PowerPoint presentation. Trent sent the pictures before noon, just as he promised—but I can't seem to get them to format. Every time I move them in the layout, they do some catawampus weird thing. After an hour of trying to figure it out, I have to admit, with a sinking feeling, that Trent was right. My idea *is* crappy.

I give up. I can't do it all.

Just then I see a Post-it note on the coffeemaker.

Charlotte,
You drank my coffee. Next time prep another pot!
XO, Mom

Then it hits me. Oh my lanta, I'm just like Mom. She doesn't know what it takes to be a cosmetologist, so she doesn't respect it. I'm guilty of the same thing. Painting and cooking and digital design—among other things—are best left to those who know what they're doing. They make it look so easy that I assumed those things were no big deal, that anyone could do them, that I could do them.

Even though it pains me to have to do it, I need to admit defeat and ask Trent for help.

I just hope it's not too late.

twenty-four

1 day to the Winter Style Showcase!

Thursday morning, I wake up rested and refreshed. I pick out a fringy sweater and put it on over gray pants and a blue tank. I wear my hair down in beachy waves and put on my signature lashes. I feel like myself again for the first time in days.

That is, until I walk into class and Ms. G sends me to Mr. Finn. All the way down the hall, I repeat in my head, "Please, God, please, let everything be okay with Shea."

"Let's start with the good news, shall we?" Mr. Finn begins, as soon as I sit down. Oh, no. When someone "starts with good news," that means bad news is coming next.

"After our recent, uh, conversations, I've spoken to a few of your teachers. Since you've encountered so many setbacks, we've decided to reimburse you the ATC bucks that Lydia used to complete her project." He gives me a big smile, then leans forward. "This is an exceptional case, Charlotte—not normal procedure here at ATC—so please don't share this with the other students."

This is great, but it's weeks too late. I think of the props, music, models, and PowerPoint design that would be better (or existed at all) if I had had that money sooner, and I feel robbed all over again. I thank him anyway, and ask if ATC bucks expire. He says they don't. At least I'll have a jump on the senior showcase.

So this is the good news. The bad news, I realize with a sinking feeling, must be about Shea.

"We have a bit of a situation," Mr. Finn says seriously. "Shea Walsh is in the hospital and won't be back in school until after Christmas break."

Hospital? That sounds serious. Oh, no. "How awful! What's wrong with her?"

"Normally, I'd prefer not to discuss one student with another, but given the situation, I'm sure Shea won't mind." He folds his hands on his desk. "She needed an emergency appendectomy. At first, she thought she had a stomach bug, so her parents simply called in to let us know she was sick. I called and left a message after I spoke to you on Tuesday. Mrs. Walsh returned my call yesterday afternoon, after Shea was out of surgery. Her appendix burst."

Poor Shea! How painful and scary! "Is she going to be okay?"

"Yes," he assures me. "It's serious, but doctors expect a full recovery. However, she won't be released for several days and will need to rest for a while after that."

"So what will she do about the showcase?" I ask, my calm voice the complete opposite of how I feel inside. "It's tomorrow. This has all been very challenging, Mr. Finn."

"I understand, Charlotte." Mr. Finn gets up and opens his closet door. "I hate to have to break this to you, especially given your string of obstacles . . ." So he's adding to the string? If only obstacles were pearls! "However, Shea has sent in the dresses." He pulls a garment bag out of the closet and drapes it over the chair next to me. Yes! I'm not totally left in the lurch.

"She's also passed along her talking points for her part of the presentation." Then he hands me an envelope with my name on it. Another lean-across-the-desk serious look: "I know this wasn't what you were expecting, but I'd like to ask one more favor: That you merge her speech with your own for the sake of the presentation. Obviously, Shea will have to work out a make-up presentation with her program director when she returns."

I take the envelope. Actually, this is a good thing—Shea's info can give me ideas for my own speech. Plus, I'll only have to share the spotlight onstage with one other person, so it'll highlight how much my team has had to overcome. Maybe this won't be so bad.

"There's one little problem," Mr. Finn adds, almost as an afterthought. "The dresses aren't exactly . . . finished. She was still working on them when she got sick."

Not finished? What the hell?

He hurries on. "I've spoken to Ms. White"—the fashion design instructor—"and she says that if you bring them to the lab today, someone should be able to finish them." He looks down at his notes. "Shea has, uh, basted the skirts, so all that needs to be done are the final stitches."

Basting? I remember Mom basting the turkey on Thanksgiving, but somehow I'm guessing that turkey basting and dress basting are not the same thing.

I thank Mr. Finn, tell him I'm on it, stuff the envelope into my purse, and drape the garment bag over my free arm. He thanks me for being such a great team player. If only he knew the half of it!

The fashion design lab is a total zoo. There's fabric and whirring sewing machines and designers scrambling all over the place. As soon as I walk in, they freak. "Get out!" one girl yells. "You can't see our designs yet!" How was I supposed to know I entered a super-secret workshop? Gabriella runs over and takes me out into the hall, closing the door behind us.

"Sorry about that," she says. "We're just kind of protective about having a big reveal."

"I wasn't snooping." I unzip the bag. "Mr. Finn told me to come here and—"

"I know. Ms. White told me." She takes the first dress from me. "That sucks about Shea."

"Yeah, it does." We both hold the dress and inspect it. Seems fine to me. I would've liked more beading and sequins, but overall, it's pretty much what I imagined. At least it's all intact.

"Shouldn't take too long to do this. I just have to sew it on the machine and rip out the basting." She drapes the dress over her shoulder and looks at the others. "These are all pretty straightforward. I should have them to you by the show."

"Should"? Not "will"? And what if something *else* happens? At least now I have the dresses in my possession. If I hand them over and Gabriella doesn't have time or doesn't care or *she* gets sick or something, I'm screwed.

"So all you're going to do is sew over where it's already sewed?" I take the dress from her.

"Pretty much." She grabs the straps. "Basting is done by hand. The final stitching is done on the machine. It's stronger."

I hold firm to the skirt and tug. It seems strong enough to me. Kaylee only needs to wear it onstage for about a minute. Who cares if the stitches are perfect? Nobody in the audience will be able to tell. "I think I'm just going to keep them as is. They look good enough to me."

She tries to get the dress back. "Shea will have a cow if she finds out."

I don't let go. "She's not here, so it's not her call."

"Are you sure?" She pulls the dress toward her.

I gather as much of the fabric as I can into my arms. "Yes, I'm sure."

"Whatever." She finally lets go. "I have a lot to do. Doesn't break my heart to cross something off my list."

And that's that.

— ✖ —

Less than twenty-four hours to go. Where am I?

Hairstyles and makeup—check.

Dresses—check.

Candy accessories—check. Lydia will be over tonight to help me hot-glue them to combs.

Props—not yet, but maybe Lyd will help with that, too. I hope.

PowerPoint—Mental note: *Talk to Trent and finish tonight.*

Music—Find out if Mackenzie already uploaded to the server.

Speech—Finish tonight and practice.

Rest and Relax—after the showcase. Looks as if I won't be sleeping again.

—— ✱ ——

When I finally get back to the program, everyone is milling around, gathering supplies and setting up their stations for tomorrow. It reminds me of Pringle's just before a snowstorm—lots of frantic grabbing, and Byron and one of the Emilys almost get into a fight over what they call "the only good" wet brush. Luckily, Shelby lets Emily use hers.

I ask Mackenzie if she's uploaded the music or if I should do it. Ms. G overhears and says, "I have you down for live music."

"No, you don't," I argue. "Mackenzie changed it almost two weeks ago." I turn to Mackenzie. "I told you to get Ms. Garrett a revised form. That day. The day we chose the music. You said you would. You did it, right?"

I glare at her. *You'd better say "Right!"*

"I just thought you were being bossy, as usual." She holds up her phone. "But I have it right here. Can't we change it now?"

"We have to buy a license!" I practically yell. Everyone stops what they're doing and stares.

"License?" Mackenzie acts as if this is the first time she's ever heard the word.

"Oh my lanta!" I throw my hands up and start pacing.

"Yes," explains Ms. G. "It's not that expensive, but it has to be done to legally play a song in public."

"Oh."

Oh? That's all she has to say? She was in charge of one thing! One thing! She didn't even have to *do* it—just give the song and artist's name to Ms. G. That's it! How are we supposed to have ballerinas dance to *no music?*

Ms. G must see that I'm about to explode because she has me sit down at my station. The others lose interest and go back to their own projects. "We can talk to Mr. Finn," she says, "and see if you can use the music we plan on playing as the audience is seated."

I take a few deep breaths. Maybe that'll work. At least it's music. Something is better than nothing, right? I ask to hear it.

"So we can't use the song *I* wanted?" Mackenzie seems disappointed. Like *I'm* the one nixing her song.

"No," Ms. G and I echo each other.

When Ms. G plays the music, I think I'm going to cry. It's not woodsy or fantastical. It's not beautiful or melodic. It's upbeat and techno and loud. It's more like catwalk music for a fashion show. Which is what it should be! It's perfect to get the crowd pumped up for the showcase. It totally sucks as a bubbly tune for ballerina fairies to frolic in an enchanted candy forest.

The bell rings, and Ms. G asks us, "So what do you want to do?"

"Ask Charlotte," Mackenzie snarks. "She's the boss."

"I don't know," I say. And I don't.

— ✳ ⁓

I find Trent in the cafeteria. There are no seats around him, so I just squeeze in by his elbow, invading his personal space, crowding the guy next to him, and blocking everyone trying to walk behind him.

"What's the matter? You look upset." How does he know anything's wrong? I did a spectacular job of pulling it together before going to lunch.

I tell him about the formatting issue, my music—or lack thereof—and that I need to work in more pics of Shea and Mackenzie. Although I'd rather feed Mackenzie to a family of rabid skunks right about now. The guy next to Trent tries to scoot away from me, but there's no room. Several people squeeze past me, almost dumping their trays on me. They all seem annoyed. I apologize, but keep talking and don't move away. The whole time Trent listens and wordlessly eats his sloppy joe. Finally I say, "So can you help me?"

He polishes off one of his milks, sighs, and says, "Do you want me to just do the PowerPoint for you? I can hammer it out in a couple of hours."

"First of all, I don't have enough ATC bucks right now to pay you."

"How much have you got?" He wipes his mouth on a napkin and throws it onto his tray. He smells good, like Axe and soap. I'm preoccupied by that longer than I should be, but I snap out of it and remember that I'm going to be reimbursed. Still, the ATC bucks aren't in my account yet, so I answer him with a pretty measly number. He swallows. "You're a tough negotiator, Charlotte Pringle, but you have yourself a deal."

"Seriously?" I'm stunned. "You'll really do it? What about music?"

"I just said I would. And, yes, I'll figure *something* out for music."

"Can you have something to show me first thing tomorrow?" A guy at the table behind us gets up and knocks into me, which pushes me into Trent. I apologize.

Unfazed, he shakes his second milk carton and opens it. "No can do."

"What? Why not?" I realize I've never actually seen his work. What if it's as careless as Carter's? I can't risk it. I'd rather have my catawampus slides than misspelled, inconsistent ones.

"I have a lot to do, too. I'll get it done, but maybe not until tomorrow morning's lab, tomorrow afternoon at the latest."

"What if you have problems? What if you can't get—"

"Cut it out! I've got it, okay?" He chugs his carton of milk.

Isn't that what the pool said—*When will Charlotte cut it out?* Ralph won by answering *never*. I guess that's right. If I cut it out, it means I quit. Nobody's ever won anything by quitting. I'll *cut it out* after I win the showcase. Maybe. Right now I need to keep on top of things.

"Don't tell me to *cut it out*! My whole presentation has been a nightmare. You have no idea how important this is. So I'm going to have to approve the pictures and proofread your work, and—"

Even though he still has a third full carton of milk and half a sandwich left, he stands, and I have to look up to meet his eyes. He grabs his tray. "I know what I'm doing. Trust me."

I get up and follow him. "Why should I? I hardly know you, and I've never seen your work. What if you can't spell?"

He buses his tray. "You. Are. Infuriating." His eyes look grayish-brown today, and there's light stubble on his clenched jaw. He storms out of the cafeteria and leaves me standing there with my mouth open.

I'm infuriating? He's the one who's infuriating! He expects me to just trust him? He's so sure he has it all under control. How cocky is that?

But I have no choice. It's either trust him or have no PowerPoint.

And he did send me the link and the photos I asked for on time. He went the extra mile for the hospital fund-raiser, too. If I trust him, it might just turn out okay.

In the middle of the crowded cafeteria, as several people step around me to get to the garbage can, I realize something else: I want him to do it because I want to see him again.

— ✳ —

Lydia shows up with a Napanelli's pizza. Buffy, tail wagging, power-sniffs her and leaves slobber all over her jeans. "It's okay," she says, "these are my painting pants." Then she scratches behind Buffy's ears and says, "I've missed you, too, Buff."

After we eat, she helps me glue the flowers to combs and pins, so I can put them wherever I want in the models' hair. Then she volunteers to help with the props.

I show her the mess. "See, I told you they were bad."

She inspects a lollipop. "Uh, yeah. That's an understatement."

"Thanks a lot."

She laughs. "I have a few ideas, though," she says. "Rather than repainting them, we could wrap the lollipops in colored cellophane to cover up the oopsies and twist-tie it like a candy wrapper, and then let's use red duct tape over the candy cane swirls to make them more uniform."

"Wow! That's genius, Lyd! But where are we going to get the stuff?"

"At the dollar store," she says, grabbing her keys from her coat pocket. "But we'd better hurry. They close in an hour."

Lydia's right. The dollar store has rolls of cellophane

wrapping paper for five bucks, and colored duct tape for three dollars a roll. We get everything we need for less than twenty-five dollars.

"You're the bargain shopping master," I say in the car on the way home. "If only you'd been with me when I went to Michael's." I tell her about my experience with the vest lady, and she laughs.

We're still working on the candy canes—in the kitchen, though, because it's gotten even colder than before—when Mom gets home. "Hey, Lydia! Long time no see!"

"It's been a while." Lydia smiles and tears off another piece of tape. "Good to see you, Kim."

"Props are looking good, girls." Translation: *Much better than they did yesterday.*

"Thanks, Mom," I say, then add, "Sorry about your coffee."

"No problem." She shoots me a sly smile. "You can prep the pot for the morning. I'm tired and going to bed." Mom grabs a glass of wine and her e-reader. "Good night, girls. Tell your folks I said hi, Lydia."

"Will do."

After Lydia leaves, I get Mom's coffee ready and go to my room to work on my speech. Shea's info outlines the reasons for her choices, the styles, the fabrics, and the more technical terms like "bodice" and "serging." The rest of it—the overall theme, and our take on it—is all me. It sounds a little stilted, but it's informative and professional.

I choose my outfits for the morning—one for school and

one for the showcase—and practice my speech a few times in the mirror. I poke at the puffy circles under my eyes. Lydia called it right the other day—I look raggedy. All these late nights and stress are taking their toll on my skin.

My clock reads 2:29 a.m. The showcase is actually later *today*!

Win or lose, by this time tomorrow, I'll know the results. Of the showcase.

Of the bet.

Of my future.

twenty-five

0 days to the Winter Style Showcase!
Today is the day! OMG!

Friday morning I load my car before I do my hair and makeup because it's starting to snow, and I can't have a wet, flat, sticky mess on the most important day of the year. Mom offers to help, but I need to organize it my way, both in my car and in my head.

Then I dress in professional salon attire—black dress pants, a fitted white button-down shirt, and silver jewelry with just the right amount of bling.

"Good luck!" Mom calls when I'm walking out the door. "See you tonight."

The cos lab is swarming with people. First, there are the models. They show up as blank canvases—clean faces and hair—just as instructed. Then, there's us. Judging by how snappy everyone is and by how fast they're running around, the whole class feels like I do—excited, nervous, and more than a little nauseated. Finally, there are the five judges— four women and a guy. They're salon owners and educators from Jackson, Lansing, and Ann Arbor. Even though they're talking and joking with Ms. Garrett in the reception area, they are terrifying. They hold more than coffee cups in their hands—they hold my future.

Just before we get started, Ms. G asks what I've decided about music.

I arrange my chalks on a paper towel and say, "I've decided to trust a guy."

She winks at me. "Hope that works better for you than it ever has for me."

Oh my lanta! *Thanks, Ms. G! As if I weren't worried enough already!*

Then she announces, "Ladies and gents, are you ready?" Several of us nod, and I take a deep breath. "Many think the competition is tonight. While that is true, the serious work starts now—with part one—away from the audience. You'll complete a total style package for your model—makeup, hairstyle, and manicure."

Although poised as always, Ms. G's voice shakes a little. She must be nervous, too. "The judges, who will walk around the room, will score you on technique, professionalism, creativity, overall aesthetics, and adherence to theme. Remember, you may only use the tools at your stations. You should be prepared. You will be penalized for extraneous talking, so speak only when necessary and only to your client, no one else."

She starts the clock with spirit fingers and a cheery, "Ready, set, go!"

The morning flies by. And it's like a dream come true. First, I do Kaylee's makeup—moisturizer, foundation, eyeliner, sparkly lashes, several eye shadows, a dash of mascara, brow pencil, an appliqué, a few more accents, a touch of blush, and shimmery highlighting powder. Her lips—liner, color, gloss, all layered to look ombre—really finish the look. Perfect!

I use brighter colors in Kaylee's hair than on Wednesday so they will show up better onstage. I chalk and dry, curl and backcomb, sweep and pin, and finish with spray and the sugar flower combs. I'm pleased, so I hope the judges are, too. But I can't tell from their stone-serious expressions.

I try not to look around at my classmates too much, but I can't help it. Country braids, simple middle part with a daisy headband, cascading curls with upswept sides, and one badass bouffant. None of those worry me at all. Toby and Byron are going all-out silver and neon, including lips and hair, which is interesting. I wonder how that's all going to look put together. Shelby and Taylor go with pinks and a few other pastels. I hope that's not too close to ours. Joelle and Tasha's Medusa and feathered Hera look like something Tyra would go gaga over—I'm talking TV show professional.

The competition is off the charts.

Then there's Mackenzie. Her style looks nothing like her design. In fact, she has the whole hairline pulled up into a faux French braid, which hides almost all of the highlights I helped her with on Wednesday. I desperately want to tell her to leave the back down to accentuate what's already been done, but I'm not going to lose points over it. I keep my mouth shut and work on Kaylee's nails.

Over the Iridescent Iris base, I paint the candy swirls

and stripes I imagined in the props, except this time, I execute it all perfectly. Just as I'm finishing the top coat, Melody and Lily show up. Mackenzie is still slaving away on those pointless braids, so I decide to do Lily's hair. Mackenzie can do her nails. She's better at nails, anyway.

Lily wiggles and wants to get down from the chair and run around and touch everything. Trying to stay professional and avoid excess chatter, I give her a Tootsie Pop from my purse, which buys me the time to pull her hair into a high pony tail and put a few curls in it. When the candy's gone, she goes to sit in Melody's lap, but almost immediately insists that I do Melody's hair, too. Since I only have one model and Lily's hair didn't take long, I have time. Melody flashes me a smile. She knows this wasn't in my plan, but it keeps Lily happy long enough for me to swipe some blush across her cheeks and a quick coat of polish on her nails.

I curl Melody's strawberry blonde locks into spirals with a wand. Since I have a couple more sugar flowers left, I sweep up each of the sides. It's nothing spectacular, but it's pretty. She likes it, and I think I even see one of the judges smile in our direction for a split second.

During lunch, I look for Trent, but he's not in the cafeteria, the digital design lab, or the sound booth. What if he's not here at all? What if he's sick? What if I don't have my PowerPoint slides or my music? Other than the style and speeches, those are the most important elements of the entire presentation!

After our other classes, about three p.m., we have dress

rehearsal. It's supposed to be a run-through to iron out any technical glitches and make sure everyone is on the same page. When we get to the auditorium, it's all set up. The backdrop, which was painted by the multimedia artists, looks as if it's straight from a Disney movie. There's a wooded area with a little cottage and a castle high on a mountain and flowers and butterflies and magical flying fairies. It's beautiful.

There's also a ridiculous papier-mâché rock right in the middle of the stage. I ask why it's there and the set team practically bites my head off. "It's for depth and dimension!" It's a rock, and it's right where my models will be dancing. I move it off to the side a little, but about a minute later it's back where it was.

Team by team we run through our programs. While one team is onstage, the next is waiting in the wings. The rest of the teams sit in the audience and watch. At this point, there's little danger of anyone stealing another team's details.

Shelby, Taylor, and Gabriella are first. I have to admit that their presentation is nice. They stick with the song "I Can't Help Myself" and they have a pink Cadillac wooden prop that they set up in front of the rock, so nobody notices it. Their models also dance—a version of the twist. And their speeches and PowerPoint are overall professional. They're definitely formidable opponents.

The Emilys, not so much. Their speeches ramble on, and their designers' dresses look as if they copied them from Dorothy in *The Wizard of Oz*. Except, instead of ruby slippers, their models wear red cowboy boots and dance to country music. They use the rock to prop up their boots and pose. It's okay, I guess, but it's going to take a lot more than mediocre to win.

Joelle and Tasha have a really fierce style. The dresses are really detailed, and their music is intense. However, I'm not seeing how the myths fit with the theme. It'll be interesting to see what the judges think.

We're up after Toby and Byron, so I don't see their run-through. They must've raced through it. I heard their loud techno music, but by the time we got backstage, they were coming off, high-fiving each other. I have to admit, though, their costumes are certainly original. I would've thought that all that silver, even with splashes of neon, would be boring, but it looks pretty cool.

When Mackenzie and I get onstage, I call up to the sound booth, "Trent? Are you up there?"

A different, yet also familiar voice, calls back, "No. Trent's busy." Oh my lanta! It's Carter Reed. Just what I need!

"Did he give you my PowerPoint?" *Please say yes. Please say yes.*

"No."

"No?" My voice cracks. I'm about to melt down. "Have you heard from him? Do you know when it'll be ready?"

"No clue," says Carter pointedly. "It wasn't my job to follow up on it, remember? I expected something a bit more *professional* from *you*."

There's a collective "ooh" from the audience.

What an asshat. I hate him so much. I want to scream and throw the giant, ugly rock through the sound booth window. Instead, I sit on it and lean forward, putting my elbows on my knees and cupping my face in my hands.

Lily runs around onstage, Melody chasing after her.

"Charlotte?" It's Lydia. She's here! She touches my shoulder and asks, "Are you okay?"

"No," I mutter into my knees.

"We're on a tight schedule," says Carter, like God on high. Or the Devil in Hades.

"Give her a minute, will ya?" Lydia yells. She must know who it is, too. *Go, Lyd!* Then to Ms. G., "Can someone else go next, so Charlotte can regroup?"

Ms. G sends the next team on—the bikers—and then meets my team in the wings. "You guys are going to have to go without your PowerPoint. Just do the best you can. It'll all come together tonight, I'm sure." She doesn't sound convincing.

But we do what we can with what we have, which isn't much. There are no pictures, no music, no designers, and only two and a half models. I tell Kaylee to just pretend to change her hair because I won't be able to redo it.

Mackenzie's speech is pretty lame, but she says she's going to tweak it after rehearsal. I hope she does. I'm going to practice more, too, to combat my nerves. We go through everything several times to get the timing of the speech, the dancing, and the quick change right. But we get it.

In order:

1. I introduce Kaylee, talk about what I did and then move on to Shea's contributions.
2. Then I talk about Lily.
3. Mackenzie takes the mic and says her part.
4. Then I talk about Kayla's dress, and reintroduce Kaylee, giving all the info on her second hairstyle and the final dress.

As Kayla dances, some of her braids loosen. I tell Mackenzie, hoping she sprays them down. At this rate, they won't last the night.

Once rehearsal is over, I change into my dress and heels, redo my hair, and freshen my makeup. I ask Mackenzie when she's going to change, but she says she already has. Does this girl own anything other than khakis? We're grouped in teams in the band room, waiting for the show to start, when Trent finally shows up.

"Oh my lanta, where have you been?" I screech when he comes through the double doors. My heart races. I'm not sure if it's from relief, or nerves, or because the buffalo-check dress shirt he's wearing brings out the green in his eyes.

"Sorry," he says immediately. "I'm sure you're freaking out." That's an understatement.

"Uh, yeah," interrupts Mackenzie. "We're super stressed over here."

"I had a lot to do, not just for you guys," explains Trent to all of us. "But it's done. I've already uploaded and tested it in the sound booth. And it's perfect. You're all set."

"Did you use the pictures I wanted?" I ask. "And what about music?"

"Didn't you hear me?" he says. "I said it was perfect."

"I heard you, but—"

"And if you don't like it, there's no hope for you whatsoever."

"You are so full of yourself, you know that?"

He just stands there and looks down at me. One part of me wants to slap him. Another part wants to hug him—or kiss him—but I refuse to let my head go there. Well, maybe for a few seconds, but I quickly recover.

Lydia whispers in my ear. "Say *thank you*."

Right, right, of course. "Thank you," I say. "I hope it's good."

"You couldn't just stop at *thank you*, could you?" He shakes his head.

"Well . . ."

"You're welcome," he says and walks away.

twenty-six

Around 5:00 p.m., a guy from Subway delivers a ten-foot sandwich. Snow falls off his boots in chunks as he stomps through the backstage door. "It's really coming down out there. The weather guys got it wrong last week. *This* is the Snowpocalypse!"

"How much snow is there?" Ms. Garrett asks, as she pays for the food.

"Only a few inches right now, but it's just getting started," he says.

Ms. G tells him to be careful, and I text Mom and Dad to tell them the same thing. Mom texts that she's on her way back from Kalamazoo, while Dad and Pops will head over from the store. Oliver and Nina are coming to the showcase, too. Dad texts me the same thing five minutes later.

Even though my stomach is doing flip-flops, Ms. Garrett insists that everyone eat something. "We don't want anyone passing out onstage, now do we?" she says. *Of course we don't.* And after a sandwich and a bag of chips, I do feel much less jittery.

Five minutes to curtain time, Kaylee runs into the band room to tell me something—but I never get to hear it, because she slips in a puddle of melted snow before she can get to me. In what feels like slow motion, her arms flail and her face contorts. Her legs go out from under her, and suddenly she's splayed like a newborn giraffe on the floor, surrounded by mangled and broken sugar flowers.

I rush over. "Are you okay?"

When I try to pull her up, she yells out in pain.

"My foot." She reaches for it and winces. "I hurt my foot." Then she breaks down.

There's only a week before *Nutcracker.* She can't afford an injury. Kayla tries to comfort her. "Maybe it's not that bad. It could feel better by tomorrow. You could be back dancing by Monday." The braids Mackenzie did are still loose and uneven. Now pieces of hair have fallen into her face.

When Kaylee tries to stand and can't, Kayla insists that she go to the hospital and get it checked out. By then, Ms. Garrett is there and agrees. "I'll get the car," says Kayla.

"No!" I can't lose both my models minutes before the showcase!

But when everyone looks at me as if I'm totally heartless—as if I'm going to force Kaylee to hobble across the stage—Lydia steps in. "Without any models, Charlotte and Mackenzie don't have a presentation at all. I'll take her."

"Thank you, Lydia," says Ms. G. The rest of us thank her, too.

"No problem." Lydia grabs her purse. "Everything is under

control here. Well, except for this." She tells Kaylee she'll pull the car around and pick her up at the back door. In the meantime, Kayla and Mackenzie help her slip out of her dress and into her regular clothes.

And I thought things couldn't get any worse.

Then, out of nowhere, Melody says she'll stand in. "It'll be easier to corral little peanut here"—she gestures to Lily, who we just realize is picking sugar petals off the floor and eating them—"if I'm onstage anyway."

"Really? You'd do that?" I'm impressed that she's willing to step up, and we're lucky that she can fit into Kayla's dress, but to me, that isn't the point. The makeup and hair are what's important—and there goes my perfect updo, limping out the door. I did Melody's hair for fun, not for the competition.

I start to hyperventilate.

Ms. Judgy-hippie said that once you lose control it's hard to regain it. *Breathe, Charlotte,* I tell myself. One breath, two . . .

Kayla assures me that she has the quick dress-change covered, and gets into the first outfit.

If only I felt confident about her hair. The flower combs are slipping down and her braids are falling out. Did Mackenzie even spray it at all? I smooth the fly-away pieces over the braid with the sugar-flower combs, slip them back in place, and cover her head in hairspray. Mackenzie gives me a dirty look, but I don't care. She should've fixed it this afternoon.

Ms. G reminds me that the judges have already seen my final hairstyles, that the presentation is the icing on the cake.

"It's only one-fifth of your showcase grade," she says. Which is kind of her, but it's not about the grade. It's about placing. It's about winning. It's about being able to call the shots in my own life.

Ms. G hurries out to tell the other teams that I'll be going last. Mackenzie and Kayla take our place in the lineup behind the stage.

Melody puts on her dress and washes the pink gum paste off Lily's mouth. "It'll be okay. We've got this." She's so nice. I wonder if she has any idea how much I want to believe her.

In the suddenly quiet dressing room, I sit Melody down and take a look at her hair. Then I get what tools I have out of my purse and amp up her glam. I brighten a few sections of her hair with chalk. (Lily wants a couple streaks, too.) Then with a comb and some hair spray, I give her more height in her crown, and redo a few curls. I'm able to salvage one of the flowers from the floor—she says she's okay with it—and add it to the other two. My appliqué is gone, but I have an extra pair of lashes. A little more shadow, blush and shimmer, and she's good to go.

Then the three of us make our way backstage. Kayla is already there. I look at each of them, and then crouch down to meet Lily's eyes. "You look pretty," I tell her. "You're going to be terrific." Then I straighten up. "And so are you," I tell Melody and Kayla. "Thanks again, both of you. I couldn't have done any of this without you." Which is so true!

The sound of applause drifts toward us.

And then: "Charlotte and Mackenzie, you're up next," whispers the stage manager.

I'm trembling so much my speech paper flaps. Making sure nothing embarrassing could possibly happen tonight, I sweep my hands down the back of my black dress and check my shoes for toilet paper—just in case. Then I ask Melody if I have any stray lettuce in my teeth. She shakes her head.

I take a deep breath and stand as tall as I can.

"And now, for our final presentation," I hear Mr. Finn say. "Shea Walsh, this team's fashion designer, is currently on medical leave, so she won't be here this evening. Charlotte Pringle and Mackenzie Moore, the stylists responsible for hair, makeup, and overall concept, will be doing the work of three. Let's give them a hand!"

As the applause subsides, I hear some instrumental Irish-sounding flute music. It's subtle and melodic and mysterious and beautiful. What is this? Then I realize that it's the intro for the PowerPoint playing on the giant screen. Our Power-Point. Trent found the perfect music and figured a way to license it. I feel a smile spread across my face.

I *tap, tap, tap* my way across the stage with Mackenzie and wait behind the podium as the slides begin. It starts with Shea. There are pictures and captions of Shea measuring models, sewing at a machine, sewing by hand, holding pins in her mouth, and on her phone in one of our meetings. The last two get good laughs.

To segue to cos, there's a pic of Shea and me with that

awful first round of dresses. We're both frowning. Another picture comes in from the right and bumps that picture over. It's of me the day I had horrible bed head. The caption: *Good projects take lots of trial and error.* The next caption: *And even more hard work.* That stays through several pictures of Mackenzie (always in khakis) and me doing hair, manis and pedis, and tweaking the models' hair on Wednesday. There's even one of the mannequin hand poking out of my backpack.

The next picture is from Monday's run-through. I'm in jeans, doing a really bad leap across the stage. The caption reads: *Charlotte jumps in 110%.* When did Trent take all these pictures? No wonder it felt as if he was always around. He was.

The grand finale is from the hospital event. It begins with the benefit's name and date. There's a slide of me applying Sarah's lashes in her hospital bed. *Charlotte displays a passion and a heart for what she does.* There are a few long shots of Shelby and me getting the group ready. There's a group shot, then a few pics of us dancing. And finally, there's the posed picture of Sarah and me. There is an audible "awww" from the audience.

The final slide is a quote: *"I love helping people feel good about themselves. Everybody deserves that." –Charlotte Pringle*

As the music ends, I realize three things: First, Trent is just as good as he said he was. Second, he made me look amazing—much better than I am, I realize. (Is he in the sound booth? The audience? It's so dark, I can't see anyone.)

And third, I am speechless—which is tragic, because I'm standing on a stage in front of hundreds of people about to give *a speech*.

Our team is waiting in the wings for a signal to start.

But our speeches aren't right anymore. Kaylee's gone. Kayla's wearing her dresses, and Melody's wearing Kayla's. In all the chaos of trying to get the models straight, Mackenzie and I never rearranged our talking points.

We're going to have to wing it.

Mackenzie waits. She clearly hasn't figured out that the order has changed. Now that Kayla is first, she should start. I signal for her to go. She looks at me like she doesn't get it. The music is playing on a soft loop in the background and nothing is happening!

Nothing!

Everyone waits. It's awkward.

Finally, I start, "Hello, everyone!" The audience chuckles. "I'm Charlotte Pringle, and this is Mackenzie Moore." I point to her. "Our first model tonight is Kayla Wyatt. Isn't she lovely?"

The audience claps for Kayla as she dances onto the stage. Mackenzie realizes that she should be talking and looks at me expectantly. In order to make the transition seamless, though, I start with Shea's dress. "Shea Walsh, our fashion designer, created this dress from satin, sequins, and iridescent tulle."

Kayla slowly turns. "She meticulously cut and surged each petal of the skirt. It's perfect for a pixie frolicking in the enchanted forest." Kayla leaps and does a pirouette.

Mackenzie must think I've taken her spotlight because she's visibly pissed. I try to hand her the microphone, but she pushes it back to me. I try again, and she does it again. Awkward! "I'll let Mackenzie tell you about the cosmetology portion of Kayla's style." I shove the mic into her hand.

She takes it. Seething, she says, "First, I foiled pink and blue highlights into the sides and top of her hair. But Charlotte stepped in and redid them."

Oh my lanta! No, she didn't!

"I did her makeup, though," she says curtly. Instead of discussing technique and the fine points of Kayla's features, she rattles off a list of the products she used—brand and color—as if that matters. "Then I French braided her hairline and twisted the back up into an intricate updo." *That's* what that mess was supposed to be? "But Charlotte had to 'fix' that, too!" She even uses air quotes.

Mackenzie has moved beyond throwing me under the bus. She's hijacking it, backing it up, and hitting me again—in front of the whole school and all of our families!

"Charlotte did pretty much everything. The end. I'm out!" She literally drops the mic and walks offstage. Kayla glides offstage behind her.

Melody waits in the wings for a signal to keep going.

The stage is empty, except for me. The music continues playing.

Why doesn't this stage have a trapdoor? I could use one.

I want to run to the nearest bathroom stall and cry my

eyes out. Or crawl under the gigantic fake rock.

I deserve to fail. I've been a spoon-licking tyrant who's refused to listen or cut anyone some slack. Even my best friend couldn't confide in me because she knew I wouldn't understand. And I didn't.

I deserve to lose. Mom is out there in the audience probably devising unspeakable tortures like liberal arts colleges, advanced math classes, and sensible shoes. She's right. There are a lot of talented people at ATC, and I've never given them any credit.

I deserve to crash and burn. The spotlight is on me. Sweat rolls down my temples and down the small of my back. The auditorium is silent—awkward, embarrassing silence—as the entire audience watches me. My family, Shelby, Trent, Carter, and every classmate who's witnessed not only my disastrous team meetings, but my epic walk of shame. They're all out there, waiting and probably laughing their asses off.

Then I hear the words "Stop, drop, and roll." Is that Pops, or is it just in my head? Wherever it comes from, I get it now. Sometimes you can't control what's going to happen. Sometimes you can't even plan ahead. You just have to act in the moment.

I need to stop trying to control everything. Sometimes I have to drop my plans and roll with what comes.

Stop, drop, and roll.

So that's what I do.

I crumple my speech and throw it to the floor. "The next model is Melody. She's from our child development program." Melody glides into the spotlight. I describe the techniques I used to create this "sweet, yet classic hairstyle fit for a playful quest in an enchanted fairyland or a date with a handsome prince."

Kayla slips out of her dress in the wings as Melody glides past the rock. She might not be a dancer, but she moves fluidly around the stage, turning and stopping and posing at a candy cane. The pint-sized fairy Lily mimics her every move. The crowd loves it.

When Lily notices what Kayla's doing, she stops following Melody and sheds her clothes, too. Melody is ahead of her and doesn't see right away. But I see. Oh, how I wish I don't, but I do. Lily flits across the stage like a naked cherub.

Then it gets worse. Kayla is so busy watching what's happening onstage, she doesn't realize that she tears the back of the skirt completely off the bodice when she steps into it. *I should have had Gabriella sew over the basting*, I think. There's a flurry in the wings as other designers try to salvage the dress.

I continue to ad lib the hair style and makeup I did for Melody and Lily. ". . . to complete the sophisticated look of this sparkly pixie, I backcombed and smoothed across the crown . . ." That's not exactly what I did to Melody—more like Kaylee, who's not even there—but nobody is listening to me. Not with a stripper fairy center stage. Once Melody notices her naked shadow, she tries to take Lily's hand and lead her into the wings.

But Lily loves her moment in the limelight and refuses

to go. She screeches and pulls away. Now the chase is on—around the gray papier-mâché rock and across the stage. The crowd is cracking up. I'm stammering over my words, trying to keep it together, but failing miserably.

Melody catches Lily and scoops her up. Screaming, Lily pulls at Melody's hair, yanking out every flower and throwing them to the floor. Melody tightens her hold and whips her head back and forth, trying to avoid the clawing fists, but within seconds, her hair looks as if it's been through a tornado.

Finally, Melody manages to get Lily into the wings.

We still have Shea's other dress, even though it's in pieces. My (two) hairstyles and the best makeup I've ever done are sitting in the emergency department at Allegiance. Every single one of the models is either hurt, naked, melting down, or a mess right now. Two partners and a myriad of other team members have bailed.

Yet the music plays on and here I am.

I keep trying and trying to force a plan that just isn't meant to happen.

I give up. So what if I visit a few colleges? Is that so bad? Why not see what's out there?

Maybe Lydia and I can still be PICs of some other kind. Partners in cashmere, maybe. Or crème brulée. Or coaxial cable. Who knows? It doesn't matter. We'll figure out something.

What's beyond the World According to Charlotte? Could it include different ways of doing things, like store displays and school projects? And other people, too, like Nina and Hannah and Melody and Shelby and Trent. I won't know until I give them all a fair chance.

So much for my Grander Plan. Maybe I should just cut it out and see what happens. Starting with this nightmare of a presentation.

I hand the microphone to Mr. Finn and *tap, tap, tap* straight to the band room. I close the door behind me and exhale. Funny; I could cry now, but the tears don't come. Instead I'm overcome with relief. It's over. Disaster or not, it's over.

twenty-seven

I sit alone at the back of the auditorium for the awards. Melody and Kayla left because of the weather, and Lily's dad carried her to the car—he was surprised she lasted as long as she did with all the excitement and no nap. Her mom apologized for the meltdown, but I said Lily was a doll and thanked her for letting her be in the showcase. I have no idea where Mackenzie went, and I haven't seen Trent. I assume he's in the sound booth, but maybe he left, too. I wouldn't blame him if he did.

The crowd chatters around me, no doubt speculating who will win. I've pictured these awards so many times—standing onstage with Lydia, accepting first prize, basking in the glow, knowing that we'd nailed it. Having our whole futures—planned and on track—ahead of us.

Instead, I'm imagining countless boring college visits and fights with Mom, trying to convince her that cos really *is* the right choice for me. I wonder if there's a super-secret extra poll about how many things could and did go wrong during my presentation.

Mr. Finn taps his mic, and the crowd settles down.

I half-listen to his lame attempts at humor and his long-winded gratitude speech to "the judges, the staff, the parents, and our community." When he takes the envelopes from Ms. Garrett and Ms. White, I feel shaky.

I know I'm not going to win, and there's some relief in knowing that the worst is over. But deep down, there's a part of me still hoping. I've wanted this for so long, worked so hard. Until the names are read, anything's possible.

He opens the first envelope. After what feels like ten minutes, but is probably only a few seconds, he announces third place: Joelle and Tasha and the Bodacious Bodices. Their work was pretty amazing. I'm actually surprised they didn't place higher. They run onstage amid the cheers and applause, and Ms. G and Ms. White drape medals around their necks and hand them each an envelope. Mr. Finn tells the audience that third place winners get one-hundred-dollar gift cards—to Ulta for the cos team, Jo-Ann's for fashion design. Everyone applauds again.

Rachel from custodial services is sitting in front of me. She must've heard clapping behind her because she turns around and says, "Hey, Charlotte! I liked your presentation. Your dress looks nice on you, and your earrings are very sparkly." She's wearing a cable-knit sweater dress and knee-high boots, and her hair is curled.

I smile. "Thanks, Rachel. You look really pretty tonight, too." I wish everyone could only see what Rachel sees.

The audience settles down when Mr. Finn says, "And

now for the first runner up . . ." He opens the envelope and smiles. It's Toby and Byron and the Polyester Psychos! I guess their urban robot theme was pretty cool after all—lots of silver paint, neon lips and hair color, and break-dancing models. Who would've thought that slacker Toby could pull off second place?

They also get medals, but instead of gift certificates, the instructors hand them prize packages filled with "tools of their trades." Toby and Byron fist pump when they open professional hair dryers, flat irons, trimmers, and a comb and brush assortment. The designers rave over their sewing machines and notions kits, whatever those are.

It turns out that they edged past Joelle and Tasha because they had more service points. They went to a juvenile detention home and cut kids' hair.

Maybe Toby isn't such a slacker after all.

Mr. Finn rambles on about what a fantastic job everyone did, a bunch of BS about how we're all winners. He uses so many stock phrases and takes so long to get to his point that his speech is more annoying than it is suspenseful. I notice people shift in their chairs all around me.

". . . and the winners of this year's Arts and Trade Center Winter Style Showcase and one-thousand-dollar college scholarships are—"

I already know what Mr. Finn is going to say before he says it.

"Neon Taffeta, Shelby Cox, and Taylor Biggs!"

Their background music plays, and a whole section of the

audience stands and cheers. "Be sure to watch for these girls on Channel 6, JTV, and M-Live next week!" Mr. Finn adds.

Shelby, Taylor, Gabriella, and their other designer hurry down the aisle and onto the stage, where Ms. Garrett and Ms. White hug each of them and place their medals around their necks. Their prizes can't be handed to them. They're wheeled out on tables. Gabriella won a really fancy, high-tech sewing machine that makes the crowd go "ooh!" and a bigger notions kit. Shelby and Taylor each won rolling cabinets with everything needed "to take the state board exam and to set up a professional station."

They stand arm in arm and beam. Cameras flash everywhere.

It's as bright and exciting as I imagined it would be. Except Shelby Cox won. She's standing in the spotlight—in her darling peacock pumps—with everything she needs to propel her into a cos career. And I'm in the back, in the dark, alone. I didn't even place.

I stand, force a smile, and clap. I knew it was coming. I did.

But that doesn't make it easier.

What's worse is that I know Shelby deserves it. She and Taylor worked well together. They didn't compete for a guy, argue over ATC bucks, micromanage each other, or challenge Gabriella every step of the way. Nobody walked out on their meetings. And nobody felt like calling them out for acting bitchy.

Except for me. And I was wrong.

A lump forms in my throat. *I will not cry. I will congratulate the winners, and I'll do my best to mean it.*

After all, I wanted the interviews and prizes so I could brag about being the best. Shelby will appreciate the time in the TV studios because that's where she really wants to be. And the scholarship might be her only shot at college.

Mr. Finn taps his mic. "Could I have your attention for one more moment, please?" The crowd settles down.

"This semester's showcase has had its share of unique circumstances. The style design department and the ATC administration would like to recognize one student who had to roll with the punches a bit more frequently than the norm and has adapted to all the changes. As a result, we've adapted, too.

"Starting this year, we will be awarding a special prize at each showcase for the person or team who encounters added challenges, forges ahead, and overcomes.

"Our first recipient fought through team adjustments, loss of funding, and many last-minute snafus—and still gave her all onstage." Is he talking about *me*?

"Her presentation, though at times painful to watch"— the audience laughs—"perfectly illustrated the tenacity and adaptability her instructors and I have witnessed these past few weeks.

"Please give a round of applause for our first 'Through Thick and Thin Award' winner, Charlotte Pringle! Charlotte, will you please come up here?"

This was not the award I'd pictured myself getting. I

wanted to be recognized and remembered for excellence in cosmetology, not for being a such a colossal failure that people can't stop talking—and joking—about it. But, on the other hand, at least some people noticed what I was up against, and maybe that I wasn't to blame for *everything*.

About halfway down the aisle, I hear Pops say to Dad, "*Our* Charlotte? Adaptable? Who knew?"

The audience rises again and applauds.

When I get onstage, both Ms. G and Mr. Finn hug me. Ms. G hands me a bottle of thickening hairspray and a pair of thinning shears wrapped together with red ribbon. Ha! "The Thick and Thin Award"! Clever! And Mr. Finn gives me a certificate and a twenty-five-dollar gift card to Meijer. Dad will love *that*.

A few cameras flash.

I take the mic from Mr. Finn and say, "Thank you! I gladly accept . . ." What was this award officially for again? Something about overcoming obstacles? Whatever they call it, I'm calling it the same thing Grandmother would. ". . . the booby prize!"

The crowd laughs, and from the corner of the stage Toby calls, "You mean the *booty* prize!" He shakes his ass, and everyone who hears him cracks up. Except Mr. Finn.

Ms. G takes the mic and instructs everyone to "drive carefully, as the roads have become quite slick." Then she thanks everyone, Ms. White thanks everyone, Mr. Finn thanks everyone . . .

And to all a good night.

⌣ ✳ ⌢

In band room, while I'm gathering my stuff, Mom bursts into the room, strides over to me, and wraps me in a hug. I can't remember the last time Mom hugged me. I'm not sure how to react.

"That was the biggest train wreck I've ever seen." She laughs into my hair.

"Thanks, Mom." I let out a deep sigh.

She pulls away and sits in a chair while I shove everything into my purple duffel. "But it also took my breath away." I stop in my tracks. She tugs me over to sit next to her, and makes sure I hear what she has to say. "Those pictures— they were amazing. You're really in your element here. Even more than at home or at the store. I'm sorry I haven't noticed before." The words "I'm sorry" echo in my head. "And you with those kids at the hospital—wow! You really made an impact."

She couldn't have gotten that from *my* presentation. It must have been how Trent portrayed me. That PowerPoint must have been even better than I realized. Mom doesn't apologize or change her mind easily. If Trent's still around, I need to thank him. I don't see him, though.

"Thanks, Mom." This time I mean it.

And I can't stop from asking: "So, does this mean the bet is off? I can skip the college visits, even though I didn't place?"

My mother grins. "Oh, no! I never said that. A bet's a bet." They will never make a Hallmark or Folgers commercial based on our mother/daughter moments. Not ever. "But we might be able to reschedule them—after the hair show."

"Deal!" I say. Shelby is on the other side of the room packing up her stuff. Her mom is riffling through her cabinet and commenting on every product and styling tool when Ms. G comes into the room. Then Mrs. Cox and Ms. G hug and make small talk and beam at Shelby.

A month ago I would've assumed Shelby's win was because of Ms. G's friendship with her mom. Now I know better. Shelby's a good cosmetologist. She deserves this, and more. She should get a shot at college if she wants it, and since she just won a thousand-dollar scholarship, maybe her mom will let her go.

My phone goes off, so I grab my purse. "Mom? Is there any way I could bring a friend when I visit Grandmother and the colleges?"

"I don't see any reason why not. Who? Lydia?"

"No, somebody else." I wave across the room to Shelby, who's stuck between her mom and Ms. G, talking loudly and laughing about beauty school "back in their day." I mouth "Congratulations!" and she mouths back "Thanks."

I finally unearth my phone. I hear Mom's go off, too. We both have texts.

We read them at the same time. "Oh my lanta!" I yelp. "Nina's water broke."

twenty-eight

Dad and Pops burst through the band room doors. "Did you hear?" asks Dad.

"Yes!" Mom says. "What happened?"

"When the show was over, Nina asked Oliver to take her home. She didn't feel very well," says Dad. "So they left before the awards."

"By the way, kiddo"—Pops puts his arm around me—"that was quite a show!"

"Yeah . . ." What else can I say?

"What about Nina?" Mom looks as if she's about to jump out of her skin.

"Well, I guess they got home okay, but as soon as Nina got out of the car, *splash!*" Dad gestures as if he's talking about a bomb or fireworks, not amniotic fluid. "So they jumped back in the car and went to the hospital."

"Okay," says Mom, taking command. "Let's get Charlotte packed up so we can get out of here and up to Allegiance."

"I haven't set foot in a hospital since Caroline died," says Pops, "and I'm not about to start now."

Dad picks up a couple of my lollipop props. "Fine. I'll drop you off first."

While we're scraping off and loading the car, Mom gets a frantic call from Oliver. Nina doesn't have her glasses, and even though her contacts are killing her, she refuses to take them out. "How am I supposed to *see*, Oliver?" I hear her through Mom's phone.

Oh my lanta! Here we go!

When Mom hangs up, she says, "I'll run to Ollie and Nina's, grab Nina's glasses and some sweats for Oliver. Then I'll go home, change my clothes, and pick up a phone charger, my e-reader, and whatever anyone else needs in the meantime. Looks like it's going to be a long night." She fishes her keys from her purse and heads to her car.

Dad slams my trunk. "Want me to follow you home before taking Pops home? It's pretty icy."

"No, it's fine." The sooner I can get out of the freezing wind the better. "We're all anxious to get to the hospital. It'll be faster if we split up."

"Okay." He hugs me. "Good job tonight. I'm proud of you."

Good job is a stretch, but I'll take it. "Thanks, Dad."

When I get in the car, Dad adds, "Wait for Mom and ride with her."

I say I will. Then I start my car and crank the heat.

The roads are slicker than I thought. I grip the steering wheel tightly and slow down. I repeat the Michigan winter slogan from driver's ed.: *Take it slow in ice and snow.*

I laugh when I think about how sure I was that I was going to win tonight. The only first I got was the first booby prize. I know Mr. Finn and Ms. G probably thought they were doing something nice, but to me, it's a reminder that my project was a disaster. If I'd really overcome obstacles, I'd have won. Winning despite challenges is the definition of overcoming, not falling on your face. I set a new goal: to win the senior showcase. Except this time I won't micromanage our team, and I'll stop, drop, and roll as much as humanly possible. Or at least as much as Charlotte-ly possible.

After a week of late-night work sessions, all I want to do is watch mindless TV in the hospital waiting room with the rest of the family, and wait for the newest Pringle girl to make her debut. None of that has anything to do with me. It's a relief not being "on," not having a Grand Plan. All we can do is wait. My niece has her own Grand Plan.

At the first intersection past the school, Dad and Pops go left, and I drive straight ahead. In the middle of the intersection the back of my car fishtails a bit, but I get through okay.

About a half mile away there's a snowdrift across the road. It looks pretty minor—about an inch, two tops, but when I hit it, I lose control of my car.

Oh, shit! Oh, shit! Oh, shit!

I slide sideways. No matter how I turn the wheel, I can't regain traction.

I hit a speed limit sign and land solidly in the ditch.

I'm shaking. My heart is racing.

The car behind me stops, and the driver rolls down her

passenger window. I roll down mine, too. "You okay?" she asks.

"Yeah," I say. "I'm going to call my dad. He's just ahead of me."

"Okay, hon. Take it easy." She rolls her window back up and continues on. I roll mine up, too—it's freezing.

Several minutes and a few more cars pass as I frantically search for my purse and my phone. My wipers are still on, back and forth, back and forth, swishing away the melting snow. My heat is on full blast, but my car hasn't warmed up enough yet. It's still blowing cold air.

I find my purse and dig for my phone. Where is it? I can't find it. My hand reaches from pocket to pocket, zips and searches and re-zips like it has a mind of its own. Why didn't I just let Dad follow me?

There's a knock on the window, and my heart starts racing again.

"Charlotte? Are you all right?" It's Trent. He's wearing a black ski jacket and thick gloves. There's a giant 4 x 4 truck in front of me, belching exhaust in my headlights.

I roll down my window and nod. "Uh-huh. Not sure about my car, though."

"It looks okay from here," he says, "but we won't know for sure until I pull you out of there. You should be back on the road and on your way in a little while."

The snow is still coming down hard. I don't want to *be on my way*. Alone. Just to wind up in another ditch. Besides,

Trent's already done enough. I owe him so much already. The last thing I need is for him to rescue me—again.

"You don't have to do that," I say. "I'll just call my dad." As soon as I find my phone.

"Does he have four-wheel drive?" he asks.

"He has Triple-A." Then I blurt, "My sister-in-law is having a baby right now. Our whole family's trying to get to the hospital."

"Whoa," he says. "Let's not waste time, then. It'll be hours before a tow truck will get here in this weather. I'm sure they're swamped. I'll just take you there. You can deal with your car later."

That's the best idea I've ever heard. After all the embarrassing things that have happened lately, I'm tired of trying to save face and be brave. I want out of this ditch and into some warm clothes ASAP.

I unbuckle my seat belt, and he opens the door. When the dome light pops on, I see my phone, right in the console where I usually put it.

Phone, purse, and keys in hand, I start to step from the car—until I remember that I'm in three-inch heels in the middle of a snowbank. Trent notices, too, and says, "Want some help?"

"How, as in you'll *carry me*?" Um, no, thanks!

"It's either that or trudge through this." He stares at me. "And with what you're wearing, I wouldn't suggest it."

I ignore him and get out of the car as gracefully as I can.

Bare legs, three-inch heels, and over a foot of snow are not a great combination. I yelp. He tries to take my arm, but I pull away.

"I can do it." I take a step and lose my shoe in the snow. Because my skirt is too short to allow me to bend over, I crouch down to dig it out, yelp again, and drop my phone. By the time I've collected everything I'm soaking wet, and I'm not just shivering, I'm shaking.

"What, is this a new workout? Snow squats?" he teases.

"Shut up." I wade out of the snowbank onto the slippery road, then take tiny baby steps to keep from falling.

He holds my arm to steady me. This time I don't pull away. I do not want to fall on my butt. Not on an icy road. Not in front of him. Not in this skirt.

Even though I'm about to die of hypothermia, the dim light from a decorative lamppost in the next yard and the snow silently falling all around us are beautiful, as if we're inside a snow globe. Maybe even a little romantic. Then a gust of wind blows snow up my skirt and I brush away the thought.

When we get to his 4 x 4, I realize that it's practically a monster truck. In pants, I could just make it up—but this skirt is way too tight and short. There's no step, no running board, no anything. "How do you get up there?" I ask, teeth beginning to chatter.

"In a skirt? No clue. I've never worn one." He laughs. "Need a boost?"

There is no modest way to get into this truck without

revealing everything, and tonight's been embarrassing enough already.

Next thing I know, his arms are around my lower back in a warm, gentle hug. His eyelashes catch a few stray snowflakes. He's so close that I see a spray of freckles across his pink nose and cheeks, and his breath smells like peppermint.

He's going to kiss me. I'm sure of it this time. He's caught up in the snow globe, too. I close my eyes, tilt my head, and wait. Ready. He holds me even tighter. I must be really numb because it feels like I'm floating.

Trent grunts. "Can you help a little bit, please?"

I open my eyes. Oh, God! He's not kissing me. He's lifting me into the truck! I reach in, grab the steering wheel, step onto the floorboard, and slide onto the seat. "Thanks." I scoot over to make room for him.

Please, please, please don't have noticed my premature kiss pose—again.

He says nothing, just turns the blasting heat vent toward me. *Thank you!*

I call my dad. "Charlotte? Where are you?" He sounds panicked. "You're not on ninety-four, are you?"

"I'm fine," I say. "But my car's in a ditch. Not on ninety-four. Why?"

"There was an accident," he says. "Your mother"—*Oh, God! Mom. Accident. I-94. No!*—"is stuck in traffic. She says it's a skating rink out there. It's closed for miles. Where are you?"

I tell him what happened and that Trent's taking me directly to Allegiance.

"You're lucky he was right there," Dad sounds relieved. "We'll call Triple-A later. Just as long as you're all right."

"I am."

"So who's this *Trent*?" Dad asks. "You know him, right? He's not just some random guy in a four-by-four?"

"Yes, I know him," I say. "He did the PowerPoint for my showcase presentation."

"Oh, wow," Dad sounds impressed. "Someone special, then?"

"Dad!"

"Sorry."

I change the subject. "So Mom's fine?"

"Yes. She's just going to be a while."

"How's Nina?" I ask.

"Haven't heard," he says. "Oliver's with her. I'm on my way to the fourth-floor waiting room now. It's just off the elevator. Can't miss it. See you when you get here. Take your time and avoid ninety-four."

When I hang up the phone, I text Mom, briefly explaining what happened and asking her to bring me a change of clothes.

I set my phone on the seat and turn to Trent. "Thank you for doing this. And for the PowerPoint. I owe you big-time."

"Don't worry." He keeps his eyes on the road, but smiles. "I'll add it to my invoice."

Great! This will probably cancel out all my ATC bucks— and then some. It's fitting, I decide, that the biggest loser will have the biggest deficit.

"Where did you get all those pictures?" I ask after a moment.

"I took most of them, but I also got a few from class-mates." He turns on his blinker to turn left. "We all stock-pile pics on the server because we never know what we'll need."

"That's cool." Digital design sounds less competitive than cos. Or is that just me? For the senior showcase, maybe I could work *with* Shelby, instead of *against* her.

"I'm glad I took a ton at the wellness fair and around school," he continues. "I was able to do some trading." The truck slides a little on the turn, and I steady myself against the armrest. "Don't worry—we're fine. I love driving in this stuff."

"I'm glad *someone* does." He laughs. I've only been driv-ing for two years. Last year, I just had my learner's permit, and I refused to drive when it snowed. Now that I've slid off the road, I hate it even more.

The rest of the way to the hospital Trent and I talk about our families. I learn that he's the youngest of six kids—the only boy—and he has two nephews and a niece. He has two dogs—a German shepherd and a Yorkie—and his oldest sis-ter is a cosmetologist. "She's a lot like you," he says. Stylish? Smart? Fun? "She's bossy, too."

As he laughs—what is with this guy and his laugh?—I fume and turn on the radio. Some country tune blares out, and I immediately hit the button for my favorite rock station. Before Arctic Monkeys can even finish their guitar solo, Trent changes it back. "My truck, my station."

"And *I'm* bossy?" I tap the rearview mirror. "Might want to look in the mirror." He just grins.

The ashtray of the truck is full of individually wrapped peppermint Life Savers. He offers me one. I unwrap it and pop it in my mouth just as he turns into the hospital parking lot.

He pulls up to the front entrance and I open my door. It's a long way down. I brace myself for an awkward dismount, but before I realize it, Trent is there helping me down, in much the same way he'd lifted me up, only slightly less awkward.

Before he lets go, he whispers softly into my ear, "When I kiss you, you won't have to guess if it's coming." I melt. "You'll know. Because you'll initiate the kiss."

He knew!

"Never!" I push him away.

"Gonna!" I slam his truck door.

"Happen!" I stomp through the automatic entrance and into the hospital lobby.

Is he watching? Will he follow? I refuse to turn around. When I get to the elevators, I push the button for "Up," then sneak a look. He's not there.

Just as the elevator dings and the doors open, I realize that I don't have my purse or my phone. I hurry back outside, but Trent's truck is gone.

twenty-nine

I step out of the elevator onto the fourth floor about 10:30—still freezing and, now, fuming as well—and as soon as I enter the waiting room, I spot Dad on the phone. Holding a full bottle of water, he mouths *Mom*, but before he can end the call, a nurse hurries in and asks, "Is this Charlotte?"

"What's the matter?" I ask.

"Nina is asking for you."

Me? Why? I leave my coat with Dad and follow the nurse through some locked double doors—we have to be buzzed through—down a hall and into a labor-and-delivery room. I peek around a pastel printed curtain at Nina lying in bed. Oliver is sitting next to her looking sort of rumpled.

"Hey," I wave.

"Charlotte!" Nina is crying. "I can't do this!"

Oliver leans forward and takes her hand. "Oh, Neen . . . What can I do?"

"You've done enough, thank you!" She pulls her hand away. To me she says, "My eyes are dry and scratchy! I forgot to grab my glasses. And *he* just doesn't get it. And then, they put an IV in my arm, and he almost passed out. The nurse told him to sit down. He can't even handle an IV—how's he going to be able to handle . . . you know?" She bursts into tears.

I *do* know. I saw the movie. An IV is the least of the horror.

I sit on the edge of her bed. "First of all, pull yourself together."

Oliver objects. "Don't talk to her like—"

"Shut up, Oliver." Nina wipes her eyes with the edge of the sheet.

I stare into Nina's eyes with faux-seriousness and intone, "Take a full cleansing breath in." She has to giggle. Still imitating Ms. Judgy-hippie, I add, "No, Nina, I'm serious." She does it. "Now exhale all the negative shit from the day."

After a few rounds of this—in which I drop the soothing voice and we all relax, even Oliver—I convince Nina to take out her contacts. I tell her that Mom will be there soon with her glasses, and in the meantime, she can close her eyes and try to sleep in between contractions. I don't need to remind her that she should rest up before it gets harder; she already knows that. She listens to me, and Oliver seems impressed.

Soon the nurse comes back to check in.

"How's she doing?" I ask, all professionalism.

"Going much faster than usual. This baby is anxious to get here." After a few more questions from me—How dilated is she? How far apart are her contractions? Can she have ice chips?—the nurse asks Nina if she wants an epidural.

"Oh, hell yes," Nina says.

I see the contraction on the monitor before Nina says anything. It's a big one. Soon she's panting, her eyes pressed closed. "Relax, Nina. You're tensing." She does. I breathe along with her. Within a couple of minutes, the pain has passed.

Oliver watches this all like a spectator, pouting a little because it's clear that Nina no longer takes his birth-assist skills seriously. I have to agree with her—who faints at the sight of an IV? We see them on TV all the time. But I still feel kind of bad for him. I mean, this is his daughter, too.

While we wait for the anesthesiologist, I continue channeling Ms. Judgy-hippie and breathing with Nina. In between contractions, I tell her about my booby prize, then about sliding into the ditch and Trent rescuing me. I don't tell her about the kiss fiasco.

The nurses ask Oliver and me to leave while they start the epidural—it's hospital policy. As we walk down the hall to the waiting room, Oliver hugs me. "Thank you," he says. "Before you got here she was miserable and hysterical and, well, mean. I didn't know what to do."

"I'd say that if you'd skipped the Wings game you would have, but I'm sure you've already heard that." We tap the automatic door opener and walk through it.

"Only about a million times."

The waiting room is pretty empty. There's a guy curled up on a tiny love seat with a flimsy blanket, and he doesn't look comfortable. Dad sits on the floor with his back against the wall and his legs stretched out. In his hands is a copy of

People, and next to him is his empty water bottle, a granola bar wrapper, and—

"Where did my purse come from?" I ask as I grab it.

"Trent brought it," Dad replies, as if they're best buddies or something.

I try to sound nonchalant. "Really? Where is he?"

"He's getting your car out of the ditch." Dad turns the page. "Another day, another celebrity break-up—"

In a flash I pluck the magazine from his hand. *"What?* You asked him to get my car?"

Dad shrugs. "He offered."

"Oh my lanta! *Dad!"*

As Oliver smirks, our father reclaims his copy of *People,* but before he can open it again, Lydia walks in. She looks wiped.

"Lyd! What are *you* doing here?"

"I've *been* here!" she tells me. "For hours. The ER is over-the-top cray tonight."

"Thanks so much for taking Kaylee. I really appreciate it."

"No problem. Her ankle's going to be okay—it's just a little sprain. Don't know if she'll be able to dance on it, though. Her parents took her home a little while ago." She looks at me expectantly. "So how did it go?"

I duck the question. "How did you know we would be here?"

"Nina's Facebook status said that her water broke. And she checked in here."

"Sit down," says Dad to Lydia. "How's life been treating you?" Uh-oh. He's been alone in the waiting room too long.

Lydia joins Dad on the floor. He asks about school, her parents, and Patti Cakes. And she actually answers him! She doesn't snap or accuse him of prying or anything.

Mom rushes in as if she's run all the way from the interstate. "What's going on?" she pants. She's carrying enough bags of supplies for a two-week trip.

The sleeping guy sits up, says, "End of the second period, the Wings just scored." We all look from him to the documentary about narwhals on TV. Then he mumbles something incoherent, leans against the wall, and pulls the blanket up under his chin, still sound asleep.

Oliver fills her in, including telling her that I was the only one who could calm Nina down, and that Ms. Judgy-hippie's breathing exercise helped him, too.

"See?" she says to me. "You *were* the right person to go to that class." More like the only person who didn't have plans, but it turned out pretty well. I won't admit that to Mom, though.

Then she reaches into one of the tote bags and hands me a pair of jeans, a baggy T, and some casual tennis shoes. I knew she had a diabolical plan to get me in comfortable shoes! But after a whole day in these heels, I'm grateful. I grab my purse and go to the bathroom across the hall, where I change and pull off my false eyelashes. Then I wash off my makeup with a wet paper towel, put up my hair, and cover my face with moisturizer. The hospital air is totally dehy-drating.

The nurse returns and says we can go back to see Nina. Mom and Oliver are off like a shot. I sit down with Dad and Lydia.

Within a few minutes, my phone pings from the front pocket of my purse. The last person to touch my bag was Trent. He carried it all the way up to the family waiting room. Did he hold it like a sack of potatoes, all cute and goofy, like the last time he carried it through the hospital? Did he snoop around in it?

I peek inside, as if I'd be able to tell if he had. There's an envelope in there. I open it and find an invoice from Trent Rockwell Creations. It's dated three days ago.

Here's where I find out how much I'll be in the red.

Then I notice the total amount due: *One kiss.* Payment due: *At **client's** discretion, and not a moment sooner.*

"What's that?" Lydia asks.

"Just a bill," I say, but from the way my pulse is fluttering, I really should say it's a love note.

"Who texted you?"

I check. "Oliver. Nina's getting closer. She wants me to go back there."

"What are you waiting for?" Dad asks. Lydia starts to shoo me down the hall. But they don't know. They didn't see the movie. I'd rather stay here and learn about narwhals and see the baby after her bath. I'm scared.

But I go anyway. It's okay to be scared, to not know what's going to happen, to not be in control.

I stop, drop, and buzz the door to labor and delivery.

"May I help you?" says the box on the wall.

"I'm here for Nina Pringle."

"And your relationship is?"

"She's my sister."

thirty

That movie Ms. Judgy-hippie showed us is a crock of crap. All it showed was blood and goo and pain and horror. But in real life, childbirth is so much more than that. It's waiting—lots and lots of waiting—for the next contraction, for ten centimeters' dilation, for the doctor to arrive. (It never takes that long on TV.) It's seeing people you thought you knew become better versions of themselves, full of surprises. It's meeting a whole new person, and falling instantly in love.

Nina is a warrior. After she's been laboring for over eight hours, the contractions get really intense. She doesn't whine. She doesn't complain. She focuses and breathes—which sometimes sounds like humming—and does what she needs to do.

Then, when she's clearly mentally and physically exhausted, she pushes. If someone were filming for one of those classes, it might seem gory—primal—but as the moment grows closer and closer and adrenaline surges through the room, it's amazing and beautiful and impressive as hell.

My dumbass goon brother doesn't pass out. He whispers

sweet things to his wife, cuts the cord when his daughter is born, and cries harder than the baby.

Mom doesn't tell Nina what to do or criticize anyone. She says nothing—but she grabs my left hand and nestles it under her chin and beams so wide I think her cheeks might rip open.

Then Nina snuggles her wide-eyed, scrawny newborn—skin to skin—and thanks God for epidurals. Her hair is sweaty and clinging to her face. She looks kind of pale and overall spent. But she's the prettiest I've ever seen her.

The baby is wrinkly and gooey and kind of blue. Her head looks like a muskmelon, and she has Vaseline-looking goop in her milky eyes.

She's absolutely perfect!

Ms. Judgy-hippie needs a lesson in childbirth. It's not about being prepared for what's going to happen. It's about going in blind and being knocked off-kilter and getting caught up in the messy moment, even though nothing will ever be the same again. It's way better than a stupid documentary. Hell, it's even better than a flipping Folgers or Hallmark commercial.

"Do you want to hold her?" the nurse asks me after Oliver and Mom have each had their turns.

"Sure." I take the tiny, squirmy, wrapped-up bundle—carefully, so I don't break her. I've never held a baby this new before.

"What's her name?" I ask.

Nina says, "Caroline Olivia Pringle."

After Grandma! Pops and Dad will love that. I wonder who won the pool.

"Beautiful!" Mom leans in to kiss the baby in my arms—my niece!—and starts singing "Sweet Caroline." Then the nurses join in, "Ba ba ba." Mom keeps humming the song, but softer, like a lullaby. One of the nurses sways to the tune as she tidies up around us.

⁓ ✳ ⁓

Oliver and I go out to tell Dad. Blanket guy is gone. The TV is now showing an infomercial for some Secrets 2 Success weight loss program. It looks like a scam.

Dad and Lydia are both smiling as if they've been up to something.

"Lydia has some news for you." Dad gathers his garbage—four empty water bottles, two granola bar wrappers, and a banana peel—and says, "I'll let her tell you. Because *I'm* going to meet my granddaughter." He stops at the trash can by the elevators on his way down the hall with Oliver.

"Your dad and I have been talking all night, and we might have a solution to my parents' problems." Lyd looks happier than I've seen her in a very long time.

"See?" I break in. "I told you my dad would—"

"It's not money, Charlotte," she says. "It's space."

"Space?"

"Yes." She moves her purse, so I can sit next to her. "Your dad says he's been stressed about who's going to run the bakery/deli full-time now. You know, since that Hannah girl is moving, and Nina's going on maternity leave."

"So you and your mom are coming back to Pringle's? Yay!"

"Listen, will you?" she snaps.

I zip my lip.

"All that subcontracting and synergy stuff from school has really sunk in," she explains. "Your dad has a bakery with no one to run it, and we have a bakery business with no building. I suggested that we subcontract the space from him. That way we can keep Patti Cakes, but with less overhead so we can pay off our debt. And he'll get more business without all the staffing and ordering hassles."

"Oh my lanta, Lyd! That's a fabulous idea!"

"Your dad and I are going to talk to my mom and dad about it later today."

"Awesome!" I high-five her. "We'll get to work together again!"

She smiles. "He also told me about the showcase."

"He did?" I hide my face behind my hand. "Everything?"

"Of course." She nods. "We had a lot of time to kill. I'm sorry I wasn't there."

"It was like a runaway freight train," I say. "You couldn't have stopped it. I'm glad you're here now, though."

"Me too."

Then I see my keys sticking out of my front purse pocket. I grab them. "When did these get here? I thought Dad gave them to Trent."

"He did," says Lydia. "Trent just brought them—and your car—back."

"When?"

"He was by the elevator when you walked in here. You didn't see him?"

"No." Is he still here? Can I catch him?

"Your dad offered to pay him, but he said you'd take care of it. What does that mean? What's going on with you two?"

I don't explain—or even think. "I'll be back," I say, racing for an open elevator. (Much easier in tennis shoes.) Some nurses are getting on, but they hold it.

Since it's so early in the morning, I'm sprinting through an empty lobby and parking lot. It's stopped snowing, and the roads are scraped. Trent's truck exits the parking structure. I run, flailing my arms and yelling his name, but he turns the other way.

The sky is pink and purple and blue as the sun peeks around the buildings downtown—seeming even brighter because of the snow (and probably my sleep deprivation). It's really still and quiet. Too quiet. I'm standing there in the middle of a practically empty visitors' lot—ultra awake— without a coat. It's cold, but I hardly feel it.

I missed him. Again.

Then I see the rear bumper of his truck and taillights. He's backing up on Michigan Avenue. Good thing there aren't any other cars on the road right now. He backs past the entry drive and then pulls in. I watch and can't help smiling, no matter how hard I try not to.

He rolls down his window. "I thought that was you," he says over the rumbling engine, "but I'd already started turning. What are you doing out here?"

"I want to talk to you," I yell. "About that bill."

He sighs. "Charlotte, it's been a long night. Just forget it, all right?"

"No! I won't forget it." I open the door to his truck. Since I'm wearing jeans now, I'm able to get a foothold and climb up. I stand on the floorboard holding on to the sides of the cab and stare at him. His hair is tussled, cute. And he still smells like peppermint.

"What are you doing?" He shifts the truck into park. "Be careful."

"I want to dispute the total on that invoice. We never discussed payment, and for you to assume—"

"I know. I know. I should've known you'd freak out. I shouldn't have—just forget it," he says. "You don't have to—"

"Do you really think that creating a stunning PowerPoint presentation, rescuing me from a snowbank, driving me across town in a blizzard, returning the purse I left in your truck, pulling my car out of a ditch, and delivering it to me entitles you to *one kiss?*"

He tips his head back and bangs it on his headrest repeatedly. "You're killing me! You know that? I was just trying to . . . *argh!* You're imposs—"

I lean into the cab, cup my hands behind his head, and kiss him full on the mouth.

He wraps his arms around my waist, pulling me into the

truck. The steering wheel digs into me, so he scoots to the middle of the seat. I tumble in next to him, and he kisses me back.

His lips are soft and strong at the same time. I melt into him. I become part of the navy blue pleather. I could kiss him forever.

Then he pulls away. "I've never seen you without makeup."

I cover my face. Oh my lanta! I forgot. I must be delirious from lack of sleep.

He pulls my hands away, smiles, and kisses my nose. "Stop. I've wanted to kiss you since the first time we talked, in the hallway. I'm glad I didn't have to do it with one eye open." When I look confused, he adds, "You know, to guard against the tarantulas!" I swat at him, and he laughs.

"You're infuriating!" I say.

"You like infuriating. Admit it."

"Never!" I do my best not to smile, but it starts to peek through. He kisses me again. "Hey! I've already paid my bill. *In full.*" He pulls away in a huff. I'm not sure if he's joking. I tell him I was, but he still pouts. I lean in and kiss him and keep kissing him until he kisses me back.

Then I hear Mom. "Charlotte?"

Mom, Dad, Lydia, and Oliver are standing outside of Trent's truck. Their faces contain about a million questions.

Except for Dad. He says, "Nina's resting. We're going for breakfast. You guys coming?"

I look at Trent, and he nods. "We'll follow you."

We invite Lydia to ride with us. She hands up my coat

and purse first, and I help her climb up. About halfway down Michigan Avenue, I ask Trent, "Are there any other cute digital dudes in your class? You know, that aren't cheating, lying asshats like Carter Reed?"

"Maybe," he says. "Why?"

"Charlotte," Lydia warns. "You're taking over again."

"Just wondering," I say. "Lydia and I like to date friends."

"So we're dating now?" he asks.

"No. Just planning ahead," I say.

"Is she as difficult as you are?"

Lydia laughs. "Nobody's *that* difficult."

"Hey, I'm turning over a new leaf. I'm going to roll with the punches now."

"Cool!" Lydia punches my arm.

"Ow!" I throw a jab her way.

"Hey! What happened to rolling with the punches?"

"I'm still me. I can't help it. That's how I roll."

Acknowledgments

ओ

Heartfelt gratitude . . .

To my agent Sara Crowe and my editor Sharyn November for being my champions in turning this story into a book. Your guidance and expertise astound me. To the entire Viking team for making *Charlotte* your own, but especially Nancy Brennan and Eileen Savage for my amazing cover design.

To the inspiration behind ATC: Jackson Area Career Center (JACC) for offering options and career training to high school (and adult) students. Both of my daughters are working in their chosen professions because of the training they received there. Avery is now a Certified Nursing Assistant (CNA), and Sylvia is a cosmetologist. To the instructors Sylvia had in cos: Ms. Romanowski, who passed away while I was writing this book (Cancer sucks ass!); Ms. Taylor and (the real) Ms. Garrett, who both inspired my fictional Ms. Garrett character; Mr. Kinch, who inspired my Mr. Finn. Thanks for all you do! You enrich our community.

To early readers Lulu November and Tirzah Price. Lulu,

thank you for touching base with your aunt and for your insightful perspectives. Tirzah, you rock in so many ways, my dear. To continual supporters Ed Spicer, Ann Perrigo, Sally Kruger, and Katie Dersnah Mitchell. Thank you for being friends to book people everywhere. You don't just promote reading; you inspire generations.

To my friends who keep me sane, which is a long list because it takes a village. The entire VCFA community for their unwavering encouragement, especially Cori McCarthy, Amy Rose Capetta, LoriGoe Perez, Debbie Gonzales, Melanie Fishbane, and Tim Martin. The Binder community. The Michigan and Northern Ohio SCBWI chapters. My bestest friends Vicky Lorencen, Kristin Willcut, Brenda Sas, Barb Garner, and most of all, Pat Gallagher, who gave me the idea to call a bakery Patti Cakes, and her husband, John Wald, a fellow author.

To my family: my parents, Richard and Linda Rumler; my husband Larry; Alex, Paige, and Arthur; Max and Madalyn; Sylvia, Zack, Walter, and Winston; Avery and Iris; Paisley, Penny, Oliver, and Karen. My life would suck without you.

To subscription services that free my brain space from meal planning: Hello Fresh, Door to Door Organics, Graze, and Naturebox. And Birchbox, too. Thanks for enabling my hermit ways.

To readers, reviewers, bloggers, booksellers, librarians, and teachers who have read and recommended *45 Pounds*. Without you, there wouldn't be another book.

I love you all!

About the Author

K. A. BARSON is also the author of *45 Pounds (More or Less),* about which *VOYA* said: "This powerful and poignant novel is a book readers will not want to wait to finish, and when it is done, they will pick it up again." She has an MFA in Writing for Children and Young Adults from Vermont College of Fine Arts. Kelly Barson and her husband live in Jackson, Michigan—the setting of both of her books—surrounded by their kids, grandkids, a pack of dogs, and one unexpected cat. She feels more like herself when her hair is purple, but it has also been pink, blue, orange, red, and many shades of brown. Visit her website at www.kabarson.com.